THESE
HEALING
HILLS

Center Point
Large Print

Also by Ann H. Gabhart and available from
Center Point Large Print:

Love Comes Home
The Innocent

Writing as A. H. Gabhart:

Murder at the Courthouse
Murder Comes by Mail
Murder Is No Accident

**This Large Print Book carries the
Seal of Approval of N.A.V.H.**

THESE
HEALING
HILLS

ANN H. GABHART

CENTER POINT LARGE PRINT
THORNDIKE, MAINE

ISBN: 978-1-68324-543-8

Library of Congress Cataloging-in-Publication Data

Names: Gabhart, Ann H., 1947– author.
Title: These healing hills / Ann H. Gabhart.
Description: Center Point Large Print edition. | Thorndike, Maine :
    Center Point
Large Print, 2017.
Identifiers: LCCN 2017028422 | ISBN 9781683245438
    (hardcover : alk. paper)
Subjects: LCSH: Large type books. | GSAFD: Love stories. | Christian
fiction.
Classification: LCC PS3607.A23 T48 2017b | DDC 813/.6—dc23
LC record available at https://lccn.loc.gov/2017028422

To the nurses in my family—
Kathy,
Glenda,
and Chrissy—
and all the dedicated nurse-midwives
in the Frontier Nursing Service

No one comes here by accident.
—Frontier Nurse saying

1

May 15, 1945

Francine Howard stepped off the bus into another world. She should have been prepared. She'd studied the Frontier Nursing information until she almost knew it by heart. That should have given her a glimpse into this place.

Hyden was in the Appalachian Mountains, but it was still Kentucky. While she lived in Cincinnati, she had spent many summer weeks on her Grandma Howard's farm in northern Kentucky. But somehow the train from Lexington to Hazard and then the bus from Hazard to here had transported her away from everything she thought she knew about Kentucky and dumped her out in a place that looked as foreign to her as the moon.

But wasn't that what she wanted? To be in a new place long before Seth Miller brought his English bride home from the war. That might not be long. The war in Europe was over. Now, with all the firepower of the Allies focused on the Pacific, surely an end to the terrible war was in sight.

When the news flashed through the country last week that Germany had surrendered, Francine celebrated along with everybody else. How could she not be happy to think about the boys coming home, even if Seth's last letter had changed everything? Seth might finally be on the way home, but not to her.

The news of his betrayal hadn't taken long to circulate through Francine's neighborhood. Not from Francine. Seth's little sister took care of spreading the news. Alice had shown everybody the picture Seth sent home of him with his arm around this English woman. She'd even shown Francine.

"I know you and Seth used to date when you were in high school, but he didn't give you a ring or anything, did he?" Alice must have seen the stricken look on Francine's face, because she pulled the picture back quickly and shoved it in her pocketbook.

"No, no ring." Francine managed to push a smile out on her face and salvage a little pride.

Alice fingered the clasp on her purse. "You want to see the picture again? I jerked it away pretty fast."

"I saw it. She's very pretty."

She'd seen enough to know that. The woman had barely come up to Seth's shoulder. Petite with curly blonde hair and a dimpled smile. Nothing at all like Francine with her plain brown hair and hazel eyes. Just looking at the woman's picture had made her feel tall and gawky. In heels, Francine was nearly as tall as Seth.

Built strong, Grandma Howard used to say. Her grandmother told Francine she was pretty enough, but a person didn't want to be only for pretty like a crystal bowl set on a shelf folks were afraid to use. Better to be a useful vessel ready to be filled with the work the Lord intended for her. Back in her neighborhood, Francine had felt like a cracked bowl somebody had pitched aside.

People sent pitying looks her way. Poor Francine Howard. Going to end up just like Miss Ruby at church, who cried every Mother's Day. No husband. No children. No chances.

But where one door closed, another opened. If not a door, a window somewhere. Another thing Grandma Howard used to say. The Lord had opened a way for Francine to escape the pity trailing after her back home. The Frontier Nursing Service. She had a nursing degree and she could ride a horse. She needed an adventure to forget her bruised heart.

An adventure. That was what the woman had offered when she came to the hospital last November to recruit nurses to train as midwives at the Frontier Nursing Service in Leslie County, Kentucky. The need was great. The people in the Appalachian Mountains didn't have ready access to doctors the way they did in Cincinnati.

At the time, Francine imagined it might be thrilling to ride a horse up into the hills to deliver babies in cabins, but she gave it little consideration. Seth would be home from the war, and she planned to have her own babies after they got married. Babies she might already have if not for the war or if she hadn't let her mother talk her out of marrying Seth before he went overseas. Then everything might be different.

Everything was different now as she stood in front of the drugstore, where the bus driver told her she needed to get off. She had no idea what to do next. The people on the street were giving her the eye but staying well away, as though her foreignness might be catching. She squared her shoulders and clutched her small suitcase in front of her, the larger bag on the walkway beside her. She tried a smile, but it bounced back to her like a rock off a stone wall. Somebody was supposed to meet her, but nobody stepped forward to greet her.

She blinked to clear her eyes that were suddenly too watery. Francine wasn't one to dissolve into tears when things went wrong. She hadn't even cried when she read Seth's letter. What good would tears do? Prayers were better. But right at that moment, Francine didn't know whether to pray for someone to show up from the Frontier Nursing Service or for a train ticket back to Cincinnati.

"She must be one of those brought-in women."

The man was behind her, but she didn't need

to see him to know he was talking about her. She was a stranger. Somebody who didn't belong. At least not yet.

First things first. If nobody was there to get her, she'd find her own way to the hospital. All she needed was somebody to point the way.

A man came out of the drugstore straight toward her. "You must be one of Mrs. Breckinridge's nurses."

"I'm here to go to the midwifery school." Francine smiled at the tall, slender man. "Somebody was supposed to meet me."

He didn't exactly smile back, but he didn't look unfriendly. "Been a lot of rain. The river's rolling. Probably kept them from making it to see to you. Do you know how to get to the hospital?"

Francine looked around. "Is it down the street a ways?"

"It's a ways, all right. Up there." He pointed toward the mountain looming over the town.

Francine peered toward where he was pointing. High above them was a building on the side of the mountain.

"There's a road, but since you're walking, the path up the mountain is shorter." The man gave her a dubious look. "You think you can make it?"

Francine stared at what appeared to be steps chiseled in the side of the mountain. "I'm sure I can." She tried to sound more confident than she felt.

"The path is plain as day. Don't hardly see how you could stray off'n it. But tell you what. Jeb over there is headed that way. He can take you on up."

The man he indicated with a nod of his head was the last person Francine would have considered following anywhere. In spite of the warm spring day, he wore a coat spilling cotton batting from several rips. A felt hat perched on top of a tangled mass of graying hair, and his beard didn't appear to have been trimmed for months. Maybe years. With a shotgun drooping from the crook of his arm, the man appeared anxious to be on his way and not at all happy to be saddled with a brought-in woman.

But what other choice did she have? She leaned over to pick up her other bag, but the man from the drugstore put his hand on it first.

"Don't bother with that. Somebody will bring it up to you later."

She left it, wondering if she'd ever lay eyes on it again as she fell in behind the man named Jeb. Back home, daylight would have a couple more hours, but here shadows were deepening as the sun slid out of sight behind one of the hills that towered around the town. Jeb gave her a hard look, then turned and started away without a word. Francine slung her purse strap over her shoulder, clutched her small suitcase, and hurried after him.

She had to be insane to follow this strange man away from town. He could be leading her to some godforsaken place to do no telling what to get rid of this interloper slowing him down. Not that he set a slower pace for her. She had to step double-quick to keep up. Nor did he offer to take her suitcase or even look back to see if she was still behind him. He didn't have to look back. He could surely hear her panting. Where were those horses the Frontier Nursing brochure promised?

When the path leveled out for a few paces, Francine caught up to the man whose pace didn't change whether the way was steep or level. She could at least try to be friendly. "My name is Francine Howard."

She wasn't certain, but she thought he might have grunted. She was certain he did not so much as glance back over his shoulder at her and that, in spite of the path taking a sharp upward turn, he began moving faster. His foot scooted on the trail and dislodged a rock that bounced down toward Francine. She tried to jump out the way, but she wasn't quick enough.

The rock landed on her toe. She bit her lip to keep from crying out. Mashed toes practically required a good yell. She set down her suitcase and rubbed her toe through her shoe. Her fingers were numb from clutching her suitcase handle and she could see nothing but trees. No wonder they called this place Thousandstick Mountain.

This many trees had to make a lot of sticks.

She'd been totally mistaken thinking her visits to her grandmother's farm would prepare her for Leslie County. Everything wasn't straight uphill there. A person could walk those rolling hills without losing her breath. Trees didn't close in on you and make you wonder if you'd ever see sunshine again.

She gave up on her throbbing toe and massaged her fingers. She started to call for the man to wait, but she kept her mouth closed. The path was plain, and while the shadows were lengthening, it wasn't dark. How far could it be? People obviously traveled this way all the time, and the man's footprints were plain as day on the muddy pathway.

The Lord had pointed her to the Frontier Nursing Service. He wasn't going to abandon her on this mountain. Francine ignored the little niggling voice in the back of her mind that said the Lord had given her a guide. Her task was keeping up.

Too late for that now. The man was gone. Francine rotated her shoulders and picked up her suitcase. Time to carry on. Find her place on this mountain.

She started climbing again, slower now as she looked around. Thick green bushes pushed into the path with buds promising beauty. Rhododendron. She couldn't wait to see them burst into bloom. Delicate white flowers near the path tempted her to step into the trees for a better look, but the thought of snakes stopped her. Snakebit and alone on this mountain might not lead to a happy outcome.

At first, the man's footprints were easy to follow, but then the way got steeper and nothing but rocks. No sign of the man ahead of her. Worse, the path split in two directions. Even worse, the shadows were getting darker. It could be she should have run to keep up with silent Jeb after all.

Even standing on her tiptoes, she couldn't see the hospital up ahead as the trees and bushes crowded in on the path here. Both traces went up, so that was no help. She had no idea how high this mountain was. She might be climbing all night. But no, she'd seen the hospital from town. It couldn't be much farther.

Francine set her case down again and chocked it with her foot to keep it from sliding away from her. The word *steep* was taking on new meaning.

With her eyes wide open, she whispered, "Dear Lord, I know you haven't left me alone here on this mountain. So can you point the way?"

She stood silent then. She didn't want to miss a second answer if the Lord took pity on her after she'd foolishly trusted too much in her own abilities instead of scrambling after her mountain man guide.

Just when she was ready to give up on divine intervention and pick a path, she heard whistling. Not a bird, but a man. And the sound was coming closer. The Lord was sending her someone to point the way. Certainly not Jeb coming back for her. She couldn't imagine that stone-faced man whistling the merry tune coming to her ears.

"Hello," she called. She didn't want the whistler to pass her by without seeing her.

The whistling abruptly stopped. Francine called again. This time an echoing hello came back to her, and a gangly boy, maybe fourteen or fifteen, scrambled into view down the path to her left. His overalls were too short, showing a span of leg above well-worn shoes, but the best thing about him were his blue eyes that looked as friendly as a summer sky.

He skidded to a stop and stared down at her. "You lost?"

"A bit," Francine admitted. "Could you point me the way to the Hyden Hospital?"

"I reckon you're one of Mrs. Breckinridge's brought-in nurses." He gave her a curious look. "Do you catch babies?"

"I'm here to train to be a midwife." Francine smiled at the idea of catching babies. "At the hospital. Is it much farther?"

"Not all that far, but night might catch you. You best follow me." He came on down to her and started up the other path. "Weren't nobody down there in town to show you the way?"

"I was supposed to follow somebody named Jeb, but I didn't keep up."

The boy laughed. "That Jeb. And I reckon he never said word one. Jeb, he ain't much of a talker. Not like me. My brother used to tell me I jabbered as much as a jaybird that had been sipping out of a moonshine still. At least that's what he said before he went off to fight the Germans. That's been nigh on four years now, but I'm still a talker."

"I was very happy to hear you whistling a few minutes ago." Francine picked up her bag and followed the boy. "My name is Francine Howard. Do you have a name other than Jaybird?"

"Jaybird might be better than what folks call me. Woody. Woody Locke. Sort of sounds funny when you say it, but my pa was Woodrow. Woodrow Locke, that's a fine name. One I reckon I can take on after I get a little older." His voice softened, turned somber. "Now that Pa passed on last year."

"Oh, I'm sorry." Francine felt an answering wave of sympathy. Her own father had died two years ago.

"Ma says the Lord calls people home when he's ready for them, and we shouldn't look askance at the Lord's doing." The boy looked over his shoulder at her. "I get in trouble all the time asking too much about everything. Pa, he used to say I had a curious mind, but Ma gets worn out by my wonderings."

"That's how you learn things." Francine couldn't keep from panting a little as she climbed behind Woody.

The boy noticed. He looked stricken as he turned back to her. "Give me that case. My ma would slap me silly if she saw me letting you lug that thing and me with two free hands."

"Thank you." Francine handed it to him. "But maybe you should just tell me the way now. You need to go on home before night falls so your mother won't worry."

"Ma don't worry none about me. She sent me up here to get some medicine for Sadie. That's my little sister and she's been punying around. The nurse over our way said she needed some ear drops she had run out of in her medicine bag. So I came on to fetch them. Sadie being the youngest and all, Ma babies her some. We all do. She ain't but four, nigh on five."

"But it will be dark soon."

"Dark don't fret me. I can find my way light or night. But Ma knowed I'd probably find a spot in town to spend the night 'fore I head on up the mountain come morning. Get me out of chores." He grinned at Francine and turned back up the path. "I oughta be shamed about that with Ma having to do them, but I laid in wood for her this morn and she milks the cow most every night herself anyhow. She'll have a list of chores a mile long to make up for me being late home, but she wouldn't want me not to help one of you nurses. No sir. I'd get in way more trouble if I didn't see that you made it to where you're going."

"You don't have any other brothers at home?" Walking uphill after him was easier without carrying the suitcase, but it didn't seem to slow Woody down at all.

"Nope. It's just me and Sadie now. Ruthie, she went north to work in one of the airplane factories and Becca got married and moved over to a mining camp in Harlan County. Ben, he's the oldest. He joined up with the army after Pearl Harbor. I been telling Ma I'm nigh old enough to go fight the Germans and the Japs too, but Ma don't like hearing that. Says she's busy enough praying that the Lord ain't ready for Ben to go home with Pa." He looked back at Francine again. "Ben's the one what says I jabber like a jaybird. Guess you can see why now."

"I always liked jaybirds." That made Woody laugh. "Where is your brother? In Europe or the Pacific?"

"Europe last we heard. We get letters now and again, but places where he might be are all cut out of them. He's a medic. Ma's right proud that he ain't just over there shooting people, but that he's doing some healing too."

"That does sound good. I'll add my prayers to your mother's for his safety and that he'll get home soon."

"That's neighborly of you. I'll tell my ma."

They stepped out of the trees to see the hospital on the side of the mountain. Not that big, but sturdy. Substantial and a little surprising. A road circled right up to its door. To the side was another building connected by a covered walkway. That must be where she'd be living for the next few months.

She'd loved working with the mothers and babies back in Cincinnati. And odd as it was here on this mountain with the long-legged boy beside her, she was looking forward to learning how to catch those babies, as he had said.

New life. And not just for the babies, but for her too. A new life in a new place. A window of opportunity for her to climb through. If only she could stop looking back at the door she had dreamed of walking through with Seth.

After she thanked the boy, she watched him disappear back down the hillside. Then she took a deep breath, squared her shoulders, and walked straight toward the hospital doors.

2

June 11, 1945

Ben Locke stared up at the stars glittering overhead, the same stars that spread across the sky over his Appalachian home. The moon rising later that night would spill light down on those hills the same as here in this country so far across the ocean. Not at exactly the same time, he supposed. Here it was already the deep of the night, while there twilight would just be settling in. He could almost hear the clang of his mother's bucket as she headed out to the barn to milk the cow. The hens would be cackling as Woody checked their nests for eggs. Or maybe baby Sadie was old enough to do that now. Her fifth birthday was last week. She wouldn't know her big brother when he got home.

Just the three of them at home, unless Becca was visiting from the county over. Hard to think about Becca being a married woman when she was just a girl in pigtails last he saw her. Harder to think about never seeing his pa again. How could he go and drop down dead back there with his hands on the plow while Ben was here at war with bullets and shrapnel flying? It didn't seem right.

Not that he hadn't seen plenty of dying. Some

of them boys with the peach fuzz of youth on their cheeks. Not much older than Woody now. As a medic with his troop, he'd done his best to keep them alive until they got back to the doctors and the hospitals, but sometimes there was nothing to do but hold their hands and look them in the eye while they died. And hope you wouldn't be next.

Thank God the shooting was over here. He could lie out under the stars without worrying about incoming bombs or night raids. Hitler was dead. The Germans defeated. But he was still half a world away from home. And on the other side of the world in a different direction, the war raged on.

Ben's stomach clenched at the thought of being sent to the Pacific. The only place he wanted to go was home.

His mother told him the mountains sent tendrils up out of the ground to wrap around a man's ankles and keep him tied to the place. He hadn't believed it then. Not that he didn't love growing up on the mountain, even if a body had to work hard to scratch a living out of the stingy ground. But a boy could be free on the mountain. He had thought then that once he was grown, he could do what he wanted. He could pull his feet loose from those mountain roots.

He'd never once thought that a war would yank him all the way across the ocean to Africa and

France and Germany. Places he'd read about in schoolbooks but had no idea that he'd ever walk on their dirt. But a man had to stand up and be counted when war came calling. That didn't keep him from wishing the war over. From wishing for home.

He shifted on the blanket he'd laid out on the ground. Not the softest place, but at least out here he could breathe. His company had laid claim to a building, but too many people were stretched out end to end inside there, breathing the same air and some of them smelling up the place. After four years living in foxholes and crawling across whatever was in the way between you and the enemy, a good number of the men didn't worry much about finding soap and water. More dirt would just be coming their way on the morrow.

Paper crackled in his pocket. Woody's letter. The boy was as much of a jabber box in writing as he'd been back on the mountain before Ben left for the army. Fifteen now. Eight years Ben's junior. The kid wrote more than his mother did. Her letters were generally short, with a few lines about what she'd been doing, like planting beans or sewing a dress for Sadie. Then she always ended with the same words. *We miss you, Ben. I pray every day for you and for the war to be over so you can come home. You take care of yourself, do your duty, and don't forget us back home. Love, Ma.*

As if he could forget. Back home had stayed with him on the ship crossing the Atlantic and marched beside him every step since, through one battlefield after another. Back home was an ache in his heart that never went away.

On the other hand, Woody's letters were a full page, front and back, of scribbles about all kinds of goings-on. He put back home right in front of Ben's eyes with his scrawled words. Ben sat up a little and pulled the letter out of his pocket. He unfolded it, but he couldn't make out the words. He moved over by a fire one of the men had started up in the yard. He poked the glowing coals until a flame flickered up and gave off enough light to see the loopy writing across the lined paper.

Hello, Ben. I'm not married yet, but I guess I'm next in line after you since Ruthie and Becca done went and got hitched. I reckon you need to go first so you best come on home and start sparking some girl around here so I can have my turn. I turned fifteen back the first of June. Not that anybody hardly noticed with Sadie's birthday coming up next week. Ma did make me a cake and I picked some ripe strawberries in the garden row. Bet you haven't tasted a good strawberry since you left here.

I reckon Sadie'll already be five before you get this what with it having to get all the way across the ocean to you. She's been a little puny with the croup, but a nurse has been coming up to see about her. The nurse says Sadie will probly get better when full summer gets here. Spring's the worst time for croup, it seems.

Speaking of nurses, I come across a lost one a couple weeks back. She tried to follow Jeb up the mountain to the hospital, but you know how Jeb is. You remember him, don't you? Works some for Mrs. Breckinridge making rock walls and such. I help him now and again when Ma can spare me. That Mrs. Breckinridge has a thing for rock walls. Says they keep the mountain from sliding away and taking her house at Wendover with it. You might figure out why that works since you went off to Richmond to college that year before the Army. What with how Pa has passed on, I'm not expecting to get to follow in your footsteps there, but Ma makes me keep going to school here. I'll probly be the oldest boy there come next school term. But Ma says Pa didn't want none of us to go to the mines so we'll have to learn how to do something else. I told her I can join the Army but she's not too keen on that either.

Anyway, if you remember Jeb, you can imagine how he wasn't too worried about some brought-in woman tagging along behind him. He told me later she oughta kept up. But don't worry. I knew better than to leave her stranded there in the woods. She'd come down from the north to learn about catching babies. While we were climbing up Thousandstick Mountain, I told her about you and how you always called me a jabber jay. Bet you thought I might grow out of that, but instead I just seem to be getting worse. Ma says maybe I'll end up a preacher or a lawyer. Both of them have to have some ready words.

Nurse Howard laughed about that jabbering and said she always liked jaybirds. She hardly talks funny at all. Not like those nurses from over in England. I've seen her a time or two since then and she always asks after you and says she's still helping Ma pray you home.

Well, I done jaybird pecked all the words I can fit on this piece of paper. Come on home as soon as they'll let you.

Woody Jabber Jay

Ben folded up the letter with a smile and stuck it back in his pocket. Maybe Woody would turn out to be a preacher. Getting strange women to pray for him. Not that Ben was turning down any prayers. Not after what he'd seen in the war. He'd been raised on prayers.

"What's got you grinning so big, Locke?" Sergeant Wilkerson squatted down beside Ben next to the coals. "Some girl writing you love notes?"

"Afraid not, Sarge. I don't have a girl pining after me back in the States." Ben gave a little laugh. "Just a letter from my brother."

"That's better than some girl. Brothers won't be writing you no Dear John letters." Sarge poked at the fire with a stick. "How's things in the hills of Kentucky?"

"They're making it. You ever been to Kentucky?"

"Can't say that I have." The sergeant stared at the flames he'd stirred up. "Texas is my stomping grounds. Got a pretty little wife and a boy getting ready to start school next fall waiting for me there. Been way too long since I've seen them."

"The army ever lets us go, you ought to bring them to Kentucky. The mountains are extra pretty in June with the rhododendron blooming and everything green and growing."

"Right now any place in the good old U.S.A. sounds good."

Ben could agree with that. "You think they'll ship us to the Pacific?"

"Hard to know. But soldiers go where they're sent." The sergeant threw his stick in the fire.

"Yes, sir." Ben sat up a little straighter.

Sergeant Wilkerson stood up. "But we wouldn't mind it if they sent us on home, would we, Soldier?"

"Not at all."

"You best get some shut-eye, Locke. None of us are going home tomorrow. That you can be sure of. You'll have to pull duty somewhere."

Ben watched the sergeant disappear back into the house. He didn't follow him. Instead he rolled up his jacket for a pillow and stretched out where he was. He'd slept in lots worse places in the last few years. And there on the ground with the stars overhead and Woody's words bouncing around in his head, he could dream of home.

3

June 28, 1945

"Fran! Fran!" Rocky Catlett raced into the gathering room where Francine had just slipped off her shoes and collapsed on the couch after her shift at the hospital. "Willie sent me to get you."

Francine sat up. "What's happening?" She stuck her tired feet back into her shoes even before Rocky answered.

"She says if you scrub up extra fast, you can assist with Tassie Jackson. She's almost ready to deliver." Rocky was even newer to the midwifery school than Francine, but they were both already getting hands-on experience assisting the other midwives.

Francine forgot how tired she was as she followed Rocky back through the walkway to the hospital.

Rocky looked over her shoulder. "Hurry, Fran! We don't want the little fellow to get here before we get there."

Fran. Nobody called her Francine here. Not from the first minute she had shown up at the hospital. That night Willie, the nurse-midwife calling for her now, had met her at the hospital door and ushered her over to the nurses' quarters

31

at the Mardi house where several women were eating in a kitchen area. They got her a plate and welcomed her in, but even before she knew their names, they were changing hers.

"Francine." A woman, who looked older than the others around the table, narrowed her eyes as she studied Francine. "No, that won't do."

"What's wrong with Francine?" she asked.

One of the other women spoke up. "Too fancy. Around here, you need a better name, Francine Howard. Everybody has one. Mine's Thumper. That's because I'm always banging on a typewriter up in the office. Lennie was the one who lowered that moniker on me, wasn't it, Bucket?"

Bucket and Thumper? Francine began to feel as if she had followed Alice down the rabbit hole to Wonderland. Eventually, she found out Bucket was Dorothy Buck, who was supervisor over the nurses, and Thumper was Lucille Hodges. But all that was later. That night her head was spinning as she tried to take it all in. Even Willie, who was trying to make Francine feel welcome, had a strong English accent that added to the strangeness of it all.

Willie was the one to come up with the name suggestion. "We don't have a Fran."

"Well, now we do." The older woman slapped her hand down on the table like a judge deciding a case. "Welcome to the Frontier Nursing Service, Fran."

And just like that she'd become a new person. Fran Howard. She didn't mind the name. Fran was much better than the Howie somebody suggested later on. But Fran was already on people's tongues by then.

Her mother would hate it, but then her mother was back in Cincinnati with her new husband. She wasn't likely to ever climb Thousandstick Mountain to see Fran or Francine. She had written only once. A very stilted letter, since she was vehemently against Fran going off to what she called the wilds of Kentucky. A place where every man had a gun in one hand and a bottle of moonshine in the other. That was what she had harped on when she found out Fran had applied to the Frontier Nursing Midwifery School.

"I have it on good authority that people down there don't like strangers. They're hillbillies, Francine." She had stopped pacing in front of Fran to glare at her. Since her mother barely topped five feet tall, she always made Francine sit down whenever she was lecturing about something so she wouldn't have to look up at her. "Are you hearing what I'm saying? Hillbillies."

She spit out the word. Francine didn't argue with her. She simply waited until her mother ran out of words, then finished filling out the application and sent it off. When the acceptance letter came, she ignored her mother's tears and dire warnings and packed her bags. Because of the same tears and histrionics, Francine had kissed Seth goodbye and let him go off to war to find a different bride.

Perhaps he would have anyway. Anybody could look at that picture Seth's sister had and know he'd traded for a cuter model.

Women weren't models of cars to be traded, she reminded herself. They were to be loved and cherished. The way Mr. Jackson did his wife. The man stopped pacing outside the delivery room when he saw Fran and stepped in front of her.

"The wife, she is going to be all right, isn't |she, Nurse Howard? She was punishing really bad before they took her back and the other nurse told me to stay out here."

He looked so upset that Fran couldn't push past him, even if the delay might make her miss the birth. Mrs. Jackson had come to the hospital a week ago to be near the doctor when her time came since she'd had problems with delivering her first baby.

"Better safe than sorry," Willie had told Fran when she explained the case. "Most birthings do fine in the mother's house. Actually better than fine, but a few cases call for more observation. Tassie Jackson is one of those."

Now Fran patted Mr. Jackson's arm. "Nurse Williams and the doctor are taking care of Tassie. We'll let you know how things are as soon as we can."

"I reckon there ain't nothing for me to do but stand here and talk to the good Lord." He looked worried again. "I ain't always done what I oughta. Do you think the Lord will want to hear anything I have to say?"

"I think he will." Fran smiled at him. She didn't add that the Lord's answers weren't always what a person might want, but no time for that kind of thinking right now. Her denied prayers about Seth had nothing to do with Mr. Jackson's.

Rocky stuck her head out the door. "Come on, Fran." She disappeared on the other side of the door again.

"You go on now." Mr. Jackson looked at the door with a mixture of longing and apprehension. He twisted his felt hat in his hands.

She started to push through the door when he said, "You won't let her die on me, will you?"

Fran wanted to assure him they wouldn't, but it was better not to make promises. Sometimes things did go wrong. She kept her smile bright. "Dr. Randall is a fine doctor and Nurse Williams is the best midwife here. It won't be long now."

She scrubbed up and stepped into the delivery room. Willie looked around at her. "Thought you weren't going to make it. The head's crowning."

Willie was a short, stubby woman. She claimed that made her perfect for nursing. She didn't have to bend over to get to her patients, and if they were tall, she could always stand on a chair.

Her given name was Beulah, but the Willie nickname came from her last name, Williams. Now she moved around beside Mrs. Jackson, who was draped in sheets, and motioned to Fran. "Take over at the business end there, Nurse Howard. You've got to catch your first baby sometime, and Mrs. Jackson's been asking for you, haven't you, dearie?"

Mrs. Jackson bobbed her head before another contraction came on and she groaned.

"You're doing a bang-up job, Mrs. Jackson." Willie mopped the woman's brow with a damp cloth. "Just a few more pushes now and the little tyke will be ready to meet his mama face-to-face."

Fran's heart bounded up in her throat. She clenched her hands to hide their trembles as she moved into the midwife's position. What if she did something wrong? But no, Willie was right beside her, and Dr. Randall standing by if needed. Everything was happening the way it should. The way a dozen other births had gone while she had assisted Willie.

"Give us another push, dearie," Willie said. "You're being a real trooper here."

The baby's head slipped out and Fran supported the weight of it as she maneuvered the little fellow's shoulders. One more push and the shoulders were free. After that the baby came in a rush. And while Fran's hands weren't trembling

36

now, inside she was all atremble as she held this new life. She wanted to break out in song.

"He's a beautiful little boy," she said.

Mrs. Jackson laughed and panted at the same time. "My Jim is going to be happy about that. Our other one is a sweet girl."

"Get on about what needs doing," Willie reminded Fran softly.

Fran snipped the cord and handed the baby to Rocky, who had her hands out ready. The baby let out a lusty cry that brought a smile to Fran's face as she massaged Mrs. Jackson's abdomen to help her pass the placenta. The baby kept crying as Rocky wrapped him in a blanket to show his mother before she began cleaning him up.

"Let her see his fingers and toes," Willie said. "Yes, every one perfect, dearie. You did a right fine job with this one."

Fran knew she was talking to Mrs. Jackson, but she couldn't stop smiling herself.

Willie noticed and said, "You'll never tire of hearing that first sweet warble of life after you usher a baby into the world. Each and every time will bring that heart smile."

Later, after baby and mama were settled and father was by their bedside, Fran fell into her own bed. As she lay there, she remembered Woody's question that day she met him on the mountain. *You catch babies?*

Fran whispered a prayer of thanks that, yes,

she did catch babies. Then she turned over and went to sleep without once thinking of Seth and his pretty English bride for the first time since she'd come to the mountains.

4

July 9, 1945

"But what am I supposed to wear?" Fran asked Willie.

Early that morning Bucket had told her Mrs. Breckinridge wanted Fran to come for tea at Wendover. And as Willie explained to Fran when she asked about skipping her duties at the hospital, if Mrs. Breckinridge wanted something, it was done. No arguments. No excuses.

Not that Fran was arguing or trying to avoid going. She looked forward to the chance to talk with Mrs. Breckinridge again. She'd met her shortly after arriving in Leslie County when a young courier named Abigail had escorted Fran to Wendover. Abigail brought a horse for Fran, who felt her riding ability was being tested. Fran hadn't been on a horse for several years, but she hadn't forgotten how to sit in a saddle.

When Abigail called the horse Pinafore, Fran couldn't keep from laughing at the odd name. Abigail smiled and said Mrs. Breckinridge named all her animals, even down to her two dreadful geese, Jack and Jill.

"They should be named Wicked and Mean. You have to watch your back every second when those nasty geese are around or they'll take a plug out of you." Abigail rubbed her arm and shivered. "The sly things don't bother Mrs. B, but I'm telling you, if we didn't know how she loved those two, we would have already had roast goose for dinner."

That day Fran was welcomed warmly by the founder of the Frontier Nursing Service. Mrs. Breckinridge's house, all logs and windows, seemed to belong on the mountainside. Several other buildings were scattered on the same hillside. A barn for the horses. Quarters for the young couriers like Abigail who ran errands for the nurses, took care of the horses, or did whatever was needed. A log office building, and all the necessary shelters for chickens, cows, horses, and those geese Abigail had wanted to roast.

Now, Fran was feeling a little like a cooked goose as she helped Willie strip and remake one of the hospital beds.

Willie laughed at the look on Fran's face. "Ease up, girl. You're not being ordered to the guillotine. It's tea. Mrs. Breckinridge has tea every day when she's home at Wendover. The woman does love her tea. It's one of the first things the courier girls learn to do when they get here. Steep and serve tea. And trust me, some of those girls have never served anybody before. They mostly come from families with servants to serve them."

"Then why are they here? I've heard they don't get paid anything."

"Heavens, no. Bucket says they fight for the chance to volunteer. Some of the early couriers from back at the beginning in the thirties ask to sign their daughters up for the chance to follow in their footsteps while their girls are babes in the cradle. It's quite a bragging point in some corners of society to claim time spent working with Mrs. B's nurse-midwives here in the mountains." Willie shook her head a little as she tucked a corner of the sheet tightly under the hospital bed mattress. "That woman could talk a queen into trading in her crown for the chance to curry some horses for a few weeks."

When Fran didn't say anything, Willie pitched a pillow across the bed toward her. "Not to mention getting nurses like the two of us to come to this outpost of poverty to wear out our boots walking up mountains."

"Why are you here, Willie?" Fran fluffed the pillow and positioned it just so on the bed. "You're a long way from home, and babies are born in England too."

"So they are." Willie put her fists on her hips and stared out the window. "But I like to feel needed and around here we're needed. You've surely seen that in the time you've been here." She looked back at Fran. "Turnabout is fair play. Why are you here?"

"To go to the midwifery school." Fran spoke quickly. She hadn't told any of the people here about Seth's betrayal.

"A fast answer and no doubt a true one." Willie narrowed her eyes on Fran. "But why do I think there's more to our Frannie than she wants us to see?"

Fran started to deny Willie's words, but Willie held up her hand to stop her. "Don't be searching for any half-truths to tell me. None of my business and whatever brought you here, I'm glad enough for it. None of us are here by accident. You've surely heard that time and again since being here."

"I have, but sometimes it's hard to know the Lord's true intent for your life." A year ago Fran would have never imagined herself working in a small hospital on the side of a mountain.

"Hard for us. Not for the good Lord. We needed more nurses, and from all appearances, you're going to make a fine midwife once you finish your training. How many babies have you delivered now?"

"Six, and I assisted when Dr. Randall delivered two of the more complicated births." The necessary number was twenty, but some of those had to be out on district in the mothers' homes and not in the hospital.

"If I were to guess, I'd say that's why Mrs. B

wants you to come to tea. So she can determine which nursing district can use you."

"Oh, I hope so. I like the idea of taking care of people in their homes."

"You'll see some sights. That's a sure thing." Willie folded a blanket and laid it over the foot of the bed. "Some sorry sights. I worked the Possum Creek district for a while and I like it better here at the hospital where they have to come to us."

"Don't you like the mountain people, Willie?"

"It doesn't matter whether I like them or not, as long as I fix what's broken or sick. I'm a nurse. Not their best friend."

"Can't we be both?"

Willie frowned a little. "I don't think so. I don't even think they want us to be both. They appreciate our nursing. I have no doubt of that, and you won't have to worry about anybody bothering you out on district as long as you have on your Frontier Nursing outfit. But we come from one way of living and they have totally different ways."

"Different? But aren't people mostly the same no matter where they are from?" Fran scooped up the dirty linens and followed Willie out of the room. "I mean, below the surface in our minds and hearts where it matters."

"I can see you want to think that, but no. These people aren't the same as us. They're mountain. They have a hard life, but they seem

43

tied to it. To embrace it even. Whatever happens. Sickness. Death. Poverty. They accept it all as what the Lord meant to be." Willie looked back over her shoulder at Fran. "How they can think the Lord intended them to shoot one another for some reason nobody can remember, I cannot understand."

"Do they do that?" Fran dropped the dirty linens in the bin for the laundry woman to collect later.

"That and more. You'll see."

Willie's words sounded like an ominous warning. One Fran didn't want to hear. But Willie should know. She'd been in the mountains for years, while Fran had only been there a few weeks. What did she really know about the people? She hadn't even known Seth. She thought he was loyal, a man who kept his word.

Often when she lay down after a shift at the hospital, the thought ran through her mind of what she was doing in such a foreign place. But then when she got up and peered out her window, something about the sight of the mountains settled her worries. It might be different when she was working in a district and climbing up to the mountain cabins to take care of people. Then she might see what Willie saw.

"Don't be getting on the judgment train." Her grandma's words echoed in her head. *"The good Lord is the only one fit to take it down*

44

the tracks. Worry about your own doings. Not that of others."

Grandma Howard's words had been popping up in Fran's head often since she got to Hyden. Her grandmother would like this place, with the lavish blooms on the mountainsides and the people who had few pretensions. She would understand how the steep ground would make hard living. Fran could almost hear her grandmother telling her she didn't have to know everything about the mountain people. She wasn't there to study them. She was a nurse and soon would be a midwife to help with their babies and everyday ills.

That was why she was here. To close the door on her life in Cincinnati and find a new way to live. If, at times, that felt frightening, she would pray for more courage. It wasn't the Lord who had deserted her and not kept his promises. It was Seth.

Seth hadn't shown up in Cincinnati with his English bride as yet. At least not before the last letter from home. Her mother didn't believe there was an English bride. She told Fran she'd thrown away her chances by running away. Her mother dismissed Seth's letter breaking off their engagement as something Fran misunderstood, in spite of his words on the paper, plain as day.

She blamed Fran instead of Seth for cheating her out of the chance for grandchildren. That had always been her mother's way. She saw her own injury in everything, without considering the sorrow others might be feeling.

Fran shook away thoughts of her mother as she pulled on the blue riding trousers and white shirt to go to Wendover for Mrs. B's tea. It didn't seem the best outfit for tea, but it was what Bucket told her to wear. The matching vest and tie had no feminine frills, but nurses didn't need frills. Nurses needed to be all business. The boots went up to Fran's knees. Not only necessary for riding, but good protection against snakes. That's what Bucket had told her the day she gave Fran the Frontier Nursing outfit to wear when working out in the districts instead of the hospital.

"Snakes?" Fran had shivered and looked behind her, as though expecting snakes to be creeping toward her in the hospital hallway.

Bucket laughed. "One slithers in on occasion, but the boots are for when you're on the trails. Most snakes are harmless enough, but you'll see a few copperheads and rattlers up in the hills."

Fran shivered yet again. "I don't like snakes. Of any kind."

"Nor do I, but you get used to them." Bucket patted Fran's shoulder. "I've found you can overcome a great many imagined dangers in this world. Generally while we're imagining one thing, a real difficulty we haven't even considered pops out at us."

"Like a snake in the grass?"

"True." Bucket laughed. "That can be a difficulty to a number of the nurses here. And not only them, but their horses as well. I've had my horse run all the way to the next mountain when a snake rattles at him."

"What did you do?"

"Held on. What else?" Bucket gave her another pat. "That's all you need to do, Fran. Just hold on. You'll learn the mountain ways."

That might be easier than knotting the fetched tie required with the outfit. Fran always looped something wrong and ended up with a strangling knot. She'd watched her father put on his ties at times, but that wasn't a skill she'd thought to ever need. She gave it one more try in front of the small square mirror on the wall in her cramped sleeping room with barely space for the narrow bed, chest, and chair. The room was for sleeping, and by the time Fran finished her duties at the hospital, that's all she wanted to do. The gathering room was for socializing and eating.

She tightened the uneven knot. It wasn't right, but it would have to do. She refused to chase Willie down at the hospital to retie it. Best to smooth it down flat against her shirt and head toward Wendover. She hadn't been assigned a horse yet, and no courier had come for her the way Abigail had on her former trip. This time she'd have to walk the four miles, so she needed to get started. She didn't want to be late.

The July day was hot, with a few white clouds floating by that looked close enough to touch. When a storm would settle on the mountain, Fran felt as though she were in the midst of the lightning and thunder and not below it. But the same was true when the sun came out and made the world sparkle.

Weather mattered more here than back in Cincinnati. Rains could turn creeks into torrents of water funneling down out of the hills to flood the Middle Fork River. But in the hot summer months like now, floods weren't as much a worry as getting enough rain for the gardens and crops the people depended on for food.

Fran passed a cabin next to the road where a woman sat on the porch, hulling beans. A couple of children played on the porch beside her.

"Afternoon, Nurse Howard. Come sit a spell."

Fran didn't know how the woman knew her name. As far as she could remember, Fran hadn't seen her at the hospital. But she'd been told the mountain grapevine worked better than telephones back in the city for spreading the news. And a new brought-in woman was news.

The two children stopped their play and stared at Fran. She wasn't sure if they wanted her to stop or were afraid she might. Nurses sometimes brought needles with them. "Wishing I could, but I'm on the way to Wendover to see Mrs. B. Maybe next time I pass this way."

Bucket had told her to always be neighborly, whether she felt like a neighbor or not. But the longer she was in the mountains, the more she wanted to feel like a neighbor. To belong here, where the earth met the sky.

5

The sight of the bridge swinging in the air over the river unnerved Fran. Bridges were supposed to have sturdy pilings down deep into the ground. Those bridges didn't sway and tremble in the breeze.

When she'd ridden the horse named Pinafore to Wendover, they went a different way and rode right through the river. Part of the test, Fran thought at the time, since the horses had to swim through the deep middle. The young courier had lifted her feet out of the stirrups to balance precariously in the saddle with her boots out of the water. She had grinned back at Fran as though daring her to do the same. Instead, Fran leaned forward in the saddle with her feet high behind her. She had to look something like a frog ready to hop, but she hadn't fallen off and her boots stayed dry.

The swinging bridge was different. Down below was the river. Fran wasn't afraid of the river. She could wade through it and swim if it got too deep. But she would have to backtrack a ways to go down to the river. The bridge was right in front of her. People walked across it all the time. All the time.

"One step, then another," she whispered. But to

her nervous eyes, the bridge looked a mile long. That was a lot of steps.

She gingerly put one foot on the bridge and then forced the other foot to follow. The bridge felt even less substantial than she'd imagined. Fran clutched the rope side and tried not to look down. But she couldn't help herself. Several men paused in their fishing to peer up at her. One of them yelled something, but she couldn't make it out. Probably something about being a brought-in coward.

Fran pulled in a deep breath and took two more quick steps. The bridge bounced to life with seemingly one aim. To shake her off. She grabbed the rope side with a death's grip, afraid to move either direction.

A laugh behind her startled Fran. When she jerked around to see who was there, the bridge wobbled under her feet again. An old woman stood at the edge of the bridge with a basket looped over her arm.

"First time on a bridge like this'n?" the woman asked.

Fran dared a slight nod. "It doesn't seem all that sturdy."

"That bridge has held up plenty of bigger folks than the slip of a girl you are."

"I'm not all that little," Fran said.

"But some smaller than an elephant."

"An elephant has been across here?" Fran couldn't imagine such a feat.

51

"Not that I've heard tell of, but 'twouldn't surprise me if Mary Breckinridge brung one in. She takes a fancy to all sorts of unusual things." The woman eyed Fran. Her bonnet shaded her face, but it was easy to see the deep wrinkles creasing her cheeks. Her eyes were an odd coppery color that made Fran think of lion pictures she'd seen.

But her eyes were striking for more than their color. While the old woman's shoulders were humped over a bit and her knuckles were thick with arthritis, her eyes looked like those of a young woman. Bright and glaring as she watched Fran, hardly blinking at all.

Fran had the feeling the old woman thought she was one of Mary Breckinridge's odd things. She decided to go along with her. "Like me."

A smile lifted one corner of the old woman's lips. "Like you. But I'm thinking you ain't as unusual as some of them others. 'Cepting for being scared of high places. These here hills ain't a very friendly place for a body fearful of being high."

"I'm not afraid of heights."

"Are ye sure of that?" The old woman clucked her tongue, then set her basket down and moved onto the bridge. She grabbed the rope handhold and jumped on the bridge with both feet.

Fran clamped her lips together to keep from shrieking. When the swaying slowed, she admitted, "Well, except those heights that wobble and sway."

The old woman twisted her thin lips to the side and gave Fran a considering look. "I like a body who tells the truth even if it has to be shook out of 'em. So I'll cure you of the fear you're having."

"How's that?" Fran thought she might just have to stay on the bridge until somebody pried her hands loose from the rope rails and carried her off.

"The bridge ain't shaking. It's dancing. You gotta dance with it, girl. Let your feet find the rhythm. If you pay some mind, there's rhythm nigh on to ev'rything."

"Dance, huh?" Fran kept her eyes on the old woman. "But I've never been much of a dancer."

"Ain't nobody what can't dance if'n they turn their feet loose. The good Lord built tappin' to music right in our toes."

Fran swallowed and gripped the side tighter.

"Don't be afeared. Give it a try." The woman took a couple of steps toward Fran. She moved with the ease of a child and the bridge barely shivered.

Fran followed her example and forced her foot forward. The bridge dropped down a bit but then seemed to lift up to meet her next step. The swaying did have a certain cadence that might make one think of dancing. She looked back toward the old woman, who had moved off the bridge. "I see what you mean."

"Good to know you kin take advising."

"Yes, thank you." She took another step or two, but then thought she should say who she was. "I'm Nurse Howard, by the way."

"I knowed who you were."

"But I don't know you."

"If that ain't the truth." The old woman picked up her basket and walked away from the bridge.

Fran watched her disappear into the trees without looking back. Maybe it was rude to ask a mountain person her name. And if the woman didn't want to tell her, that was her right. Fran wasn't treating her. She was being advised by her. Advice was something Fran needed if she was going to figure out these mountain people.

Down below, the fishermen, no longer worried about their lines in the water, stared up at Fran as though she were the best show they'd seen for a while. Either that or they were hoping the bridge would win and pitch her off in the river.

That wasn't going to happen. She shut her eyes a moment and let the sway of the bridge soak up into her feet. And then she danced across, barely skimming the railing with her hand.

The men down below yelled something. Fran wasn't sure what, but it sounded like a cheer of some sort. Maybe they hadn't wanted her to fall after all. Maybe the people here wanted to help her as much as she hoped to help them.

She stepped off the bridge, relieved to feel solid ground under her boots. The mountain granny's idea of dancing had gotten her over the bridge, but now she needed to do some fast walking. Willie said Mrs. Breckinridge had no use for those who were late. When Mrs. B wanted something done, she wanted it done yesterday.

Fran kept a wary eye out for those geese Abigail had warned her about as she rushed up the hill past the cluster of buildings toward the Big House. Again she was struck by how well the house fit there on the mountain.

"You're on time." Mrs. Breckinridge stepped away from a tree beside the path. "I like that in my nurses."

"Oh." Fran put her hand over her heart. "I didn't see you there."

"Sorry. I didn't mean to startle you." Mrs. B moved down on the path beside Fran. She wore a blue-striped dress with a full white apron. She swept back a few wisps of gray hair that had escaped the bun at the nape of her neck and looked back up the hillside. "I was just out here communing with Brother Lawrence while the girls get the tea ready."

Fran peered up the hill too, but she didn't see anyone. Not even a goose or a chicken.

Mrs. B stepped back off the path and laid her hand on the trunk of a huge beech tree. "Meet

Brother Lawrence. He's stood guard in this spot for a very long time. Well before I came here to disturb his solitude."

"The tree?" Fran couldn't keep the surprise from her voice.

That made Mrs. B chuckle. "I like naming my friends, don't you?" She pointed toward a cow grazing on the hill below them. "See, down there. That's Gretchen. A fine milk cow. Something every house needs around here. I seem to recall you're a city girl. Have you ever milked a cow?"

"No. I used to watch my grandmother milk on her farm, but she never let me try."

"She should have, but learning to milk is no problem. It's all in how you squeeze." She held up her hands and demonstrated. "You're not the first nurse to come to us without knowing the basics of mountain life."

She stepped down on the path and started toward the house. She wasn't very tall and a bit thick around the waist, but in spite of being in her sixties and having once suffered a broken back from a fall off a horse, she moved with only a minor limp.

She looked back at Fran. "I hear you had trouble on the bridge." When Fran couldn't hide her surprise, the woman went on. "News can come up the mountain fast as lightning. Best you remember that when you're out on district. Eyes and ears are all around. I expect all my nurses to uphold a strict standard of proper behavior and gentle care of these dear people here."

"Yes, ma'am."

When they reached the house, Mrs. B turned to give Fran another curious look. "How did you overcome your fear?"

"An old woman gave me some advice."

"And what was that?"

"She said I should dance across the bridge." That sounded a little silly when she said it, but Mrs. B only nodded her head as if it was what she expected to hear.

"And since you're here and not clinging to the side of the bridge, you must have done what she said."

"I did."

Mrs. B laughed out loud. "Granny Em is far afield today. She's not often on this mountain. She must have been looking for some rare herbs."

"She didn't tell me her name."

"Didn't or wouldn't?"

"Well, wouldn't, I suppose."

"That's Granny Em. But if she took the time to help you, feel favored. She doesn't take to all the nurses."

"Is she a healer?"

"She knows some good ways with herbs and delivered her share of babies as a granny midwife before I brought in you nurse-midwives. There have been times when she didn't favor me so much, even though I rode up every trail and where there weren't any trails, talking with all the granny midwives before I picked this spot for the Frontier Nursing Service. Most of them are fine with us here, but it's the smart nurse who listens to advice when it's given, whether that's from a mountain granny or from somebody like me who knows the better ways."

"I want to be a good nurse-midwife," Fran said.

Mrs. B leveled her gaze on Fran for a long moment. "Yes, I can see you do. I think it's time you moved out into one of the districts. Maybe Beech Fork. Betty tells me a number of mothers are ready to deliver in the next few weeks there. You can get your quota of births and then take the exam to get your midwifery certification."

"Thank you. I look forward to getting to know the people here."

Mrs. B's eyes narrowed a bit. "Yes, I think Betty Dawson will be the perfect teacher for you. Have you met her?"

"I don't think so."

"No matter. You will. But come." Mrs. B reached for the doorknob. "The tea will get cold. I've instructed the girls time and again to use the cozies, but some of them can't remember."

6

August 2, 1945

"Give me my gun!"

Ben looked up from notating the vital signs of his last patient. The panicked voice came from the tent next door, where a makeshift ward had been set up.

No enemy fire was downing soldiers now that the war was over, but plenty of men still showed up at the medical tents due to various and sundry other ills and accidents.

Ben ran toward the ward. In between the man's yells, he could hear a nurse trying to defuse the situation. A loud crash indicated the soldier was having none of that.

"I'm not dying without my gun," the man screamed. More crashes and the sound of broken glass.

A couple of patients pushed out through the tent opening. One of them grabbed Ben. "Nurse Bertram ordered us out, but you gotta help her. It's Jeffries. He's gone bonkers."

The tent sides shook. Ben pulled away from the man and ducked inside. He knew the soldier. Private Jeffries had come in with a fever caused by an infected cut left untreated too long. His sergeant reported that the man showed signs of shell shock. Now the fever must be pushing him over the edge.

The nurse was scrambling up from where the man had knocked her against one of the tent poles. Nurse Bertram was tough, but Jeffries was a bear of a man. Way bigger than even Ben. No way could he physically subdue him without help.

Ben stepped up behind Nurse Bertram. "I'll try to talk him down, but you better get a sedative."

"Right." With a curt nod, she slipped past Ben. Jeffries turned on Ben. The soldier's face was flushed and he was trembling all over.

"Stand down, Private." Ben barked the order like a sergeant might.

It almost worked. The soldier went ramrod straight and raised his hand to salute. But then a truck backfired outside the tent and pushed him back into the war zone in his head.

"The Krauts are out there." The private's eyes went wide as he stared at Ben. "You're not Sarge."

"You're right, Private Jeffries. But your sergeant brought you here. You're in a medic tent. The war is over."

"You're lying. You're one of them." The man made a sound something like Ben had once heard from a wildcat caught in a trap back home.

"Watch out, sir!" a soldier in the bed beside

Ben warned. A full cast on his leg must have kept him from escaping the tent with the other men. "He's about to blow."

"Keep your mouth shut!" Jeffries lunged up the narrow aisle toward the kid who spoke up.

Ben stepped in front of Jeffries and gave him a hard push backward that barely slowed the man down. Nurse Bertram needed to hurry with that sedative.

"Come on, Private. I'll help you look for that gun." That slowed him better than the shove but only for a moment.

"You're trying to trick me. That's what the enemy does. Tricks you. Then they shoot you." His face changed, looked tragic. "They killed all my buddies. My brothers. All of them." The anger came back. "But they won't get me without a fight."

He roared like an enraged bull this time and came at Ben. The beds crowding in on both sides of the aisle left little room for escape. Besides, he couldn't scoot out of the way and let the big man change his focus to the kid in the bed again. One messed-up leg was enough.

Ben blocked the man's way. "Easy, Private. We're on your side."

The man wasn't hearing anything except the battle in his head. He lowered his shoulder and banged into Ben.

Ben couldn't keep his feet. The man was too

heavy. He tried to catch himself as he fell, but then Jeffries came down on top of him. It didn't help that the bone snapping in Ben's arm sounded like a rifle shot.

Nurse Bertram was back with her syringe. Ben squirmed out from under the big man as the nurse found a place to stab the man with her needle.

Even before the drug had time to take effect, the soldier went from enraged to crying. "I never wanted to kill nobody. Not even those Krauts. I'm sorry."

The nurse got him up and, with the help of a doctor who appeared on the scene, led him back to his bed. "It's all right, Soldier. You'll be going home soon. Things will be better then." Nurse Bertram's voice trailed back to Ben.

Ben wondered if that was true. They all said the word "home" like it was a cure for everything. Home. If they could only get home, everything would be good. But Private Jeffries would still have those memories lurking below the surface. Ben too. The things they'd been through couldn't be brushed aside.

Holding his injured arm to his chest, Ben leaned against the foot of an empty bed and looked across at the young soldier. "You okay, kid?"

"You mean besides having a broken leg?" The kid smiled a little. "My leg bone made an even bigger crack than your arm."

"Lucky no shell-shocked guys were around you

at the time then." Ben tried a smile back at the kid but couldn't quite push it out on his face. He felt dazed. He started to reach up to see if he had a lump on his head, but he didn't want to turn loose of his arm.

He pushed away from the bed and the tent started spinning. War was a funny thing. He had gone through almost four years of stepping around land mines, diving for cover when the bombs started falling, and dodging bullets and shrapnel to pull wounded men back to safety without much more than a scratch. Not one battlefield wound, and now he'd been taken down in the middle of a hospital tent.

The kid kept talking, but Ben couldn't make out any words. He sat down on the bed. They'd get to him when they had time. Hadn't he done enough making one man wait with no more than a broken bone to stop another man bleeding? That's how you did things. Took care of those in the most need.

He had a banged-up arm, but he didn't have a broken mind like Jeffries. Like so many other men he'd seen in the field hospitals, tormented by seeing their friends die in front of their eyes and by the noise of death. Ben had heard it too. Death waiting in every explosion.

Nothing like the peace at home. He shut his eyes and let his mind drift to keep from thinking about the pain starting up in his arm. He was on the wooden porch in front of his father's house. His home. He had known no other except for those months he'd spent in a dorm on the Richmond college campus before the war. And then his home, if you could call it that, was the army, among his brothers in arms.

He didn't want to think about arms right now. Not his broken one. And not the arms that killed. Home. Better to let his mind drift to home.

He shut out every thought of war and imagined the cool mountain breeze on his face. Dawn was pushing back the shadows of night. The house perched high on the mountain like a bird on a branch. The morning sun bathed the porch in light when it slid up over the neighboring mountain. A mourning dove cooed and then a cardinal added its trilling song. Ben pulled in a deep breath and could almost taste the green pushing in on him from every side. From the open door behind him came the smell of biscuits in the oven and the rustle of his family coming awake like the morning. His father stepped out on the porch behind him.

His imaginings crashed down around him. Even after he did finally make it home, his father would never step out behind him. Instead he had stepped ahead of him into heaven.

But his last words to Ben before he climbed on the train to go to the army camp rang in Ben's ears. "A man does what a man has to do for his family. For his country. You do that and make me proud, son."

"Ben, talk to me." Nurse Bertram's voice brought him back to the hospital tent. Her cool hand touched his brow. "Did you hit your head?"

"I don't know." He tried to remember, but everything kept slipping away. "My arm hurts."

"Your arm is definitely fractured, but let me check your head." Her fingers explored through his hair on the back of his head. "Nasty lump there."

He winced. "Easy."

"Don't be such a baby." She pulled her hand back and flashed a light in his eyes.

"I'll just lie down here and rest awhile."

She put her hand under his arm. "Nope, Soldier, come on. No sleeping for you. You've got a concussion and we need to find a doctor to do something about that arm."

"If it's all right with you, I'll just go on home and see about it."

She laughed as she got him up on his feet. "This may be your ticket home, but we better work on you here. Are you sure you even have doctors back in the hills where you're from?"

"Doctors are kind of rare, but we have nurses. Frontier nurses. They ride horses to your house." Ben bumped against the bed. Everything was spinning again.

"Horses, huh?" She guided him past the beds.

"Maybe you can go home and be one of those nurses."

"No, that won't work. They're all women and right now I don't think I could stay on a horse."

"If I didn't know better, I'd think you'd been into that moonshine they say you have in the hills."

Ben tried to shake his head, but that made the room spin more. He shut his eyes and stayed still a second until the nurse eased him forward. "Nope. My pa never had a still. Never made any moonshine. Didn't believe in it."

"I see. And what do you believe in, Soldier?"

Her question circled in his head, spinning like the tent was spinning. He wasn't sure what to answer. He wasn't sure she even expected an answer. "The Lord" would have been the answer his father could have given without thinking twice. Ben could echo his pa, but shouldn't a man have his own words?

"Home," he finally said, barely above a whisper. "The hills of home."

7

August 28, 1945

Fran shot Woody a hard look after he let out a laugh when the cow at the Beech Fork Center swished her tail right in Fran's face and then tried to step into the milk pail. Fran managed to grab Bella's foot and save the milk. Milking wasn't as easy as Mrs. Breckinridge had made it sound or as Fran's grandmother had made it look.

"I'm sorry, Nurse Howard." Woody managed to gasp the words between his guffaws. "But watching you milk is a belly jerker."

"I'm glad I'm giving you such amusement." Fran wasn't a bit amused. As much as she liked Woody, she didn't need his appraisal of her milking ability. She was actually proud she'd figured out how to strip milk from Bella's teats. Unfortunately, Bella wasn't the most docile cow. At times, Fran was sure the cow was laughing at her, just like Woody.

Woody's house was up on the mountain in their district. To help pay for his family's yearly subscription fee for treatment, he came by a couple of times a week to bring them coal for the cookstove and to keep the weeds back from their cabin, but he claimed milking was women's work.

"Didn't you have no cow where you come from?" Woody asked.

"No."

"That's the wondering thing for me." He stepped over and stroked Bella's neck.

That distracted the cow enough that she stood still so Fran could finish milking.

"What's that?" Fran glanced up at Woody. She liked hearing the boy's wondering. Sometimes it led down some interesting paths to start her own wondering.

"How folks can live in places where there ain't no cows or chickens. Ma says that everything there in the city has to be store bought. Even potatoes and other sass."

Fran still didn't know why the mountain people called gardens "sass patches," but every family had one. They had one at the center too. Beans, tomatoes, cucumbers, and more. Raising your own produce was necessary here in the mountains where stores were scarce and money scarcer. But Fran hadn't expected harvesting and canning vegetables to be part of her nursing duties.

"It's a different world in the city." Fran stood up and whisked the milk bucket out of the way before she smacked Bella's rump and let her head back out in the pen. "There's no room for farming, although some people did plant victory gardens during the war."

"It's a fine thing the war is done with, ain't it?"

Woody plucked a grass stem and chewed on the end of it. "All the way done with. Ma and me danced around the cabin last night after one of the neighbors brung the news. 'Course we already knew Ben was on the way home. Had you heard about that? Got his arm broke and wasn't much use to the army over there. Leastways that's what he said in his letter."

"When do you expect him?" Fran headed toward the house to strain the milk through cheesecloth. Betty needed some to make potato soup. Then Fran would take the rest to the springhouse behind the cabin. That water coming out of the heart of the mountain kept things cool.

Woody trailed after her. "Hard to say. He said traveling army schedule is a mite uncertain. You'll like Ben."

Fran looked over her shoulder at Woody. "If he's anything like his brother, I'm sure I will."

"He ain't nothing like me. He don't say anything unless he's really got something to say. Sort of like Pa was. And you know Ma. She's like that too. Don't know what happened with me. Could be one of you nurses brung me out to the house in your saddlebag."

"I think your mother would know about that." Fran laughed. She'd heard about mountain children believing babies came in the saddle-bags, since sometimes the nurses carried the

69

babies to or from the hospital that way if the little ones needed extra care.

"She gives me that 'Ma' look when I say things like that. What she claims happened was that she went to a camp meeting over in the next county the week before birthing me. Said all those preaching words must have turned me into a jabber jay."

"Maybe you'll make a preacher someday."

"Ma used to say I might, but Pa said a man had to be called to preaching and then let the Lord put the words in his mouth. Not just jabber on like me."

Betty Dawson heard Woody's last words and looked around from the stove when they came in the door. "Your father was a wise man, Woody. Now, did you have a reason for coming down to see us?"

She didn't smile. Betty was a short, spare woman who rarely saw the humor in any situation. She kept separate from any of the mountain ways and advised Fran to do the same.

"I can admire their fortitude and love of family," Betty had told Fran when she first moved into the district cabin to finish her training under Betty's supervision. "But that doesn't mean I have to approve of their ways. Nor should you. Our job is not to pass judgment but to try to educate them in better hygiene."

Now her words stopped Woody at the door.

He looked down at his feet as if realizing he was barefoot and mountain while they were shod and city. Fran wanted to take him by the hand and invite him in to share their supper, but it was Betty's center. Not hers.

"Yes'm. I do have purpose in my trip down here. Ma's jarring up some pickles and wanted to know if you'd like some."

"Thank her for us," Betty said. "Your mother makes fine pickles, but tell her not to short herself."

"Yes'm. I'll tell her."

When Woody still hesitated in the doorway, Betty raised her eyebrows. "Anything else?"

"Well, she was thinking if you were up our way making your rounds and wanted those pickles that you might come by to check on Sadie."

Fran felt a pang. She should have already asked Woody about Sadie. They'd been treating the little girl for a bad summer cold that was settling in her ears. "I can come up and see her right now if she's sick."

"Ma said tomorrow would do. She thinks Becca might show up tonight and that way you can give Becca a once-over too."

"Becca?" Betty frowned a little. "Your sister?"

"She's moving back home for a spell. You heard about that mine cave-in over in Harlan, didn't you? Killed three men stone dead."

"We got the news," Betty said.

"A terrible thing. Was your sister's husband one of them?" Fran had heard some of the mountain men talk about being down in the mines. Their very words about blasting into the mountains for coal and making their ways through dark tunnels far underground made her shiver. Even worse than the sight of the green snakes that liked to sun on their porch steps.

"Carl was one of the last ones out. Said he could hear the tunnel crashing in behind him when he run out. The other miners in his crew went back to working, but Carl couldn't make hisself go back down in there. Just couldn't do it."

"So they're moving in with your mother?" Betty asked.

"Just Becca. Carl is heading up to Ohio to find work. But Becca wants to stay close to Ma until the baby comes."

"Then we do need to see her. Is she well along?" Betty said.

"Hardly worth speaking about yet. Ma says it could be a Christmas baby, but Ma says you nurses like to get an early start watching out for the babies."

"Tell your mother we'll be up that way in the morning. Now you'd better go on before dark catches you." She stared at Woody until he gave a halfhearted wave and, with a "yes'm," backed out of the door.

"That boy would spend the night if you gave him a minute's encouragement," Betty muttered before she turned her disapproval on Fran. "And it could be you encourage him too much. You need to keep a professional distance to do your job properly."

Fran barely stopped herself from saying "yes'm" like Woody. "He's a big help around here."

"True." Betty blew out a breath with the word, as though she hated to admit it. "Best get that milk strained. And what about the horses? Did you give them their feed and pick their hooves? You know they have to be ready in case somebody comes for us."

"I took care of them and fed the chickens and picked some beans. Looks like the beets could be ready." Fran carefully attached the cheese-cloth to the side of the crock with clothespins and slowly poured the milk through.

"Beets. I don't know why I let Em talk me into planting them. I don't even like beets. Do you?" Betty was the only person Fran ever heard call Granny Em by her name without the granny title.

"They're not my favorite, but I can eat them."

"Good. Then I won't have to. Have you seen Em lately?"

"Not this week, but the courier here last week . . . what was her name?"

"Hilda. Or maybe Wilma."

"No, Hilda is right. Anyway, she saw her down at the river. Said she was turning over rocks."

"Probably hunting something vile to put in her concoctions. She no doubt drank some of it and had to take to her bed." Betty shook some salt into the pan with the potatoes and set it on the stove. "We best go by and see about her tomorrow after we check on Sadie. Make sure she hasn't poisoned herself." A frown furrowed Betty's brow. "But Sadie. That child worries me. Maybe we should go over our notes about her after we eat. You best light the lamps."

Being out on district was totally different from working in the hospital. There the patients came to them and they contained them in beds all close together. Here they went to their patients, with nothing close about any of it. At the hospital, other nurses were around. Willie. Bucket. Rocky. Although Hilda had reported that Rocky was being assigned to the new Possum Center soon. She'd have a good time with the nurse-midwife there, Edie Marston. Fran had rarely seen Edie when she wasn't smiling.

Smiles didn't come as easy to Betty. But smiles weren't why Fran was there. Betty knew her business when it came to babies, and even if she could be a little prickly, she made sure their patients got good care.

But the biggest difference was how here at the center, something always, always needed to be done. No courier girls here to help care for the horses or run errands. They came by now and again with messages and supplies, the way Hilda had last week. Sometimes they slept on the couch if it was the edge of dark. Dark was what the mountain people sometimes called night.

In the mountains, dark could fall quickly like a woolen blanket dropped over the hills. Other times, night slipped in and settled down over the trees and houses like a mother gently tucking a cover around a sleeping child.

Hilda hadn't spent the night. She headed back to Wendover without the first worry of twilight catching her. She'd brought them the news about the terrible bombs dropped on the Japanese cities that ended the war. Atomic bombs. Some means of destruction never used before. Hilda claimed the bombs wiped out whole cities and killed over a hundred thousand people.

After she left, Fran and Betty couldn't believe Hilda had her story straight. No one bombing raid could kill that many. But when they turned their battery radio on before they went to bed, the story of the bombs and the Japanese surrender came through the airwaves.

The news flashed through the hills. Men shot guns up in the air and the children banged sticks on kettles and fences. The end of the war called for noise and celebrations. Woody and his mother weren't the only ones dancing for joy.

The people needed good news after the mine tragedy in neighboring Harlan County. No mines were dug into the hillsides in Leslie County, but Betty said it was only a matter of time until train tracks were laid to Hyden. With a way to haul out the coal, the mine companies would follow.

But now no noise of trains or mines disturbed the peace of the countryside. Fran liked stepping out into the twilight and hearing the night creatures. The whippoorwills. The frogs in the nearby creek. An owl. A chorus of dogs barking back and forth between the cabins in the hills. Sometimes she could hear a mother calling in a child from play. Good sounds and so different from what she might be hearing if she was in Cincinnati.

This night as she carried the milk out to the springhouse, she couldn't keep from thinking about Seth and how she had expected to be welcoming him home after the war. She'd often imagined them setting up housekeeping somewhere near his parents and her mother. She would still work as a nurse, but only until the babies came.

She looked up toward the stars beginning to show in the darkening sky and thought about how she used to wish on a star when she stayed at her grandmother's farm. *I wish I may. I wish I might. First star I see tonight.*

The stars had seemed brighter there on the farm, the same as here. No streetlights to dim their glitter. She couldn't remember what childish wishes she might have made then. She made no wishes now, even though she felt a stab of sorrow for what might never be. A baby of her own.

But she'd heard over and over how nobody came to the Frontier Nursing Service by accident. The Lord wasn't in the wishing business. He answered prayers. Sometimes in ways a person couldn't imagine. Perhaps the Lord had put her right where she was supposed to be.

8

August 29, 1945

The next morning, Fran was up before the sun to get what the mountain people called a soon start on their nursing rounds. But first she had to milk Bella again. That had to be done twice a day. Morning and night. But at least this time she didn't have an audience, although she could never be sure of that here at the center. People came seeking help at all hours.

Fran only lacked ten deliveries having the required amount for her training. Most of the deliveries in their district in the last couple of months had been routine. Only two women had been carried out to the hospital. Routine was good. That's how births were supposed to be, but they were never ordinary. Each time Fran helped a baby come into the world it was a marvel. A miracle of life.

But being a nurse-midwife here in the mountains was much more than delivering babies. Willie was right about the things she would see and treat. A bean up a child's nose. A broken bone. Gunshot wounds. A chopped toe. Lung ailments. Worms. Stomach problems. Anemia. Bee stings. Sometimes it made Fran's head spin.

It was hard to imagine one person being able to handle everything at one of the centers by herself, but Betty said that if Fran stayed on in the mountains once she received her certification, she might be assigned to a center alone.

If she stayed on. Fran hadn't thought about that. She simply thought about each day that came. Could she meet the challenges of whatever happened? A new infection to treat. The proper medicine to ask the doctors to prescribe. A chicken to pluck for their dinner. Lamps to fill with oil. Pills to count and keep in their pharmacy cabinet. Mice to keep out of their supplies. Records to keep on each patient.

Betty was even more inept than Fran with the housekeeping and stock tending. Before Fran moved in to the center to take the extra bed, a neighborhood girl stayed at the center to tend to the cooking, the garden, and the livestock. Betty made no secret of the fact that Fran's abilities fell far short of the mountain girl's.

But she was learning. Betty might not hand out many compliments, but she rarely found reason to fault Fran either. Except in the way Fran wanted to learn more about the mountain people.

As they saddled their horses to head up to the Locke house, Betty once again took the opportunity to lecture Fran against embracing mountain ways.

"You have to remember you're a nurse. An

educated nurse-midwife." Betty looked over at Fran as she mounted her horse, Moses.

Fran led her horse, Jasmine, in a circle to calm her. Jasmine was a tough little mustang, but headstrong. Fran stroked the horse's dark brown neck and whispered some nonsense words.

"Don't take all day with that horse. You need to let her know who's boss." Betty frowned at Fran and continued her lecture. "The same as you have to let the people know you're the one with the medical expertise. Not them. You have to remember your training and not listen to the people here. They're a superstitious lot who depend on old wives' tales for cures. Last winter one of the men told me he'd cured the cramps in his feet by putting his shoes upside down under the bed." Betty made a sound of disgust.

"What could it hurt if it worked?" Fran swung up into the saddle and patted Jasmine's neck when she danced to the side. Finally, the horse settled.

Betty clicked her horse forward, then turned to give Fran a hard look. "See, there's your problem. It didn't work. The only thing that could do is keep mice from nesting in his shoes. The cramps in his feet went away because I told him to drink more water and eat some pickles."

Eating pickles was Betty's answer to various complaints, from morning sickness to asthma. She pushed greens too in order to strengthen women weakened by bearing and nursing one baby after another.

"For the potassium," Fran said.

"Yes. The people here don't have the means to have fresh fruit all the time. They do have their vegetables and fruit in the summer, but they need better diets all year long. Some of them appear to subsist on gravy and biscuits."

"I suppose they have to make do with whatever they have."

"So they do, but that doesn't mean we can't enlighten them about proper diets and necessary hygiene. We have to make the changes we can." They rode their horses into the creek bed and started climbing. When the creek was low like now, it made the easiest way up into the mountains. "That's our duty as nurse-midwives."

"Yes, of course."

"A better diet. Shoes so the children won't get worms. Vaccinations. Emphasizing safety around the fireplaces. We suffer a bit with the heat now, but I can assure you these warm months are the best times here. Things get considerably harder when winter blows back our way. Ice and snow are not strangers to these mountains."

"Are you able to make the rounds then?" Fran remembered how sometimes a heavy snow could shut down Cincinnati.

"Babies don't check the weather when they decide to be born. We go where we're needed.

The horses have special winter shoes to help in the ice and snow. But if the horses can't go, we walk. Wouldn't it be nice to have one of those jeeps out here?"

"They have a couple at Wendover and the hospital now."

"Named, I suppose," Betty said.

"Naturally." Fran laughed. "Mrs. B does like naming things. Woody says one of them is Clara Jane and the other Diamond Lil."

"I could use a Diamond Lil about now." Betty slowed her horse and pulled a handkerchief out to dab her face. "It must be going to storm, as close as it feels this early in the day."

"I hope so. Everybody's sass patches need rain."

"See, there you are." Betty shook her head. "Calling gardens sass patches. I'm beginning to think you must be from Harlan instead of Cincinnati."

"Do people come to the midwifery school from Harlan or here in Leslie County?"

"Not as far as I can recall. Mrs. B brought in all her nurses. In the beginning, most were from England. Then she found a few New Yorkers like me to recruit. Mrs. B has a way of making it sound like such an adventure. Did she recruit you?"

"A different woman presented the program. Said she was a frontier nurse in the thirties. The best time of her life."

"I suppose she promised you a horse and a dog too."

"I have the horse." Fran stroked Jasmine's neck and let her move over to a pool in the creek to take a drink. Betty let Moses drink too. "But how come you don't have a dog?"

"Never cared much for dogs. Way too many of them around here, with hounds on every porch." Betty pulled on her reins and started up the creek again. "I guess you like dogs." She said it like that might be a character defect.

"I do, but I've never had one. My mother said town was no place for a dog." Fran looked at the land around the creek. "Here seems a perfect place."

"A perfect place for the dog to bring home ticks and fleas." Betty snorted. "I think Mrs. B put that in about a dog for every nurse, just to recruit those girls like you who have romanticized ideas of owning a dog. Back when England first went to war and most of the English nurses headed home for the war effort, she was desperate for nurses to fill their places. That's why she started the midwifery school. But now with the war over—praise the Lord—we should have an abundance of staff."

"Brought-in women."

"You are hopeless." Betty kicked her horse out in front.

Fran smiled. She was hopeless, but she liked

83

the mountain vernacular. The poetic sound fit with the hills and hollows. Granny Em's rhythm.

Cincinnati seemed far away as she followed Betty out of the creek and onto a rocky trail. The city might have a rhythm too, but few stopped to listen for it. Not even Fran when she was there. She'd been busy planning ahead. Everything she'd done had a reason for it. All leading to her imagined future with Seth. She wasn't sure she'd ever stopped to take in the blessings of whatever moment she was in.

Not that what she was doing now didn't have purpose. It did, but here the very landscape made you stop and pay attention. A person had to look and listen when out on the trails. Your horse's hooves clattered on the rocky trails and splashed through creeks. Birds sang you along the way and sometimes signaled your progress to those ahead. Flowers bloomed in abundance, watered by Mother Nature. Boulders and trees some-times blocked the paths, and it didn't do to think about what the blackberry bushes might be hiding in their tangle of briars. But most of all, a person had time to think while riding up and down the hills.

At a cabin near the trail, a couple of children paused from playing in the dirt to wave. Betty reined in Moses and Fran followed suit. The mother came to the door carrying a baby. One delivered by Betty before Fran came to the district.

"You're out right early." The woman stepped out on the stoop. "Are you needing a drink or some eats?"

"That's kind of you, Mrs. Newcomb. We'll come back this way another time." Betty knew how to talk with the mountain people, even if she didn't embrace their ways. "But how is little Marcus doing?"

"He's thriving, Nurse Dawson." When she held the baby up for them to see, he kicked his legs and giggled. "He's done learnt to crawl. I have to set one of these'n to watching him so's I can get my work done." She nodded toward the little girls who had edged back toward the stoop closer to their mother. The oldest one might be five, but in the mountains, children learned responsibility early.

"It's good you have help then."

The woman smiled. "That's ever bit the truth. I couldn't make it without my Deena and Lydia here."

The two little girls looked like they got two inches taller under their mother's praise.

"We best be on our way." Betty flicked her reins to start Moses moving.

"You headed up to the Locke place?" Mrs. Newcomb asked. "I hear tell Sadie is punying around. I'm glad my girls do fine."

"Healthy children are a blessing." Fran spoke for the first time as she turned Jasmine to follow Moses.

"That's the good Lord's own truth," Mrs. Newcomb called after them. "You tell Ruthena if she needs anything to let me know. Anythin' at all."

Fran smiled and waved. She knew Mrs. Newcomb meant it. Neighbors on the mountain took care of one another. But then she could almost hear Betty and Willie reminding her that sometimes the neighbors carried on long-running feuds too. That was one of the things Mrs. Breckinridge told her nurses to strictly avoid. Feuds and paying any notice to moonshine stills they might accidently run up on as they went about their rounds. The nurses were to turn a deaf ear and a blind eye toward that sort of thing.

They were there to serve the mothers and children who lived in their district. Sometimes the people's cabins were within hollering distance of one another. Other times the houses were high in the hills, surrounded by trees and hidden from the world, like Woody's house. A long climb from the center, but through a beautiful stretch of woods. Woody said Granny Em's cabin was a half-hour ride beyond his home, even higher up.

Granny Em told Fran she liked being high where she could just pitch her troubles out the window and let them roll clear to the hollow, never to be seen again. She did, as Mrs. B said, seem to favor Fran. She'd stepped out from beside the oak tree in the center's yard to meet Fran when she first rode up to Beech Fork a couple of months ago.

When Fran asked her how she knew she was coming, Granny Em laughed. "I don't have a special seer's eye, if that's what you're hinting at. But I got eyes and ears to watch the signs. A body can figure out a heap of things by watching the signs."

Fran had no idea what signs she could have watched to know when Fran would arrive at the center. But then, there was the mountain girl told to give up her bed at the center. And Woody had been at Wendover and had probably heard she was on the way. The boy wasn't exactly closemouthed about anything he knew.

She had no doubt he had shared with every-body on the mountain how inept she was at milking, since several of the women had given her some hints on dealing with a cranky bovine.

They still had a mile or so to go when a loud hello sounded behind them. They turned their horses to wait. That kind of hailing generally meant somebody had a need.

A man riding a mule bareback appeared around a bend in the trail. The mule's neck was lathered around the reins.

"The folks down yonder said you headed

up this way," the man said when he got closer. "Good thing. Saved me some time."

"Is your wife having problems, Mr. Nolan?" Betty asked.

They'd checked on Mrs. Nolan the end of last week. The girl, little more than a child herself at age seventeen, was expecting her first baby.

Ira Nolan wasn't much older and looked beside himself as he pulled up his mule. "Her back was hurting some last night and then today she started punishing bad. My sister said I better fetch you even if it weren't the time you set for it all to commence."

"Babies don't always cooperate with our time schedules, Mr. Nolan. But don't you worry. She's far enough along that everything should be fine even if she is in labor." Betty used her most calming voice.

"You are coming now, ain't you?" He looked between them with near panic that they might not listen. "Both of you." He settled his gaze on Fran. "My woman was askin' for you."

Betty spoke up before Fran could. "I'll come now, and Nurse Howard can come after she checks on a sick child." Betty turned away from the man toward Fran and lowered her voice. "Since this is a first baby, I'm sure you'll have time enough to make that visit. You best go on to check on Em too if nobody's seen her up that way. From there you can take the trail across the hill to the Nolans instead of going back down to the center. That will save you a good hour."

"Do I know that trail?" The mountain paths still confused Fran.

"You have your map, don't you?"

"Yes." Fran thought of the paper carefully folded in her saddlebag with the traces and creeks marked. She'd studied it time and again, but most of the markings remained a mystery to her.

"It's time you figured out how to find your way on the hills." Betty's mouth tightened with irritation. "Try to keep the direction in your head. The Nolans are due west of the Locke cabin."

"All right." Fran looked around. The sun was to her face. East. She just had to go opposite that.

Betty sighed as she turned Moses to follow Mr. Nolan. "Try not to get lost."

9

Jasmine whinnied and jerked her head when Betty turned Moses to follow Mr. Nolan back down the trail. Fran kept a firm hold on the reins. The horse tossed her head again and only grudgingly started on up the mountain.

She was a surefooted little horse but ready to shy at most anything. So far, Fran had only been unseated once, when a dove flew out of a rhododendron bush directly in front of them. Fran, as startled as Jasmine by the sudden whir of wings, slipped out of the saddle when the horse reared, with no harm done except to her dignity. Jasmine hadn't even run away, but turned to nuzzle Fran's shoulder as if wondering why she was sitting on the ground instead of in the saddle.

"I hope you know where you're going, little horse." Fran leaned down on the horse's neck close to her ear. "I'm not sure I do."

Fran could get lost in a minute. She tried hard to get her directions straight. East, west, north, and south. But where she needed to go was often some spot between north and south, east or west.

Betty told her to learn the creeks. Cutshin. Bear Branch. Chokeberry. The creeks all ran into the Middle Fork River. At least Fran did know the river. She'd even learned the best crossing places. But the creeks were different. They all looked alike. Water tumbling over rocks, downhill. Her father had once told her about the Continental Divide, where all the water flowed south on one side of it and north on the other. Or was it east and west?

That didn't matter here in the mountains. She did know up and down. Just not north and south. At least not after the trail made a few twists and turns.

East and west, she reminded herself. Check the shadows. Moss on the north side of the tree. North, east, south, and west. That should be easy enough.

Right now she wasn't worried. Unless she'd gotten completely off the trail, the Lockes' place was not that far up ahead, and if need be, she could retrace her way to the center. What made her throat tight was the thought of finding her way over the mountain to the Nolans'.

She didn't want to let Lurene Nolan down. Betty could handle the birth, if indeed Lurene was in labor, but Fran had promised the young woman to be there with her. Betty was all business and Lurene needed somebody to hold her hand and let her know she could get through this. Her mother had died some years before of tuberculosis, leaving a young Lurene to grow up in a house of men. Her father and brothers were little help to her now. She needed a woman's touch. And not just Betty's businesslike get-this-done-and-over-with touch, but a sweet touch of love. Fran could almost see Betty frowning at her silly thoughts.

A baby coming safely into the world was their business. Not filling in for mothers long dead. Other women in the neighborhood could do that if such was needed. But Fran couldn't see why their business couldn't include a gentle touch of caring. One woman to another.

Fran could learn from the women. She had never carried and birthed a baby. Neither had Betty or most of the frontier nurses. It was no wonder the mountain women sometimes looked askance at them giving out advice on caring for their little ones with no hands-on experience with children of their own. Fran wanted to go past the textbooks and lectures. She wanted to embrace how the mothers felt. That would better equip her to help them deal with the labor and birthing pains.

In the Cincinnati hospital, the doctors generally put the mothers into a twilight sleep to lessen the pain of labor. Births followed a more natural path here in the mountains. The mothers accepted and endured the pain of labor, but they welcomed the nurse-midwives to ease the baby's path into the world.

Fran caught a whiff of smoke right before she broke out of the trees into the clearing around the Lockes' place. A sturdy two-story log house sat squarely in front of her, with various outbuildings around it. A garden patch looked good, in spite of the scarcity of recent rains. Woody had to be carrying water from the creek to keep it green.

Smoke in the air meant Mrs. Locke was cooking or perhaps heating her laundry water in iron kettles over a fire in the yard.

"Hello." Woody swung down out of a tree to land in the path in front of Fran.

Fran was ready with a strong hold on Jasmine's reins. "You're giving Jasmine a panic."

"She's fractious for sure." Woody reached to touch the horse's nose. "Reckon I could ride her on to the house?"

"Sure. My legs could do with a little stretch." Fran swung her foot over and slid off the horse to the ground. "Don't you have a horse, Woody?" When she thought about it, Woody was always walking when she saw him.

"Naw. We have the mule, but he ain't much for riding. Does a fine job plowing and hauling wood. That sort of thing. Ma traded off Pa's horse after he passed. Said the Waynards over in the next holler needed her worse than we did. Pa always said Ma was generous to a fault. He pestered her some about that, but he didn't really mind." He stroked Jasmine's neck and grinned over at Fran. "I'm hoping Ben will want a horse when he gets home. Make getting around these hills a mite easier."

"I suppose so." Fran handed the reins to Woody. Jasmine stood still for him to mount. "She never stands that still for me."

"She's just tuckered out from climbing the mountain." He looked around. "Where's Nurse Dawson? Ma sent me out here to watch out for you in case you'uns needed help carrying your saddlebags or anything."

"She got called to a laying in." Fran smiled as she walked along beside Woody on Jasmine. Betty wouldn't like her using the mountain term, but Betty wasn't here.

"It's good you come on. Sadie is punying around for certain. She won't even go crawdad hunting with me at the creek. They're plenty easy to catch right now with the water so low. You think it's gonna rain soon?" Woody looked up at the sky and didn't wait for her to answer. "The sunrise was kinda red this morn. That sometimes means rain on the way."

"I hope so. Our garden at the center could use a good soaking."

"Yeah. Ours too. I've 'bout broke my back hauling water for Ma's tomatoes. And if the late corn don't get a dowsing soon, we won't have naught but nubbins."

Woody peered up at the sky again, where a few white clouds floated along and offered not the least threat of rain. The boy sighed. "Pa always said it rains easy when it's wet and hard when it's dry like now."

"Your pa sounds like he was a wise man."

"He was that. Everybody said so. He knowed a lot about everything, but he always said a man could learn more. That's how come Ma is making me keep on with school."

"School's in session now, isn't it?" When Woody nodded, Fran went on. "Then how come you're not there?"

"A man can't be expected to go every livelong day. I wouldn't get nothing done if I did that. I figure I can learn all the teacher knows to teach me, going a couple days a week." At the porch, Woody slid off the horse. "Mr. Harkins is fine with that. Claims it's some quieter on the days I ain't there. He's about give up on getting me to talk proper. You know, not saying 'ain't' and the like, but if I did that, folks would think I was putting on airs, sure as anything. I'll wait till I go to lawyering school to start city speak."

"Woody!" Mrs. Locke came to the door. "Stop talking poor Nurse Howard's ear off and go fetch some water from the spring."

"Yes'm." Woody picked up a couple of buckets and headed away from the house.

"Don't concern yourself, Mrs. Locke. I'm always glad to have Woody catch me up with

95

what's happening." Fran climbed up on the porch steps. "How are you doing?"

"I'm fine enough." She lowered her voice. "It's Sadie that's fretting me."

Ruthena Locke was tall and bone thin, but there was a strength about her that went deeper than muscles to her very core. She would do whatever had to be done for her family. No doubt had done as much all her life. Things were hard for her without a husband, but somehow with Woody's help she kept things going. She couldn't be much past fifty, but deep lines creased her face. They weren't smile wrinkles. Shadows under her faded blue eyes indicated the woman hadn't been sleeping well.

"Is she eating better?" Fran picked up the saddlebag Woody had laid on the porch. Her routine nurse equipment filled one side of the saddlebag and the midwifery supplies the other.

"She ain't an easy child to feed." Mrs. Locke let out a sigh. "She can mess with a spoon of beans till she nigh on wears them out."

Fran looked past Mrs. Locke to where Sadie played with a rag doll on the porch. "Maybe with the vegetables coming on in your garden, she'll have more of an appetite."

"She does favor sweet potatoes and corn." Mrs. Locke looked out toward her garden. "We've been putting rain in our prayers at the church. And we've been praying for you too, Nurse Howard."

"For me?" Fran was surprised. She didn't know anyone knew she was in need of prayer. After all, she hadn't shared her grief over Seth's betrayal with anyone.

"Yes'm. We pray for all the nurses what come up here to Leslie County. We know mountain life ain't all that easy for folks what weren't raised here. It's hard enough for those of us born to it."

"I like the mountains." Fran gazed toward the hills rising up beyond the garden patch.

"I can see that." Mrs. Locke smiled. "Our petitions to the Lord are working. Our prayers will surely help my Sadie too. I know they will. I've done been promised it wasn't the tuberculosis and she had a shot for some other worries." Her smile disappeared.

"The vaccinations help." Fran looked past Mrs. Locke toward the open door. "Woody says I might need to see your other daughter too."

"I did think Becca might be here today, but she ain't showed up yet. She and her man must have decided to stay another day or two with his folks 'fore he brings her over here. His people live a good piece across the mountain."

"Send word when she gets here and we'll come back. Woody says she's not far along."

"She's got a good climb yet ahead of her for sure before she gets her baby here, but come along and see what you think of Sadie. I've done had you standing on the steps past time." Mrs.

Locke stepped back and lowered her voice to a near whisper. "The child grieves after her pa. She ain't never been a young'un to clean her plate, but it weren't till Woodrow passed on that things got worse for her. She was her pa's little girl more'n any of the others."

The girl didn't show any sign of hearing her mother, but Fran thought maybe she had from the way she hugged her doll close when Fran stepped across the porch to squat down beside her. The child was fair of skin and her hair was more white than blonde. She didn't favor Woody all that much, except for eyes the color of a summer sky.

Most of the mountain children they treated were all arms and legs, but Sadie took slender to a different level. She looked almost fragile. She didn't seem to have the energy or the will to run, wade in the creek, or climb trees. When Fran and Betty came to check on her, she was generally on the porch or on the floor in the front room, playing with her doll or helping her mother fold towels or break beans.

"Are you drinking your milk like Nurse Dawson told you?" Fran asked.

"As much as I can." Sadie peeked up at Fran, then stared back at her doll.

"I imagine a glass of milk will taste good with whatever your mother is baking." Fran smiled up at Mrs. Locke.

"I do have pies in the oven. I'd best go check on them." Mrs. Locke glanced back at Fran as she started toward the door. "You will share a slice with us, won't you, Nurse Howard? Woody come across some windfall apples yesterday."

"That sounds delicious." Maybe she could get Mrs. Locke to wrap it up to take with her. She still had to check on Granny Em before she headed to the Nolans'.

After Mrs. Locke went inside, Fran put her hand on Sadie's forehead. Even though the child didn't feel feverish, she reached into her bag for her thermometer.

"I helped Ma wash the apples, but Woody says he did the hard part, fighting off the waspers for the apples and getting stung for his trouble." Sadie shivered a little. "I don't like waspers and bees. Ma said he should have shooed them off the apples before he picked them up. She says Woody always goes at everything full tilt and that some of these days he's liable to fall clear off the mountain in his hurry. I hope not, don't you? I wouldn't want to lose Woody."

"Nor would I." Fran shook down the thermometer with a couple of quick flicks. "Did the sting get all right?"

"Ma made a paste of baking soda and water. Says that takes out the swelling."

"Your ma knows." She put the thermometer in Sadie's mouth. "Now keep that under your

99

tongue and let's see who can win the quiet contest."

Fran held the child's wrist and counted her pulse. Then she checked her fingernails. Pink, as they should be. Her eyes were clear. No sign of nits in her hair. Betty had already given Sadie medicine for worms. She peered in Sadie's ears with a scope. A little red. The girl had chronic earaches that Betty said were probably due to her tendency to croup or perhaps some sort of allergy. Plenty of plants blooming all the time to make that a probability.

Fran took the thermometer out of Sadie's mouth. She had a slightly elevated temperature.

"I won, didn't I?" Sadie said.

"I don't know. I think maybe your doll was quieter."

Sadie giggled. "It's hard to win against Priscilla. She's always real quiet. Even when she's talking to me, can't nobody else hear her."

"What does she say?"

"All sort of things." Sadie held the doll close. "Secret things."

"Oh, then I'll just have to wait until she tells me herself. But has she been feeling bad? Does she have any pains anywhere?" Fran put her stethoscope on the doll's chest and then on Sadie's chest and back. No congestion.

"Let me ask her." Sadie whispered into one of the doll's black embroidered ears. Then she held the red embroidered mouth close to her ear. "She says her ear hurts a little and sometimes her stomach feels funny."

"Funny? How funny?"

"Like she can't drink any more of that milk less'n she has cornbread with it."

"Or pie?"

"Or pie."

"Then I think we're in luck. Here, let me fix her ear." Fran started to pretend to put a drop in the doll's ear, but then stopped. "But maybe first, you can show her how to tilt your head to let the drop go down the right way to help."

Sadie held her head to the side to let Fran put in the drops and then held up her doll for the pretend drops.

Fran smiled and started packing up her nurse's bag. "I think you're both going to be just fine. If you drink your milk."

Sadie looked around as though to be sure nobody else was close enough to hear. "Priscilla wants to know something."

"What's that?"

"It's one of those secret things so's you can't tell. Not even Ma." Sadie's eyes shifted to the side again.

"All right." Fran hoped that was a promise she could keep.

"Does everybody die and go to heaven?" Sadie fastened her gaze on Fran. "Even if they don't want to?"

Fran knew Sadie wasn't asking just about heaven. "Is Priscilla worried about somebody dying?"

"Pa did already, and Ma says everybody dies." A tear slid out of Sadie's eye and down her cheek. "She says Pa is happy in heaven. I want Ma to be happy, but I don't want her to go up there with Pa. Is that bad?"

Fran laid her hand on Sadie's cheek. "No, honey, that's not bad. And your ma may want to go to heaven someday to be with your pa, but she's not wanting to go right now. She wants to stay here with you for a long time yet."

"Are you sure?" Sadie clutched Fran's arm. "Priscilla says you're a nurse so you should know 'bout these kinds of things."

"I'm sure." Again she hoped her words would stay true for this mountain family. "You can tell Priscilla that." Fran softly poked the doll's chest. "Now, let's go eat some of that pie."

Sadie ran on into the house while Fran packed up the rest of her instruments.

"It ain't good to make promises you can't keep."

Fran looked up. Granny Em was at the corner of the porch.

10

"I didn't exactly promise," Fran said.

"Sounded like a promise." Granny Em stepped closer and stared up at Fran. She was so short her shoulders were barely higher than the porch floor. "To her."

"What would you have had me say instead?" Fran sat back on her heels. The old woman looked a bit pale and her cheeks were hollowed out, as though she hadn't eaten well for a few days. But those odd golden-colored eyes had plenty of snap.

"Best tell the truth as how the world is a hard place. Leastways up here in the hills." Granny Em's glare got fiercer. "You need to learn that if'n you're gonna be any count to us here."

"I do want to be a help." Fran didn't shy from the old woman's stare. "But I don't think it would be helpful to Sadie to paint a dark picture of her future. It's not unrealistic to think her mother will be here to take care of her for years to come."

Granny Em made a sound somewhere between a laugh and a sound of disgust. "I'm reckoning you still believe in fairy tales. And true love. All that nonsense."

Fran wondered if she should answer at all as she considered her words. She didn't believe in fairy tales and she knew that love could end up far from true. "I don't think the love of a mother for her child is nonsense. A mother's love can be considered pure love. Like that the Lord has for us." Too late Fran remembered Mrs. Breckinridge's instructions to not talk religion, politics, or moonshine with the mountain people.

"More nonsense." Granny Em slapped her hand down on the porch. "Don't need you preaching at me."

"You're right. I'm sorry." Fran turned back to packing her instruments. The contents of the saddlebag had to be evenly weighted in both sides to keep from breaking down her horse.

Granny Em watched her a moment. "Surprised you, didn't I? You was thinking I'd be the one shouting hallelujah at every camp meeting. Maybe handling snakes."

"No, no. I hadn't thought about that at all." Fran tried to turn the conversation. "Are you feeling well? We hadn't seen you for a while, so Nurse Dawson worried you might be feeling poorly."

"Then why ain't she the one here checking on my well-being?"

"She had to attend a more urgent call."

"The Nolan girl is having her baby, I reckon. I knew that girl lost her notching stick."

"Notching stick?"

"What she used to count up the months."

Granny Em laughed. "Or could be you nurses is the ones what counted up wrong."

"Babies sometimes come early."

"That they do. And sometimes old folks like me don't buy into the nonsense preachers talk down."

Fran knew she should be quiet, but she couldn't seem to stop the words as she looked at Granny Em. "Are you saying you don't believe in God?"

"Never said no such thing. Fact is, me and the good Lord come to a fine understanding up here on this mountain more years ago than I can remember." Granny Em laughed. A rusty sound. "Guess I lost my notching stick to count up my years."

"You don't know how old you are?"

"Oh, I know within a year or two. Ev'rything weren't writ down back when I was born, like as how it is these days with your certificate papers. Folks might scribble a name down in the Bible if'n they could write or knowed what year it was. But my folks' house burned down and they couldn't rightly remember what date they wrote down. Calendars never meant a lot to us. We lived by the seasons. I was born around corn-planting time. That was good enough."

"I suppose so." Fran stood up and towered over Granny Em on the ground. She felt like she should bend back down, but she needed to get moving.

"You staying for pie?" Granny Em headed for the porch steps. "Ruthena makes a fine apple pie. Better'n most."

When Fran hesitated, Granny Em went on. "If you're wonderin' how I knowed Ruthena had a pie, that ain't no mystery. I got a nose. Yours must not work too good if'n you can't smell a pie fresh out of the oven. And if you're thinkin' you need to move on to see to little Lurene Nolan, I figure you've got plenty of time for a slice of pie. First babies take a while. 'Course you might get lost. Seeing as how you get some confused even on trails that are plain as day."

"I'm not good with directions," Fran admitted.

"You jest need to learn the mountains. Remember that rhythm I told you about some time back when you was stuck on that swinging bridge."

"I don't see how a trail could have a rhythm." Fran placed her saddlebag on a straight chair on the porch and followed Granny Em inside. The apple pie did smell delicious.

Granny Em looked around at her with a shake of the head. "Guess you need to learn to use your ears too. Ev'rything has music. Horse hooves. Wind in the trees. Water in the crick. That's rhythm."

"Given by the Lord." Again the words were out before she could bite them back. Maybe she was preaching at the old woman.

"I ain't denying that." Granny Em almost smiled. "Not at all."

After she ate Mrs. Locke's pie that was as good as Granny Em said and drank some of the cool springwater Woody brought to the house, she gave Mrs. Locke more drops for Sadie's ears and headed out over the mountain toward the Nolans'. She guided Jasmine along the ridge Woody pointed her toward and listened to the horse's hooves on the hard ground. She could hear that rhythm and the one in the light breeze tickling through the leaves overhead. But she couldn't see how any of that could help her find her way.

As if to prove her right, the faint trail was suddenly swallowed by a patch of blackberry vines. She reined Jasmine in and pulled the map out of her saddlebag. She stared at the lines and markings and then looked around. Nothing seemed to match. She folded the paper and stuck it back in the bag. Better to just keep heading west. She could watch shadows to figure that out. But first she'd have to get past the briars.

She turned Jasmine down the hill and let her have her head as they maneuvered through some rhododendron bushes. At least they weren't briars. Fran tried to be thankful for that as she dodged and ducked away from the branches that snatched at her hair and arms. Jasmine wasn't any happier and stopped in her tracks. Fran could almost hear the horse wondering what Fran had gotten her into, as she twitched her ears and swished her tail at a horsefly that was tormenting both of them. Fran smacked at the bug and knocked it into the bushes.

"Just a little farther, Jasmine." Fran stroked the horse's neck. When that wasn't enough encouragement, she flicked the reins and prodded the horse with the toes of her boots. Not something Jasmine appreciated. She moved but headed directly toward a tree, where Fran barely ducked under a low-hanging limb.

But they did make it to the other side of the bramble thicket. Except there were more thickets ahead and no sign of a trail. None. Jasmine nibbled at a clump of grass and Fran didn't try to stop her. She could hear the horse chewing the grass and remembered Granny Em's rhythm, but chewing rhythm was no help.

She held her breath and listened for running water. If she could find a creek, that might pinpoint where she was on the map. Except that part about all the creeks looking alike. And that she couldn't hear a thing except a woodpecker working on a tree. A definite tapping rhythm there. She shook her head to forget Granny Em's rhythms. Fran didn't care about rhythms. She cared about finding the trail to the Nolans' cabin.

A crow cawed almost directly overhead. If Fran didn't know better, she'd think that old crow was laughing at her. Maybe the whole woods was. The whole mountain. Maybe that was Granny Em's music.

She couldn't hear a creek, but somebody might hear her. She called out a loud hello. Nothing but silence answered her. Why weren't there any mountain people around? There were always mountain people around. Except they probably had more sense than to end up in the middle of briars and brambles.

"Well, Jasmine, it's up to you and me to figure out which way to go. West. That's what we want. And surely there are ways around the brambles." Fran pulled up the horse's head. "You're a smart girl. Pick an easy path."

Fran could almost hear her grandmother's voice in her ear advising the easy path wasn't always the best and that when in doubt it was good to ask the Lord's guidance.

Grandma Howard prayed regular as clockwork. It didn't matter if she was having easy times or hard times. *In all things be thankful.* Fran did some regular praying. She whispered thanks over her food and most days expressed gratitude to the Lord for each new morning, but she wasn't praying the way her grandmother did. Not soul-stirring, stopping-and-listening-for-answers-back kind of praying. She didn't have time during the day with all her tasks, and at night she was asleep the minute her head hit the pillow.

But she hadn't forgotten her grandmother's teachings about the Lord. How he was a ready help in times of trouble. And wasn't she in trouble? Lost here on the side of a mountain in the middle of a blackberry patch.

"Let me see a trail, Lord. To the other side of the mountain. I did promise Lurene I'd be there to help her." Fran softly spoke the prayer aloud. Seemed to make it more real, even though she knew the Lord could hear unspoken prayers. "So if you could just give me a sign about which way to try?"

As if Jasmine understood Fran's prayer and was ready to be that sign, she raised her head away from the grass and began moving down the hill and then zigzagging back up to get past the brambles. And there on the far side of a huge rock was a bare trace of a trail. The ground was packed hard, but a few hoof tracks were still visible from the last time the trail had been muddy. That proved people, not just raccoons and foxes, used the trail. The path twisted around through more boulders, but it appeared to be generally westward. Fran breathed out a long breath of relief and looked up toward heaven with a whispered thanks.

A rattle jerked her attention back to the trail at the same instant Jasmine reared at the sight of the coiled snake in front of them. Fran kept her seat, but there was no holding the horse as she veered away from the snake into the bushes again. Fran pulled on the reins, but Jasmine jerked her head and kept going. They slid down a steep incline through brush. Jasmine was practically on her side and Fran's leg banged against the rocky cliff.

"Whoa, girl!" It was no use. In her panic, the horse couldn't get her footing.

Before the horse slipped and perhaps rolled on Fran, she slid out of the saddle. She couldn't stop Jasmine. Better to fall where she didn't see any rocks. And the snake was up on the trail. She wouldn't think about it having a friend down in the brambles. That was another thing her grandmother used to say. When you saw one snake, be assured there were two.

With Fran no longer yanking on the reins, Jasmine recovered her balance enough to scramble to her feet. Fran whistled, but the horse showed no sign of hearing as she took off across the hillside at a good clip. Fran whistled again, but the snake rattle was still echoing in the horse's ears. She didn't stop. At least the horse seemed no worse for the fall. Not if the way she was speeding out of sight was any indication.

Fran ran her hand down her legs. She too appeared to be all in one piece. Nothing bent or broken. Just a nasty bump where her shin banged against a rock. A scrubbed place stung on her arm, but everything was in working condition. She stood up and brushed off her pants, thankful her hands had escaped injury. A midwife had to protect her hands and not get scratches or cuts that might transfer an infection to the patient. That was one of the first things Mrs. Breckinridge had told her.

Fran ran her fingers through her hair to rake out a few twigs and leaves. Nothing for it except to walk. She could hope Jasmine would be waiting over the ridge, but she couldn't depend on it. The mare would either make her way back to the center or somebody would find her and bring her back. Mountain people knew their horses and everybody else's too. Fran's biggest worry was her saddlebag falling off into a briar patch. In case that happened, Fran started across the ridge the way Jasmine ran away to watch for it.

Her leg ached and she must have tweaked her ankle. Sweat dripped down her face, and when she wiped it away, her handkerchief showed traces of blood. She dabbed at a scratch on her cheek. She must look like she'd been fighting wildcats. But at least she didn't hear any more warning rattles or spot any snakes.

If only she could see Jasmine up ahead, nibbling on grass and waiting for her. But all she saw were more bushes. A mosquito buzzed in her ear. She swatted at it and then at a fly on her cheek.

Just when she thought things couldn't get any worse, thunder sounded in the distance. She peered up through the trees at dark clouds sweeping in from the west, bringing a wind with them to ruffle the leaves over her head. Surely after being dry for weeks, the drought wouldn't pick now to end.

It did no good to stand there wishing for a horse or a mountain man to appear out of nowhere to point the way. Rain or shine, she had no choice except to hoof it. She ignored the pain in her ankle as she headed across the ridge.

It was going to be a long, hard walk. She hadn't gone far when the clouds pushed all the way across the sky to cover the sun. Now she didn't even have shadows to point out the way west. But what could she do except keep walking? Lurene Nolan was counting on her.

— 11 —

A week ago, when Ben stepped off the ship back on American soil, he didn't kiss the ground, but he felt the joy of it all the way from his toes to the top of his head. Plenty of times he'd feared he might die on foreign ground, but he'd made it through the war.

He had to smile at the irony of his arm in a cast and his head still aching at times from the concussion. Who'd have thought he would make it unscathed through battle after battle only to get a stint in the infirmary for being KO'd by an overgrown, shell-shocked grunt. But the injury had put him on a faster track for home.

Home. That word had echoed in his mind for years. If only he could breathe the mountain air once more. He wanted to see his mother push the hair back from her face and give him that smile he'd sometimes earned as a boy when he'd done her proud.

He wouldn't see his father's smile or feel his work-roughened hand clamp down on his shoulder. The truth of that was a pain that got sharper with every mile closer to home.

For a while, he might need to step into his father's shoes to help his mother carry the load of trying to feed the family on their hillside farm. But he couldn't imagine continuing forever in that role. Barely scraping a living out of the hard ground. With few prospects for finding any paying jobs except in the mines. And yet the mountains called to him.

How could he want to be in a place and at the same time want to leave it behind? That question had trailed him all the way across the country after he got his discharge. His gun was gone, leaving his shoulder strangely light. He still wore his uniform, but he was no longer in the army. He was simply Ben Locke, ex-soldier without a job.

But he was alive and this day he wouldn't worry about the future. Not while he was getting off a train in Harlan to climb on the bus for Hyden. Almost home. That was what he needed to think about. Already home with the hills rising up around him. With people clapping him on the back and welcoming him back to the mountain fold. Glad he made it home. Thinking he was the same wet-behind-the-ears kid he'd been when he boarded that train in 1942 to go off to the army. A lifetime ago.

But none of them were the same. Not those who went or those who stayed at home. The war left its mark on a person. On a country. Now he simply wanted to shrug off the last four years like taking off a coat that had gotten too heavy. It wouldn't be that easy. But today with his feet touching home ground, he'd push aside all the bad he'd seen. He wouldn't think about what he'd do in the days ahead. He would simply soak in each moment.

He leaned back in the bus seat and let the voices of the other passengers swirl around him. Easy conversations about how they needed rain. Sad talk about a mine cave-in. Behind him, a grandmother sang softly to the young boy in her lap. Not a song Ben had ever heard. The woman was probably making it up as she went along, but the rhythm of her words wound through his head and made him remember being that child in his granny's lap, hearing a song about the mountains.

He shut his eyes and took in the sounds and the smells. Some not so pleasant, as the man across the aisle obviously didn't see the need in wasting soap. But Ben was used to that. And the air coming in the bus windows brought the scent of trees and animals. Home.

When he climbed down off the bus in Hyden and looked around, not much had changed in the years he was gone. More cars and trucks. Fewer horses. Some people on the street he didn't recognize. Or that didn't seem to recognize him but noted his uniform and gave him a nod anyhow. Plenty of others he did know.

In the general store, Mr. Saunders looked the same behind the counter as he had the last time Ben lifted a soft drink out of his cooler. Only this time he wouldn't take the coins Ben pulled out of his pocket.

"No sir. That army money's no good here today." The man smiled so big Ben could see where he'd lost a tooth. He came out from behind the counter to pump Ben's good hand up and down. "Mighty fine to see you back home, Ben. All in one piece. Heard you got wounded, but bones knit good as new. Fell out of a tree and broke mine when I was a boy. Works fine." He flexed his arm. "Better than having your arm shot off."

"Can't argue that." Ben had seen too much of that.

"Grab you a candy bar there to go with that drink." Mr. Saunders pointed to a rack of candy. "Least I can do for a returning soldier."

Ben took him up on the offer.

"Guess you're heading up to the homeplace." Mr. Saunders's smile faded. "Sorry about your pa. That was a real shock. He was a fine man."

"Yes." Sadness stabbed through Ben. His father being gone wasn't new. He'd known about it for months, but being back in the mountains made the pain fresh again. To give himself a minute to get his emotions under control, he popped off the bottle cap with the metal opener on the side of the cooler and took a long drink before he said, "Yes, he was."

"You hang around, somebody'll be coming by

to give you a lift up toward your place. A few folks has got hold of some trucks that can make it over rough ground. 'Specially when it's dry like this. That Mrs. Breckinridge got her nurses a couple of them army jeeps. Guess you know how they can go."

"Been in a few of them." Ben took another drink.

"Good for the nurses to make their rounds."

"No nurses on horseback anymore?"

"Still those too. Nurse Dawson out your way goes on horseback. Can't remember if she was the nurse at Beech Fork before you went to the service or not." Mr. Saunders leaned back against the counter and twisted his mouth to the side as he tried to remember. "You recall?"

"Been too long ago. Most all of them were from England back then."

"That's right. Mrs. B got her midwife training overseas. She claimed there weren't any like schools here, but now she's started her a midwifery school up there at the hospital. Had to, she said, seeing as how the English nurses mostly headed home to help their own people with the war going on." The storekeeper nodded toward Thousandstick Mountain. "Girls is coming in from different parts of America these days to go to her school. Still brought-in, but not clear from way across the sea."

"Woody wrote me about some of them."

"That Woody." Mr. Saunders laughed. "He knows everybody. If you ask me, the boy's got a future in politics. He can glad-hand with the best of them. You're gonna be in for a surprise when you see how he's done about growed up. And little Sadie isn't a baby no more. I did hear she was feeling poorly." The man reached into a jar of penny candy and scooped some out into a paper bag. "Here. Take this for her. She's partial to peppermint."

When Ben started to reach into his pocket, Mr. Saunders held up his hand.

"I done told you your money's no good here today. My treat."

"Thank you." Ben set his soda bottle down to put the candy in his duffel bag. He already had a doll stuck in there for Sadie and scarves from France for his mother and Becca. He'd snagged a surplus flashlight for Woody.

"Don't worry. Come tomorrow you come on back down and I'll be more than happy to let you spend some of that army coin burning a hole in your pocket."

"Guess I'm through collecting from the army," Ben said.

"Don't be so sure 'bout that, son. Old FDR fixed you up pretty good with the GI Bill before the Lord called him home. With that, you can go on back up to Richmond and finish out your schooling. Wasn't nothing like that for them boys

119

in World War I, that's for sure. But we didn't have Franklin Delano then either."

"Did you serve in the army?" Ben finished off the drink and racked the bottle in the return box.

"Naw. I slipped through both times. A hair too young then. A hair too old this time." Mr. Saunders shook his head. "Didn't grieve none about that. Never had no hankering to go to war like some. Happy as a bug in a rug right here selling folks stuff."

"Or giving it away." Ben held up the candy bar.

"Only on days of note." The man laughed. "You sit a spell here, and if nobody else comes along, I'll run you partway up the hill after I close down the store."

"I appreciate the offer, sir, but I'll just head on shanks' mare and see if I remember the trail home." Ben smiled, a little surprised that "shanks' mare," the mountain lingo for walking instead of riding a horse, had risen so easily to his tongue. It was as if he'd reached inside his head and flipped a switch. Back to his mountain upbringing after being gone so long.

He hadn't lost who he was in the army, but he'd learned to talk like everybody else there. Soldiers needed to understand one another. Especially when it was his job to bind their wounds and keep them breathing. Best not use confusing words at times like that. But here now, he could settle back into his home skin at least for a little while.

The mountain trail felt good under his boots. Different from the places he'd been. Places he could never have even imagined when he last walked down this mountain. Not that things were exactly the same as he headed up into the hills. A tree down here. More bushes there. A spring flood had pushed out a new gully down the hillside. A rock slide in a different place. But the ancient rocks and dirt underfoot were the same. The squirrel chattering at him from the treetop might be a few generations removed from the one that had fussed at him when he was leaving, but the chatter sounded the same. Now he was coming. Coming home.

He stripped off his jacket. He might like the feel of the mountain under his feet, but that didn't make the air any cooler. When a rumble sounded in the distance, Ben peered up through the trees at the sky. The sun was still shining but clouds were spreading up from the west. He hoped he didn't get caught in a gully washer, but if he did, so be it. He'd just keep going, even if he did turn out to be sorry for not waiting for that ride up the mountain in one of those trucks. Even a horse might make the trip faster.

Woody had been wishing for a horse, but if a man could find a wide enough swath of cleared ground, a motor car would be better. Ben liked driving the trucks in the army when the occasion arose. Going home didn't mean he had to go back in time. He could bring a little of the modern world with him, along with that horse for Woody. A boy needed a horse. And a dog of his own. Rufus, his pa's coonhound, had to be way past young if he was still living. Ten anyway. Only good for sleeping on the porch these days. Not a boy's dog.

Ben made a list in his head of things he could do when he got home. A horse. A motor car. A dog for Woody. A puppy for Sadie if his ma didn't fuss.

The rumble of thunder edged nearer. Ben figured he was still a good hour's walk from home. Maybe he should have shopped for a horse in Hyden before he started up the mountain. That would have made Woody even happier to see him.

Then as if his thoughts had summoned it, a horse came crashing through the underbrush. Foam flicked back from the horse's mouth to spot its neck. Reins hung loose and the saddle was empty.

The horse skidded to a stop as it eyed this obstruction in his path.

Ben put his hand out to the animal's nose. "Easy, girl."

The dark brown mare seemed ready enough to be captured. A pretty little horse.

"Where's your rider?" Ben took the reins and stroked the mare's neck. The saddlebag looked familiar even if the horse didn't. A frontier nurse horse. "Think we'd better go find her?"

Ben looked around. Hard to know for sure where the mare had come from. Up or down. Maybe across the hill. He tried to think what house the nurse might have been coming from or going to. Could be his mother's house. The storekeeper had mentioned Sadie wasn't feeling pert.

The poor woman might be lying somewhere hurt. He shouted out a hello, but the only answer was a blue jay's surprised squawk.

Ben threw his duffel bag across the horse's saddle and led it back the way it had come. The mare came calmly enough. If he remembered right, and he was sure he did, a spring bubbled up out of the hill not too far away. As a boy he'd roamed all over this hillside and knew every rock and crevice. Back then the spring never failed to have a little pool in front of it even in the driest seasons. The mare could use a drink and so could he. The nurse, if she hadn't already made her way to a house somewhere, could be that direction the same as any.

12

Fran fought her way through yet another thicket of rhododendrons. As beautiful as they were when they bloomed, right now she wished they weren't quite so prolific on this hillside. Each time she had to plunge through one of the thickets, she shook the branches and stepped gingerly. It was too easy to imagine more snakes hiding under the bushes. Actually she was sure her imagination was more than right about plenty of things scurrying around near her feet that she didn't want to know about. Thank goodness for boots. But she couldn't see any way around some of the thickets without a long walk uphill, and maybe not then. She did manage to ease past the blackberry brambles.

She paused in the deep shade of an oak tree. Plenty of acorns adorned its branches. A sign of a bad winter on the way, according to Grandma Howard. She should ask Granny Em if she believed the same. If she ever saw Granny Em again. If she ever saw anyone again. Could be she might wander around on this hill forever and die of thirst.

She was thirsty. And completely and thoroughly lost. Where were the mountain people when she needed one of them to point the way? She didn't care if they did laugh at her for being such a tenderfoot that she let her horse get away from her. Not that most of them would laugh at her out loud. They'd keep their faces straight while laughter built up in their eyes. No telling how many stories they were already telling on this inept brought-in nurse.

Fran wasn't worried about that. She just wanted to find her way over the mountain to the Nolans' house. She looked behind her. She supposed she could go back to the Locke house and get Woody to escort her along the right paths. She stared at the thickets she'd just fought through and had some doubts of being able to retrace her steps.

Another rumble of thunder sounded closer than it had a moment ago. A breeze sprang up to ruffle the leaves. And cool her face. That felt good, but it might not be good if she got caught in a storm. Fran wasn't afraid of storms. Not when she was watching them from inside a house. But out in the middle of the woods on the side of a mountain might be a different matter.

She could almost hear Betty saying it would be good practice. A nurse-midwife couldn't let anything stop her when she was called to deliver a baby. Storms. Floods. Snow. Sleet. Fran wiped her forehead again. No worry about snow on this day. But the trail might as well be under a couple of feet of snow. It was just as hidden from her.

Young Mrs. Nolan would have her baby and

Betty would be back at the center drinking tea before Fran found her way out of this overgrown wilderness. If only Jasmine hadn't run away. The mare was going to be in trouble next time she wanted an extra carrot or apple.

Fran tucked her handkerchief back in her pocket. While she couldn't see any sign of the sun through the dark clouds, the storm had blown in from the west. Maybe if she kept the wind in her face, she would be going in the right direction.

She picked out a tree a good way ahead. That's what Betty told her to do to keep from walking in circles. Walk toward something and when she reached it, walk on toward something new in the right direction. West.

She squared her shoulders and pushed through the undergrowth toward the tree. The wind stirred the leaves, then seemed to tease her by first blowing her hair back from her face and then whipping around to blow strands into her eyes. She hooked her hair behind her ears and kept walking toward the tree. She dared not take her focus off it, because one tree had a way of looking much like another.

No birds sang or squirrels chattered. Even the wind suddenly deserted her as everything went still. She felt totally alone in the world.

No, not alone. Never alone, her grandmother would tell her. Who was always there through every storm? Through every dark night? Fran whispered one of her grandmother's favorite Scriptures. "The Lord is an ever present help in danger."

She might not have the words exactly as they were in the Bible, but the thought was there. The prayer was there. She pulled in her breath and thought only of those words, while the wind seemed to hold its breath too.

What was that sound? Could she be so thirsty she was imagining the sound of water like a man in the desert seeing a mirage? Not a creek running over rocks, more like a trickle out of a pipe. She shut her eyes. Why closing her eyes helped, she didn't know, but it did. The water was up the hill to her left. Not too far. She moistened her dry lips and hoped it wasn't her imagination.

Then a fresh wind gust ripped through the trees, bringing the scent of rain. She might not need a spring. Water might dash down on her at any minute, but she headed up the hill anyway.

Lightning lit up the sky. Earlier in the summer before the dry days of August set in, she'd watched a storm from the door of a cabin high on the mountain. The storm clouds had settled down around the cabin and set it to shaking with thunder booms and lightning streaks. She didn't want to think about the storm settling around her now in the same way.

A few fat raindrops slipped down through the trees to plop on her head. She kept going toward where she'd heard water. Springs often bubbled out of a rocky place. There might be a ledge she could take shelter under, like an old bear. As long as the bear hadn't beat her to it.

And sometimes springs could mean people fetching water. Somebody who could get her back on a trail. She tried to remember the map that was in the saddlebag she fervently hoped was still on Jasmine. Seemed as though a spring was noted on the map not far from the trail she was supposed to take toward the Nolans'. So maybe all was not lost. Fran kept climbing. It was good to have a purpose. Then as quickly as she felt better, she remembered that moonshiners often located their stills near water. This overgrown hillside would be a perfect place to hide away from the law. Her steps lagged a bit.

The moonshiners wouldn't shoot her on purpose. Not while she was wearing the Frontier Nursing outfit, but it would be good to let them know who she was. If anybody was at the spring.

"Hello," she shouted. The wind whisked away the sound. So she shouted it again.

No answer, or none she could hear over the noise of the storm. She called out her hello again. Some nurses sang when they were going over the mountain trails just to let the mountaineers know they were about, but singing would be useless in the storm. Nobody could hear her. But she shouted out another hello anyway.

• • •

The mare jerked her head up.

"What's out there, girl?" Ben held the horse's bridle to keep her still while he listened.

A gust of wind swept through the trees. Ben raised his head up to get the full benefit of the cooler air. He'd been in storms overseas. Sandstorms in the desert. Rainstorms in France. Firestorms in battle that had nothing to do with nature and everything to do with man. But a lightning storm on a mountain was different. Sometimes the clouds would drop their fury right down on a person until his skin tingled.

The lightning must have been what had the mare's ears perked and her nostrils flared. She stamped her feet and tried to shake free of his hold, but he hung on. "Easy."

Then the wind took a pause and a shout came up from below them. A woman's voice. The horse whinnied. Perhaps recognizing his thrown rider.

"Hello," Ben called back. "Do you need help?"

"No." A second later a different answer. "Yes. Please don't shoot me."

Ben wasn't sure he heard her right. The wind was picking back up. Maybe that had distorted the words. He wasn't in a war zone now. No reason to shoot anybody.

"Why would I shoot you?" Better not to think about the times he had shot to kill. Not now on his first day home. Not with the sudden crack of lightning. The woman's startled shriek was drowned out by thunder that sounded too much like a bomb.

He pulled in a breath and let it out slowly. He wasn't on a battlefield and this woman wasn't the enemy. The thunder subsided to a rumble. "Do I need to come help you?"

"No, I'm coming toward you. If I can get through these blackberry bushes."

"Best go round," Ben called back to her, but a new clap of thunder covered up his words. The mare whinnied again and danced to the side. That lightning strike was way too close. He searched his memory of the hillside for a place to wait out the storm. He seemed to remember a rock ledge with a hollowed-out cave not far from the spring, but he couldn't desert the woman.

He held the horse and waited. Rain came down in a hard dash, soaking the cast on his arm. There was no help for that. It was time the cumbersome thing came off anyway. He'd tried to get them to remove it before he got on the ship for home, but the doctors said another week or two would guarantee the bones had knitted as they should.

"Come on, woman. Hurry up," Ben muttered under his breath. She must be a city girl. Getting unseated from her horse and then unable to find a path up the hill. But he could hear her getting closer.

Then she stepped out into the small opening around the spring. Wet locks of brown hair stuck to her cheeks and forehead. She shoved them back and picked a briar out of her hair. A few bloody scratches stood out on her face and arms. She had on the frontier nurse's uniform of blue pants and vest over a white shirt. She stopped and stared at him with wary eyes, her face showing a mixture of relief and apprehension.

She was surprisingly attractive. Ben didn't know why he was surprised. Maybe because the frontier nurses had all been much older than him before he went to war. But that was years ago now. He was older. They could be younger than he remembered. At least this nurse surely was.

She was very slim, but there was something enticingly feminine about her standing there in the rain watching him.

"You must be Woody's brother." When she smiled, her face lit up.

13

Even without the cast on his arm to give her a clue to who the man in front of her was, Fran would have known. His eyes were that much like Woody's except a darker blue. Eyes so blue she couldn't help but note their color even in the darkening air of the storm.

He had Jasmine. The horse tried to toss her head at the sight of Fran, but the man held her tight with his good arm.

"My talkative brother. Seems he must have been talking to you."

"He simply said you were on the way home." Fran kept smiling as relief washed through her that she wasn't facing down a moonshiner. A returning soldier from the war was much less threatening, even if he wasn't smiling. And no wonder. She had to look a mess, with hair plastered down on her head in the rain and bloody scratches decorating her face and arms from fighting through the brambles.

He, on the other hand, looked very handsome in his uniform, standing there as though the rain was no bother at all. Some mountain girl would be eager to welcome him home. Woody hadn't mentioned whether his brother was committed to a girl or single. It wasn't information she needed to know, but looking at him, she couldn't help but be curious. And a little envious of whatever girl might be waiting for him to make it home from the war.

She pushed that thought away before Seth's betrayal could stab her again. She had worries enough without that. Instead she looked at Jasmine and was very happy to peer past the soldier's duffel bag on the saddle to see her saddlebag still there. She hadn't lost her midwifery equipment.

"Thank you for catching my horse. A rattler frightened her into making a sudden detour." She stepped over to rub Jasmine's nose. "Without me slowing her down. Bad girl."

"I doubt petting her nose will convince her you mean it."

"Probably not. But she's a good horse most of the time. I like that she has spirit."

"A skittish horse can be dangerous on a mountain path." The man frowned. "Especially to an inexperienced rider."

"I'm not inexperienced." Fran gave the man a look. "Lots of horses don't like snakes and even the best riders get thrown now and again."

"True enough." He said the words, but he didn't look as though he believed them.

It didn't make any difference what the man thought of her riding ability. She didn't need to convince him of anything. She just needed her horse and the way to the Nolans' cabin pointed out. But first she'd get a drink. She might be soaked on the outside, but her mouth was dry.

She stepped past him to where a trickle of water tumbled out of a ledge of rocks and gathered in a pool. Fran cupped her hands to catch some water for a drink. After she had slaked her thirst, she splashed cold water on her face. That made her feel better and ready to move on.

The man watched her without a word until she reached for Jasmine's reins. "The storm's not over." As though to prove his words, lightning lit up the woods and thunder crashed down around them almost at the same time. "We best take shelter."

"I don't think there's anywhere to take shelter."

"There used to be a small cave not far from here."

"Big enough for Jasmine too?"

"Jasmine?"

"My horse."

"We'll find out." He looked back at her as he started away from the spring. "I'd let you ride, but it's a steep climb. Best for you and the horse both if you walk."

Fran followed him. It wouldn't do Lurene any good for Fran to get struck by lightning. As if she'd called it, the lightning cracked again, with thunder shaking the ground. A sheet of rain dashed down through the trees, mixed with hard pellets of hail that stung her arms. Jasmine whinnied, but the man kept going, forcing the horse to scramble along behind him. Fran trailed them, taking care to stay back from Jasmine's hooves.

Woody was right about his brother not being talkative. He hadn't even asked Fran's name, but then, she supposed she should have offered that. His name was Ben. No way she could not know that, with how Woody was always asking if she was still praying for him. She was or at least she had prayed for him and all the soldiers whenever she hadn't been too tired to keep her eyes open at bedtime.

She remembered asking Grandma Howard once the best time to pray. Her grandmother had said, "There's no right or wrong time. Anytime can be the best time. Or all the time. Me, I'm partial to walking prayers."

"Walking prayers?" That had been a puzzle to Fran.

"Those a person can say while she's busy doing what has to be done. Like when I'm walking to the barn or the garden. Grabbing minutes with the Lord. His children don't have to set up appointments for him to pay attention. He's always ready to bend down his ear to us."

"Like you do for me?" Grandma Howard had smiled and laid her hand on Fran's head. "Something like that, for sure. Only better."

Fran said one of those walking prayers as she followed Woody's brother. For safety in the storm. To eventually find her way to the Nolans' cabin. For Lurene Nolan to have an easy delivery whether Fran was there or not.

Woody's brother stopped and motioned her past him toward an overhang with a hollowed-out depression under it. She tried not to think about what else might be taking shelter under the ledge as she stepped into the small cave. Snakes. Bats. Spiders. All things she'd rather not face nose to nose. At the same time, the lightning flashed so brightly she saw spots. She shouldn't look askance at the shelter the Lord was providing.

The man stepped in behind her and pulled Jasmine partially under the overhang too. "We can wait out the storm here."

They stood shoulder to shoulder, so close Fran could hear him breathing. Jasmine snorted and then settled with her head turned toward the earthen wall behind them. The wet-horse smell mixed with the musty odor of the cave and that of their wet clothes. Fran shifted a bit to breathe the rain smell outside the cave.

"It's a little close in here, but the storm won't last long," Woody's brother said. "By the way, my name is Ben in case Woody didn't tell you that."

Fran looked around at him. He had to bend his head a little to fit under the overhang. "He did tell me, Mr. Locke, when he asked me to add my prayers to your mother's for your safety."

"With a mother and a frontier nurse praying for me, no wonder I made it home." Finally the man smiled. "And if it's not against your rules, Ben will do."

Lightning flashed to let her see how the smile lit up his eyes as well. A friendly smile that showed he was trying to put Fran at ease, huddled there in the little cave with him.

"I don't suppose there are rules against using first names." Fran wasn't sure about that, but it sounded too unfriendly to claim such a rule. She turned to stare back out at the rain.

He was silent a moment, as if waiting for her to say more. Maybe call him by his name, but she stayed quiet. If she was standing there with Woody, she could have been chatting along easily enough, but his brother was different. A man instead of a boy. She had to consider proprieties. The air under the ledge seemed to grow heavier and not merely because of the storm.

Finally he spoke up. "All right then. So, are there rules against telling your own name, Nurse? It seems odd to know your horse's name and not yours."

"I'm sorry. I didn't intend to be rude." She hoped he wouldn't notice the flush warming her cheeks. "I'm Francine Howard, but everybody calls me Fran." Her cheeks got hotter as she imagined Betty's disapproving glare for telling the man her first name. She tried to backtrack. "Or Nurse Howard."

"Glad to make your acquaintance, Nurse Howard."

She was relieved he chose the more formal address, but the relief was short-lived. "Francine is a lovely name."

"Thank you."

What else could she say? She couldn't take back her words now. She should have simply said Nurse Howard. Betty said the families they treated had no need to know their given names. She would probably tell Fran to step out into the storm instead of standing so close to this man that she could feel the cast on his arm against her back and feel his breath against her hair.

Her heart rate accelerated, but it was only her concern about whether being scrunched into a hole in the hill with a man was improper. That and the lightning and the worry of spiders crawling on her. She should simply turn her face to the wall like Jasmine and ignore it all. Even the man beside her. Or perhaps think of him as a patient. She could ask him about his arm, how it was healing.

He spoke before she could figure out something safe to say. Something that Betty might approve. "Why did you think I might shoot you?"

"I've been told it's best not to startle anyone

out in the woods." She tried to think of the most diplomatic way to explain. "We know the local people would never harm us nurses, but they are wary of strangers coming up on them unexpectedly. And with the storm and rain hiding the noise of my approach, I thought it sensible to shout out a warning."

"A warning?" He sounded puzzled.

"Maybe warning isn't the right word. I just wanted to let whoever might be there know they didn't have anything to worry about from me."

"Why would they be worried about you? You nurses haven't started carrying guns, have you?"

"No." Fran shook her head. "We don't need guns."

"Might come in handy against a rattlesnake."

"We just take detours around them. Sometimes long detours." Fran couldn't keep from smiling at that. "Jasmine shies easily, but she seems calm enough now."

"I guess she's not hearing any rattlers."

A shiver went through Fran at the thought. "I hope not."

"Then again, it might be hard to hear them over the rain."

Fran started to jerk around to see if he was serious, but then decided to keep her calm. "Horses know, rain or not."

"You could be right." He sounded amused again. "So you didn't have a gun to shoot anybody yourself and you wanted to make sure nobody shot you."

"Better safe than shot."

"Plenty of soldiers I've known would agree with that. But there's no war going on here."

"No wars like you've been in, but there can be other conflicts or problems a person might stumble up on. Especially at a remote spring or creek."

He suddenly laughed. "Of course. I guess I've been away too long. You were worried about moonshiners."

His laugh sounded like Woody, and if he went home and told this story to Woody, the whole mountain would know about it by next week. Maybe sooner. Not only had she gotten thrown from her horse and lost, she was afraid of moonshiners. Not one of her better days.

"I guess it is funny." She managed a laugh too. Might as well laugh at herself first. "I'm still getting used to mountain ways."

"Not everybody who lives in the hills is a moonshiner." He wasn't laughing now. Instead he sounded a little offended.

"I didn't say they were." She started to apologize, but she hadn't accused him or anybody else of being a moonshiner. It was certainly a fact of mountain life that moonshine was made in some of the hollows and on some of the hills. If he grew up here, he had to know that.

An uncomfortable silence pushed into the cave with them. Fran had no problem imagining the man's frown, even though she didn't look around at him. Instead she shifted a little toward the outside of the cave. Rain was still peppering down, but no hailstones bounced off the rocks. The lightning and thunder sounded more distant.

"It looks like the storm is passing. I thank you kindly for catching Jasmine and guiding us to this shelter, but I should move on. A baby is on the way over the next ridge." At least she hoped it was over the next ridge. She didn't really want to ask him for more help, since his mood seemed to have darkened, but she'd be foolish not to ask for directions. "Can you point me toward where the Nolans live?"

"Nolans?"

"Woody told me they lived west of your place. I was just there checking on Sadie."

"Is she all right?"

"Trouble with her ears. Nothing serious, but she does seem to have one problem after another. Your mother is trying to get her to eat more." Fran twisted to the side to look at him. "You coming home might be the best medicine for her. She misses her father."

"I can't step into his place."

"I didn't mean that you should, but having you home will be a good distraction for her sorrow." She softened her voice when she saw the sadness settle on his face. "And perhaps for you as well. It must be hard for you to come home and not see him here."

He tightened his mouth as though he didn't want to admit any struggle, but his eyes gave him away. She let him pretend what he wanted and said, "But about the Nolans?"

"Name isn't familiar to me."

"Well, they are young. I think she was an Abrams. Lurene Abrams."

A look of recognition and surprise settled on his face. "Lurene Abrams is having a baby? She wasn't but thirteen when I left. Not even as old as Becca."

She started to tell him Becca was in the family way too, but decided that wasn't her place. "She's young, but some mothers are younger. So can you point me toward where she might live?"

"Maybe. For a price."

"A price?" She stared at him. She had yet to meet the mountain man unwilling to point out the way she needed to go to this or that patient's cabin. "I don't have any money with me."

"I don't want money."

14

Ben bit his lip to keep from smiling at the look on the nurse's face. Nurse Howard. Francine. Fran. He supposed he should be ashamed of himself, but she shouldn't be so ready to jump to conclusions about mountain people. His people. He'd put up with enough of that in the army when he told people he was from the Appalachian Mountains. Outsiders were always ready to judge.

Then again, she was right about the spring being a possible hiding place for a still. It could be he should have let out a shout before he walked up to the spring. A nervous moonshiner was apt to shoot first and ask questions later. That would have really been something. Make it home from the war only to be shot on the way up the mountain toward home.

But whether she was right or not, that didn't mean he couldn't still make her at least think twice before she branded every man in the mountains an outlaw. The way she was looking at him right now, it was evident she was doing plenty of wondering about him.

He had to give her credit though. She stood her ground and was doing her best to stare him down. It wasn't hard to imagine her thoughts.

Alone in the woods with a man she didn't know. Thinking he might be about to force himself on her.

He let her think it. He thought about it himself. A kiss would be interesting. He tried to remember the last time he'd kissed a girl. There was Ginny here at home. They'd kept company before he went to the army. But he'd asked for no promises and she'd made none. His mother wrote that Ginny got married a couple of years ago. Moved to Perry County. Probably had a kid by now. Then there'd been that nurse in France who grabbed him and planted a kiss on him when Germany surrendered. Not sure that counted as a real kiss.

Kissing this woman he'd just met wouldn't count as a real kiss either. But it was an interesting thought. Not one he had any intention of carrying out and not what he really wanted from her. Could be, he had let her stew about it long enough. She might even now be feeling around behind her for a loose rock to knock him in the head. She didn't look like the wilting type.

"You think you could trade a little of your nurse expertise for directions?" He nodded toward the saddlebag on the horse. "You have surgical and such tools in there?"

She quit trying to edge away from him, but her frown deepened. "I can't give you my equipment."

"I don't want you to give them to me. I want you to use them."

Now she looked even more astounded. "What are you talking about? This is no place for surgery."

He smiled. "I've done some doctoring in worse places."

"That's right. Woody said you were a medic in the army." Her frown eased a bit. "So what do you want?"

"This blasted cast off my arm. You might not even need a scalpel. The rain soaked it and it's crumbling." He held his arm out toward her. The light was dim, but an accommodating flash of lightning lit up the shallow cave.

She changed right in front of his eyes from the frightened woman lost in a storm to the nurse ready to help as she reached out to prod the cast. Her fingers made impressions in the soft plaster. "How long has the cast been on?"

"A month."

"Not long enough. Bones take a while to knit." Her voice had no give. "You need to go to the hospital and get a new cast."

"I'm going home. Not to the hospital, and the cast is coming off whether you cut it off or I do." He kept his voice every bit as sure as hers.

She shifted her gaze from his arm to his face. Again the lightning cooperated to let her see he meant it.

"That's your decision, but I can't do something that might be harmful. You don't want to have a crippled arm."

"You and I both know a wet cast is not a good cast." He softened his look on her. "I'm asking you to help me."

She didn't shy from his gaze. "Do you give your word you'll not use your arm until you get it checked out?"

He was still holding the mare's bridle with his good arm so he held up the arm with the cast and kept a solemn face. "I give my word, Nurse Howard."

"All right." She breathed out a long sigh. "I'll probably get reprimanded for this."

"I'll tell them I did it."

"I don't lie or ask others to lie for me."

"Ever?"

"Lies just double back and make things worse."

"You sound like you're speaking from experience."

She had been looking around, perhaps considering where to perform the cast removal, but now her look shot back to his face and then quickly away, as if his remark had hit too close to home.

"Everybody has been lied to at some time, don't you think?" She didn't wait for him to answer. "We'll have to do something with Jasmine. You can't hold her while I'm cutting on your cast, and it would be better if you were sitting down." She peered toward the back of the shallow cave.

"The storm is letting up."

"It's still raining."

"Rain won't hurt your horse or us. As long as the lightning moves off. I'm guessing you've been wet before."

She almost smiled. "I think we're both already soaked. Okay, I'll tie Jasmine up to a tree and you find a place to sit. The rain might help keep everything clean. We don't want an infection. But I'm sure you know that after working with the injured in the war."

"Yes." He could tell her about some of the things he'd seen. Gangrene. Shrapnel embedded in muscles. Men screaming. He shut his eyes and pushed the memories aside. "I do know."

"Good." She gasped as she ducked past Ben out into the steady downpour. She clucked her tongue at the mare and eased her out of the shallow cave where she attached the reins to a branch. The horse shivered as the rain peppered down on her, but then lowered her head to nibble at a bush.

The nurse got her saddlebag and stepped back into the cave to open the pouches. She pulled out scissors and some cotton that she stuck in her pocket. After she slid an apron over her head and tied it behind her back, she poured alcohol on her hands and a scalpel. He'd done the same thing with various instruments out on the battlefield.

"If you run out, I can try to find some moonshine." He stepped closer to her.

"The alcohol will be fine, but they tell me moonshine works in a pinch." She held the scalpel to the side as she answered evenly. She obviously wasn't going to let him goad her into saying something she might regret. She was a nurse now. He was the patient. "Did you pick out a place to sit?"

"I can stand and lean against the rock here."

She flashed him an irritated look. "I know you can stand, but I want you to sit. You'll need to rest your arm on your leg to steady it. If you don't want to cooperate with my orders, I'll leave you to your own devices and continue on to deliver a baby."

"Is that your bedside manner?"

"When necessary." She didn't smile.

"All right. Why don't we step out into the rain, Sergeant Howard?"

She didn't flinch when he said *sergeant*. "A sensible choice, Mr. Locke." She nodded toward a knee-high boulder just outside the cave. "Sit there."

He should have simply pointed the way over the hill and gone on to his house where he could have easily removed the cast himself with his mother's help. He wasn't sure what had made him ask her help. She was a nurse, but he had been a medic. Still, he had asked. So now there was nothing for it except to do as she said, sit in the pouring rain, and feel more than a little foolish.

What had she gotten herself into? When Betty heard about this, she'd be called on the carpet for certain. As she should be. Removing a cast before the proper time had passed for the bones to heal. But the man was right. The cast was a soggy mess.

She was a soggy mess too. Rain dripped down into her eyes and trickled down her shirt collar. Her tie had come undone in her fight through the underbrush and now hung every way but straight. The cut on her arm was burning like fire from the alcohol. That was probably good, but it didn't feel good. Not that she was about to complain out loud. Not to this man wounded in the war.

But Woody said he wasn't wounded in battle. It was after the war ended. Fran probed the cast, looking for the best place to cut it off. She didn't want to slice open his arm. She wasn't a surgeon. She was a nurse. But here in the mountains, nurses had to do all sorts of things they might never attempt in other places. They had to treat whatever came their way. Not that this qualified as a necessary treatment. She shouldn't have agreed to do it, but it was too late to back out now with him watching her, almost daring her to get on with it.

Even as a kid, she paid no attention to dares. If she didn't want to do something, she didn't do it. So did that mean she wanted to do this? No, what she wanted was to get on Jasmine and find her way to the Nolans' house. If only she didn't have such a terrible sense of direction.

"Let me know if you feel anything." She made a slight cut.

"By then, it might be a little late."

"There is a considerable difference in a scratch and a deep cut. I will be careful, but you can help by making me aware if something goes wrong." She looked straight at him. "Understand?"

"Yes sir."

She ignored the prod. It didn't matter what he called her. What mattered was getting this foolish operation over and done with. She leaned over his arm, much too aware of how close she was to him. Something that had not bothered her in all the people she had treated in Cincinnati or the mountains. But now she could almost feel those dark blue eyes watching her. A man's eyes. Not just a patient's eyes.

She made herself concentrate on the cast. The rain had done most of the work for her already. He was right to know the cast needed to be removed after getting soaked. She shifted closer to see the cut she was making and felt his breath against her cheek. Her own breath came a little faster.

"Am I making you nervous, Nurse?"

"I'm simply trying not to hurt you." That was true, just not the entire truth. He was making her uneasy. She remembered her earlier statement about lying, but at times, the entire truth wasn't necessary. This was definitely one of those times.

Betty would say she shouldn't have put herself in such a vulnerable situation. The men they treated might be patients, but they were still men. And the nurses treating those men were still women. Not that Fran thought Ben Locke was looking at her with any kind of romantic interest. She wasn't the kind of woman who attracted men and certainly not a handsome man like this returning soldier.

"Don't be too concerned. I'm pretty tough," he said.

"Especially, I would think, after being in the war." Fran shifted her thoughts away from a man and woman alone in the rain to what he'd experienced. Always better to think about the patient rather than herself. "Woody says one of the soldiers you were treating attacked you and broke your arm."

"The kid was having a bad time."

"Was he hurt?"

"Nothing you could see, but yeah, he was hurt. Not everybody can handle seeing his buddies blown up."

"I guess not." She kept her voice low, calm.

151

For all she knew, Ben Locke might have some of the same invisible wounds. She shifted talk away from the war. "As dry as it's been, this gully washer won't cause a flood, will it?" Weather was surely a safe topic.

"According to how long it rains."

"The Middle Fork River was flooding when I got to the mountains back in May, but I'm told that since then, it's drier than normal."

"What made you come to Hyden?"

"To go to the midwifery school. I was a nurse in Cincinnati, but decided a change of scenery and learning new skills would be good."

Ben laughed. "You got that change of scenery. That's for sure."

"The mountains are beautiful. I was here in time to see the rhododendrons bloom. Since then, I've seen something new nearly every day. It's like getting a new gift to open each morning."

"I'm doubting you'll count standing out in the rain, working on a recalcitrant patient, as one of your better gifts."

"I can be grateful for the rain." She laid the scalpel aside and used her scissors on the last connections of the cast. She gently pulled the cast away from his skin.

Ben lifted his arm free with a grimace.

"Moving your elbow may be painful for a while after being immobilized so long." She soaked a cloth with more alcohol and carefully cleaned his arm. The bone felt straight when she probed his arm, and his muscles were strong under her fingers. With a bit of good fortune, he should be fine without the cast. That was a relief, because she had doubts about whether he would make the trip to the hospital for a new one.

"But it's good to move it." He pulled away from her hands and bent his elbow.

"As long as you're careful for a little longer. Remember, no lifting with that arm, and please, avoid falling at all costs. If you do trip, tuck your arm up against your stomach and protect it."

"You'd rather I fall on my face and break my nose?" He frowned as he lifted his arm in the air.

"Yes." She pulled a strip of cloth out of her bag and fashioned a sling for him. "Here. See if this works."

He slid the sling over his neck and positioned his arm in it. "You do know that doctors say a fracture that heals makes a stronger bone than before."

"That's after it's fully healed." Fran stepped back under the shelter of the cave to wrap the scissors and scalpel in the alcohol cloth.

Ben stayed seated on the rock. She knew he was watching her, but she ignored him while she packed her supplies back in her saddlebag. She positioned the bags on Jasmine, who seemed unconcerned about anything now that the thunder had retreated. Even the rain had let up until it was little more than drips from the branches overhead.

She grabbed a handful of her own hair and squeezed water out of it before she brushed through it with her fingers. Then she wrung out her tie and the edges of her sleeves and wished for a towel. Even her boots had collected water while she stood in the rain, working on his cast. Her socks squished with every step. She leaned back against the rock wall and pulled one boot off to shake a few drops of water from it.

"Best take off your socks and wring the water out of them too," Ben told her, no doubt from the experience of many marches in the rain.

Without comment, she did as he said and then pulled the sock and boot back on before doing the same with the other foot.

She turned to untie Jasmine's reins when Ben spoke up again. "Thank you, Francine."

His use of her given name stopped her in her tracks. And then she surprised herself even more by saying, "That's Sergeant Francine to you."

When he laughed out loud, she smiled at him with no thought of what was proper or not.

15

Sergeant Francine. That was the last thing Ben expected the woman to say after she'd been so stiff and uneasy while working on his cast. Nothing stiff or unfriendly about her now as she smiled at him. A smile as bright as the sun that suddenly popped out from behind the clouds and streamed down through the trees.

He should have known better than to try to get the upper hand on a nurse. He'd been around enough of them during the war to know they didn't quail at much and certainly weren't bothered by a wisecracking soldier. But those women were battle-tested. He didn't know about this Francine Howard. But she was here. Alone on a mountain, making her way from one house to another through rough country. That showed some backbone.

He was glad they could part friends, even if he'd done plenty to make her do nothing but frown and hope she never saw him again.

"Time to keep your part of the bargain." Her smile disappeared from her lips but remained settled in her hazel eyes. She pulled a folded paper out of her saddlebag. "Directions. Here's the map I have of the area. If you can show me where I am now and point the way toward the

Nolans', I'd be grateful. It can't be too much farther, can it?"

Ben studied the hand-drawn map with creeks and paths and houses marked. Easy to read for him. It was home. But a glance up at the nurse's worried face showed the marks didn't mean much to her.

He stepped over beside her. "Face that way." She turned the way he pointed. "That's west. Toward the sun heading down."

"If another storm doesn't hide it," she muttered.

"Clouds don't change it being west." He put his finger down on the place where the spring was marked and traced a line up the paper. "This is Redbud Spring where we met, but we climbed up a ways to this cave." He stooped a little to make his face on the same level as hers. "See that ledge of rocks."

She leaned forward to get a better look, then shook her head. "I don't see anything but trees and they all look alike. How do people ever figure these paths out?" No smile remained on her face. "Half the time I can't even see a path."

"I guess it helps that I was born here."

"Nurse Dawson, the nurse I'm working with, has no problem at all and she's from New York. But she says I could get lost in the backyard at the center." She sighed. "And she's not far wrong. Is there a trick to knowing your directions?"

"Just a matter of paying attention to where you are and learning a place."

"I'm trying." She peered down at the map and then back up at the trees. "Granny Em tells me to listen for the rhythm of the woods. I sort of know what she means, but I can't see how that will help me figure out how to get where I need to go."

"Granny Em? Is she still kicking?" Ben smiled. "That old woman had cures for everything."

"So far she hasn't been able to cure me getting lost. She was at your mother's house eating apple pie when I started this way. That had to be hours ago. Mrs. Nolan's baby will be long birthed before I find her place."

"Maybe you should just head back to the center then," Ben suggested.

"No. I promised Mrs. Nolan I would be there. So I will. You say it's that way." She turned to stare back in the direction he had indicated. "About how far?"

"Two, three miles. Farther than you've come from my house."

"But not that far. If Jasmine doesn't dump me again, we should make it easy enough if I can keep on the right trail."

With the tip of his finger, Ben traced off her path on the map, pointing out the landmarks. She watched him carefully, repeating some of what he said before she folded the map and stuck it back in the saddlebag. With one easy movement, she mounted her horse and did appear comfortable in the saddle.

"Thank you. And be careful with that arm."

He slid it back in the sling. "Yes, Sarge."

Another smile and then she clucked her tongue at her horse and at least headed out in the right direction. Ben watched her, feeling something like he had in the army when he pointed fresh recruits toward the battlefield. Like he should go along to guide them, protect them. To see that they made it through.

But she had made her way in the hills before he got home. If she got lost again, somebody else would find her and point her in the right direction. Home was calling him. Maybe there would still be a piece of that apple pie the nurse had mentioned. It would be good to put his feet under his mother's table again.

He slung his duffel bag over his shoulder and slid down the damp hillside until a path ran along the ridge. Then he walked fast.

It gave Ben a start at the sight of a man working on a fence around the sass patch in front of the house. He could hardly believe that man was Woody, even after the boy looked up, let out a whoop, and jumped the fence in one bound to run toward Ben.

"Ma told me to keep an eye out for you. She had the feeling you'd be making it home today.

'Course she's been saying that ev'ry livelong day for a week." Woody's smile went practically from ear to ear.

Ben dropped his duffel bag and forgot the nurse's warning as he slipped his arm free of the sling and grabbed Woody in a hug, lifting him off the ground. The boy might be almost grown, but Ben was still bigger.

The boy laughed and then pulled free to run ahead of Ben, yelling for their mother. Ben didn't run. He wanted to take it all in. The sight of the house. The smell of the rain-washed dirt. The cow mooing in the pasture and his pa's old coonhound barking and then hobbling toward him with his tail whipping back and forth.

Ben leaned down to look the dog in the eyes. "Good of you to come out to meet me, Rufus. We've both changed some since I last saw you."

The dog nuzzled his hand and then licked Ben's chin.

Ben's mother stepped out on the porch, drying her hands on her apron. Sadie leaned against her, a shy smile on her pale face. Woody came back down off the porch to take Ben's bag and circle around him like a happy puppy.

At the bottom of the porch steps, Ben stopped to look up at his mother. "Hello, Ma."

She'd aged while he was gone. New lines creased her face that had nothing to do with smiling. But a smile was in her eyes now. "Good to have you home, son."

"Good to be home."

She put her hand on the girl's shoulder and gently pushed her forward, away from her side. "Tell your brother hello, Sadie."

She was a pretty child. Her white-blonde hair lay in curls around her face, and she had her father's sky-blue eyes like Woody. Ben had gotten a mix darker. Still shy, she hunched up her shoulders and said, "Hello."

"Hi there, baby sister of mine. You weren't knee high to a grasshopper last time I saw you and look at you now. Half as tall as your ma."

She giggled a little. "Ma said you wouldn't hardly know me when you got home."

He climbed up on the porch to squat down in front of her. "Now don't you be worrying about that. A brother always knows his sister no matter how long it is between sightings of her. Think you could give me a hug?"

She stepped into his arms and giggled again. "You're wet."

He gave her a quick hug. "Got caught in that storm a while ago. Along with that nurse lady who said she'd just been here to see about you."

"Nurse Howard is nice." Sadie leaned back against Ma.

"She left here some time ago." Ma frowned.

"She should have done been on the next hill way before now."

Ben stood up. "Her horse pitched her off and ran away. I happened to come up on it and caught it for her."

Woody laughed. "That Jasmine does give Nurse Howard fits. Was she lost? Not Jasmine, but Nurse Howard."

"Actually she was."

"I was feared she would be. I should have took her over the way to the Nolans', I reckon. But I figured I'd just slow her down. Me with no horse." Woody slid his gaze over to his mother and quickly away when a corner of her mouth turned down. "She was some anxious to get there."

His mother shook her head a little. "The poor girl does get in a quandary about directions. But it appears the Lord sent a different Locke to help her out this time." She reached over and put her hand on Ben's cheek. "Your pa prayed for you every day 'fore he passed, son. And I don't have a doubt in the world that he kept on laying your name before the throne even after he was walking those streets of gold. He was a praying man."

Ben swallowed down the tears tightening his throat and managed to nod.

His mother's eyes softened on him, but no tears showed there. "I sent away a boy and you've come back a man. But good to see you haven't turned hard."

"A war can turn a man that way," Ben said.

"I know it can." She held both her arms out to him. "Grown man or not, you can still give your old ma a hug."

She was rail thin, but there was strength in her arms as she tightened them around him. Then she was stepping back. She'd never been a woman with much time for hugs, even in her gentlest moments. "I baked some pies. Come on in and get on some dry clothes whilst I put on some coffee."

It was good to be dry, even if the shirt he found in the chest was tight across the shoulders and the jeans loose in the waist. The army rations had changed his body. But if his mother kept making pies like the one she set before him, he'd find those pounds he'd lost soon enough.

They sat at the table talking about things that didn't matter and things that did while he ate three pieces of pie without his mother once saying he was going to ruin his supper.

"Becca's coming home." His mother looked toward the door almost as if she expected to see her coming in right then. "I thought she might be here today, but they must've decided to stay over at Carl's folks an extra day. He's gonna head up to Ohio and look for work."

"It's hard to think about Becca married." Ben pushed his saucer away.

"And in the family way."

"Sure enough?"

"She's young, but no younger than I was when I carried my first. She's staying here till the baby comes. Be a while. Not till December, she says. But that will give Carl time to find a job and get settled up north. All my children seem to be wanting to leave the mountains." She reached over and touched his arm. "I'm glad you let the mountains call you home."

"I wanted to see home again." There was no need in adding how, as much as he was glad to feel the mountain back under his feet, he didn't know if he could stay forever. Forever plans could wait for another day.

Sadie looked up from playing with her rag doll. "I don't ever want to leave here, Ma."

Ma smiled at her. "You're my girl, Sadie bug."

Outside the cow started bawling. Woody stood up. "You want me to milk her tonight, Ma?"

"No, I'll do it. You take care of the hog and the chickens."

Woody hesitated at the door. "You think I oughta head down to the center and milk their cow? If the Nolan woman has a long lay in, won't nobody be there to take care of Bella."

"No need going all the way yourself. Go down and see if Jeralene can do it. She used to work for Nurse Dawson there. She'll know where everything is."

"Yes'm." Woody had a bounce in his step as he went out the door. "I'll hurry back to tend to my other chores."

Ma almost laughed when he was out the door and running down off the porch.

"You must have given him a chore he favored," Ben said.

"It's Jeralene he's favoring. He's sweet on the girl."

"He says he wants to marry her someday," Sadie spoke up. "Soon as he's old enough."

"Well, that's not yet." Ma gave Ben a look. "Could be you should have a talk with the boy. Make sure he knows how to behave. That Woody is so all awhirl with ideas that sometimes he don't stop to think out things in a clear manner. He's ever bit a boy, but man enough to get hisself in a fix."

That pushed the one missing at the table back into Ben's thoughts. His pa should be the one talking to Woody. Ben wasn't ready to take on a father role. He wasn't sure what he was ready for. Maybe not anything. He just wanted to let his feet get used to home again, but sometimes a man couldn't step back from what needed to be done. He'd learned that lesson well enough in the war.

"If you think I should." Ben took a sip of coffee.

"He might listen to you better'n me. He's a good boy. I'm not saying he ain't, but he can be willful." Ma stood up to put what little was left of the pie back in the warming oven. "I guess I worry too much, even though the Bible speaks against it. But I think the Lord understands a mother's concern for her children." She laid her hand on Sadie's head in passing. "This one here gives me plenty of concern, what with how she picks at her food. Can't even get her to tuck into that pie."

"I ate some of it." Sadie looked up at her mother and back at the pie left on her saucer.

"I'll save the rest for your supper." Ma picked the saucer up. She handed Sadie a bowl of scraps. "Go on and feed Rufus. He's got his nose to the door waiting for you."

His mother watched her out the door. "She just keeps punying around. Ever since your pa died last year. Some before too. The child's never been sturdy the way you and the others were."

"The nurse I met said she had an earache."

"Ear troubles all the time. The nurse give me some drops for her." Ma leaned against the cabinet. "Nurse Howard has a good way with Sadie. Better'n Nurse Dawson, but they both aim to help her. Nurse Howard is new. Did she tell you that?"

"She said she was learning to be a midwife."

"I hope she stays on after her training. She's

165

different from some of the others. Not to say the other nurses aren't fine, but Nurse Howard has a spirit of kindness. She don't look down on us. Even Granny Em has taken to her and she don't take to many outsiders."

"The nurse said something about Granny Em being here. I was glad to hear she's still around."

"You just missed her. She was here, but headed on home a little bit ago." Ma poured them both more coffee and sat back down at the table.

"She still concocting her cures?"

"Don't make light." Ma twirled her cup in her saucer. "She knows her herbs and there's times her doctoring works as good as the nurses' brought-in pills. She fixes me up a tonic from time to time."

"What do the nurses think about that?" Ben raised his eyebrows at his mother.

"Nurse Dawson does everything she can to make sure we don't pay no mind to Granny Em. I'm thinking the new nurse ain't so set against her. If she thought Granny Em's herbs would put apples in Sadie's cheeks, she'd be for it."

"You sound like you like her."

"She's a nice enough girl. For somebody from off of here. And she's done won Sadie and Woody over." She sipped her coffee.

"She must bring them candy." Ben leaned back in his chair and thought about Nurse Howard.

Francine. Sergeant Francine. A smile tickled around his lips. He could see why people were taken with her.

"Peppermint for Sadie and she lets Woody ride her horse now and again."

"She had a nice mare."

His mother's eyes sharpened on him. "Did you talk to her long?"

"We took shelter from the storm in a shallow cave up from Redbud Spring. Then I talked her into cutting the cast off my arm." When his mother frowned a little, he went on. "It was wet and crumbling. We were in a gully washer rain."

"I see. Did she think it was knit back together?"

"She wasn't sure about that, so she fixed a sling for me. It's drying over there on the chair." He pointed toward it. "She made me promise to fall on my nose and not catch myself with my arm if I slipped." Ben smiled and flexed his arm a couple of times. "It's fine."

"I reckon you know best after your medic training." She stood up again and touched his head as she had Sadie's a moment ago. "It's good to have you here at my table. And Becca coming. It'll be nice to have the house full again after Woody and Sadie and me have been rattling around in here all of a lonesome."

She turned to pick up her milking bucket. "Best see to Blondie. I hear her mooing again."

"How come you didn't let Woody have a horse? I had one at his age."

"But Woody ain't like you. That boy wanders all over the hills as it is. No telling where he'd end up if he had a horse." She stopped at the door and looked back at Ben. "I wanted him home."

"You can't keep a person home that's wanting to leave."

"That ain't something you have to tell me. But he just turned fifteen. He's got a few more home years without no more wars to steal my boys."

"I guess you're right."

Ben followed her out on the porch, where Sadie was sitting with Rufus and Woody was just coming into sight on the path up the hill to the house. Home. A few home years. He could live with that.

16

August 30, 1945

Fran caught Lurene Nolan's baby boy just after daybreak. Granny Em had been right when she told Fran she had no need to hurry. First babies did have a way of taking their time being born. After laboring for over twenty-four hours, the young woman could barely lift her head off the pillow to look at the baby when Fran held him up after she cut the cord. The baby seemed almost as stressed and his cry was weak. Fran handed him off to Betty, who began gently massaging his arms and legs.

Betty might be stern and more than a little prickly at times, but she loved the babies.

"What a fine boy you are," she cooed. "You're going to grow up strong and able. I know a fine boy like you will. Come on and let us hear you cry. It'll be music to your mama's ears and to mine too."

"Is he all right?" Lurene whispered. She sounded scared.

The poor girl was so young. Just a slip of a girl, as Fran's grandmother used to say. But she had borne the long labor with the resigned fortitude evident in many of the mountain women.

Fran let out a soft breath in relief when Betty answered, "He's a little worn out from his trip out into the world, but he's going to be fine, Mrs. Nolan. Just fine."

As though to prove it, the baby's cries grew louder. Fran peeked over at the baby waving his arms in fury and had to smile. *That's the way,* she thought. Swing out at the world. She turned her attention back to Lurene.

They wouldn't leave until they had given her instructions on basic care of herself and her baby. Then they would come back often in the next few weeks to check on both mother and child. Lurene was fortunate to have her brother's wife, Stella Abrams, nearby to help her. The sister-in-law brought them supper last night and promised to come back to cook breakfast after she saw to her own family.

Mrs. Abrams had offered to fetch Fran a change of clothes when Fran showed up soaked to the skin. No way could Fran wear anything the tiny Lurene might have in her wardrobe. But when Betty's frown grew darker at the suggestion, Fran thanked her but refused. Her clothes would dry. She did set her boots with her wet stockings draped over them by the woodstove in the kitchen. She didn't care how much Betty frowned. Feet needed to be dry.

And the fire in the stove had to be kept up regardless of the heat in the cabin so they could have the hot water they needed. Fran had taken a pan of that water out on the little back porch that slanted a bit precariously away from the small house. She brushed off her damp clothes and combed her hair into place.

Then she scrubbed her hands and arms until they were red. Cleanliness was essential in healthy births. Last, she washed the apron she'd worn while working on Ben Locke's cast. After she wrung as much water out of it as possible, she draped it around her neck. It too would dry on her, and the apron made her feel like a nurse. She hoped it would convince Betty too, who had looked horrified when Fran showed up disheveled and looking worse for the wear.

"What in the world happened to you?"

Betty had put her fists on her hips and glared at Fran as she slid down off Jasmine. Fran handed the reins to young Mr. Nolan, who looked glad to have something to do besides wait for his baby to make an appearance.

"A rattler on the trail spooked Jasmine, and when she dived off the trail down an incline, I lost my seat. She ran off and I had to chase after her through some rough country. Then I got caught in the storm." Fran tried to shift the conversation. "Did it hit here? The lightning was awful where I was."

"It stormed," Betty answered shortly. "And I guess you were lost."

171

"I did get a little off trail."

"Why didn't you look at your map?"

"The map was in my saddlebag on Jasmine. Luckily, I happened across Woody's brother headed home from the war. He had found Jasmine and caught her. Then he was kind enough to point me in the right direction." Fran saw no need in going into details about her meeting with Ben Locke. If Betty found out about her standing shoulder to shoulder through the storm in that bowl-shaped cave or about her cutting the cast off the man's arm, she'd have to hear it from Ben Locke.

The Nolans' house was small with only two rooms, but it had porches and was spotless, as though Lurene had prepared for the nurses to be there. When the young mother had looked up from the bed and saw Fran, such a smile lit up her face that Fran didn't regret her eventful trip there.

Through the long night of labor, she'd sat by the girl, letting her grip her hands during the worst contractions while Betty napped in a rocking chair and Lurene's husband paced the night away on the porch. Now and again he tiptoed inside the house and poked his head in the bedroom door, but he seemed afraid to come nearer. Having babies was women's work.

Now at the sound of the baby crying, the young father peeked through the door again. Fran glanced around at him. "You have a son, Mr. Nolan."

He let out a whoop and ran back outside to jump off the porch. Out the window they could see him running around the yard, sending the hens, fresh off their night roosts, squawking out of his way. His hound dog joined in with a howl.

"Good heavens." Betty frowned.

But the young mother smiled as color crept back into her cheeks. "Ira gets in a whirr. My pa says he surely ain't the silent type."

"A new son is reason to get excited." Fran looked at the girl over the sheets draped in a tent over her legs.

"That's sure enough so." The girl moistened her dry lips. "If I weren't so done in, I'd be out there shoutin' with him."

"No running around like a banshee for you." Betty gave her a stern look. "You need to rest and let your body recover. Remember, you're a mother now. You have to think of your baby and what's best for him. A healthy mother is necessary for a healthy baby."

"Yes'm. I aim to be the best mother I can be to my little feller." Lurene twisted her head to peer at the baby Betty was efficiently bathing while ignoring his protests.

"You'll make a fine mother." Fran patted Lurene's leg, then massaged her abdomen to help her pass the afterbirth.

After all was taken care of, Fran gave Lurene a few sips of water. Then they helped her to the pot before they settled her back in the bed, now with clean sheets.

Betty placed the baby, bathed and wrapped in a blanket, in his mother's arm. The look on Lurene's face brought tears to Fran's eyes. Then when Ira came in, hat in hand, to shuffle over to the bed with a look of wonder as he touched his baby's face, she wanted to go over and hug them all. Instead she turned her eyes away and continued to clean up. This was their private moment.

The love between the young parents failed to move Betty. She gave the father a hard look. "You did wash your hands after you touched that dog out there, didn't you?"

He jumped away from the bed and scurried to do as Betty said. She called after him. "With soap." Then she shook her head and muttered something under her breath that Fran couldn't make out. That was just as well.

After a breakfast of eggs and biscuits with fresh-churned butter and blackberry jam, Fran and Betty watched Lurene nurse her baby. Sometimes that was simple and sometimes a baby needed encouragement to latch onto his mother's nipple. This baby had a good sucking instinct.

"If I have trouble, Stella says she'll help me."

Lurene looked over at her sister-in-law, who had brought her toddler girl with her. "She says she can help nurse him if I don't have enough milk, being so skinny like I am."

"Skinny doesn't matter. You just need to be sure you eat more than cornbread," Betty said.

"Yes'm. I remember what you said about the collard greens and eggs. We most always have plenty of eggs. And Ira, he's good at bringing home game for the table. Fish out of the river now and again and squirrel and rabbit. We eat fine."

They wrote down the little boy's weight, six pounds four ounces, and the name Lurene and Ira picked for him.

"Ira Leonard Nolan. After me and her pa," Ira said with a burst of pride. "She wants to call him Lenny."

After telling Lurene they'd be back in a day or two to check on her and the baby, Fran and Betty headed back to the center. As Jasmine tripped along behind Moses, Fran tried to pay attention to the trail since she'd have to come back up it soon, but it was all she could do to keep her eyes open.

"Don't fall out of the saddle," Betty told her. "You wouldn't be much help with a cracked head. We have clinic tomorrow."

"Nobody is expecting a baby tonight, are they?"

"Mrs. Perkins up the way is a few weeks out.

And Mrs. Tipton has been having some worrying signs of not carrying her baby to term. But with good fortune, we might get a full night's sleep." Betty looked back at Fran. "You should have napped when you could last night."

"The poor girl was scared. The least I could do was hold her hand."

"That's noble thinking, but you have to take care of yourself too. A tired nurse-midwife can make a mistake. A sleepy nurse-midwife can fall off her horse." Betty shook her head. "And we'll still have tasks to do when we get back to the clinic."

"I need a bath."

"Best milk Bella first."

Bella. Fran hadn't once thought of the cow. "Poor Bella. Her bag will be ruined, going without being milked for a whole day."

"Don't worry about that. The folks around the center will see to her. Your talkative friend, Woody, might have even come down and milked her."

"He says milking cows is women's work."

"A lot of things in these mountains turn out to be women's work." Betty made a face at Fran over her shoulder. "But you say Woody's brother came in from the army."

"Yes."

Betty slowed Moses as they stepped their horses into the creek to make the final leg to the center. The water was up a little after yesterday's rain, but still only hock high for the horses.

After settling Moses into a walk beside Jasmine, Betty asked, "Is he like Woody? Ready to talk your arm off?"

"Not at all. He seemed very serious minded."

"I suppose the war might make a man that way. More soldiers will be coming back to the mountains." Betty laughed a little. "Guess that might mean a baby boom for us in nine or ten months. If you're still here." She looked over at Fran. "Have you thought about what you might do after you finish your training?"

"I wouldn't mind staying in the mountains a while if there is a need."

"That would be up to Mrs. Breckinridge, you know. Whether she thought you were capable."

"And that might hinge on what you tell her." Fran didn't see any reason to avoid that truth. Betty was the one who would report to Mrs. Breckinridge.

"I suppose it might." Betty kept her eyes on the creek bed in front of her horse. "I can't fault your nursing ability or how you help babies into the world. It would be good if you could stop getting lost every time you go up in the hills. A lost nurse-midwife is no help at all."

"You're right. I need to learn the area. Get to know the people and where they live."

"It's all right to get to know where they live,

but it's important to keep a separation. You are not one of them. You can never be one of them. Heaven forbid to even consider being one of them." Betty shivered at the thought. "In a way you have to admire their obstinacy. Even when it infuriates you that they won't listen and learn better ways. They do endure. But no, I'd never want to live their life."

"Do you ever think about going back to New York?"

"I consider it from time to time. But I hear most of the mothers there want doctors to deliver their babies in hospitals, and midwives aren't welcomed. That doesn't mean I might not take a long break and go see my folks. Who knows? I might even find a man not scared off by a woman who says what she thinks and doesn't play flirty games. The soldiers coming home from the war might be ready for that."

"They might. Do you want to get married?" Fran had never thought about Betty pining for marriage. She seemed so capable and independent.

"It's something to think about at times." Betty swished away a horsefly. "What about you? You're a nice-looking woman. Didn't any guy ever ask you to get married?"

Fran started to think of some way to change the subject so she wouldn't have to answer, but why not talk about it? Betty didn't know Seth.

178

She did know Fran wasn't married or engaged. "One did. Before the war."

"Oh dear." Betty looked distressed. "Did he get killed?"

"No. Just found a woman he liked better over there."

"Then you're fortunate to be rid of him." The creek narrowed and Betty kicked Moses to get him out in front again.

Fortunate. Maybe she was. She wouldn't be here in the mountains if Seth had stayed true to his promises. She would have missed learning how to catch babies and participate in the miracle of birth. She would have never gotten to know these mountain people with their enduring spirit and love of family.

Fran looked at the hills rising around her and at the clear water trickling past Jasmine's legs. If not for Seth's betrayal, the mountains would have stayed just a name on a map to her instead of a place of beauty that sometimes left her breathless. Even so, she still felt the stab in her heart and the emptiness of thinking she'd never find love.

It was better not to dwell on that. To just do as Grandma Howard used to say. Live one day at a time. That was what the Lord promised and only that. And today she had helped a sweet young woman birth her baby. She'd seen looks of love. She'd heard the cry of life. And before the day was over she'd be clean again.

She felt even more blessed when they got to the Beech Fork Center to see Jeralene, the neighbor girl who had worked at the center prior to Fran being there, smiling in the doorway. She had milked the cow and had a pot of soup beans on the stove. A courier had also come while they were away to bring supplies and a few letters. One for Fran. The first letter from her mother in weeks.

Fran stuffed the unopened envelope in her pocket and took care of the horses.

Then she carried a graniteware wash pan of warm water to her small bedroom to clean up. They didn't have a tub, but a washrag did the job. She pulled off her tie and boots. When she unhooked her pants, the envelope crinkled in her pocket. She pulled it out and stood in the middle of the room to read her mother's letter.

Dear Francine,

I do hope you are ready to come to your senses and get on a train back to Cincinnati. I am sure you could still get your old nursing job at the hospital. I can't imagine you wanting to stay on with those hillbillies. I fear for your health, even for your life. But you are aware of how I feel about that, so I will tell you the news I have.

180

Seth is home from the war. He did bring that English girl with him. I can't deny Cecelia has a pretty face. She looks like some kind of doll. But trust me. Nobody wants to live with a doll.

The thing is they aren't married. She came over here to meet his parents and to see what America is like. She's very English. She won't fit in at all with his family. Not at all. Seth will see that. She will see that. Most important, Seth's mother will see that! So I'm telling you to come home right away. Seth can be yours again. I know he can. Then you can have that family you always dreamed of having. That would make me very happy.

You know I've always just wanted the best for you.

Your loving Mother

Fran blew out a long sigh and tossed the letter on the small table that held the coal oil lamp. Her poor, deluded mother. She supposed she would have to answer the letter sometime. But she definitely wasn't packing for home.

Home. As she stripped off her shirt and wrung out the washrag in the water that had cooled to lukewarm while she was reading the letter, she thought about how it would be nice to have a long soak in the bathtub back at her mother's house where a person turned on a tap and warm water poured out.

Here everything was more of an effort. Water had to be carried from springs, drawn out of a well, or caught in a rain barrel. Fires had to be built to heat that water. The only shower a person was likely to find this far out in the country was under a waterfall.

But effort was rewarded. Tomorrow at clinic, people would line up with their various ailments and she and Betty would do their best to help them all. She would make time to go back up into the hills to see baby Ira Leonard and to check on Sadie.

She would see the sun set behind the mountain and listen for the whip-poor-wills after dark. And she would be right where she needed to be. Perhaps she was home.

17

September 6, 1945

Ben hammered down a loose piece of the tin roof. The tin almost burned his hands, but the paint to seal the roof went on better when it was hot. They needed to get it done before another rain. The day he came home after that storm, his mother had three buckets under drips in the house. The roof had been prone to leaking ever since Ben could remember.

He sat back on his knees, ignoring the heat to look out across the hill. From the roof, he could see all the way down to where the Robinsons' house poked up out of the trees. That was where the girl Woody was sweet on lived. The shadow of a buzzard floating past up in the sky skimmed over him, and a cardinal trilled out its song from the edge of the woods.

Home sights and sounds. But in spite of how good it felt to be home, he couldn't deny being a little restless. He needed more, but he hadn't figured out more of what.

Woody let out a yell to bring Ben's attention back to the roof. Woody was brushing on the paint, and from the looks of it, he had almost as much silver paint on him as on the tin.

"It's hot as Hades up here." Woody swiped his forehead with his sleeve and left a smear of paint in his hair.

The boy was willing, but he had a hard time staying focused on a task from beginning to end. That had to be why so many things around the place needed work. Things that would have been kept up if Pa hadn't died.

"We don't lack much. After I hammer down a few more nails, I'll help paint."

"We should wait till sundown or a cloud to shade the roof or something. A body could die of heat prostration up here."

"I've been in worse places. You'll make it." Ben bent back to the task of nailing down the tin.

Sadie's head popped up above the edge of the roof. Ben frowned at her. "What are you doing up here?"

"Becca's holding the ladder. She said I could climb up and see what you're doing." Sadie looked at Woody and giggled. "You've got paint on your face."

"He's got paint everywhere but on the roof, I'm thinking." Ben sat back on his haunches. "You climb on back down from here before you get hurt and tell Becca to keep you on the ground."

"I think I need to be on the ground too," Woody said.

"When we finish."

Woody sighed and dipped the brush in the paint can again.

Becca called up from the ground. "I won't let Sadie fall, Ben."

As if she could catch the child should Sadie make a misstep on the ladder. They'd just both end up in a heap. Ben clamped his mouth shut. It wouldn't do any good to fuss at Becca. She wouldn't listen. Not to him. Not to their mother. She never had.

Becca had shown up with a pillowcase stuffed with her clothes and a happy smile on her face the day after Ben got home. She looked as glad to be back under her mother's roof as Ben was. Her husband, Carl, trailed after her, his smile less certain. He acted as uneasy as a toad on a hot rock and spent most of the time out on the porch. Becca said the cave-in at the mine had jangled his nerves until he couldn't hardly stand being inside anywhere. Ben could understand that. He'd witnessed plenty of jangled nerves in the army.

The morning after they came, Carl gave Becca a hug and headed to Harlan to catch a train to Ohio to look for work. Becca stood on the porch and watched him head down the trace. The man didn't look back. Becca didn't appear bothered by that. Instead, once he disappeared from her sight, she let out a long breath that sounded as much like relief as sorrow and settled in the grapevine rocker on the porch. She rocked back and forth, her hands lightly on the baby bump that barely showed under her loose skirt. She started humming a tune Ben didn't recognize and then broke out in words that were no more familiar.

Becca was the one among them who took after their pa's granny and was always ready to tap her toes to any song she heard, and if she wasn't hearing any, to make up her own.

She looked over at Ben when she'd sung through her song. "Did you know that down in those mining towns with the houses setting practically on top of one another, some folks bellyache about a body sitting out on her stoop and singing a song?"

"Is that right?" Ben leaned against the porch post and looked at this sister who had grown up while he was away. She was tall and slim like their mother and looked some like her, with her dark hair in a thick twist pinned up on her head. She'd gotten her dark blue eyes from Pa, the same as Ben. The two of them were alone on the porch.

"Every bit right. You'd think a person would want to hear something to take the gray out of those places, but some folks gather gray around them." She looked back to where her husband had disappeared into the trees.

"Didn't Carl like your songs?"

"Back when, he did."

"Back when?"

"When he was courting me. He used to play a juice harp some and was ready to do a jig at the first note of a tune. That was 'fore he went down in the mines. He said man weren't meant to spend all the daylight hours down in a dark hole with a lantern on his hat. Even before the cave-in he felt buried alive, I'm thinking. A man can't be happy that way nor nobody around him."

"I suppose not."

She stared up at him from her rocking chair. "You happy, Ben?"

He looked away from her out over the mountain. He was glad he'd gotten home while everything was still green. "I'm glad to be home."

"I reckon so am I. But happy ain't always so easy to catch and hold on to as the storybooks tell us, is it?"

"We don't live in storybooks."

"I can't argue with that. Especially here in these hills. But that don't mean we don't have stories to tell. I'm thinking you could tell plenty if'n you wanted. About the war and all." She stopped rocking and eyed him.

"Some stories are better left untold."

She watched him a long moment before she nodded a little. "I reckon we do pick and choose what we want to tell and what we don't. Me, I like turning stories into songs, and right this minute I'm catching hold of happy sitting here on this porch to sing, with nobody but that blue jay up there in the oak yonder to complain about it."

"What about me?" Ben couldn't keep from smiling. "What if I complain?"

She grinned back at him. "I'll tell you to poke your fingers in your ears and leave me be."

Ben laughed then. "Sing on, little sister."

As the week had passed, he'd heard Becca singing every day. Some of the time, she got Ma and Sadie to sing along with her. At first, Woody tried to join in until Becca put her hands over her ears and let him know he couldn't carry a tune in a bucket. That hadn't bothered Woody much. He just said if he couldn't carry the tune in it, he'd just make a drum out of that bucket. That was worse than the singing, and Ma saved their ears by producing a harmonica. With Becca's help, he was learning to make some music.

Becca had tried to talk Ben into joining the family band too, but he told her somebody needed to listen.

"No, no," she told him. "Better to jump right in the middle of the tune and be part of it."

"But I might be like Woody and then you'd kick me right out again."

"I didn't kick Woody out. Just shoved him over in a different spot. And weren't you glad? If

Woody had kept singing, old Rufus would have been joining in with a howl or two."

"A fellow has to sing the song he's got."

"I'll be listening for yours," she'd told him with a laugh.

Becca was forever ready to laugh about something and she even had a way of getting Ma to smile along with her. She could make him smile too.

So could Woody with his jabber jay talk. But right now, up here on the roof, Woody wasn't trying to get anybody to smile or doing any smiling himself. He was probably ready for Ben to go back to the army, since every day Ben found new things that needed fixing up around the place. That cut in sharply on the boy's wandering-the-hills time.

Ben picked up the extra brush and leaned over to stroke the paint on with a broad sweep. "Bet I get my tin piece done before you," he challenged Woody.

That was all it took to get Woody down to work.

They just lacked one more tin sheet when a voice called up to him. "I do hope you're taking care of that arm, Mr. Locke."

Ben stood up and looked down at Francine. He changed the name in his thoughts to Nurse Howard. Best to think of her as a nurse. Not a woman. At least not solely as a woman.

"Don't worry yourself, Nurse Howard. If I were to be unfortunate enough to fall off this roof, I'd tuck my arm up against my chest and break my face."

"Good that you remember directions." She laughed. "Is that you up there, Woody? You're looking as shiny as a new nickel."

It wasn't the first time he'd seen her since they huddled in the shallow cave to wait out the storm. A couple of days after that, she and the other nurse from the Beech Fork Center came to check on Sadie and see Becca. But the other nurse had obviously been in charge that day. Nurse Howard had shown none of her Sergeant Francine side or this friendly side he was seeing now.

In fact, when she'd come last week, Nurse Howard hadn't even glanced his way, as if she feared looking at him might get her in trouble. Nurse Dawson did keep a sharp eye on her, as though expecting Nurse Howard to make a misstep. Ben had stayed out of the way, not mentioning his arm, nor had she that day. Not even to ask if he was using his sling. Just in case the stern Nurse Dawson knew about the removal of the cast earlier than prescribed, Ben had found the sling and rested his arm in it.

"Very funny, Nurse Howard." Woody stood up. "I guess this gets me back for laughing at you milking Bella."

"I'm not laughing at you, but with you. There's a world of difference." She dismounted and tied her mare to a tree. "Jasmine missed you riding her in."

"Somebody won't let me off the roof." Woody shot Ben a look.

"Not until we're through, but that should be soon." Ben was ready to climb down himself where he could watch the nurse. See her smile close up. It cheered up the place when somebody new came to call, but then he hadn't felt much cheer when the two nurses had come together last week.

"Well, if you get down before I have to move on, Woody, you can ride Jasmine to the creek for a drink as long as you don't run her. We've got some distance to cover today back over to the Nolans' to check on baby Lenny."

Ben moved closer to the edge of the roof and looked down. "You think you know the way now?"

"I'm hoping so. I'll be ready for rattlers, and the sky is blue all the way across. I think we'll be fine. Somebody showed me the landmarks on that map." She shot another smile up toward him.

"It's hard to be ready for rattlers. You should get a dog."

"Nurse Dawson isn't fond of dogs."

The screen door slammed open and Sadie

ran out to meet her. "Nurse Howard, I've been drinking all my milk. Priscilla said I should tell you that next time you came."

The nurse gave Sadie a hug and then pointed toward Sadie's doll. "And what about Priscilla? How's she feeling? You know, about everything."

"Yes'm, she's feeling fine. Becca is teaching us a song about a frog going courting." Sadie laughed. "Ain't that the silliest thing? But Becca says silly songs make us feel better."

"I think she must be right." Nurse Howard put her arm around Sadie and they moved up on the porch out of Ben's sight. "Come on. I need to check your ears and see how Becca's doing."

Ben dipped his brush back in the paint and swiped it on the tin. He could hear the sound of the women's voices drifting up from the house below him but couldn't make out what they were saying. Still the sound was good.

"Nurse Howard's nice, and not just because she lets me ride her horse." Woody looked over at Ben. "I like her, don't you?"

"I just met her last week, Woody."

"That don't mean you can't like her. I liked her the first day she was here when I took her up to the hospital." Woody made the final swipe of paint on his tin sheet and stepped over on the last spot not painted as he backed toward the ladder. "Some folks are just easier to like than others, don't you think? Take that Nurse Dawson.

She don't like me for nothing, but Nurse Howard, she's different. She's one of them what's easy to like. I mean, for somebody brought-in."

"You could be right." Ben dipped his brush in the almost-empty paint can and then scooted the can behind him toward the ladder. "Climb onto the ladder and I'll pass you the paint. But be careful. We don't need to give Nurse Howard any extra work."

Ben held the top of the ladder steady while Woody stepped over the edge of the roof onto one of the rungs. Ben handed him the paint can and watched him climb down. Then he stepped over on the ladder and finished painting the last of the roof.

He barely had his feet on the ground when Woody jumped on the nurse's horse and headed toward the creek. The boy was apt to get paint all over her saddle. Ben would have to make him clean it and the reins when he got back if they showed traces of silver.

The sound of singing came out through the screen door. Sadie singing the song about frogs courting and then another voice joined in. Not Becca or his mother. The nurse. Francine. Ben hesitated at the steps. Maybe he shouldn't go in and disturb their fun. But it was his house, he was thirsty, and Woody was right. Nurse Howard was an easy person to like.

18

Becca and Mrs. Locke were hulling butter beans when Fran went in. Fran told them to finish what they were doing, but Becca emptied the unshelled pods out of her lap back into the bucket and jumped up.

With a little shake of her head, Mrs. Locke went on opening the hulls and dropping the beans into the dishpan on the floor beside her. "I reckon she and Sadie can take a rest for a mite. Seeing as how you've come to check on how they're doing."

"One little girl is looking good." Fran touched the top of Sadie's head. "Have you been helping your mother with the beans?"

"Yes'm. I like hulling these beans. Ain't they pretty? All purple speckled." The little girl ran her fingers through the pan of purple-and-white beans.

"They are pretty. Don't think I've ever eaten purple beans." Fran moved past Sadie to the water bucket on a little table next to the door and dipped out some water in the wash pan to soap her hands. She always carried soap with her, but here, as in most houses, she didn't have to dig hers out of her saddlebag. A chunk of lye soap was usually in a dish by the wash pan.

"They turn dirt brown when you cook them," Becca said. "Lose all that pretty color."

"But brown or purple, they taste fine. We'll give you a mess," Mrs. Locke said. "Sadie, fetch Nurse Howard a clean towel."

Fran dried her hands. She liked coming to the Lockes' house. Woody was the first person to help her when she got to the mountains, and she felt blessed to be assigned to the district where his family lived. Mrs. Locke had a way of making Fran welcome each time she came to treat Sadie. And now she would get to continue her midwifery training with Becca. Fran wasn't as sure what to think about the man painting the roof over her head, but she wasn't there to see him. If he was working on a roof, his arm must be all right.

"Sadie's had a good week." A smile softened Mrs. Locke's face. "We all have."

Fran hadn't often seen the woman smile—or frown either, as far as that went. Stoic. That was the word that described her. But now she looked almost happy.

"That's good to hear," Fran said.

"A mother likes having her children around her table."

"And it won't be long till you're a granny." Becca whirled around to hug her mother's shoulders. Stoic didn't describe Becca. Not in the least. She was more like Woody. Ready to spill over with something all the time.

Fran smiled. "Well, let's see how that baby is doing." She measured Becca's belly and listened for the baby's heartbeat. "Looks like you're doing fine. Do you have any complaints?"

"Plenty of them. Too hot. Too poor."

"Too silly," her mother put in before she could say any more. Sadie giggled.

"That too." Becca swished her skirt and did a couple of jig steps.

"I was thinking more about backaches or stomach upsets," Fran said.

"I get a mite queasy now and again and have some burning here." She touched her chest.

"Heartburn," Fran said.

"I guess, but Granny Em give me some dogwood bark to chew."

"Does that help?" It was a good thing Betty wasn't there to hear that Becca was trying mountain cures. But Fran had never heard anything about dogwood bark being harmful.

"Most of the time. Granny Em promised me it wouldn't hurt nothing to give it a try."

"You could also watch what you eat, and not eat whatever bothers you." Fran could at least suggest the prescribed way to handle heartburn.

"Yeah, that's what Nurse Dawson told me last week. She's a stiff one, ain't she?"

"Becca." Her mother's voice was sharp and her look sharper.

"Well, she is." Becca didn't take back her

words. "How come she's not with you today? Somebody on the mountain having a baby?"

"We had visitors from Chicago."

"All the way from there." Becca sounded amazed. "That Mrs. Breckinridge brings the folks in, don't she? I heard tell Mrs. Ford—you know, the wife of the fellow that makes automobiles—has been down here to check on you nurses."

"Mrs. Ford is a good supporter of the Frontier Nursing Service."

"Wouldn't it be fine to be so rich you could just sling money around wherever you took a notion?" Becca threw her hand out as if she were throwing some of that money around.

"There are all different ways to be rich, Rebecca Jane. And just as many to be poor. Most of them don't have much to do with cash money." Mrs. Locke dropped a handful of butter beans into the pan and grabbed more unshelled pods out of the bucket. She settled her gaze on Becca even as she kept hulling the beans. "Me, I'm feeling the riches of having you children here with me, and soon you'll know what that means, daughter."

"Oh, I know, Ma." Becca looked from her mother to Fran. "Don't pay no mind to me, Nurse Howard. I do have a way of running on, but I'm tickled as an'thing that you and Miss Stiff Nurse will be here to help me when my time comes

197

around. Probably have a foot of snow on the ground then."

"We'll get here somehow." Fran curled her stethoscope back into her bag.

"If'n you don't get lost." Becca grinned and lifted her eyebrows at Fran.

"I see you've heard about my tendency to do some wandering around in the woods."

Becca laughed, but Sadie stepped between them to take up for Fran. "She knows how to get here."

"I do that, Sadie. I have to know how to find my favorite patient. But don't go around telling people that or I'll get in trouble for playing favorites." Fran put her hand on Sadie's shoulder. "Now let me check those ears of yours."

Sadie's ears were clear with no sign of redness. Even better, she had some snap to her step. Becca being here and Ben too may have eased her sadness of losing her father.

"Those ears are good as new." Fran pretended to look at Sadie's doll's ears then. "And Priscilla looks fine too. Purple-speckled butter beans must be good medicine."

"We haven't eat but one mess. Priscilla don't like 'em much, but I tol' her she had to eat at least one bean. Whether she liked it or not. They aren't as bad as turnips." Sadie stuck her tongue out the side of her mouth.

"So did she eat one?" Fran poked the doll's stomach. "A bean."

"She nibbled on one a fair while."

"Then they must be extra-powerful medicine if just a nibble can keep her well. Maybe I'd better tell my next patient about purple-speckled beans." Fran started packing up her instruments.

"Woody's done rode off on your horse, so you might as well sit a while." Becca peered out the door and then pointed to a straight chair. "Sadie and me, we'll entertain you with a song or two. We might even get Ma to join in."

"I reckon I can sing and hull beans at the same time," Mrs. Locke said.

"Can we sing the frog courting song?" Sadie hopped up and down.

When they started singing "Froggie went a-courting," Fran laughed. "My grandmother used to sing that song to me. Some of the words were different, but the tune was the same."

"Oh yeah?" Becca stopped singing and grinned at Fran. "Then you have to sing them for us so we can add your verse to ours."

"I don't know if I remember." Fran hedged. She couldn't sing right here in the middle of them all, with Ben Locke right outside the door.

"You remember." Becca gave her a considering look. "You're just pulling a shy on us."

Sadie tugged on Fran's sleeve. "You have to sing it for us, Nurse. You have to."

"Don't be a pester, Sadie." Mrs. Locke spoke mildly. She emptied the hulls out of her apron and looked up at Fran. "But I'm thinkin' you might have a fine singing voice, Nurse Howard. So if'n you're a mind to, we'd be happy to hear you sing it for us."

"Oh yes. Please, Nurse Howard," Sadie begged. "Pretty please with sorghum molasses on top."

Fran laughed. "I don't guess I can turn down sorghum molasses. I'll sing it through once. It's real short, and then you can sing it with me. All right, Sadie?"

Sadie's eyes sparkled as she nodded.

Fran felt silly, but then sometimes it was good to be a little silly. She cleared her throat and sang her grandmother's words.

"Froggie went a-courting, he did ride. Uh-huh.
  Uh-huh.
Froggie went a-courting, he did ride. Uh-huh.
Jumped so high he thought he'd fly. Uh-huh.
  Uh-huh.
Went right up and hit the sky. Uh-huh.
Bumped his head and said, 'Oh my.' Uh-huh.
  Uh-huh."

Sadie bounced up and down and clapped her hands. "I can sing it now. Uh-huh."

They were singing the verse again when Ben stepped inside. Fran let her voice fade away as warmth exploded in her cheeks. Betty was right. She did forget her position sometimes.

Sadie ran over and grabbed his hands to pull him into the room. "Nurse Howard just taught us a new verse to the froggie song. You want to hear us sing it?"

"I heard you when I came in just now." Ben's lips turned up a little as he looked at Fran. "Didn't sound like anything I ever heard a sergeant sing. Sergeants mostly bark orders."

A smile tickled Fran's lips, even though she knew she shouldn't grab the bait he was shaking in front of her with the talk of sergeants. "Orders you followed?" She swept her gaze across his face and to his arm.

"I generally got in trouble if I didn't."

When he laughed, Fran couldn't keep her smile under wraps. She did have the sense to keep her head ducked so the man couldn't see her eyes.

"What are you talking about?" Becca sounded bothered. "Us singing don't have a thing to do with your sergeants."

"I think we might've come in late to this particular story, Becca." Mrs. Locke didn't stop shelling her beans, but Fran knew she was watching her.

"If it's a story, I want to hear it." Sadie jerked on Ben's shirt.

"Watch out. You're liable to get paint on your baby doll," Ben warned her. "And could be I'll tell you the story some of these days. Or maybe Nurse Howard will."

"Maybe." Fran didn't look up as she took extra time buckling her saddlebag.

Ben Locke changed the whole feel of the room when he stepped inside, bringing in the smell of the outdoors and the sweat of working. But it would be the same with any man coming into a room full of women. It was only their meeting in the woods that had her feeling so off balance.

But she was the nurse. It was up to her to get the balance back right. Betty would have told her it was up to her to keep things in balance from the start. Fran straightened up and looked at Sadie. "It's not that good a story, Sadie. I just told your brother to keep his arm in a sling a little longer, but as you can see, he's not good at following a nurse's orders. I'm glad you did and that your ears are fine this week."

"My arm is fine too." Ben held out his arm and twisted it back and forth.

"Did you go to the hospital and let them x-ray it?" Fran finally looked directly at Ben. That was easier to do when she was talking like a nurse instead of singing about frogs going courting.

"I haven't had time to make the jaunt down that way, but Granny Em came by. She said it appeared to be healed nicely."

"Granny Em?"

Mrs. Locke looked up from her beans. "Granny Em has a right good feel for bones."

"I'm sure she does, but an x-ray might confirm that." Fran kept her voice even. She didn't want Mrs. Locke to think she was dismissing Granny Em's doctoring skills.

"Now, Ma, you know the nurses don't like us to depend on mountain grannies instead of them." Something about Ben's voice changed, as though he'd heard disapproval in Fran's voice, even though she had intended none.

Fran wasn't sure what about the man made her so nervous. She had treated plenty of the mountain men and their wives without feeling a bit shaky about her skills. But when Ben Locke settled his gaze on her, she seemed to lack sureness about anything. Maybe because she knew he'd had medic experience in the army. She didn't want to believe it had anything to do with his dark blue eyes.

"Not at all," she said. "We're not in competition with anyone. We merely want to do our best to be sure everybody gets proper care."

"Well said, Nurse Howard. Did you have to memorize that when you came to Hyden?" The smile in his eyes was gone.

This time Fran didn't shrink from his direct look. "No. No, I didn't. But it is true for all the nurses I've met."

Sadie hugged her doll close and scooted over to lean against her mother.

Mrs. Locke looked ready to say something, but Becca gave Ben's arm a whack. "What's wrong with you? Don't be running the nurses away. Granny Em's fine, but I want the nurses here when little Carl is ready to show his face."

"Don't worry, Becca. We'll be here if someone comes after us, but it will be a while yet." Fran pushed a smile out on her face as she looked at Becca and picked up her saddlebag. "Nurse Dawson or I will be back to check on you in a couple of weeks. If any of you need something before then, just send Woody down for us."

She looked out the front door, relieved to see Woody back with Jasmine. A strained silence had fallen over the room where moments ago all had been friendly and easy. Maybe Betty was right. Maybe she was wrong to try to be friends with her patients. Just get the job done. But she'd always thought smiles were part of the job.

She directed a big smile toward Sadie. "You and Priscilla keep drinking your milk."

"Yes'm." Sadie didn't move away from her mother.

Mrs. Locke's eyes narrowed as she stared past Fran toward Ben just inside the door. But he wouldn't stop Fran leaving. He appeared more than ready for her to be gone. She was definitely more than ready to be gone. He had changed from friendly to antagonistic in a heartbeat, but being in a war could make men volatile. She knew that, for it had surely changed Seth from a man of promises to a man of betrayal. She needed no more of that.

She kept her eyes away from Ben as she stepped past him.

19

"The heat up on that roof must have addled your brains." Becca glared at Ben after the door shut softly behind the nurse. "What's the matter with you?"

He didn't answer Becca because he didn't know what was the matter with him. Something about Francine put him on edge. Not Francine. Nurse Howard. He wasn't on a first-name basis with the woman. Wouldn't likely ever be on a first-name basis with her. She wasn't one of them. She was from beyond the mountains, where people didn't understand mountain ways.

He'd come across that enough in the army. Always having to prove he had enough sense to do whatever needed to be done. Not having money didn't mean a man didn't have brains. His sergeant had accused him of having a chip on his shoulder and maybe he did. Maybe he'd let it show with the nurse. That didn't mean he wanted to admit it.

"Well?" Becca wasn't one to let something ride.

"I said what I thought. She had no reason to be bothered." He should have kept quiet. That sounded lame even to his ears.

"Times is when a body don't let out ev'ry

thought." His mother looked up from her beans. "Run after Miss Nurse, Sadie, and tell her to wait a minute for that mess of beans we promised her. Becca, get a sack out of the drawer for me."

Sadie slipped past him to go out the door, her eyes too big, as though he scared her.

He met his mother's steady gaze. "I'm sorry."

"It ain't me you need to say that to." She slipped a couple of handfuls of beans into the sack Becca gave her.

"Some things are best left alone," Ben said.

"Could be you're right." His mother peered out the window and then handed the beans to Becca. "Appears she's waiting. Run these on out to her."

"Should I tell her we're sorry?" Becca took the sack of beans and shot Ben a look. "That Ben's sorry?"

Ben shut his eyes a second to hide his irritation. He'd known it would be different coming home to a houseful of women after living with his army brothers for years. Women were always ready with hurt feelings. Men just socked somebody in the nose if they got mad. Could be somebody should have socked him in the nose for upsetting the nurse. She hadn't intended to rile him. He wasn't even sure what had poked those rude words out of him.

"I can do my own apologizing." He reached out and took the sack from Becca when she started to step past him. "Here. I'll take them out to her."

Becca gave him a look as she handed over the sack of beans, but for once, she kept her mouth shut.

He stepped out on the porch in time to hear Woody say, "You ain't mad, are you, Nurse Howard? I took a little while coming back from the creek. You said you didn't want Jasmine tired out."

"I'm not upset. You did exactly what I asked. Jasmine needed a drink." The nurse didn't seem to notice Ben on the porch as she reached for her mare's reins. Instead she looked at Sadie beside her. "You best back up, Sadie. Jasmine can be a little fractious at times. Except when Woody is riding her."

"But ain't you gonna wait for the beans, Nurse?" Sadie stepped over behind Woody.

"Thank your mother for me, but I'll try those purple beans another time." She put her foot in the stirrup and mounted her horse in one graceful movement.

Ben couldn't keep from admiring how she sat in the saddle. She really was lovely, even with her hair tucked up and wearing her frontier nurse blue pants and vest. It might be interesting to see her in a dress going to a dance. He put the brakes on his thoughts. He was here to apologize. Not ask her to a dance.

"No need to wait." He held up the sack of beans. "Here they are."

For a few seconds, he thought she was going to flick her reins and take off. But then she relaxed her hands and turned toward him with that same forced smile she had given him inside. "Then, I'll be glad to take them. I'm sure Nurse Dawson and I will enjoy them for our supper."

He stepped over to the woman on the horse, too aware of Woody and Sadie watching him. Watching them. He could take care of that. "Woody, go find some coal oil to get that paint off your face, and Sadie, you get on back in the house and help Ma."

Ben waited until Sadie scampered back into the house and Woody headed toward the shed with a curious glance over his shoulder. Becca was probably watching out the window, but at least none of them were right there peering over his shoulder.

He handed the sack of beans to the nurse. "Ma says I need to apologize for speaking my mind."

"This is your house, Mr. Locke. You are free to say whatever you want." Her voice was stiff.

"Free. That's a good word. Free." He put his hand on her horse's nose when the mare turned toward his voice. "And home. They were words to dwell on while I was over there."

Her voice softened and her smile looked almost genuine. "Now you have both. Home and free."

"So I do. But sometimes I still need a sergeant to keep me in line. Ma. You."

"I'm not a sergeant and I do well to keep myself in line. Nurse Dawson is always telling me I forget my place at times."

"What is your place?"

She looked a little puzzled by his question. "Sometimes I wonder." She looked away from him, then out toward the mountains. "But I do love it here. The trees. The hills. Even the rocks."

"The snakes?"

"The snakes not so much." She patted her mare's neck.

"What about the people?"

She let her gaze come back to him. "I like the people too. I admire women like your mother, and how could I not love youngsters like Sadie. There is something real about the people here."

"People aren't real where you come from up in the city?"

"I guess that did sound foolish. But whether you like me saying it or not, the people here are different from the people I grew up with."

"Yeah, they probably had shoes."

She kept her eyes locked on him. "You have shoes."

He lifted his foot up. "So I do. Compliments of Uncle Sam. But it could be I ought to take them off since I seem to keep sticking my foot in my mouth. Shoe leather is tough on the teeth. Then again that's something else outsiders don't expect us mountain folk to have. Teeth."

She frowned a little at that, but instead of responding, she twisted around in the saddle to stuff the sack of beans in the top of the saddle-bag. "Tell your mother thank you for me. She has a generous heart."

"And I act like I have no heart at all." Ben reached for the mare's bridle before the nurse could turn the horse away.

"I wouldn't say that. I see your heart for your family. For the mountains." Her polite smile came out again as she looked at his hand on her mare's bridle. "It's been a pleasure talking with you, Mr. Locke, but I need to be on my way."

"Sure." He turned loose of the bridle and stepped back. "But I am sorry, Sarge. Really."

An actual smile slipped out on her face. "You're going to have to stop calling me that."

"But weren't you the one who told me to call you Sergeant?"

She shook her head. "A momentary lapse of good judgment."

"What's the matter? Can't nurses have fun?"

"Of course. The same as sergeants, but I'm guessing your sergeants in the army let you know when it was time for fun and when it was time to attend to your duties. I need to be about my duty as a nurse." She turned her horse's head and flicked the reins. The mare cantered out of the yard.

"Don't get lost," Ben called after her.

"Very funny." She looked over her shoulder at him. "We'll be fine as long as the snakes stay out of our path."

He watched her out of sight with an odd urge to trail after her to be sure she didn't meet any of those snakes. But he didn't even have a horse. And no reason to feel responsible for her. She'd traversed these hills through snakes and more before he got home. Other people had pointed her in the right direction if she got lost.

But it was time to go hunting a horse. Or a truck. Maybe both. A man couldn't always go shanks' mare. He'd done enough walking the last few years to last a lifetime. He didn't have to walk now. He stared out at the trail the nurse had disappeared down. The storekeeper said folks had trucks that could go most anywhere. If he cut a tree here and there, he could probably get one of those trucks nearly up to the house.

With the way people were going to automobiles, they'd be building roads. Until then, a man could get plenty of places by driving in creek beds. If a man had a motor vehicle, he could drive clear out of the mountains, if that was what he wanted to do.

For three long years he'd thought about coming home and now here he was thinking about leaving. Maybe that was why the nurse seemed to be drawing him. Because she was from beyond the hills. But she'd come here by choice.

He'd come home by choice. Wanted to be here with his family. It was just that he wasn't sure what the future could hold.

If only his father were still there to help him get his head straight. To figure out what he should do. Ben shut his eyes and remembered his pa now and again taking a rest on the porch. Back then, Ben could talk any problem out with him. Most of the time, his pa would open up his Bible to help find the answers.

Trust in the Lord with all thine heart; and lean not unto thine own understanding.

That was one from Proverbs Pa liked to point out to Ben. Trust. Believe. Listen. That was his father's way. Ben had carried a Bible all through the war, and while he hadn't opened it as much as he should have, whenever he did, it was as though his father was sitting down right beside him to point out Scriptures he needed to see. Psalm 46:1 pulled him through some dark days. *God is our refuge and strength, a very present help in trouble.*

With the thought of that verse, he could almost hear his pa speaking in his head. *The Lord was with you over there, son, but you got to remember he come home with you too. The good Lord is everywhere around us. You just have to be still and listen for him.*

"You done been staring down that empty

213

path a long while, Benjamin." Somebody spoke up behind him. Not Becca or his mother.

Granny Em leaned against the side of the porch watching him. He had no idea how long she'd been there.

"Here you ain't been home but a week and yo'r feet done wanting to go wandering."

He wasn't surprised to see her there. Granny Em had a way of appearing out of nowhere ever since he could remember. His mother, she with the generous heart the nurse had spoken about, had claimed the old woman kin even without any blood ties. His father had been a bit warier of the woman's ways. Ben tried to remember why, but nothing came to mind other than her way of coming up on him unawares. That had always irritated his father.

"My feet are right here at home." Ben stepped back toward the porch.

"Then it must be that girl what was drawing your eyes."

"She was here to see Becca. Seems a fair nurse."

Granny Em's eyes crinkled up in a smile. "For a brought-in girl, she ain't bad. Did Becca tell her about the dogwood bark?"

"Dogwood bark?"

"Good to settle the upheavals in a body's stomach that a baby comin' can cause."

"You'll have to ask Becca about that. I was up

214

on the roof when the nurse went inside. Trying to stop it leaking before the next rain."

"Climbed down pretty quick then, I'm thinking." The old woman raised one eyebrow at him.

"We got finished."

She stepped back and peered up at the roof. "Appears you did. But you should have used tar. That shiny paint won't be no help."

"It's what Pa always used."

"And always had leaks." She headed toward the steps. "I reckon I better go see what Becca told the girl. See if them nurses are ready to run me off the mountain."

"I don't think anything could do that, could it?"

"That other nurse, the one that weren't here today, would like to, but this'n that was here, she'll stop and talk to a feller." Granny Em shot him another smile. "Appears she's more than ready to stop and talk to some fellers."

"She likes Woody."

"Most ev'rybody does that. The boy ain't never met no strangers. But I'm thinking that ain't the only feller that girl is ready to spend some words on. It ain't all nursing with her. Times is she even pays some mind to what I has to say to her." The old woman grabbed hold of the rail next to the steps and pulled herself up. She looked back at Ben. "And she ain't particularly hard on the eyes neither."

With a cackle something like a hen that just laid an egg, she went on into the house. Ben didn't follow her inside. He'd had enough of women for a while. Instead he walked off down the hill to find somebody with a horse to sell. His ma wouldn't worry about him. She'd know he'd be back.

But it could be the next time Nurse Howard came to see Becca, he'd be better served to find something to keep him busy out in the field or woods. Hard on the eyes or not.

20

As soon as Fran was out of sight of the Locke house, she slowed Jasmine to a walk. The day was hot and the way across the mountain long. Riding from patient to patient gave a person plenty of time to dwell on words misspoken and mistakes made. At least Betty wasn't with her to point out every wrong.

Not that Fran could see any problem with singing with Becca and Sadie. A harmless bit of fun. Ben Locke was who complicated things. He was different from the other mountain men she'd met. Different from any man she'd met, with those dark blue eyes that had a way of seeing through her. Past her polite exterior. Down to the quick.

And calling her Sarge. That made Fran shake her head, even as a smile tugged at her lips. Sarge Howard. It might be nice to be a sergeant for a while. To order things done and watch them happen.

She had always been the one taking orders. From her mother, who had continually needed something. Fran wondered if her mother's new husband tried as hard to keep her happy as Fran's father had. Her father was such a dear man, working two jobs so that he could give Fran's mother her every desire.

Then he had died without warning. Left for work one morning the same as any other day but never came home. A heart attack at his desk. Sudden. Final. Leaving Fran and her mother alone, with Fran the one to try to please her mother. Something she was never able to do.

She'd grown too tall too soon. As tall as her mother at age nine, and a head taller than her by the time she was twelve. Her mother hadn't quite known what to do with such an awkward, overgrown daughter, when what she wanted was a feminine replica of her. Someone who could wear lace and ruffles. Not someone who liked riding pants and horses.

Her father told her she was pretty, but all fathers said that. Grandma Howard told her pretty on the outside didn't particularly matter. Pretty on the inside is what mattered to the good Lord.

Fran tried to remember if Seth had ever told her she was pretty. He might have at that high school dance where she wore a red chiffon dress with a swinging skirt. She had felt almost pretty that night, in spite of her mother saying the dress was a disaster. Fran had bought it at a secondhand shop without getting her mother's approval.

"Why did you pick out something so bright? You should have looked for a neutral color or pastel. In that red, you're going to stand out like a sore thumb. You're more of a beige kind of girl."

A beige kind of girl. Even now Fran could hear those words just as her mother had said them. Fran had almost called Seth and claimed some sudden illness to keep from going to the dance. But instead she'd wiped away tears and stared at herself in her dresser mirror. Her dark brown hair curled softly around her shoulders. The result of hours in curlers. Her lipstick and fingernail polish exactly matched the dress.

She didn't feel a bit like a sore thumb. Tall and too slim. Feet entirely too big. Knees knobby but out of sight under the swishy skirt. When she heard the doorbell ring that meant Seth was there, she pulled back her shoulders and lifted her chin. Even a beige kind of girl could wear red sometimes.

Fran had turned away from her dresser mirror a different person than when she'd first looked into the mirror with tears in her eyes. She might not be the prettiest girl at the dance, but she was going to be a girl at that dance. She wasn't going to hide in her room and be invisible in front of the beige walls.

That night, Seth had first mentioned getting married someday. It seemed like an affirmation of Fran's decision about the dress. They were only seniors. They had many years to go before actually standing up in front of a preacher, but the promise was there. Somebody did love her.

Her future was set. She was going to be Mrs. Seth Miller and the best wife and mother ever. Nothing like her own mother.

The war changed all that. Seth changed all that by falling out of love with her.

Fran waved away a horsefly buzzing Jasmine's ears. Who knew? Maybe he had never really been in love with her. They'd made promises as kids. Neither of them were kids now. He'd gone through a war and found a new love. And look at her. Here riding a horse across a mountain to a house where she had delivered a baby.

She remembered what Willie had often told her while she was training at the hospital. *No one comes here by accident.*

That sounded like something Grandma Howard would tell her. *The Lord has his mighty hand on your shoulder, child. Trust him to guide you to the paths you need to walk.*

"But does the Lord know how easy I get lost?" Fran spoke the words out loud as if her grandmother could hear her.

It wasn't hard to imagine her grandmother's answer to that. *You might be confused on how to get to some place, but with the good Lord beside you, you're never lost. He'll hold a light to your path, just like the Bible says.*

She stopped at the spring to fill up her water bottle and let Jasmine get a drink. She tried not to think about being there with Ben Locke. But somehow he kept pushing into her thoughts. She needed to push him right out again. Better to think about the bluebird flying by or the woodpecker knocking against a tree. And to be thankful that so far the snakes were staying out of sight.

Jasmine was climbing the last hill to the Nolans' when Fran saw Ira riding his mule toward her. Her heart sank when she saw how he was kicking his mule to make it go faster. Something must be wrong.

"Nurse Howard," the young man called. "I knowed you were aiming to come today, but Stella told me to find you fast as I could to hurry you on up. It's Lurene."

"What's wrong?"

"I don't know. Stella says she ain't doing right."

Fran kicked Jasmine to a trot. What if she'd done something wrong or not done something right when the baby was born? But Betty had been there looking over her shoulder. She slid off Jasmine at the doorstep. A man, perhaps Lurene's brother, looked way too grave as he took Jasmine's reins. "I'll see to your horse, Nurse. You best see to Lurene."

Inside, the newborn's mewling cry and the sister-in-law's toddler's wail greeted Fran. Stella looked around at Fran and then turned back to the girl in the bed. "Hold on there, Lurene baby. The nurse is here."

Lurene's face was white against the pillow. Fran washed her hands as fast as she could and laid her hand on the girl's face. "What's happening?"

"I been bleeding some." The girl's voice was barely a whisper.

"How long?" Fran pulled back the cover. The sheet was stained a fresh red. She'd examined the placenta after the birth. It had looked entire, but obviously something was wrong.

"It weren't so bad till a little while ago." Lurene licked her lips. "I maybe done too much."

Stella spoke up. "The girl was mopping the floor. I reckon she didn't know no better."

"I didn't see what it would hurt," Lurene whispered. "Can you bring Lenny to me? I can't abide him crying like that."

"Don't you be worrying about him, sweetie." Stella folded a damp washcloth and laid it on the girl's forehead. "I'll nurse him and my Cassie too."

Fran reached out to stop the woman. "First, get a clean towel or two for me." Then she turned to Ira, who had followed her in. "Find something to prop up the end of the bed. Some wood chunks or rocks. Anything, but hurry."

The man didn't move as he stared at the blood on the bed. When he began to wobble on his feet, Fran shoved a chair under him and dug smelling salts out of her saddlebag. She waved it under his nose and he jerked back.

Fran leaned down right in his face. "You pull yourself together, Ira Nolan. Lurene needs your help."

Stella brought two iron pots from the kitchen. "Will these do, Nurse?"

Fran pulled the cover back over the young mother's legs and looked at Ira. "Help me lift the bed."

Once the foot of the bed was elevated, the bleeding slowed. Ira stepped out on the porch while Fran massaged Lurene's abdomen to get the girl's uterus to contract. She looked over at Stella, nursing the newborn while her little girl sat on her lap. "Does anybody close by have a vehicle? We need to get Lurene to the hospital."

"Joseph Brown down the way has a truck, but he can't get it up here."

"Then we'll have to get Lurene to it."

"If that's what needs to happen, I best get my man to gather the help. Ira is next to useless right now and little wonder, I reckon."

The woman set the little girl out of her lap and carried the baby with her to the door where she hollered at her husband.

As Fran kept up the massage, she hoped she was making the right decision to transport the girl to the hospital. She had no doubt that was where Lurene needed to be, but would the trip down the mountain be too much for her?

The girl was quiet now, her eyes closed, but then her eyes popped open as she looked straight at Fran. "I don't want to die, Nurse Howard, and leave my little boy motherless the way I was. He'd not have the first memory of me. I'd be like a wisp of morning fog forgot soon's the sun comes up."

"The bleeding is better, Lurene. We're going to get you to the hospital where the doctor can take care of you."

"I don't want to leave my baby."

"He will go right along with you so that you can keep nursing him."

"Will you fetch him there in your saddlebag?" A ghost of a smile settled on Lurene's lips. "That's how I used to think babies came. In them saddlebags."

"He'd fit easy enough." Fran smiled at the girl. "But this time he can ride along with you when we carry you out."

"I reckon it might be better if you take him. I ain't got the strength to raise my hand to scratch my nose. What if I let him slide off in the bushes?" A tear slid out of the corner of her eye and down her cheek. She didn't rub it away. "Could be he oughta stay here with Stella. I might not have nothin' for the poor babe."

Fran looked across the room at Stella, who had come back inside. She held the now-sleeping baby, while her own little girl clutched her mother's apron.

Stella nodded a little. "I kin take that on if need be."

Fran examined Lurene's breasts. She had milk, but would she have the energy to nurse the baby? But the girl needed the baby with her. Else she might just fade away.

Fran took the baby from Stella and laid him beside Lurene. "No, he wants his mother."

When Lurene lifted her hand to cradle the baby's face, he turned to nuzzle her side. The young mother blinked away tears. "But I don't want to risk his breathing."

"Nor do I. We'll take him with us and ask the doctor what's best. If he says Lenny would be better off with Stella here, I'll bring him back up the mountain."

"You wouldn't get lost with him, would you?" The girl's lips turned up in a smile, but there was a spot of worry in her eyes.

Fran laughed. "I tell you. A person gets confused on a trail a couple of times and everybody in Leslie County hears about it."

"That's the mountain grapevine for you." Stella smiled at Fran and then leaned over Lurene. "Don't be worryin' yo'r head about it, Lurene sweetie. Hal will go on down the hill with you so's he can bring back news and little Lenny if'n the doctor thinks that's best."

The men carried a cot over from Stella's house. Lurene was so slight that it was no problem using the child's bed. Ira picked Lurene up like he was handling a butterfly and carried her out to the cot. Fran and Stella had helped Lurene into a clean nightgown and wrapped her in a quilt. A couple of pillows kept the girl's legs elevated.

Ira, Lurene's brother, and two neighbor men picked up the corners of the bed and started down the trail. Two other men trailed along behind them. One of them carried Fran's saddlebag while Fran kept a constant eye on the baby beside his mother. She'd wrapped a sling around the baby and looped it around Lurene's neck to be safe. Even so, she wanted to be ready if one of those carrying the bed stumbled and perhaps jostled the baby out of Lurene's arms.

Jasmine nickered in the lot behind her, but Stella's husband promised to bring the horse back to the center. Nobody said much as they made their way down the path. After they went a ways, the two extra men traded out with two who were carrying the bed, but Ira wouldn't trade out. He stayed at his corner closest to Lurene's head.

"She ain't heavy," he said.

A dark cloud seemed to hover over them all.

The girl was so slight. The journey to the hospital might be too much for her. Fran second-guessed herself with every step. What if she had done something wrong when she delivered her baby? What if Lurene couldn't handle the trip to the hospital?

Lurene must have felt the sorrow trailing along with them. With typical mountain woman spirit, she whispered to Ira. "Sing for little Lenny. I reckon I don't have the strength right now, but I want fun in his ears."

"What you want me to sing, li'l darling?"

"How about that elephant song?"

One of the other men chuckled. "I know that one." He started singing.

"If you should meet an elephant on a summer's day,
What would you do? What would you say?"

Ira picked up the tune.

"I'd say, 'Good morning, Elephant, how do you do?
I'm glad to meet you, Elephant, I'd like to dance with you.' "

"Do the skunk." Lurene was smiling.

Then they were all singing to the girl as they went down the mountain. One of the men looked around at Fran. "Join right in, Nurse. It'll make the walk go faster."

She didn't know how long it had been since she sang a song along with others except for hymns in church, but for the second time in the day, she started singing and it felt right. Songs belonged here in the mountains.

"If you should meet a stinky skunk on an
    autumn day,
What would you do? What would you say?
I'd say, 'Good morning, Stinky Skunk, how do
    you do?
I'm glad to meet you, Stinky Skunk, I'd like to
    dance with you.' "

They came up with all sorts of animals and kept Lurene smiling until they got to the truck. There they loaded the bed into the back of the truck. Lurene's brother crawled in the front and Ira and Fran in the truck bed, one on either side to steady the cot. Ira leaned down close to Lurene and sang a song right into her ear.

Fran caught enough of the words to know it must be a love song he'd come up with especially for Lurene. Her heart ached for the young couple, and she closed her eyes as an old church song came to mind about the Great Physician. She prayed he was near for Lurene and would hold his healing hand over her.

At the hospital, they rushed Lurene into the examining room ahead of all the others waiting there. Willie came out a little later to let Fran know Lurene was going to be all right but would need to stay at the hospital a few days to build up her strength.

"You look a mess." Willie stared down at Fran's bloody apron that she hadn't thought to take off.

Fran slipped it over her head and folded it. "I guess I do."

"You want to get a shower and stay here tonight?"

The thought of a shower was tempting, but Fran shook her head. "No, I better not. Mr. Brown, who brought us in his truck, says he'll give me a ride most of the way back to the center. Betty won't know what happened to me."

"She'd survive. Probably be glad for the time alone."

"Not if she has to milk the cow."

"Wouldn't hurt her."

Fran smiled. "I've got a ride. I'd better take it. Tomorrow I might have to walk the whole way."

"Whatever you think best."

"You will send me word about Lurene? Did I do right having the baby come too? She had a sister-in-law there on the mountain who offered to be a wet nurse for him."

"The baby needs to be with his mama. We'll

take care of them. Don't you worry." Willie gave her a hug. "You know we love the babies as much as their mamas do. Somebody will be rocking that little fellow all night long."

Fran looked back at the hospital as she rode away in the neighbor's truck. It might be easier to take care of the mothers and babies there, but she liked being out at the center. She looked over at the silent man with his eyes on the road. Lurene's brother had crawled in the back of the truck. For a crazy moment, Fran thought about asking Mr. Brown if he knew the song about Froggie going courting. But instead she looked out at what passed for a road as they wound their way around curves and through creeks back to the center.

When she saw the roof of the center and heard Bella mooing, she felt at home.

21

September 20, 1945

"The pups are 'round back in the shed. Not much count for huntin' but you might teach 'em to herd cows. A mix of shepherd and collie, best I can figure." The man led Ben around his house that was mostly log with an extra room tacked on with plank siding.

Shorty Johnson's yard was full of rusty plows and other farm tools. When the man noticed Ben looking at the piled up offerings, he said, "If'n you need something for yo'r farm, I'm getting rid of all this stuff. Cheap. Motor vehicles is the coming thing. Like that there truck you just bought off'n me. This other stuff you could practically steal from under my nose." He waved his hand over at the plows. "Nothin' wrong with 'em 'cepting some surface rust that'd come right off when you commenced to plowing next spring."

"I'll keep you in mind if I hear of anybody needing one," Ben said.

"You do that. Just tell 'em to come see Shorty whatever they need, and if I don't have it, I can get it." The man stopped in front of Ben and yanked a red bandanna out of his pocket to wipe his face. "It's a scorcher today for September."

Shorty was a big man, as tall as Ben and twice as wide. How he came up with the name Shorty was a mystery, but one Ben wasn't interested enough to hear. The man's shirt was crusty with sweat rings that made Ben just as glad they were doing their dealing out in the open air.

He hadn't come looking for a pup, but when the man mentioned he had some, it seemed a good time to follow through on the idea of getting Woody a dog. Rufus, poor old fellow, just wanted to be left alone to live out his final days.

Last week Ben had brought home a horse. A five-year-old gelding with some snap to his step. Ben and Woody had ridden Captain down the hill this morning. Then Woody had hoofed it over to the nurses' center to take them some pickles while Ben came on to Shorty's. He hadn't seen Nurse Howard since he'd made that lame apology to her. Better that way.

Ben told Woody not to tarry and get on over to Shorty's a few miles on down the creek to ride Captain home in case Ben made a deal with Shorty for a truck. And he had. Not a new truck. Those were few and far between, since the factories had just started up making cars and trucks again after making tanks and planes during the war.

But it looked rugged enough. A 1940 Chevrolet that sat high off the ground. He wouldn't be able to drive it all the way up to the house without clearing out some trees, and come a washout, not at all. But a spot down at the bottom of their property would make a good place to leave the truck.

If he headed back to college, he could use the transportation. With the GI Bill dangling out there, it seemed next to foolish not to grab it and try to make something of himself. The trouble was, he wasn't exactly sure what he wanted to make.

A teacher? He wasn't overloaded with patience for youngsters. He had no feeling for being one of the lawyers about town or a banker all dressed up in a suit, strangled with a tie and shut up inside an office all the livelong day. He had his medic training. But what good was that except in the army? The nurses around here were all female. And it took a lot of years to make a doctor. Maybe he should just be a trader like Shorty. A better-smelling trader.

The tan-and-white pups tumbled out of the shed when Shorty opened the door. One of the fuzzy balls of fur ran straight to jump up on Ben's leg. The pup's brown eyes were bright and his tail whipped back and forth at lightning speed. The very thing for Woody.

Ben picked up the pup. It didn't smell too good either after being shut up in the shed with what looked like five or six more pups. But the pup

233

wriggled with excitement and tried to lick his chin. Ben couldn't keep from laughing.

"Appears that one likes you." Shorty peered over at him, his trader face on. "But you might best take two. Dogs is some like people. They need company."

The pup made a high-pitched whine and a yellow-and-white dog sitting off to the side yipped. Ben had noticed the collie lurking close the whole time he and Shorty haggled over the truck price. Never close enough to be touched, but always in sight.

Now Ben nodded toward the collie. "Is that the mother?"

"That?" Shorty gave the dog a look and spat on the ground. "Naw. That's one from last year's bunch. He's nigh on useless. I'd a done got rid of him 'cept he's a right fair snake dog. But snakes ain't so much trouble. They keep the mice in line. That one. He just eats." He nodded toward the dog. "I'd shoot him, but he ain't worth the bullet."

The dog's ears drooped a little as if he understood the man's words.

Ben stepped toward the dog and squatted down to hold out his hand. The dog slunk toward him, his tail between his legs.

"Look at that." Shorty whistled. "That dog ain't never come to nobody. He's commonly a standoffish critter. Half wild."

Ben put the pup down and stroked the dog's head. The dog eased closer to him and lifted up his paw to touch Ben's arm. "How much you want for him and the pup?"

"You take that dog off'n my hands, I'll throw in the pup for nothing. I'll throw in two pups for nothing."

Ben thought of Sadie. Why not? Ma might kill him, but two pups couldn't be much more trouble than one. This other one, the sweet dog looking at him with dark yearning eyes, he didn't intend to keep. He knew the perfect person for him. Somebody who needed a snake dog while she was traversing all over these hills.

Could be she'd turn it down. But how could she refuse a dog that appeared to know your every thought? Francine wouldn't. Her given name slipped right into his thoughts.

"Has he got a name?" Ben asked.

"Naw. I jest call him 'Dog.'"

The dog shied a little at the man's voice, almost as if he expected a kick to follow. Ben stood up and the dog scooted around behind him.

Shorty pulled a length of rope out of the shed and made a loop in it. "You'd better slip this on his neck to keep him from running off."

Ben didn't think he would, but he stroked the dog and murmured to him as he looped the rope over his head. The dog sat down, not bothered at all.

"So what other pup you want?" the man asked.

Ben peered through the door of the shed. "That littlest one there." He pointed.

"The runt. I figured it'd end up like that 'un there with nobody wantin' him." Shorty reached in and grabbed the little pup by the scruff of the neck. "But here he is."

Ben stuffed the littlest pup down inside his shirt and carried the other one. The dog trotted along beside Ben, not even pulling against the rope.

When they went back around to the front of the house, Woody was waiting beside Captain. That was a relief. Ben hadn't wanted to leave the horse there. He didn't trust Shorty not to trade him off.

"Wow! Is that yours?" Woody's eyes were big on the truck. They got bigger when he saw the pup and the dog. "And you got dogs too? Two of them?"

"More like two and half." Shorty laughed behind Ben. "How you doin', Woody? Ain't seen you around for a spell."

"Been busy 'round home," Woody said. "Didn't have nothing to trade nohow."

Ben frowned over at Woody. What could the boy be trading with Shorty? But that wasn't a question he'd ask in front of the man. Instead, he opened the truck door and fished the runt pup out of his shirt to stick him on the floorboard with the other pup. He snapped his fingers at the dog and he jumped right in. The dog settled on the seat while Ben pushed back the pups to climb in behind the wheel.

"You know how to drive that, Ben?" Woody asked.

"I know how to drive it." Ben slammed the door shut. "You bring Captain."

Woody mounted the horse and turned to look in the truck window. "You getting a dog for Becca too?"

Ben almost smiled. "Becca doesn't appear interested in pups. Sadie can pick first and you can have what's left."

"The big one's yours then?" Woody said.

"Nope. I've got somebody else in mind for it." He looked at the trader. "Thanks for the dogs, Shorty."

"I'm obliged to you fer carrying them off. You let me know when the boy here is ready for some wheels."

"A horse will have to do him for a while."

"Well, I got bridles and sech too. Out in the barn. You name it. Shorty sells it."

Ben motioned Woody to get on the road and then shoved the floorboard gearshift into reverse to turn around and follow him. That rascal pup came over under his clutch. He grabbed the dog's tail and pitched him out of the way. The pup yelped and started scrambling back over the gear shift to get under Ben's feet again.

It looked to be a long ride back to the house. With a sigh, he jerked the pup away from his feet and back on the other side. The pup was about to come back again when the older dog put his nose in front of the pup with a low growl. The pup retreated to settle down by the little runt scrunched up against the door.

"Good dog." Ben rubbed the dog's head. The dog sat up straighter in the seat and panted happily. Ben's imagination might be working overtime, but he thought the dog smiled. For certain, Ben was smiling as he looked back out at the road. "Wonder what she'll name you."

The dog closed his mouth as if considering an answer.

"Maybe I'll just tell her your name's Sarge. How do you like that, Sarge?"

The dog started panting again. Maybe the name fit. Sarge and Francine. That would bring that smile to her lips Ben liked seeing. Wasn't anything wrong with liking to see somebody smile.

He was going to be bringing smiles all around with this truckload of canines. Sadie's face would light up for certain when she saw the pups. She'd pick the runt. That was just Sadie. Feeling for the lesser thing. The frisky pup would suit Woody best anyway.

"You think you'll suit her, Sarge?"

The dog stuck his head out the window to let the wind brush his fur back. A person didn't have to be mountain to appreciate a mountain dog. Ben tapped his fingers on the steering wheel and began humming. It took a minute for him to realize what he was humming. That silly song he'd heard her singing with Becca and Sadie. Froggie went a-courting.

He shook his head. He wasn't a frog and he wasn't going courting. He was just giving this dog that needed a home to somebody who needed a dog. Besides, he remembered that song from when his grandmother sang it to him. That courting frog got eaten by a duck.

22

Fran straightened up to stare down the row of late beans and wished she hadn't planted this extra row when she first moved into the center with Betty. The early beans had already been picked then and it had seemed reasonable to replant the row for a fall crop. At the time, it was something of a lark to plant beans. Now it was just one more chore on her long list, and she was tired.

Nothing in the Frontier Nursing brochure had said a thing about breaking her back picking beans. Or milking cows. Or carrying water from the spring. A nice long hot shower sounded like heaven right then, but the only shower she'd get here was standing out in the rain or pouring a bucket of water over her head.

A breeze blew against her face, as fresh as the mountain trees it had just swept through. Here and there, a few of those trees were sporting red and yellow leaves. Fall was not just coming anymore. It was here. With winter ready to chase in behind it. Betty warned her of that every day.

"Just wait until the snow starts falling and you have to break the ice in the water bucket. Then these mountains might not seem so pretty to you," she'd told her just that morning when they rode their horses through a particularly colorful stretch of trees on the way back from ushering the Tipton baby into the world. A pretty little girl to join her two sisters and three brothers. But everybody—mother, father, and siblings—seemed entranced by the new addition to their family.

Children were a poor man's riches. Mrs. Breckinridge had told Fran that when she stopped by to visit the center last week. She'd come to give Fran the details about her trip to Lexington to take her final exam to be a fully qualified midwife. Then she'd talked to Fran about her future with the frontier nurses. It seemed Betty was anxious for an extended vacation to visit her family in New York.

"You know the people here in this district now," Mrs. B said. "You could continue their care without the upheaval of them having to get used to a different nurse. Betty tells me you have excellent nursing skills."

Fran had been surprised to hear that kind of praise from Betty. But when she thought about it, Betty rarely complained about her nursing abilities. Instead, she harped on Fran being too interested in the mountain culture and continually warned her not to listen to their different ways and superstitious cures.

Fran had to admit some of the cures went past

odd to bizarre. One father insisted the drop of his toddler's blood on a grain of corn he fed to a black hen had cured the boy's lingering cough. As long as the mother dosed the child with the medication Fran prescribed, it hardly mattered what the father fed the hen or what color that hen might be.

The boy being well was what mattered most. As long as the people allowed her to treat them, she could abide their folk cures, agree that some had merit and ignore the ones that didn't but were harmless. Betty, on the other hand, was ready to lock horns with the people if they mentioned any mountain cure.

Mrs. Breckinridge had a rule for her nurses not to talk politics, religion, or moonshine. Mountain cures might be added on to that, except as nurses they had to know what doses their patients had tried before they were called in. While it was easy enough to dismiss the black hen cure or putting hair clippings under a rock to keep away headaches, other cures like peppermint tea for an upset stomach had merit.

Fran would be ready to try that one herself. Or Granny Em's dogwood bark remedy for heartburn. It seemed to work for Becca. Last week when she and Betty went to the Lockes', they'd found Becca up in a tree picking apples.

Betty lectured the girl. "Falling out of trees is not advised for expectant mothers." Betty had given Becca a stern look. "You do have brothers who can pick those apples for you."

"Those boys are never around when you need them, and I've got a hankering for one of Ma's pies." Becca slid down out of the tree and landed on her feet light as a cat. She flashed Fran a big smile. "Have you seen Ben lately?"

"Not since the last time I was here." Fran pulled her saddlebag off Jasmine and followed Becca up the porch steps.

"Yeah. That day we give you the speckled butter beans. Did you like the brown things?"

"They were good. Thank you." Fran looked over at Betty as she dismounted. "You remember the purple-speckled beans I cooked for us."

"Oh yes. They made a substantial meal with cornbread," Betty said. "Your mother is kind to share her garden produce with us."

"Ma says what's the use of having a sass patch if a body can't share the plenty of it. But I weren't sure Ben actually give you the beans that day." Becca gave Fran a sideways look. "He seemed a mite perturbed after you rode off. Can't imagine what his problem was, can you?"

"You'd have to ask him that, but he did give me the beans." Fran could feel Betty watching her as they went inside.

Sadie looked up from helping her mother roll out pie dough with a smile that turned shy when she saw Betty behind Fran.

In the bedroom, Fran stuck the ends of her stethoscope in her ears and told Becca to take some deep breaths while she listened to her chest. She hoped that would get Becca to switch to talk about the baby and not Ben Locke. Fran was relieved he wasn't there. At least that was what she told herself, even as her grandmother's warning slipped through her head that the worst person to lie to was yourself.

Becca waited until Fran had listened to her heart and was ready to listen for the baby's heartbeat. "We didn't know where he'd got off to that day. But then he brung home a horse."

"I'm sure that made Woody happy."

"Oh, we all were." She shot Betty a smile. "I reckon if Mary the mother of Jesus could ride a donkey all the way to Bethlehem, there ain't no reason I can't ride a horse, is there, Nurse?"

"If the horse is gentle." Betty didn't smile. "And you don't do something foolish like fall off."

Becca cradled her growing abdomen with her hands. "Don't worry, Nurse. I aim to do ev'rything I can to be a good mother to this little fellow."

"You have no way to know you're carrying a boy," Betty warned. "It's best to be open to having a boy or a girl."

"I'd welcome either one, but I just know this first one is a boy. The way he kicks around in there."

"Could be a girl just like her mama." Fran laid the stethoscope on Becca's belly. "Now be still a minute so I can hear the baby's heartbeat." After she listened, she pulled the earpieces free and held them out to Becca. "Nice and strong. You want to hear?"

Becca shook her head. "Ain't no need. I hear his heart beating right along with mine. That's a mama thing. Guess the two of you wouldn't know about that, not having had no babies of your own."

Becca hadn't meant the remark to be hurtful and there was no reason it should have been. But it stabbed Fran then and lingered even now. *No babies of your own.*

Seth's image flickered through her thoughts before she pulled in a long breath and leaned down to pick more beans. Jeralene, the girl who helped them now and again with their chores, was coming later to help them string up the beans for shucky beans. Not that it sounded hard. Just break off the ends and thread them on a cotton string to hang to dry. That had to be less work than canning them by boiling the jars of beans for hours. Of course, Betty warned her it took some taste adjustment to actually like shucky beans. But then Betty warned her about everything. And picked the easier chores. She was inside counting pills or who knew what. Maybe taking a nap.

Fran yawned. She could use a nap after being called out at midnight for Mrs. Tipton to have her baby. Then the woman hadn't had a minute's trouble. When Fran told her that, Mrs. Tipton pointed to the next room where the other children waited to welcome their new sister. "I've done had a mite of practice."

Now Fran needed some practice sleeping before the morning. She hoped no emergencies popped up to take them out this evening. She planned to ride back up to the Nolans' in the morning to check on Lurene. She'd already been to see her once since the doctor declared her well enough to go home from the hospital. She had a ways to go to build up her strength, but Ira had been right there with Lurene, doing whatever necessary for the girl and his baby.

Fran's bucket was almost full of beans when a truck roared up the creek toward the center. She still hadn't quite gotten used to the mountain people using creeks for roads, but often as not that was the smoothest places for a vehicle to run. She didn't look up even when the truck stopped in front of the house, but kept picking to finish out the row. Betty was inside. She could take care of whatever the people needed.

She was yanking off the last bean pods when somebody spoke up behind her. "Nurse Howard, I thought I saw you out here."

She knew his voice at once. She straightened up and turned toward where he waited at the end of the garden. A fine-looking yellow-and-white collie sat on the ground beside him, its tail swiping back and forth across the grass. She wiped her hands on her pants and brushed the hair back off her forehead. Not the best time to meet up with Ben Locke again. But then, what difference did it make how she looked? She didn't need to impress him. She was his family's nurse. That was all.

She picked up her bucket and walked toward him. "Hello, Mr. Locke. Is something wrong with Sadie?"

"She's fine. Becca keeps her busy with something all the time so Sadie can't mope." He made a little face. "As far as that goes, Becca keeps us all busy with something. She wears me out sometimes."

Ben Locke smiled then, and in spite of herself, Fran's heart did a little stutter step. The man had the most remarkable eyes, and when he smiled, it was like the sun coming out in that dark blue. She set her bucket down and pretended the bean picking was the reason she needed to catch her breath.

"Did you get Sadie a dog?" She held out her hand toward the dog. It was better to look at the dog instead of Ben Locke's eyes. The dog gingerly sniffed her hand and then gave her fingers a lick. That made Fran smile. "He must like the smell of beans."

"Or the one picking the beans." When Fran looked back at him, he rushed on as if he'd said something he shouldn't have. "Why don't you get somebody to pick the beans for you?"

Fran shrugged. "Jeralene Robinson does help us some. And Woody comes by now and again to help with this or that chore."

"I'm betting especially when Jeralene is here." Ben smiled a little. "Ma says he's sweet on the girl."

"That's not surprising. She's pretty as a spring flower."

"But very young. Both of them."

"I've seen some very young mothers here in the hills."

"Exactly," Ben said.

"Oh." Her cheeks warmed to embarrass her even more. She was a nurse. Talking about such things as the consequences of young love was part of her job and no reason for blushing. "I'll talk to Jeralene when she comes by later. She's supposed to show me how to string up shucky beans." Fran pointed at the bucket.

Some high-pitched yaps came from the truck in front of the center. Fran peered around Ben toward it. "Is that your truck?"

He looked over his shoulder at the truck too. "Yep. Just bought it today."

"It's making some unusual noises."

Ben laughed. "Come on and I'll show you what's yipping."

He started toward the truck. The collie dog reached a paw out to touch her hand before he followed Ben. With that kind of invitation, how could she refuse? She picked up the bucket of beans.

"Let me carry those for you." Ben reached for the bucket, his hand brushing hers. The dog wagged his tail and bared his teeth in a funny dog grin.

"Is he smiling?" It was easier thinking about a smiling dog than how the mere touch of Ben's hand had her feeling breathless again. What in the world was wrong with her? She barely knew the man.

"This one is an interesting dog. I think he does smile and I wouldn't be all that surprised to hear him talking."

"A talking dog? I've seen a lot up here in the mountains, but not that." Fran laughed.

"You're right. That is a little far-fetched. Could be Sarge only reads minds then."

"Sarge?" Fran gave Ben a look.

"That doesn't have to be his name. Just one I thought might fit." He stopped beside the house. "You want me to put these beans on the porch?"

Fran looked toward the house, hoping Betty

wasn't peering out the window at Fran and Ben, side by side. She must be asleep or she'd be right there in the door, sending Ben on his way if he didn't need nursing care.

"Just leave them there in the shade." Fran nodded toward a tree. "From the sounds coming from your truck, you'd better go check that out." The yipping was getting more frantic. "You must have a puppy in there."

He set the bucket down. "Puppies. As in two. Ma is gonna shoot me, but I had in mind to get one for Woody. Then the guy talked me into two."

"Or three." Fran looked at the dog walking beside them.

"We need to talk about that."

"Are you saying you have more than three?" She didn't wait for him to answer but stepped up on the running board to peer in the truck window. A fluffy pup jumped up on the door and yapped even louder. Another pup was on the floorboard, its tail between its trembling legs.

Fran wanted to pick up the timid puppy, but she didn't feel she should open the truck door. So instead she lifted the yapping puppy out through the window. "They are the cutest things. Sadie is going to be one happy little girl when you get home with these."

23

The pup wiggled all over and tried to lick her face. That made Francine laugh. The dog beside Ben surprised him by easing closer to the woman to lean against her leg. The other pup, left alone in the truck, began whining. Ben could sympathize. He was feeling a little left out too.

He wanted to be like the collie and step closer. Brush shoulders with Francine. Her laughter lit up her face and made her eyes sparkle like creek water chasing through the sunshine. He kept smiling too like some kind of idiot, but he didn't try to wipe the smile off his face. It felt too good.

She must have heard the other pup whine, because she pushed the pup she was holding into Ben's hands and opened the truck door to scoop up the other puppy.

"Aww, poor little thing is scared to death." She rubbed the puppy's ears. "I bet he's never been away from his mother."

The pup in his hands was going crazy trying to get back to Francine, so he put him back in the truck. "You've had your turn," he told him. He ignored the pup's wails as he looked back at Francine stroking the runt pup and wished for a turn of his own.

It could be he'd made a mistake bringing her the dog. He wanted her to have the dog, but he should have let Woody bring it. This woman was messing with his heart's equilibrium like no female he'd ever met. Some things were best avoided. Like poison sumac.

But he was here now and nothing for it but to clamp down on his feelings and play out the scene. "That was the runt of the litter, but I'm thinking that's the one Sadie will want. She has a soft place for little things."

Francine held the pup up to her face and the pup licked her nose. "Goodness, I've never had such a face washing."

The dog at her feet lifted a paw to touch her leg as if to keep her from forgetting about him. Ben restrained the impulse to reach across and do the same by touching her arm. He'd come to give her a dog. Nothing else. Especially not his heart. He needed to stop thinking of her as Francine with the eyes that made his knees weak. She was Nurse Howard and that was all.

She leaned down to pat the collie's head.

"Be careful. He might snap at the pup," Ben warned.

But the dog just nosed the pup and then pushed past it to nuzzle Francine's arm.

"Oh, he's too good a dog for that." She straightened up after ruffling the collie's ears and handed the pup back to Ben. "Thank you

252

for bringing them by for me to see, but did you need anything else? Is your arm bothering you?"

"I'm not in need of your nursing services." At least that much was true. "It's this dog." He nodded toward the collie. "He needs a home. His owner was threatening to get rid of him once and for all."

"You mean shoot him?" She looked horrified.

"That's one way to get rid of a dog."

"A sweet dog like this?" She laid her hand on the collie's head as if to protect him.

"Dogs are almost as plentiful as rocks up here in the hills. And this one can't even earn his rations by claiming to be a hunting dog."

"Collies are herders, aren't they?"

"Some are. Don't know if this one is. The man I got him from said about all he could say for him was that he was a snake dog."

"He kills snakes?"

"I don't know. I haven't seen him in action. He could just bark at them."

"As long as he kept them out of the paths, I'd be happy. Good dog." She stroked the dog's head. "When Jeralene gets here, I'll ask if she knows anybody who wants a dog."

When she straightened up, the dog put his paw on her leg again.

"I think he likes you." The dog wasn't the only one. Ben hesitated, feeling like a school-boy afraid to ask a girl to the church picnic.

"The fact is, I told him on the way over here that you'd be the perfect person for him."

"Me?" Her eyes flew open wider as she looked from the dog to Ben. She shook her head. "Oh, no. As nice as he is, I can't have a dog."

"Why not?" He fastened his gaze on her and she didn't look away. "I know Mrs. Breckinridge is fond of animals and that some nurses have dogs like Sarge here."

"Did you name him Sarge?" She looked down at the dog, but not before he saw the smile sneaking out on her lips.

"Seemed a good name."

"He doesn't look much like a Sarge to me."

"No?" He watched her stroking the dog and smiled. "The thing is, he made me think of this nurse I know. A person wouldn't be thinking she looked much like a Sarge either."

"You have to stop calling me that." She looked up at him. "Please."

"Fair enough. I slipped the name right off you onto the dog. I'm thinking he'll like the name and being your dog."

"I told you I can't have a dog."

"But I didn't believe you and neither did Sarge. Just look how he's watching you. He thinks he's yours already."

She looked sorry as she shook her head. "Nurse Dawson doesn't like dogs. She would veto the idea hands down."

"Who gave her veto power?"

"She's my supervisor while I'm training."

"Supervising your nursing, but not your life. You can make some choices on your own, can't you? Like what you eat for breakfast or how to keep snakes out of the yard."

She smiled then and he was pretty sure he had her convinced, even as she shook her head again. "But I've got to go to Lexington next month to take my midwifery exam. I couldn't ask Nurse Dawson to take care of a dog while I was gone."

"We'd be glad to keep Sarge for a spell in that event. But the dog's yours. He hasn't taken his eyes off you since we got here, and he really doesn't want to go home with these noisy pups." Ben nodded toward the truck where the pups were making a racket again.

"You're very convincing, Mr. Locke." She laughed. "All right. But if Nurse Dawson makes me sleep on the porch, I'm going to blame you."

"Porches make a fine sleeping place this time of the year. You can hear the frogs in the creek and the owls on the hunt."

"Are you sure you're not a salesman?" But she was still smiling.

So was he. Inside and out. He knelt down in front of the dog. "She's the one I told you about, Sarge. You take good care of her, hear?"

The dog barked twice, almost like he was saying "yes sir," and licked his hand. Guess that made Ben the general. Then the dog moved closer to Francine. It was useless, Ben trying to keep her given name out of his thoughts. As long as he could keep from saying it out loud.

Ben stood up and opened the truck door. He pushed the pups back and climbed in. He felt a wet spot under him where one of the pups had obviously needed to be out on the ground instead of in the truck, but even that didn't wipe the smile off his face.

Before he could think better of it, he leaned out the window. "The Hoskins over in the next holler are having a sorghum stir-off next week. If nobody's having a baby, you and Sarge ought to come."

"I don't know that family. They must not live in our district."

"Probably more over toward Possum Bend, but it's not all that far."

"I'd get lost for sure trying to get there." She shrugged with a smile.

"We could swing by and get you." He couldn't believe he was saying that, but he wasn't sorry. Not a bit. But at the same time he figured he'd better add on some words to keep her from thinking he was asking her for a date. She'd never say yes to a date. "Becca and Woody want to go. Not sure about Ma and Sadie, but we can always make room for one more." He patted the ledge of the open window. "I got a truck."

Color bloomed in her cheeks. "I would like to see how they make sorghum. If we don't have a laying in then."

His own cheeks felt a little warm too. Maybe three years toting a gun across Europe had made him forget how to talk to a woman. He slid the pups back over on the passenger side and pushed in the clutch. He'd said enough. Maybe too much. He shifted the truck into gear and with a wave let the truck roll away from her. He looked in the rearview mirror before he got out of sight. She was still standing there, her hand on the dog's head.

"Take care of her, Sarge." He felt silly saying the words out loud, but nobody was around to hear him except the pups and the Lord. And the good Lord heard everything, whether you said it out loud or just let it sneak through your head.

He hadn't gone far when he spotted Granny Em walking up the creek with her gathering basket on her arm. She was moving slow, like each step cost her more effort than she had to give.

He tapped the brakes and rolled to a stop beside her. "Want a ride up the hill, Granny?"

She stepped over to the truck. "Benjamin Locke. What you doin' with this contraption?"

She sounded surprised, and as best Ben could remember, surprise wasn't something Granny Em often showed. She was like an ancient pine tree that just stood still in its place and took in everything that went on around it. Not that Granny Em stayed in one place. She might be on any hill on any day. The years piling up on her hadn't stopped that.

His mother said the old woman might have been married once upon a time, but it was so long ago, nobody was sure. And Granny Em never admitted to it. Some even claimed she'd had a baby once that hadn't survived. Others weren't sure she hadn't just crawled out of a cave up here on this mountain already old.

But she had aged while Ben was gone. Wrinkles lined every inch of her leathery face now. Her shoulders were stooped and she favored one of her legs with a limp. Her hair was a bush of gray tucked into a bun at the back of her neck with plenty of unruly strands springing free of her hairpins.

In spite of her unkempt appearance, she had an air about her. Mountain pride, Ben's mother called it. As necessary as food and water if a woman was going to survive in these hills.

"I bought me a truck," he told her now. "Get on in and you can be the first person I give a ride. Just watch out for the pups."

"Pups." She tiptoed up on the running board to peer inside. Her wrinkles crinkled up in a smile. "Well, if you ain't about to set Ruthena on her ear with them critters."

"But Sadie will be happy."

"That child'll be in hog heaven for sure. What with two of 'em."

She stepped down off the running board to open the door. Ben held the pups back while the old woman set her basket in the seat and clambered in beside it. She moved spryer than he thought she could. But then she was so thin, she didn't have much to lift up into the truck. He had to wonder if she'd been eating anything.

He peered into her basket filled with dandelion leaves and some bark. "Find anything good today?"

"Pickings was kinda slim, but I beat the squirrels to a few hickory nuts. They's down in the bottom there 'neath those greens." She lifted both the pups up into her lap. "Looks like your pickings was some better."

"Took this one dog off Shorty Johnson's hands so he threw in the pups too." That was sort of the way of it.

"Shorty's not generally so giving." Granny Em's eyes narrowed a bit. "I'll fix you up a dose to get rid of the worms. Coming from Shorty, these'n is bound to have worms." She looked out the rear window toward the truck bed. "What happened to the other critter? He jump out the window?"

"I gave him away already." Too late he realized it might have been better to not mention the collie dog. "To somebody who needed a dog."

"I used to have a dog. Long time back. Went ev'rywhere with me. Even learned how to sniff out ginseng root. Mighty handy that way. That old dog was fine company."

"How come you never got another dog?" Ben glanced over at her. Both the pups were lying peaceful as anything in her lap.

"Too much trouble feedin' 'em. Dogs ain't good 'bout eatin' greens and the like."

"I guess not." He hit a rock that bounced Granny Em up off the seat. She kept her hands over the pups.

"I hear tell these contraptions can be a body's death." She didn't sound worried. "One way to go's as good as another, I reckon."

Ben laughed. "I'll pay more mind to the road and try to miss the bumps."

"They ain't no road out there to pay mind to. I can't see no way you can git this thing up to your house."

"Not yet. But I'll work on that."

"Roads'll ruin these hills. Cuttin' the trees and all. Trees is what holds it all in place."

"You could be right." Ben twisted the wheel to spin around one of those trees and head up the hill.

"Ain't no could be about it."

Ben didn't argue with her. The roads would come whether they wanted them to or not. That was just the way things were. When the trees got too thick, he pulled the truck between two of them and turned off the key. The truck shuddered to a stop.

"Guess we'll have to shanks' mare it from here." He got out and went around to open the door for her. She handed him the pups and he set them down on the ground while he helped her out. The woman didn't feel like she weighed much more than Sadie. "Why don't you come on up the path with me? Ma was cooking apples and green beans. She might even have fried apple pies."

"That's right temptin'." She reached for her basket. "But I reckon I'll go on in and fix up that dose for them there pups 'fore they give Sadie the worms too and have her punying around agin. If I get it done 'fore night falls, I might come on back down the hill. It ain't a far step."

"That'd be kindly of you." Ben picked up the little pup before it could run under the truck to hide. He stuck it inside his shirt.

She looped her basket on her arm and started up the hill toward her house. Then she looked back at him. "Reckon I better make three doses so's you can give one of them to that nurse girl. In case they don't have nothing for dog worms in their medicine chest." When Ben just looked at her without saying anything, she went on. "Did the girl like the dog?"

261

"How'd you know I gave it to her?"

"Some things ain't hard to figure out." She gave a little laugh as she turned back up the path toward her house. "No indeedy. Not hard at all."

24

She had to have lost her mind. Letting Ben Locke leave this dog here. The collie leaned against her leg and looked up at her with trusting brown eyes. He hadn't made the first move to run after Ben's truck. Just stayed right beside her, his tail sweeping the ground behind him whenever she touched his head.

"All right, Sarge." Fran leaned down to look the dog straight in the eyes. "We'll figure out something, but I'm warning you. There's going to be a storm when I take you inside. You better be on your best behavior."

A cocklebur embedded in his fur stuck her finger when she stroked his side. With care, she worked the hair away from the burr, one strand at a time. The dog stood still, as though he knew she was getting rid of this thing that had been sticking him. She finally worked it free.

"Wonder how a currycomb works on a dog. Could be we should go find out before we introduce you to Nurse Betty. Make you as handsome as possible." And maybe she'd just stay outside until dark and then sneak the dog into the house.

She smiled, thinking about him sleeping on the rug beside her bed. How had Ben Locke known she wanted a dog? Thinking about Ben brought up the other reason she had to have lost her mind. Saying she'd go to the sorghum stir-off with him. Not with him. With his family. A great deal of difference there. A great deal. It was best if she didn't let herself get swept away by those blue eyes. And that he'd brought her a dog.

She'd never had a dog. Ever. Even though she'd begged for one for years when she was a girl. That and a horse. At least until she turned twelve and faced the fact that no way in the world would her mother let her have either one. When she went crying about that truth to her father, he shrugged and told her she'd have to claim her grandmother's old hound dog and pony as hers.

But Fran did better than that. She hadn't gotten the dog, but that next year she found a job at a nearby stable where rich girls boarded their jumping ponies. The pay wasn't much, but along with mucking out stalls, she got to exercise the ponies.

Now she had a dog. A smart one too that did seem to almost read her mind. She talked to him as she combed through his fur and worked out more cockleburs and beggar lice. The dog's ears drooped a bit now and again, and he whined once when she accidentally yanked his hair, but he never tried to get away.

"We can't count on Betty seeing how smart

you are, Sarge. I can't believe he named you Sarge! That man won't ever let me forget telling him to call me Sergeant." She couldn't keep from laughing a little. Sarge showed his teeth in his funny dog grin as if laughing along with her.

"We could change your name. How about Prince?" She sat back and gave him a once-over. He was small for a collie. Probably mixed with something else, but hard to tell what. Shepherd maybe. The tip of his left ear bent over a little, while the other ear stood up tall. Now that she'd smoothed down his fur, she could see his ribs showing. She needed to search him out some biscuits or cornbread. "How do you like that name? Prince?"

The dog gave a full body shake. She knew it was only because she'd quit brushing him and he was settling his hair back down the way he liked it. Even so, she had to smile. "Okay. Not Prince. Sarge, it is."

She liked keeping the name Ben had given the dog. She liked knowing why he'd given the dog that name. But she wasn't about to tell anybody else that. Not even Ben Locke.

First things first. She had to figure out a way to get the dog past Betty. She remembered the notice she'd seen on the bulletin board at the hospital that had made her go to the meeting about the Frontier Nursing Service:

ATTENTION! NURSE GRADUATES WITH A SENSE OF ADVENTURE! YOUR OWN HORSE, YOUR OWN DOG, AND A THOUSAND MILES OF KENTUCKY MOUNTAINS TO SERVE. JOIN THE FRONTIER NURSES BRIGADE AND HELP SAVE CHILDREN'S LIVES.

"That's what I'll tell her. I got the horse. I got the adventure and the thousand miles to get lost in. But I was promised a dog too, and now I have one. A dog named Sarge."

Since she was at the barn, she fed and watered the horses. Jasmine did a little dance at the sight of the dog, but then leaned down to touch her nose against Sarge. The dog didn't seem a bit bothered. Moses had no interest in anything but his feed.

Fran went to get water on the way to the house. Sarge lapped the water in the pool below the spring as if it had been too long since he'd had a drink. Fran thought about maybe using some of the water to give the dog a bath, but he didn't smell bad and he looked good now that he was brushed. She was the one who needed the bath. What he needed was something to eat.

"Come on, Sarge. We can't put it off forever. Let's go introduce you to Betty. Just don't get bothered if she gets bothered." Fran picked up the bucket and headed for the house. She rehearsed the part about how nurses were promised a dog. Somehow she doubted that was going to sway Betty. Could be she'd have to go to a higher power to get permission for Sarge to stay. Mrs. B had made the horse and dog promises.

When she came around the garden, Betty was standing on the back porch, her fists propped on her hips. The thunder was about to commence.

"I guess there are all different kinds of adventure." Fran touched Sarge's head. "We're about to have one of the kind that aren't all that fun. Like falling off your horse into a blackberry patch. But I did that and survived." She squared her shoulders and kept walking. The dog stayed right on her heels.

"Where did that come from?" Betty pointed at the dog.

"Somebody dropped it by here." Fran thought it better not to say exactly who. "Said the poor thing needed a home. Its owner was going to shoot him." Fran hoped to tap into Betty's sympathetic side.

But it didn't appear she had even a smidgen of sympathy when it came to dogs. "You give that animal right back. You know I don't want a dog around here."

"But I do." She stopped where she was with her hand on Sarge's head. She didn't like butting heads with Betty, but she intended to keep Sarge. "I'll take care of him. He won't be a bother to you at all."

"The mangy thing bothers me just being here. It will stink and bring in fleas and no telling what else. We run a clinic here. We don't need dog hair in our medicines." Betty's frown grew fierce as she threw out her hands.

"Mrs. B has a dog." Fran kept her voice even but firm. "And now I do. His name is Sarge."

"This is my center. What I say goes. If you want a dog, you'll have to go somewhere else." Betty's voice rose.

Fran's heart sank as she thought about being moved out of this district. She wouldn't get to deliver Becca's baby or see Lurene's son grow bigger. But she didn't back down. This seemed to have become more than about the dog. "If Mrs. B says so."

Fran's measured response seemed to upset Betty even more. She practically screeched at Fran now. "It's my say-so that matters on this."

All at once a low rumbling growl started up in Sarge. Fran grabbed at his ruff, but he jerked free and streaked straight for Betty.

"Sarge," Fran yelled, not able to believe her eyes. If he attacked Betty, there would be no way she could keep him. At any of the centers.

Betty screamed and then stood frozen as if unsure which way to escape.

"Stop, Sarge." Fran set down the bucket of water and chased after him. She couldn't let him hurt Betty.

The dog slid to a stop at the steps and pounced on something. A snake crawling out from under the porch. Sarge grabbed it in his mouth and shook it furiously. Fran backpedaled and Betty jumped back toward the door, her hand over her mouth and her eyes wide.

Sarge held the snake in his mouth and wagged his tail as he looked at Fran and then Betty. He dropped it on the step. It was very dead.

"A copperhead," Betty breathed out the word.

Fran was a little breathless too. "I hadn't had a chance to tell you he's a snake dog."

"Well." Betty appeared to be searching for words. "You should have told me that first thing."

Fran looked from the snake to the dirt under the porch. "You know what they say up here in the mountains. If you see one snake, another is close by."

"If only they stopped at two. There are snakes everywhere around here." Betty stepped back into the house and then looked over her shoulder at Fran. "A snake dog might earn his keep. He can stay, but he's completely your responsibility. And carry off that snake." She slammed the door behind her.

Sarge pranced over to Fran, his ears perked

up and tail wagging, obviously very proud of himself.

Fran leaned down to scratch his chest. "Good dog. You didn't happen to herd that snake under there while I wasn't looking just so you could play hero dog at the exact right moment, did you?"

Again the doggie grin.

"Wait until Ben Locke hears this."

The thought pulled her up short. She wasn't going to be talking to Ben Locke. At least not unless she really did go to that sorghum cooking with him.

"Not with him," she muttered aloud. "With his family. I need to keep that straight, Sarge. Very straight. Now we better get rid of this snake carcass. I don't guess you bury them as well as kill them."

The dog just looked at her. She sighed. "That's what I thought."

She hooked the snake over a stick to carry it off into the woods where some scavenger could make a meal of it. She was glad Sarge followed her, his eyes peeled on the path ready to clear it of any other unsavory creatures. Indeed, he might earn his keep.

Back at the house, she found some biscuits and a sausage left over from breakfast in the stove's warming oven for Sarge. Since neither she nor Betty had cooked anything for their supper, they made do with bread and cheese. That made Jeralene even more welcome when she showed up with an applesauce cake.

They carried chairs out to the shade where Ben had set the bucket of beans and started snapping off the bean ends.

Jeralene was young, but she was right at home working on the beans. "I've been stringing beans as long as I can remember. Ma didn't let me put them on the string till I was nigh on seven. But since then, I've strung up most all we've had. We got shucky beans hanging ev'rywhere. Up in the attic. Round on the porch. Looks something like the way folks in some places string up Christmas pretties, but the beans ain't for pretty. It takes plenty to feed our bunch."

She pitched a handful of beans in the dishpan. She said it was best to get several ready before they started threading them on the string. She was a pretty girl with brown hair falling down her back and eyes brown as hazelnuts. At fourteen, she already had a woman's figure. It was no wonder Woody was struck on her.

"I see you got a dog." Jeralene nodded toward Sarge stretched out beside Fran's chair. "Who brung it to you? Woody?"

Betty spoke up and saved Fran from answering. "Sounds like the boy. He's always coming around here with something."

"Usually something good to eat, so we're the

271

better off for it." Fran looked at Jeralene as she picked up another handful of beans. "I hear Woody has his eyes on you."

Jeralene flushed a little. "He hangs around some. Ma don't mind. He takes the young'uns fishing or entertains us with stories. Pa says he's a talker."

"He is that," Betty muttered.

Jeralene laughed. "He tells me his brother calls him a jaybird he jabbers so much. Says when he has a boy of his own, he might just name him Jay. Woodrow Jay."

Fran remembered her promise to Ben to have a talk with Jeralene and this seemed the perfect time. "He'd be better off waiting awhile for that."

"You ain't got no reason to concern yourself about that with me." Jeralene looked straight over at Fran. No flush heated up her cheeks now. "Seeing as how I've got six younger than me at the house, it ain't no mystery to me how babies happen and I ain't about to have it happen to me. Leastways not for a good long spell."

"Sensible of you," Betty said.

"Good," Fran added. "You will have time to go to school if you want."

"Not sure about that." Jeralene threaded a large needle and knotted the string. "I don't know that I'd want to end up a nurse like you with no babies at all." She picked up a bean from the dishpan, stuck the needle through the middle of the pod, and pulled it down to the end of the string. "Didn't neither one of you never want to marry and have your own young'uns?"

Silence followed her question as both Betty and Fran kept working with the beans. The girl didn't mean to be rude. While plenty of new babies were born to women as old or years older than even Betty, first-time mothers here in the mountains were generally much younger.

Jeralene must have realized she had asked something she shouldn't have. "Oh, don't pay my nosiness no mind. I let my curious side get the better of me. Ma would give me a good slap over letting my tongue wag without thinking."

"That's all right," Betty said. "I'm not ashamed of being a single woman. Never met a man I wanted to marry. Not that I'm so old I might not still find a good man and have a family. I'm only thirty-two. Old to you, Jeralene, but not completely over the hill yet." Betty actually laughed. "And Nurse Howard here is even younger. What are you, Nurse Howard? Twenty-two?"

"Twenty-three," Fran said.

Betty looked at Jeralene threading the beans on the string. "See. Young enough to marry and have a houseful of children." Betty switched her gaze from Jeralene to Fran. "Pretty like you are, I'm sure you've had your chances. Me, I've never been accused of beauty."

"I'm not pretty." Fran wasn't sure why she let that out. Maybe because Betty's words surprised her so.

"Come now." Betty dropped her hands into her lap. "False modesty is not attractive."

Fran shook her head. "I've always been awkward. Too tall. My smile too toothy and eyes that don't know whether to be green or tan and with hair that won't curl. My mother never knew what to do with me. She said everything about me was too big. Even my feet."

"Sturdy feet are a plus here in the mountains." Betty picked up a bean and broke off the ends. "And a good height makes everything easier. Although frontier nurses come in every size. I can't help what your mother told you, but if you don't think you're pretty, then your mirror must be broken." Betty stated it all very matter-of-factly as she pitched the bean into the dishpan.

"Ma says that beauty is in the eyes of the beholder," Jeralene said. "But that the Lord has put something pretty in everybody."

Fran smiled. "That's a good thought, Jeralene. Thank you. And thank you too, Betty."

"Well, don't get the big head. Looks don't make a nickel's worth of difference when it comes to being a nurse. Skill is what matters then."

"Yes."

They worked on the beans without saying anything for a few minutes. Then Jeralene spoke up. "But it is nice when somebody thinks you're pretty. And Nurse Howard, Woody says his brother must like how you look. He seen him talking to you extra long the last time you went up to his house."

Fran could feel Betty staring over at her, but she kept her head bent over the beans. No need advertising the red rising in her cheeks. "He was just giving me a mess of his mother's speckled beans. We talked some about where I was going because he thought I might get lost heading over the mountain again. I am prone to get off trail."

"That you are. You need to study those maps I gave you." Betty reached for another handful of beans.

"Yes." Fran couldn't argue with that as she tried to keep her mind on the beans.

Jeralene poked the beans and pulled them down on the thread faster than both Betty and Fran could break off the ends.

Later when the shucky beans were all threaded and hanging from the porch rafters and she was getting ready for bed, Fran stepped in front of the small square mirror on the wall. She generally only used it to comb her hair and knot her tie. But now she stared at the mirror until her image got fuzzy and her face didn't even seem like hers any longer.

Betty was right. She might not be pretty like young Jeralene, but her features lined up fine.

Not a thing was wrong with her face. She wasn't Cecelia from England with a cute turned-up nose and curly hair. She was Francine Howard, Frontier Nurse in the Appalachian Mountains. And Ben Locke did think she was pretty. She didn't know how she knew that, but she did.

She turned away from the mirror with a smile. Sarge sat beside her, his tail thumping against the chair. She patted the round rag rug beside her bed. "This will have to do, Sarge."

She rubbed his ears after he circled three times to lie down. "And you know what? My face may just do too. What a day! Ushering a baby girl into the world this morning. Learning how to string up shucky beans. Getting a dog." She trailed her fingers through Sarge's fur again. "And finding out some people think I'm pretty. The capper would just be helping a baby boy into the world tonight."

Fran yawned. "I do hope that adventure waits for another day."

25

September 28, 1945

Sarge settled in at the center as if he'd always belonged there. He ate whatever Fran scrounged up for him, and before the week was out, Fran caught Betty slipping him a tidbit from her plate.

Betty wiped her hands on her napkin. "The fact that we haven't seen a snake on our porch since he's been here is deserving of a crumb or two off my plate."

Fran saw no reason to point out the nippy feel to the morning air and how snakes went into hiding in cool weather. Betty knew it was fall.

Later that day, Granny Em showed up at the center to warn Fran frost was on the way. "Best pick any sass left in yo'r sass patch 'fore the frost falls. It can come a nigh bit sooner up here in the hills than in the flat country where you're from. 'Twon't hurt the pumpkins, but best pick the beans and tomatoes, even the green ones. They'll ripen in yo'r winder or they make fine eating fried."

"I've never fried tomatoes." Fran went down the steps to stand on the walk beside Granny Em. Sarge followed to sit at Fran's feet.

"That's 'cause you's from the north, but I

allow Ruthena can show you how to coat 'em in cornmeal and fry 'em in drippin's next time you're up that way." Granny Em eyed her. "You been to see her girls lately?"

"Betty checked on Becca last week. I had to go see the Tiptons."

Granny Em nodded. "I heared they had a rash of drippy noses. Frost'll take care of that. Get rid of the ragweed. Till then they'll just need extra snot rags."

"That's what Mrs. Tipton said. About the ragweed. But she wanted me to check over the baby anyway."

"She must have jest been wantin' somebody to talk to." Granny Em made a face. "Dora Tipton knowed that baby was too new to have to worry 'bout him ragweed sneezin'."

"Could be." She hadn't seen Granny Em for over a week. "You want to come in and have a cup of tea? Jeralene's mother sent us some molasses cookies."

"Ain't got no time to be supping tea. I got to be gathering what I need 'fore winter blows in." Granny Em raised up her basket. "And you need to be gathering in that sass. Be sure to get those yams out of the ground. Frost'll ruin them quick as anything. Runs right through the vines down into them sweet tators."

"Well, let me get you some of the cookies anyway before we both get back to work. They'll get stale before Betty and I can eat them all."

"I reckon I kin take time out for one of Wyona's molasses cookies." She stepped up on the porch. "Where's that other one?"

"You mean Nurse Dawson?"

"That be the one." Granny Em peered toward the door. "She's liable to chase me off. Feared I might tell you some cure that works better'n hers."

"No, she'd glad to see you, but she's gone to Wendover today. Some visitors Mrs. Breckinridge wanted her to meet."

"Good. Then I'll sit whilst you fetch them cookies." Granny Em settled down in one of the chairs on the porch.

Fran wrapped up all but two of the cookies and sliced some bread and cheese to go along with them. Granny Em had a look about her that Fran had seen on other mountain women when she didn't see much food on their tables. The men and children ate first. Granny Em didn't have a houseful of children or a man to feed, but she still had a hungry look.

Fran had never been all the way up to where Granny Em lived. She always ran across her on a trail or the old woman showed up at the center. So she didn't know if Granny Em had a garden or chickens. She needed to ride all the way up to her place sometime to see.

When she went back out on the porch to hand

279

Granny Em the food she'd wrapped up in a tea towel, the old woman frowned. "I never knowed Wyona to make sech a big cookie."

Fran laughed. Even to her ears it sounded a little forced. "I added in a little more. You don't mind, do you?"

"I reckon not if'n you needed to get it out of yo'r way." Granny Em stuffed the food down in her basket without looking inside the parcel. She kept the basket on her lap.

Fran sat down on the top step and leaned back against the porch post. Sarge settled beside her with his head in her lap.

"I see you're already some attached to that dog Ben Locke give you." She reached out her foot to poke the dog's tail.

"He's a good dog." Fran looked up at Granny Em. "Did Mr. Locke tell you he gave me the dog?"

"Didn't have to. I knowed already when he said he got three dogs and only come back up the mountain with two." The old woman dug down into the pocket of her skirt and pulled out a little bottle. "I brung you something for it. Most likely the critter needs a good worming and this concoction'll do the trick."

Fran took it. She'd already wormed Sarge, but she didn't have to tell the old woman that. "Thank you." She peered at the brown liquid in the bottle. "What's in it?"

"Nothing that will hurt the animal. I promise you that. I give a slighter dose to Ruthena to give to them two pups Ben took home."

"That's good." Fran slipped the bottle into her apron pocket and smiled. "I wish I could have seen Sadie's face when she saw those pups."

"I weren't there, but Ruthena said she might near cried to see Sadie so joyful. And Ruthena don't cry easy."

"You don't either, do you, Granny Em?"

"I can't recall shedding tears for some time. Though I might near did last week when a fox carried off my fav'rite hen."

"Do you have other hens?"

"None that lay regular like Hortense. I done threatened them others with the stew pot more'n once."

"Guess that would be better than the fox getting them."

"They'd be somethin's meal either way." She pushed up from the chair. "I best be on my way. Daylight's wastin'."

Fran shoved Sarge off her lap and stood up too.

"What'd you name the creature?" Granny Em poked Sarge with her toe again, but he didn't seem bothered by her.

"Sarge. Mr. Locke gave him that name." Fran held her breath, waiting to see if Granny Em knew why. She always seemed to know every-thing, as though news traveled to her on the wind.

"I reckon he brung that name home from the war."

Fran hid her smile, relieved at last to have some sort of secret from Granny Em. "That could be it. He did name his horse Captain."

The old woman turned a sharp eye on Fran, but she didn't say any more about the name. She started away across the yard toward the creek and then looked back. "I reckon I'll see you at the sorghum stir-off on Monday."

Fran hid her surprise. But she supposed Ben Locke had to tell his family he'd invited her. To join them. Not him, Fran reminded herself one more time. "It's a possibility. If Mrs. Garnett doesn't go into labor."

"Won't be no worry then of you missin' out." Granny Em spat on the ground. "That woman's gonna have a November baby. If she's telling you sooner, she done messed up her notching stick." She held up her basket a little. "Thank ye kindly for the vittles."

Fran watched her until she was out of sight. She couldn't keep from wondering about the| old woman. She didn't seem to be related to anybody on the mountain, and that in itself was strange. Most of the families in their district had plenty of kin living nearby. But Granny Em seemed to be a solitary figure. Would that be how Fran ended up? A solitary figure. Always walking alone.

As if sensing her thoughts, Sarge whined and touched her leg with his paw to remind her he was there. Even more, making her remember who had given him to her.

She shook away that thought and touched the dog's head. "My dog and me. And we've got work to do. Time to saddle up Jasmine and see how all our people are doing."

She didn't feel lonesome as she turned toward the barn. She had purpose. A reason for being there. One of the Tyler boys needed the stitches taken out where he'd fallen off a porch and gashed his head. Chesley Smith had a gunshot wound from accidently shooting his foot. No telling what other needs she'd find today.

She let her eyes feast on the beauty of the mountain behind the center with trees every shade of orange and red. A buzzard floated on the wind currents high overhead. Awkward on the ground but graceful as a ballet dancer in the air. A crow cawed as it flew past, and an orchard oriole sang out in the apple tree.

Fran walked over to the apple tree to search for windfalls. Most of the apples had already been dried or canned, but she always seemed able to find a few more. Sarge nosed one out first and lay down to chomp it while Fran waved away the bees buzzing around the bruised apples to pick up a couple for her and Jasmine.

Late that afternoon, after she finished her

rounds, she milked Bella and then headed for the chicken house to gather the eggs for breakfast. With the days getting shorter toward winter, the hens had already gone to roost on the long poles across one end of the shed. In the shadow of the mountain, night fell like a curtain dropping. Fran was counting their hens and wondering if she could pack one of them up the mountain to Granny Em to replace the hen the fox had stolen when a hello sounded outside.

In her head, she ran through the women expecting babies and came up with nobody due for weeks. But babies didn't always stick to schedules. Or there could be other sickness or an accident to call her out. She ducked out the short door, careful not to jostle the six eggs in her basket.

Woody was sliding off his horse in front of the center. Betty, back from Wendover, stepped out on the porch and pointed toward the henhouse. Fran breathed a sigh of relief. If something was wrong, Woody would have told Betty. Instead, he headed toward Fran carrying something wrapped in a dish towel. Maybe if Mrs. Locke had sent something good for their table, Betty might not be too upset about Fran giving away most of the molasses cookies. Betty liked her sweets.

Sarge ran ahead to greet Woody, who petted him with one hand and balanced the dish with the other. Fran hurried to take the dish before whatever offering he was bringing ended up Sarge food on the ground.

"It's fried green tomatoes." Woody pointed to the dish. "Granny Em said you didn't know about frying tomatoes, so Ma fixed some up for you to give 'em a try."

"She shouldn't have, but thank her for us." Fran peeked under the towel at the crusty slices of green tomatoes. Didn't look too appetizing, but looks didn't always reveal taste.

"She said to tell you they're better hot, so you might want to warm 'em up in the skillet."

"Okay." Fran put the towel back over the dish. "Everybody all right up your way?"

"We're good. Even Sadie ain't punyin' around. She's been so busy thinking up new verses to that froggie song she's forgot about being sick. She's about to drive me crazy with it."

Fran laughed. "You don't like singing?"

"Not the same livelong song all the day long. Besides, I can't sing a lick. Ma says I take after her pa that way, but that he played the harmonica. She give me Grandpa's harp so I could give it a try." Woody held his hands up to his mouth like he was blowing into a harmonica. "Maybe I'll learn a tune you can jig to."

"I don't know how to jig."

"Oh, anybody can jig. That's just an itching in your feet when you hear the right tune."

"You learn to play that jig tune, then we'll see." Fran laughed again. Woody always brought on smiles.

"That's what Ben said too." Woody gave her a sideways look. "Maybe you two could learn a jig together."

Her cheeks warmed. She tried to cover it up with another laugh. "I imagine he could find a better partner. Somebody who knew what she was doing."

"I reckon so. Guess I better get on home before the owls go to hunting. Them big old things flying out of a tree in front of you can spook your horse about as bad as a rattler." He headed toward Captain, who was nosing around the yard for a sprig of grass. Woody looked back at Fran before he mounted the horse. "I about forgot. Ben told me to tell you we'd be by to get you Monday morning early. To go to the sorghum stir-off. Ma said for me to invite Nurse Dawson too."

Woody glanced toward the house. Betty had gone back inside and shut the door. "I don't reckon she'd want to come anyhow. She ain't much for studying on mountain ways."

"I'll ask her for you."

Woody shrugged his shoulders. "If you want to. I reckon there'll be room in the back of the truck."

Extending the invitation to include Betty

might make it easier to say she was going. Plus that made Ben asking Fran merely a neighborly gesture. Nothing personal. She needed to remember that. Nothing at all personal.

Fran touched Sarge's head as she watched Woody ride off. She could still be grateful for a good dog by her side.

26

October 1, 1945

Monday morning Fran was up well before daylight to milk Bella and take care of the horses. Even Sarge looked sleepy as he trailed after her. Fran had awakened every hour after midnight, worried she might oversleep.

Just as Woody thought, Betty had no interest in seeing sorghum being made. "But if they offer you a jar, you take it. It's delicious on a hot biscuit."

Fran was surprised when Betty didn't name over a dozen reasons Fran shouldn't go. All she did was insist Fran wear her Frontier Nursing outfit of pants and vest along with the fetched tie.

"I'll stand out like a sore thumb," Fran said.

"Exactly." Betty leveled unsmiling eyes on Fran. "That's what you want. Even the roughest mountain men up here respect that outfit. That's what lets us travel alone through these hills without the first worry anyone will bother us. But we have to dress so the home people recognize us as nurses."

"I'll be with the Locke family," Fran said. "I

hardly think I have anything to worry about with them."

"Nothing but perhaps your own foolishness. I hear it was Ben Locke who brought you the dog." Betty raised her eyebrows and gave Fran a disapproving look.

"It was, but I told you he was simply trying to find a home for Sarge."

"Indeed that is what you said." Betty waved her hand to dismiss any further argument from Fran. "You're of age. Do whatever you want there. You wouldn't listen to me anyway."

"Giving somebody a dog doesn't mean a thing. Dogs are traded or given away all the time." It sounded like a good argument to Fran, even though she didn't consider Sarge an ordinary gift.

"That's certainly true. A dog on every porch. Sometimes a half dozen when there's scant food for their children. If I stay in these mountains a hundred years, I will never understand these people." Betty heaved a sigh. "But never mind that. I agree the Lockes are fine, upstanding people. I have no concerns about you going with them. Other than you getting too attached to that family. Maintaining a professional distance enables us to make decisions based on knowledge rather than emotions."

"Yes, of course." No way could Fran argue with that. A nurse-midwife needed a clear head and eyes undimmed by tears.

"Good that you keep that in mind." Betty went on. "But the Lockes won't be the only ones at this sorghum making. The Hoskins live in a different district where some of the people may not recognize you. So who knows what might happen if you didn't have on your nurse outfit. A new woman in their midst. A new, attractive woman."

"I can't imagine anybody bothering me."

"Then you don't have much of an imagination." Betty's eyes narrowed on Fran. "I've lived here longer than you, and it takes no imagination at all to know someone will be passing around moonshine in mason jars before the day is through. A man drinks much of that, he can forget every shred of decency."

So with the sun just up, Fran was on the porch in her nurse uniform when the truck bounced down the ruts that passed as a road and stopped by the yard gate. Ben leaned out the window. "Climb in."

The cab was full with Becca and Granny Em. Woody, Mrs. Locke, and Sadie, in the bed of the truck, waved her toward them.

She turned to tell Sarge to stay, but Woody yelled, "Sarge can come too. We brung a rope to tie him if he gets to be a bother."

Sadie spoke up. "They wouldn't let me bring Buttons." She made a sad face.

"She's too little. She'd get trampled for certain," Mrs. Locke said.

"And she had to stay home to keep Bruiser company."

"Bruiser?" Fran laughed at the name. "You named that little pup Bruiser?"

"I named him for the future." Woody jumped out of the truck and lowered the tailgate. "Just wait. He'll be a bruiser."

When Fran patted the truck bed, Sarge jumped in and then watched Fran scramble into the truck before he danced over to see Sadie.

"Nurse Dawson didn't want to come?" Mrs. Locke asked.

"She thanks you for the invitation, but she decided to stay here in case someone needs something."

"If they do, they'll be needing it at the Hoskins stir-off. That's where everybody will be." Woody slammed the tailgate shut and clambered back into the truck.

"Hang on," Ben called back to them as he shifted the truck into gear.

"You ever rode in the back of a truck before?" Woody asked.

"Just once." Fran's ride with Lurene Nolan down the mountain to the hospital wasn't a good memory.

Now she wasn't sure where to sit or stand. |Mrs. Locke perched on a wheel well and held onto the sides of the truck bed. Sadie sat on a folded blanket in front of her. Woody took up a position behind the truck cab.

"You can stand here behind the cab as long as you're ready to duck if tree limbs hang down over the road. Or sit on the other wheel well over there." Woody pointed.

"Maybe I should try that." Fran settled on the opposite wheel well from Mrs. Locke.

"It's a bumpy ride but a mite faster than walking." Mrs. Locke smiled over at Fran. "We would have let you ride up front, but considering Becca's condition and Granny Em's age, we give them the front."

"That's fine. This is fun." And it was fun to feel the wind blowing her hair back from her face. Sarge stepped up beside her, leaned his head over the edge of the truck, and panted into the wind.

The sorghum making was well under way when they got there, with the field already crawling with people. Horses and mules were tied to trees near the clearing, and children and dogs ran helter-skelter everywhere.

After Ben parked the truck alongside some other vehicles, he came around to open the tailgate and help his mother and Sadie out of the truck. Woody had jumped out before the truck came to a complete stop and run into the middle of the crowd.

"That boy." Mrs. Locke shook her head, but

she was smiling. "Acts like I never taught him nothing."

Fran sat down on the tailgate and scooted out of the truck bed before Ben could offer to lift her down the way he did Sadie and his mother. Best to keep that professional distance Betty talked about.

Not so easy to do with this family. Becca grabbed her in a hug. "I'm so glad you came. I'm figuring we might even have time for a song or two on the way home, or would if Ma would let me ride in the back. Granny Em's not much for singing and Ben's got to be the strong, silent type here lately. I remember he used to sing before he went off to the army." She gave Ben a look. "I guess he's forgot how."

"I haven't forgot anything. Around the house there's not an inch of quiet time to squeeze in a note, what with you and Woody always jabbering." Ben laughed.

Fran felt better just hearing him laugh, the same as she had that day out in the woods when he'd laughed after she told him to call her Sergeant.

Ben gave Becca a playful shove away from him. "Go on and hunt somebody else to pester."

"But what about Nurse Howard? It's not nice to just leave her standin' here not knowin' nobody." Becca looked around. Her mother and Sadie had already walked away, carrying the food they'd brought to add to the lunch. Granny Em followed after them.

"I'll be fine, Becca. Don't let me put a damper on your day," Fran said.

"I can show her around." Ben looked over at Fran. "If you're all right with that, Nurse."

"I would like to see how sorghum is made." Fran kept her smile easy in spite of the way her heart started hammering faster.

"Oh no. You sound like one of those weird people from the north wanting to learn our old-time ways." Becca rolled her eyes.

"Becca." Ben's voice was sharp.

Fran just laughed. "I guess I am one of those weird people from the north."

"That did sound awful, didn't it?" Becca hunched her shoulders and made a face. "But I wasn't meaning you, Nurse Howard. No denyin' you're from the north, but we're turning you mountain." The girl's smile came back. "But trust me. Watching sorghum cook is like listening to water dripping in a bucket. Dull as all get-out."

Somebody waved and yelled Becca's name from across the way. Becca went up on her toes and waved back. "That's Maxine. I haven't seen her in forever." She gave Fran a quick look. "Tell you what. You get bored watching green juice squeezings, hunt me up."

She was off in a flash, leaving Fran alone with

294

Ben. Fran was glad when Sarge pushed against her. She put her hand on the dog's head. "Are you sure Sarge is going to be all right with all these other dogs?"

"I don't know. Why don't we ask him?" Ben squatted down in front of Sarge. "Are you going to stay with us and not get in any fights, Sarge?"

Fran twisted her lips to keep from smiling. "What's he say?"

Ben stood up. "Couldn't you hear him? He said he planned to stay right beside you. That's his job."

"He does it well." Fran scratched behind Sarge's ears. It was easier to look at the dog than into those dark blue eyes. "But what about this green juice Becca was talking about? I thought sorghum was brown."

"You are a city girl." Ben put his hand under her elbow. "Come on. It's time you found out the secrets behind sorghum molasses."

He pointed at a pile of green stalks next to what he called the sorghum press. Some of the stalks looked ten feet long.

"The cane grew over there." He nodded toward a field where nothing was left but stubble and weeds. "The Hoskins have a good flat place here for their sorghum cane. Most of us have to do hillside farming."

"I've seen that growing. You'll laugh at me, but I thought it was some different kind of

corn. I wondered why I never saw any ears."
Fran laughed at herself. "I should have asked
somebody. What happened to the leaves?"

"They strip the leaves off before they cut
the stalks. Faster to do that while the cane is
standing, but you'd best wear long sleeves and
gloves. Those leaves are rough on your skin.
After they cut the cane, they let it weather a few
days for the sugar to rise in the stalks. Then they
haul it to the press to squeeze out the juice."

Fran watched a couple of men feeding the
long green stalks between two rollers. A boy
about Woody's age was leading a mule harnessed
to a long pole attached to the press around in a
circle. The mule had already worn a circular
path in the grass.

"I guess that's mule power."

"Best power for up here in the hills. A mule
can keep going all day." Ben watched the mule
make a circle. "There were times I wished we
had a mule with our army division. Of course,
sometimes a mule can take the studs and be
more trouble than help."

"Take the studs?" Fran frowned a little. "What's
that mean?"

"I guess it's mountain talk for being contrary.
Refusing to do something." Ben laughed. "Being
mule stubborn."

"Oh. That I understand." Fran smiled and
pointed at the green juice spilling out of a pipe

at the bottom of the press into a bucket. "The squeezings?"

"Right."

Smoke drifted over from the fire. "Then they cook it?" Fran moved to get a better look at a long tin trough-like pan full of the green liquid over a slow-burning fire. When Ben nodded, she asked, "How long?"

"It takes a while. One of the old-timers here will judge when it's ready. Then they'll pour it up into jars. A lot of stirring and skimming before that."

Fran watched a woman skim green scum off the top with a large wooden paddle. Then she started stirring again. On the other side of the fire, a man worked the same kind of paddle through the green liquid. "It's hard to think about that turning into the sorghum molasses I've seen."

"It takes some doing to get it right. The same as with most things."

People milled around them. Some stopped to clap Ben on the back and welcome him home. Then they'd nod at Fran. She knew some faces, but many were new to her. Fran was right about standing out in her frontier nurse trousers. Nearly all the women wore dresses. But it wasn't a fashion show. It was a neighbor gathering, although a little courting was surely going on when she spotted Woody following Jeralene around.

The fact that Ben Locke was staying beside her was probably more the reason for the looks she was getting than her trousers. She thought she should tell him he didn't have to play host to her, but she liked him beside her. That professional distance was getting harder and harder, but Ben looked healthy. It was unlikely he was going to be her patient. And it wasn't as if he had any ideas of courting. She was Nurse Howard to him. Somebody brought-in.

27

"Do you think they'd let me stir it?" Fran looked up at Ben.

"I don't see why not." She looked so eager Ben couldn't keep from smiling at her.

Something about this woman grabbed at him the way no other woman ever had. She was different. Different wasn't always good, but with Francine it felt good. She had a way of looking at everything here with fresh eyes.

His view of it all should be fresh too after so long away, but what he kept seeing anew were all the wrong things about the mountains. Barefoot kids because they didn't have shoes. Men going to work the mines or moonshining against the law because that was the only way to make money. A place where a stretch of dry weather might mean going hungry come winter without the vegetables put up in the cellar. His ma worked dawn to dark to see that their cellar was well stocked.

He wanted to be home. He was home, but a restless feeling kept scratching at him. He needed to figure out what tomorrow held for him. Funny how he hadn't worried about that while he was in the army. Then his whole focus had been on surviving to get home. He hadn't thought about what he'd do once he was here. He hadn't considered how changed he would be from the boy who had left for the war.

He'd seen the world outside the mountains. Serving in the army opened up opportunities. He could go to school on the GI Bill, but diplomas didn't count for much in the hills.

What was it his pa used to say when Ben started worrying a problem like a dog licking a sore? *You don't have to know the last step. Just the first one. You and the good Lord can figure out the rest of it on the way.*

Today was a gift. Each day was. Plenty of soldiers' only trip home was in a body bag. They never had the chance to open the gift of this day or stand next to a pretty girl and see their world through her eyes. Best to stop fretting about tomorrow and grab hold of today.

He nodded toward one of the women stirring the cane juice. "I can ask Miss Jessie over there if you can have a turn. She used to go to church with us before she moved across the way to where her daughter lives."

"Everything is family up here, isn't it?" Fran looked a little wistful.

"Don't you have family?"

"My mother. Dad died and Mother remarried a year ago. So I have a stepfather, but I hardly know him."

"No sisters and brothers?" Ben couldn't keep the surprise out of his voice.

"Nope. But I always wished I did."

"I'll loan you mine. I figure in a week or probably before a day was over, you'd be sending them packing back up the hill to me."

"I'd give it a try with Sadie and Woody, but I'm not sure I could get Nurse Dawson to go along with the idea. Especially if they brought those new pups with them. Sarge is winning her over, but I can't see her taking in a Bruiser." Fran laughed. "But what about this stirring? You think I can do it?"

"I think you can do anything you set your mind to." Now why did he say that? He believed it, but a man didn't have to let every livelong word out into the air.

"There have been times I've wondered about that." Her smile faded for a moment, but then came back brighter than ever. "But I would like to know how to stir sorghum."

"We can make it happen."

He tapped Miss Jessie on the shoulder. When she looked around at him, she propped her paddle across the tin trough to give him a hug. "Ben Locke, if you ain't a sight for sore eyes. I hear'd you was home from the war. I prayed for you ev'ry night. Along with all the other boys over there."

301

"Thank you for that, Miss Jessie. Times were I needed those prayers."

"Could be what brung you home. And now that you're here, it's time you settled down." She gave him a look over. "I got a pretty little granddaughter what's got grown since you been away. I bet she'd make eyes at you." The woman grinned up at him and then noticed Fran beside him. "And looka here. You must be one of Mrs. B's nurses. Come for a look-see at our sorghum stir-off."

"I'm Nurse Howard." Francine held out her hand.

Miss Jessie laughed and pushed Francine's hand to the side. "We do hugs round about here, child. You at a stir-off, you have to abide by mountain rules no matter how far away you come from. You ain't one of them English nurses from across the ocean, are you?"

"No, much closer than that. Cincinnati."

"That ain't so far. Jest over the river in Ohio. Some of my folks went up there to work in the munitions factories during the war. Settled in. Ain't come back down this way yet awhile." She shook her head. "I can't imagine not having these hills around me."

"It's a beautiful place." Fran stepped back from the hug, taking some of the green stain of the juice with her. "I love the mountains."

And that's what Ben liked best about Francine.

She might not be a mountain girl, but she was here because she wanted to be. Now he just had to decide if he was there for the same reason. He couldn't believe he was even wondering about that. He was home. With his people. His roots went deep. And yet . . .

He pushed those thoughts aside as he watched Miss Jessie show Francine how to stir the squeezings without sloshing any out.

"You got to get some shoulder into it," the woman told Francine. "But keep back from the fire. Don't want to catch your skirt tail on fire." The woman laughed. "Reckon you don't have no worry about that in your men's clothes."

Francine laughed with her as she worked the paddle.

"Don't skip the corners," Miss Jessie warned. "And you gotta keep that scum skimmed off."

By the time Francine turned the stirring paddle back over to Miss Jessie, the woman was ready to claim her as a granddaughter too. Everywhere Francine went, her smile won over people.

After they ate the meal laid out on planks set across sawhorses, the first batch of sorghum was declared done and the syrup poured into jars. Then a couple of men passed out short bits of stalk for the children and anybody else who wanted to scrape the cooked syrup off the sides and bottoms of the tin cooker. Ben lined up with Francine to get a taste of the sweet molasses. He hadn't enjoyed a stir-off this much since he was Woody's age. All because of the woman beside him.

They were sitting on the tailgate of his truck in the shade, licking the last of the sweet syrup off the stalks, when a gunshot went off over close to the woods. Then somebody was screaming.

The sound of the gun shook Ben. For a few seconds he was back on the battlefield with men dying around him. Where it was up to him to keep them alive.

"Was that—"

"Gunfire." He jumped off the tailgate, his eyes searching through the people. He spotted Sadie clinging to his mother's skirt, while Ma was doing the same as Ben. Searching through the people to let her eyes touch on the ones who mattered most to her. And there was Becca with some other young women.

Then Jeralene was running toward them. Blood on her sleeve. "Nurse. You've got to help him. Woody's been shot."

Ben couldn't move. He'd seen too many boys die. He couldn't bear to watch his brother be one of them.

28

Fran ran past Ben. When he didn't follow, she looked back. At the stricken look on his face, she wanted to stop and take his hand, but every second might be vital to Woody. So instead she yelled at him. "Come on, Ben. I'll need your help."

She didn't look back again as she raced toward where Jeralene pointed. The people parted to let her through. Woody was sitting on the ground, his hand on his chest. Blood seeped through his fingers.

With eyes wide, he stared at Fran. "Somebody shot me." He sounded surprised.

Ben was there then. "Who?"

"I don't know." Woody's breathing was getting a little rougher. "I didn't do nothing, Ben. Honest."

"Shh. Lie down and stop talking." Fran gently pushed him down. "Let me look at it."

"Is it bad, Nurse?"

Ben stood up and stared at the men and boys circled around them. "Who did this?"

Nobody claimed to know.

Fran glanced up at Ben. "Let somebody else handle that. Help me with Woody." If only she had her saddlebag. She peeled Woody's shirt back. The bullet appeared to have missed Woody's major organs, but he was losing blood fast. Already he looked paler than when she'd first knelt beside him. "Has anybody got something clean? A towel. An apron."

Mrs. Locke jerked off her underskirt and handed it to Fran. Her face was grim.

"Stay with me, Woody," Fran said. "You're going to be all right."

"You bet, kid. Just be still." Ben was on his knees beside Woody again. He ran his fingers across Woody's cheek and then looked at Fran. "Is the bullet still there?"

"I would guess so, but it would be better to let the doctor probe for it at the hospital." Fran folded the material and pressed it over the wound. "We need to get him there as fast as possible."

"First, find the bleeder," Ben said.

"Bleeder," Woody echoed weakly. "I don't like how that sounds, brother."

"Army talk. That's all." Ben leaned close to Woody's face. "Now be quiet for once in your life."

People murmured around them, but Fran focused completely on Woody and what Ben had said. He was bound to have more experience with gunshot wounds than she did.

"Right." Fran looked at her hands. They were far from clean, but Ben's wouldn't be any better.

"Give me some moonshine." She looked up at the men in the circle around them. A couple of them stepped back as if wary of her demand.

Granny Em poked one of the men with her finger. "Give it to her."

When the man pulled out a flask, Ben grabbed it to pour the alcohol over Fran's hand. She found the bleeder and put pressure on it. "I'll hold it. Get your truck."

Ben touched Woody's face again. "I'll be right back. Do whatever Nurse Francine says."

"Francine?" Woody murmured.

Fran ignored his question. Not a time to talk names. "We're going to get you to the hospital and take care of this."

The men made a stretcher out of a tablecloth to carefully lift Woody into the bed of the truck. Fran crawled into the truck with him, still holding the pressure on the bleeder. She lost it for a moment and fresh blood spurted out. Then she had it again.

Sarge jumped in before the men could close the tailgate to crouch in the corner of the truck bed behind Fran. Mrs. Locke climbed in on the other side of Woody while Becca and Sadie and Granny Em squeezed in with Ben.

"This ain't the way you're supposed to ride in the back of a truck, Nurse Howard." Woody gave her a wan smile.

"I'll keep that in mind," she said.

Woody turned his head toward his mother. "Are you praying, Ma?"

"I'm praying, son."

"Reckon I should pray too. Ask forgiveness and all. Just in case."

"If you feel the need." Mrs. Locke stroked Woody's arm. "But you're a good boy. The Lord knows that."

Ben drove fast, swerving to miss the worst bumps in the road. Fran put her knee against Woody's shoulder to try to keep him from bouncing away from her. "Mrs. Locke, move as close to Woody as you can. We need to hold him steady."

"I feel funny, Nurse." Woody's voice was weak. "Is this how you feel when you die?"

Fran kept her voice absolutely sure. "You're not going to die."

"Everybody dies. Ain't that right, Ma? Our days are numbered. Pa told me it says that in the Bible."

"The Bible does say that." Mrs. Locke nodded.

"But you haven't run out of those numbered days. Not today," Fran said. "The doctor will poke around inside you, get that bullet out, sew you up, and in a few weeks, you'll be good as new."

"I hope so. I would sincerely regret not getting to marry Jeralene." He groaned as they hit another bump. "I could write a song about Jeralene. She's so lean. And sometimes mean."

"Maybe she's the one who shot you. Singing a song like that." Fran took his pulse with her free hand. Still strong. Her other hand was cramping, but she ignored the pain.

"That might be." Woody tried to laugh but it came out a groan. "They musta shot my laughing muscle."

"Could be you should think on praying and not laughin' then." His mother sounded stern, but she brushed the hair back off his face with a gentle hand.

"Yes'm." He shut his eyes, but if he prayed, it was a short one. The next moment his eyes popped back open as he stared up at Fran. "Has Ben sung you a song, Nurse? Francine he called you. Ain't it funny that Francine and Jeralene rhyme, so guess he could say 'mean' and 'lean' for you too."

"Nobody has ever made up a song for me, but if they do, I hope they come up with something better than 'mean.' How about 'keen'? 'Or serene.'" Fran wished she had a better sense of the area so she could know how much farther to the hospital.

"I bet nobody ever give you a dog before either," Woody said.

"No." At least they were on a smoother road. That had to be a good sign.

"Reckon I should give Jeralene a dog?"

"I think you'd best be quiet awhile," his

309

mother said. "You're not making much sense."

"Yes'm. But it's hard to make sense when I'm floating up there with them treetops flying by. But I ain't seen no angels yet. Oh wait. There might be one."

Mrs. Locke looked over at Fran. "What the Lord wills."

Fran checked Woody's pulse. It wasn't quite as strong, but it was steady. She leaned down close to the boy's ear. "That's your guardian angel, making sure you're all right."

"I reckon as how it could be." Woody smiled a little. "I give her a good chase now and again, don't I, Ma?"

At last, they sped through Hyden and headed up Thousandstick Mountain. Minutes from the hospital.

Ben started blowing his horn as soon as the hospital was in sight. Nurses were waiting when they pulled up to the door. Fran sat back and let them take over as they rushed Woody into the hospital. Mrs. Locke, Ben, and the others hurried after him.

Fran scooted out of the truck bed and sank down beside the truck's back tire. Sarge rested his nose on her shoulder. She told herself to get up and go inside, but she just sat there.

A simple prayer rose up inside her. "Please, Lord, not his time," she whispered.

The daylight faded and night crept over the

mountain. She didn't know how much time went by before Granny Em came out to find her.

"I knowed you didn't leave." She squatted down beside Fran.

"Is he all right?"

"Life and death ain't in your realm, child. It never was in mine neither. You can't hide from death."

"I know that."

"Do you?"

Fran studied Granny Em's face in the light coming out of the hospital windows. "Tell me how he is."

"He's gonna live."

"Did the doctor tell you that?"

"He told Ruthena. But I knowed it already. 'Tweren't the boy's time." She stood up and reached a hand down to Fran. "If'n it were, wouldn't be nothin' none of us could do. Even as much as we all might want to."

"Are they okay? Becca? Sadie?" Fran stood up and looked toward the hospital door.

"Ben?" Granny Em peered up at her.

"Ben."

"You coulda come in and been with them."

"I wasn't sure I should. I'm not family."

"I reckon that's so, but sometimes what's in the heart matters more than what's in the blood. If'n we're not afeared of it."

Fran didn't know what to say to that. Instead

she stared down at her hand with Woody's blood crusted between her fingers. "I need to clean up."

"You're a sight, sure enough." Granny Em made a sound that might have been a chuckle. "And reek some of the 'shine. Could take the color right out of them britches you got on. Hobart stills it strong."

"Do you know who shot Woody?"

"I got some supposings, but it ain't always good to suppose." Granny Em's face changed, closed in on itself for a minute. Then she shook her head a bit. "Could have been naught but an accident. Folks get careless with firearms around here from time to time. Nothing you want to involve yourself in."

"You're right. That was something I shouldn't have asked."

"Some things are better not talked about. I seem to recall Mary Breckinridge making some such rules 'bout that."

"No politics, religion, or moonshine talk. Just nursing."

"The woman knows. She may be city bred, but she learned about the mountains 'fore she brought in any nurses. Hunted up all us grannies when she first came to these parts. Made out like she really wanted to know what we was thinking."

"You don't think she really wanted to know?"

"I reckon as how she mighta. You'd have to

ask her that. But her coming and bringing in all you others changed things. I ain't caught a baby in years." Granny Em blew out a long sigh. "Could be for the best. Hardly ever hear 'bout any birthing deaths these days."

"We have the hospital now if there are problems," Fran said. "And better ways to get mothers here."

"Like that contraption there." Granny Em pointed at Ben's truck. "You gonna head on back to Beech Fork tonight?"

"I better wait for daylight. Chances are I'd just get lost and wander around until dawn anyway."

"I could show you the way."

"You're not walking home tonight, are you? I'm sure they can find you a place here at the hospital to sleep."

"I could lay right down here under that bush yonder and have me a nap if'n that was all I wanted, but I got an old cow and my hens to tend to."

"But—"

"Don't start fretting about me. Night's the best time for traveling when a feller knows where she's going. I know the way, daylight or dark." Granny Em's lips turned up in a smile. "The moon plays that music I told you 'bout sometime back. The rhythm of these here hills. But you ought not to go till you see the folks inside. They's wondering where you went to."

"You're right."

"I nearly always am, but tell you what. If'n you go speak your piece to them in there and then want to head home, I don't walk so fast these days. A young thing like you could catch me 'fore I get to the bottom of the hill."

Fran wanted to tell her to stay, but she knew better than to argue with Granny Em. "Be careful."

Granny Em looked around at her. "Careful don't get you nothing in this life. You remember that, girl."

Fran watched her out of sight, then told Sarge to stay while she went inside to find a sink to scrub her hands and face. She ran her hands through her hair and straightened her tie. She rubbed at the bloodstains on her clothes, but that would take soaking in cold water. After splashing more cold water on her face, she still looked like she'd been keeping watch with a new mother at a laying in for days.

It didn't matter how she looked. What mattered was that Woody was going to be all right. And suddenly she wanted to be with his family and let them know she cared. Betty might be right about keeping a professional nurse-to-patient distance. She was right, but Fran was breaking all the rules with the Locke family. She did care and as more than their nurse.

314

29

Ben didn't realize how he was watching for Francine until he saw her coming down the hallway. But then she was there and he was glad.

Without thinking whether he should or shouldn't, he went to meet her. She had an outward look of calm as a nurse should, but her lips trembled when she pushed them up in a smile. She had washed her hands, but Woody's blood still stained her clothes, as it did his and his mother's.

He wanted to ask where she'd been. Why she hadn't come to wait with them. But he held back the words. He couldn't be sure she had the same need to see him as he had to see her. But her eyes did seek his and not turn away. He let her speak first.

"Granny Em says the doctor told you Woody was going to be all right." It wasn't a question, but she sounded as if she needed to be assured it was true.

"The doctor talked with Ma a little while ago. Claimed Woody was lucky. An inch or two to the right and he'd have been gone. Said it was a wonder he didn't bleed out." Ben pulled in a breath that even now felt shaky when he thought about losing Woody. "We have you to thank for that."

"Or you." She put her hand on Ben's arm. "You knew what to do."

"Too well." The gunshot echoed in his head. He'd wanted to leave those sounds behind forever. "But I didn't want to need my medic training here. Not for my brother."

"Of course not." She hesitated and then asked, "Are you all right?"

He knew what she meant, but he didn't know how to answer. The sound of that gunshot had brought back too many bad memories, but that wasn't a burden he needed to thrust off on her.

She seemed to sense his reluctance to answer and changed her question. "All of you? Becca and Sadie? Your mother?" She peered around him at them.

He looked back too. Sadie leaned against his mother, her eyes wide and scared. Becca slouched in one of the wooden chairs, obviously exhausted. His mother, on the other hand, was the strong, steady rock she always was. She'd been through her own kind of wars and dealt with each new battle with a resigned endurance.

"Go talk to them." He stepped to the side to let her past him.

She stooped to hug Sadie and then grasped his mother's hand as Ma told her what the doctor said. Last she turned to Becca and offered to find her a place to lie down.

Before Becca could answer, his mother spoke

up. "No need in that. Ben can take you and Sadie to the house now that we know Woody is going to be all right."

"I'm fine." Becca stood up and stretched her back. "I want to stay."

"What you want don't matter right now. Somebody has to go home to see to things and that has to be you and Ben. Come morning, Ben can bring you back down if'n you feel the need to be here." Ma settled her eyes on Becca a moment, then looked over at Ben. "I expect Nurse Howard could use a way back to the center and Granny Em back to the mountain."

"Granny Em left a bit ago," Francine said. "Told me to catch up with her after I talked with you and she'd make sure I didn't get lost on the way."

"No need in that." Ma's face was set. "Ben has that truck."

Becca looked ready to argue, but one look at Ma's face and she merely nodded.

"Let me find the nurse." Francine looked from Becca to Ben. "Maybe you can see Woody before you leave."

A few minutes later, a nurse led Becca and Ben back a corridor to Woody's room. Sadie, too young to visit, stayed with Ma. The nurse promised Ma she could sit with Woody through the night.

The woman Francine introduced as Nurse

Williams warned them Woody would be weak and still under the influence of the anesthesia. "Even if he's awake, he may not respond with much sense."

Becca stopped and hung back at the door into the hospital room with beds divided by curtains.

Ben put his arm around her and kept his voice low. "It will be okay."

"How do you know?" Becca blinked away tears. "Anything could still happen."

"In the army if the boys made it through the first round of treatment, they nearly always continued to get better."

"Nearly always."

"But some of those wounds were ten times worse than Woody's. Come on. Smile in case he's awake." He urged her through the door while making sure to hide the worry on his own face.

Woody looked almost as pale as the sheet pulled up over him. His eyes were closed and that made him look so young. Like a child tucked in for a nap. Woody was never that still.

The nurse checked his pulse. "He can probably hear you whether he can respond or not."

Becca blinked back tears and pasted on a smile. "Woodrow Locke, what in the world are you trying to do? Scare me to death? You know that's not good for a woman in my condition."

A slight lift of the corners of Woody's lips showed he did hear her. Ben took his hand and squeezed it. "You'll be fine as long as you do what the nurses say." Ben kept his voice light too.

"You mean Nurse Francine?" Woody's voice was barely above a whisper, but there was no denying the teasing sound in it or in his eyes when they flickered open.

Ben could feel both Becca and Nurse Williams giving him curious looks, but he did his best to act like he didn't know what Woody meant, even though he did. He had let Francine's name slip out into the open. "Whichever nurse is trying to help you."

Woody's lips curled up even more. "Francine ain't mean. She's a dream."

"I don't know what they gave you, but it better wear off soon before you get in trouble."

Woody's smile faded. "I reckon I'm already in trouble. Coy was a better shot, I'd be dead as a doornail."

"Coy? Who's Coy?"

Woody shifted uneasily as though the bed had suddenly gotten too hard. He groaned and shut his eyes. The nurse took hold of Ben's arm and pulled him away from the bed. "Not now, Mr. Locke. Questions will have to wait."

Ben took a deep breath. "Yes, ma'am. I understand."

Nurse Williams gave him a stern look. "All right then. Two more minutes. Then you'll have to leave."

"Where's Ma?" Woody asked Becca.

"She's waitin' out front with Sadie. She'll come on back to sit with you when we leave. Ma says we have to go home to take care of things."

"Good. Bruiser's probably half starved by now."

"I'll feed him a few days, but then you best get on home and do it yourself. That pup is a trial and tribulation," Becca said.

Woody was smiling again. "Just like me."

"Ain't that the truth!" Becca brushed her lips across Woody's cheek. "You do like Ben said and mind the nurses. We better go mind Ma."

The collie was waiting by the door when they went out. Francine patted the truck bed and the dog hopped in. "I can ride back here too." She started to climb into the back of the truck.

"Nope. Sarge will be fine." Ben stepped in front of her to slam the tailgate closed. "You ride up front."

"But it'll be crowded. Especially after you pick up Granny Em."

"Who knows if we'll even see her. She has her own shortcuts home, but if we do, we'll make room. Sadie can sit in Becca's lap."

"You ain't looked at me lately, Ben." Becca smoothed her dress over her growing stomach. "I done lost my lap."

"I can sit in Nurse Howard's lap." Sadie took Francine's hand. "She's got lots of lap."

"I do. And it's all yours right now." Francine stood back for Becca to get in first, but Becca motioned her toward the door.

"Sorry, Nurse Howard, but you'll have to do the scooting on the seat. I do well to climb in and cling to the door," Becca said.

So Francine ended up next to Ben. Then when they did see Granny Em making her slow progress through Hyden, Francine scooted closer to Ben to make room for the old woman. Her arm was warm against his. He gripped the steering wheel and fought the crazy urge to put an arm around her.

Instead he leaned to look at Granny Em squeezed between Francine and Becca. "Who's Coy?"

"Plenty of Coys here in the hills. Right common name." Granny Em kept her face forward.

The old woman wasn't going to give up any information easily. "You know the Coy I mean. The one that shot Woody."

"I weren't close to the boy. Didn't see 'ary a thing." She turned her head toward him. He could barely see her face in the light reflected from the dash, but he could feel her scrutiny. " 'Cepting you and this 'un here licking sorghum sticks."

Francine spoke up. "If you know who it was, Granny Em, shouldn't you tell the sheriff?"

"Folks sometimes do that." Granny Em nodded. "If they know. I told you I weren't close to the boy. Could be he can tell you more'n me."

"Could be." Ben stared out at the road as an uneasy silence settled over them in the truck.

Sadie started sniffling. "I want Ma."

"There, there." Francine stroked Sadie's head and spoke softly. "Becca and Ben will take care of you."

Ben noted her using his first name, but he didn't have time to dwell on that. He needed to take care of Sadie and Becca. Maybe even Granny Em. Francine didn't need him to take care of her, but the thought was in his head that he wouldn't mind adding her to the list. He thought about the college catalog he got in the mail a few weeks ago, but college wasn't going anywhere. The GI Bill would still be there next year if he could work out a way to go to school and take care of his family. Right now, family came first.

Granny Em gave Sadie's knee a poke. "You's too big to do all that tear making."

That just made Sadie cry harder. Francine put her hand over Sadie's knees, as if to ward off any more pokes.

"Coddling a body cheats 'em out of finding their own strength." Granny Em stared out the windshield and didn't look toward Francine.

Ben started to say something, but Francine spoke first, her voice low and even. "There are times for growing stronger and times for comforting, and sometimes both times see a few tears."

Ben could feel Francine tightening her arms around Sadie.

"And times to get on home." Becca spoke up after being unusually quiet. "This baby is kicking up a storm. He's hungry."

That made Sadie giggle through her tears and the mood in the truck lightened as Ben turned toward the Beech Fork Center.

"You can let me out and I can walk from here," Fran said. "You'll get home faster that way."

"Oh, me and little Carl won't starve that fast," Becca said. "Will we?"

"No not that fast." A smile was in Fran's voice. "But you do need to eat, and remember, smaller meals to keep the heartburn down. That and Granny Em's dogwood bark."

Francine was making peace with Granny Em, but Ben still had questions that he was going to ask the old woman before she headed up the hill to her cabin. She knew more than she was telling.

At the center, Ben stopped and opened his door. "Best you get out on this side. Be easier for Granny Em and Becca."

"Thank you for that, brother," Becca said.

Sarge leaped to the ground the second the truck stopped and sat down to wait for Francine. She gave Sadie another hug before she scooted under the steering wheel to get out.

Ben helped her down off the running board. "I'm sorry the day ended hard."

"Woody getting better is all that matters now." She hesitated, then touched his arm. "Let me know if there's any way I can help. With Sadie or Becca. I'm very fond of both of them. And Woody too."

It was on the tip of his tongue to ask if she had any little bit of that affection for him, but he swallowed the words. "You've done a lot already."

She stepped back then and he missed the warmth of her hand on his arm. Nothing for it but to climb back in the truck. Do what he had to do for his family. He needed to push these crazy feelings for her out of his head. They were from different worlds. But he couldn't keep from looking in the side mirror at her one more time as he drove away.

He got the truck as close to the house as he could so Becca and Sadie wouldn't have to walk as far. Then he sent them on ahead while he walked with Granny Em toward her place.

"Ain't no need you walkin' with me," Granny Em said. "I know the way."

Ben kept walking beside her. "You know more than that."

"Could be I do."

She didn't say any more as she continued climbing up the hill. The path was so narrow Ben had to walk behind her. He hadn't been to her place since he came home, even though his mother had suggested more than once that he go up that way to see if the old woman needed repairs done on her cabin before winter. Maybe if he had, she'd be more ready to talk now.

Ben tried to wait her out, but finally he said, "Are you going to tell me?"

She let out a sigh. "I ain't knowin' anything for sure and certain. But the Caudills' shine still got axed by the Feds a week or two ago. Could be they were of a mind that somebody told where it was."

"Woody?"

Granny Em stopped walking and turned to peer up at Ben. Just enough moonlight slipped through the trees that he could see her face.

"The boy is all over these hills. Prob'ly could lead you straight to a dozen stills. I figure he ain't the kind to tell, but them Caudills might be thinkin' diff'rent. I hear tell that trader feller you bought that vehicle from is thick with the revenuers and Woody's been tradin' with him some. Folks is wondering what he's trading." She hesitated a bare second. "Don't reckon you know?"

"No."

"Could just be purty rocks. City folks get all stirred up over shiny rocks." She grabbed his arm with her bony fingers. "But one thing you keep in mind, Benjamin Locke. Don't you be getting yo'self involved in no feud. All that comes from that is more dying."

"Whoever shot Woody needs to pay for it."

"I ain't denying that, but could be that nurse girl is right. Let the sheriff handle it." She gave his arm a shake and turned him loose. "Now ou git on home. I been goin' up this hill on my own two feet since afore your pa was born. I ain't needin' nobody to show me the way. That Sadie child might need a mite more coddling. Could be that nurse was right about that too." She peered up at him in the moonlight. "That nurse, she's a right purty thing, ain't she? You best guard your heart."

She turned to head on up the path. Then she looked back over her shoulder. "If'n it ain't already too late."

30

October 8, 1945

Woody was released from the hospital after a week. By then, he'd been up talking to the other patients more than in his own bed. The doctor said a boy his age had a way of healing faster than most.

Ben was there when the sheriff came to talk to Woody the day after he got shot, but Woody acted like he'd never mentioned any person's name. Even when Ben asked about Coy, Woody shrugged and said he must have been out of his head. He knew some Coys but none that would shoot him. At least not on purpose. So if he thought any of those Coys shot him, it must have been an accident. To Ben's ears, it didn't sound as if Woody was lying outright, but he did appear to be skirting the truth.

Ben waited. He'd have plenty of time to question Woody once he had him alone with no other ears bent their direction to listen.

Francine had been to see Becca, but Ben was at the hospital when she came. Once Ma knew Woody was going to pull through, she came on home and let Ben go down to check on him. She claimed too much work to do before winter to spend hours sitting idle at the hospital. Not when Woody had all those nurses to see to him.

She, along with everybody else, was ready to pass off the shooting as an accident the way Woody claimed. Ben didn't swallow his story, but at the same time he wasn't exactly sure what to do about it. He had loaded his father's pistol, but the very feel of the gun brought back too many hard memories. He had come home glad to leave the war behind. He didn't want to be part of an ongoing war here in the mountains. Even so, he couldn't hide from the truth, whatever that was. Nor could Woody.

On the ride home from the hospital, Woody chattered like a nervous squirrel, filling the truck cab with words that didn't matter. Ben knew men like that in the army. Men who talked about every silly thing to keep from thinking about what might happen on the morrow. Or telling what happened yesterday.

Ben stopped him as they started down Thousandstick Mountain. "Quit blabbering just to hear your voice in your ears and tell me what happened at the sorghum stir-off."

"About all I know is I got shot." Woody spoke fast. "I imagine it was an accident."

"Or you imagine it wasn't." Ben didn't frown at Woody. He was determined to keep an even keel no matter what the boy had to tell him. "Try the truth instead of imagining."

Woody stared out the window. "I didn't do nothing wrong, Ben."

"I haven't said you did. But I need to know what's going on so I won't have to be worried about you getting shot again. Is there worry that might happen?" Ben tightened his grip on the steering wheel as he waited for Woody's answer.

"Can't really say, seeing as how I didn't expect it to happen the first time."

"So who's Coy? Was he playing with a gun and it just fired without any intent the way you're trying to make out the shooting happened?"

"No sir. I reckon he aimed to shoot me, but after I pondered it some, I'm of the mind he didn't aim to kill me dead. Coy's a right fair shot." Woody rubbed his hands up and down his thighs.

"This Coy a friend of yours?"

"Was back when he went to school. Then his pa let him quit after the fifth grade. Coy wasn't much for book learning anyhow, but he could hit a baseball a mile."

Ben blew out a breath. "I get the feeling you don't hold any hard feelings against this Coy. Not sure that makes sense."

"Well, it's like this. I figure I can hunt Coy up and we can straighten out the misunderstanding."

"What misunderstanding?"

"Coy's pa has a still up on Whistler's Ridge. I

stumbled upon it some months ago. I didn't think anybody saw me 'cause once I saw what was up, I kept my head down. It can be chancy around them stills, but somebody must have seen me around about those parts." Woody moistened his lips and looked out the window as they started through Hyden. "I don't reckon you want to stop at the store to get a soft drink. I'm mighty thirsty."

Without a word, Ben pulled into a parking spot. "You stay put," he told Woody when the boy started to pull up on the door handle.

"You act like I done something wrong by getting shot."

"Stay put," Ben repeated with no give in his voice. He didn't look back at Woody as he went into the store. The boy better know enough to do as he was told. Even so, Ben was relieved when he came out of the store with two drinks and a bunch of bananas to carry home and Woody hadn't climbed out of the truck.

He waited until they were headed out of town and Woody had downed part of the cola before he pushed him to tell more. "All right. You came across the still. I'm assuming that's the Caudills' still that Granny Em told me was raided."

"The revenuers found it and I can't imagine they coulda done that without somebody pointing the way. Whistler's Ridge is not easy to get to. You know where I'm meaning."

"I do. Pa and I used to squirrel hunt up that way now and again."

"A fire took out some of the trees back a few years and now it's growed up with every kind of bush until it's hard going."

"Why were you there?"

Woody shrugged. "I don't know. Just seems like after Pa died that I couldn't get no rest unless I was moving."

"So was Coy or his father arrested?"

"Nope. The way I heard it, they got wind of the raid in time to make themselves scarce, but not in time to move their operation. Reckon that upset 'em some."

"They were breaking the law," Ben said.

"Don't look at me that way. I wasn't making moonshine. I just happened on where it was being made. Gave that place a wide berth after that."

"But they still thought you told."

"That's the part I haven't figured out. Why they would think that."

"Shorty Johnson." Ben shot a look over at Woody as he said the trader's name.

"Oh." Woody ran his finger around the top of his soda bottle. Then he took a drink and swallowed. "That could be it."

"What's it?"

"Shorty will do 'bout anything for a dollar and some folks say the Feds are willing to pay to hunt down the stills."

"For a kid, you know an awful lot about stuff you shouldn't know about." Ben frowned as he stared out at the road.

"I'm fifteen, Ben." Woody sounded insulted. "I could go work in the mines if Ma would let me."

"No." The word almost exploded out of Ben. He pulled in a breath to calm down. "No mines. You're going to school and make something of yourself. If you don't get killed dead first."

"That's what Ma says too. 'Cept that part about getting killed dead."

"What do you have to do with Shorty Johnson?"

"No more'n anybody else. Shorty buys stuff sometimes. He's big on marbles. Collects them. Now and again, I come across an aggie marble or two that was lost who knows when in the school yard. And then sometimes if a feller takes time to look, he can snag a pretty agate rock in the creeks. Shorty'll buy those too, but I ain't never told him nothing 'bout stills. I got more sense than that."

Woody finished off his drink. "Ev'rybody knows that Shorty ain't one to be trusted, and no way was I wanting trouble with the Caudills. Coy's pa is a mean one and I hear tell his grandpa is even meaner."

Ben turned the truck down into the creek and hit a rock that bounced Woody up off the seat. He groaned and grabbed his chest.

"Sorry." Ben looked over at Woody, who still had a grimace on his face. "You okay?"

"It's a mite sore. Doctor said it would be for a spell. Don't know how much work I'll be able to do for a while."

"None. No horseback riding either or walking to who knows where to find trouble. You're going to attend to your school books for a while."

"Aww, Ben. I can't stay shut up in the house all the time."

"You can sit on the porch."

"Well, maybe Nurse Howard will come see me." Woody grinned and gave Ben a sideways look. "That'll get us all singing and feeling better. Even you."

"We're not talking about Nurse Howard. We're talking about you. So explain why you didn't tell the sheriff all this."

"You've been gone from the mountains too long." Woody jiggled the soda bottle up and down on his leg. "You must've forgot how it is. The sheriff takes Coy in, then it'll be Coy's pa who comes after me next. Better to let it be an accident. Besides, I didn't want to get Coy in trouble. Like I said, we're practically friends."

"He shot you." Ben couldn't keep the anger out of his voice.

"If I know anything, I know it was his pa that made him. Like I said, he didn't shoot to kill me dead."

"You might have bled to death if Nurse Howard hadn't been there."

"Then I reckon it's lucky for me that you're half stuck on her and asked her along." Woody grinned over at Ben.

Ben didn't smile back. "We're not through with this. But your trading days with Shorty Johnson are over."

"Good thing you got this truck first. And them dogs. Nurse Francine really likes that Sarge."

"Nurse Howard to you." Ben kept his voice stern. "And to me too as far as that goes. That was a slip of the tongue that won't happen again."

"I don't see why not. I think she's a mighty fine woman. If I weren't already in love with Jeralene, I might ask her to wait till I got a little older."

"Now you're just being silly."

"I don't know. She might could wait. She likes me." Woody tried a laugh that ended in a sharp pulled-in breath. "That laughing muscle still ain't doing so good. But I guess you're right. I was being silly. But fact is, most all Mrs. Breckinridge's brought-in nurses don't appear to be the marrying kind."

"They probably go back to wherever they're from and get married after they leave here." Ben didn't like thinking about that for Francine.

"I hadn't thought of that. Then could be you should try to convince Nurse Howard she don't

334

need to head back to Ohio. Tell her the mountains are a fine place to find a feller."

"I'm not telling her any such thing and I better not hear you saying anything like that to her either."

He'd called Woody silly, but he was the one who was silly. Forgetting to guard his heart the way Granny Em said he should. But he didn't have time to worry about that now. He had to figure out what to do about Woody. It didn't seem right to let somebody get away with shooting the boy. Not right at all. Mountain code or not. What about law and order? Maybe Woody was right. Maybe he had been gone too long.

That night his mother followed him out to the cornfield where Ben was picking corn by the full moon.

"Your pa always liked picking corn by the harvest moon. Said the leaves weren't near so scratchy. I helped him some before you children came along. And I reckon you recall spending some nights picking with him too."

"I do." He pitched an ear into the barrel on the sled hooked to their mule. "Good times."

"Your pa prayed for you ev'ry morning and ev'ry night whilst you were over there till the day he died." Ma pulled off an ear of corn and shucked it. "He was proud of you."

"I sometimes wondered if I'd make it home,

but I never thought about him not being here if I did." Ben moved down the row. His father always said steady was the best way to work.

"Things happen as the Lord wills." She pitched the corn in the barrel. "Ain't no use fighting agin what's meant to be. You were meant to come home and Woodrow was meant to go on to meet the Lord."

Ben stopped and looked at his mother. "Do you believe everything that happens is meant to be?"

She shucked another ear of corn and ran her fingers over the kernels as if she were counting them before she threw it in the barrel. At last she looked up at Ben. The moonlight softened her wrinkles, and it wasn't hard for him to imagine what she looked like back in her newlywed days as she and his pa worked together.

"You're thinkin' 'bout Woody."

"Him and others." He had too many images of wounded and dying boys in his head. He couldn't imagine the war as part of God's plan. Or Woody getting shot either.

His mother let her arms drop down by her side without reaching for another ear of corn as she stared down the row away from Ben. Finally she pulled in a breath and turned back to Ben. "Your pa was better at knowing answers from the Scripture. Me, I can't answer for the Lord. I learnt a long time back to accept whatever comes my way. Best savor the good and bear up under the bad. There ain't no changin' none of it."

"But we ought to try to change the bad. We fought a war to change the bad."

He could see his mother's smile in the moonlight. "True enough, but it's time for peace now."

"Are you saying I shouldn't do anything about what happened to Woody?"

"I'm sayin' let the sheriff handle it. If'n any handlin' needs doing. Your pa never believed in takin' the law into his own hands." She looked over toward the sled where Ben had laid the pistol. "No need to go hunting the bad."

Ben grabbed another ear of corn off the stalk. "Turn the other cheek. Is that what you're saying? What about an eye for an eye? The Bible says that too."

"So it does. The Lord also says vengeance is mine. And a man reaps what he sows." She stepped across the row and put her hand on his arm. "Just give it some time, son. Woody is gonna be all right."

"He could have died. If Nurse Howard hadn't been there, he might have."

"If you hadn't been there, he might have. But he didn't." She reached and got another ear of corn. She looked over at him as she pulled it free of the shucks. "That Nurse Howard is a pretty woman."

"She is."

His mother pitched the corn in the barrel and then studied him without saying anything.

He stopped and looked at her. "If you've got something to say, best go on and say it."

"She ain't mountain."

"No, ma'am, she's not." He turned away from his mother then to pull more ears off the cornstalks, working faster up the row. After a couple of minutes, she turned and walked back toward the house.

31

October 23, 1945

Each morning when Fran walked outside, the hills around the center were even more beautiful with the red oaks and golden maples clinging to their leaves amid the pines. Sometimes the air was so crisp and fresh, she knew if she were to walk up to the top of the hill she could see forever.

Other times fog sat heavy in the hollows and she could barely see Bella out by the fence, waiting to be milked. She didn't know how anybody could find their way on the mountains then, but whenever that familiar halloo called them out in the early morning fog, the one who came to fetch them never strayed off trail.

Late in October, they made their way to Mrs. Wyatt's confinement over on Robin's Branch with fog rising up around them before the sun came over the horizon. At the Wyatt house, Betty stood back to let Fran care for Mrs. Wyatt. Said she'd be on her own soon after she took her exam in a few days. Betty had already made arrangements to go to New York for an extended visit.

When Fran asked what would happen if she

didn't pass the exam, Betty waved away her concerns. "You'll do fine. You better, because I'm going home for a while. Maybe till the New Year. Been a while since I've been home for Christmas." Betty peered at Fran. "But that means you'll have to stay here. Becca Hayden could have a Christmas baby."

Fran's mother might not be happy about that, but Christmas in the mountains didn't sound bad at all. She did want to be here to help Becca's baby come into the world. Besides, nothing was the way it had been last year. Her mother had moved on with her life with her new husband. Fran had moved on too.

She rarely thought about home and the life she had once hoped to have, except when her mother's letters came in the mail. Her mother refused to believe Fran could be happy in the mountains and always mentioned Seth and how he had yet to marry his English girl. The woman was still in America considering his proposal, but as Fran's mother underlined in her last letter, they had not found a preacher to say the words.

Fran faithfully answered the letters without mentioning Seth or his English bride-to-be. She told her mother about the fall colors, the crisp apples their neighbors gave them, the stack cake Jeralene's mother made with caramel icing, and the babies she caught. With each baby, Fran felt more blessed to be using her hands in such a way. Perhaps it had all been the Lord's plan anyway. That would be what Grandma Howard would say.

She took over care for Woody after he came home from the hospital. The boy endured the healing process with impatient good humor. He didn't seem at all angry about getting shot. Things happen, he said. The sheriff must have agreed with him, since he decided it had to be an accidental shot. Only Ben seemed unable to accept that.

Not that he talked to Fran about what he thought, but she noted he generally had a gun with him on the rare occasions she did see him. He was busy, Becca told her. Getting ready for winter and without Woody to help, he had to work twice as hard. Fran didn't doubt that was true, but at the same time, it was plain Ben Locke was taking pains to avoid her.

That was surely for the best. While she couldn't deny how her eyes sought him out every time she climbed the hill to the Locke house, some things were better nipped in the bud. Everybody would tell her that was so if she were to ask them. Betty. Her mother, whether she knew Ben or not. Even Ben's mother, who did know Fran.

Ben's mother and sister welcomed her into their house as a nurse. That was what Betty kept telling her. Only as a nurse-midwife.

That was good. That was what she wanted to be. She had time to think about the future as she sat with Mrs. Wyatt through the long morning, waiting for the baby. It was Mrs. Wyatt's third child, but Fran worried about how big she was this time. She had suggested Mrs. Wyatt go to the hospital for the birth, but the mother didn't want to be away from her children. Then Betty, who had delivered Mrs. Wyatt's other babies with no problems, agreed that a home birth would be fine. So there was nothing for it except to wait for the woman's labor to advance and hope for another easy delivery.

Mrs. Wyatt's mother rocked back and forth in front of the fire, and each time her daughter groaned, she gripped the chair arms a little harder. A neighbor came after the other children, a girl of five who kept looking back at her mother as she went out the door and a toddler boy barely walking. The grandmother had food on the table with a white cotton cloth spread over it. Apples and winter squash. Cornbread and butter. Biscuits and sorghum. She told them to grab something to eat if they felt a hunger pang, since nobody knew when the baby would decide to make an entrance. The grandmother hoped it would be soon.

So did Fran. The water was hot and Fran had her instruments ready. She was relieved no chickens had the run of the house the way they did in some of the cabins. It didn't seem right to have to shoo hens away from her instruments, but as Betty said, the mountain folk could make pets of anything. Even groundhogs.

This house was fairly calm with the father keeping his post on the front porch with his hound dogs. Nobody seemed to mind about Sarge trailing along with Fran and opened the door to him the same as to her and Betty. Even now, Sarge was settled out of the way in the far corner, eating the biscuit the grandmother had pitched his way.

At noon the woman's contractions got stronger fast. But the baby wasn't coming. Fran checked Mrs. Wyatt's pulse and blood pressure. High but not unreasonable with the pain. Then she listened to the baby's heartbeat and position.

Fran looked over at Betty, who had been the last to visit Mrs. Wyatt. She kept her voice low. "Two heartbeats."

"Are you sure?" Betty took the stethoscope and listened. "Guess one of these little fellows has been hiding out for a while."

"Twins. I knowed it." The grandmother was up from her chair, peering at Fran and Betty. "Is they fighting over who comes out first? If that's so, them rascals'll never get along. Be like Jacob and Esau in the Bible."

Fran hoped they would have the chance to squabble with one another. That would mean they both made it out into the world as healthy babies.

"Twins?" Mrs. Wyatt breathed out the word before another contraction grabbed her.

Fran held her legs to give her some support until the pain passed. "Looks like you're going to be blessed with two babies." She kept her voice cheerful. No need worrying the mother about possible complications that might have been better handled at the hospital.

"I can't have two babies at once." Tears slid out of the woman's eyes and down her cheeks. "I can't."

The grandmother stepped over to her daughter. "Now, you stop carrying on like that right now, Delora. If'n the Lord gives you two young'uns, he'll supply you the ability to take care of them."

"But I'm jest so tired, Ma. I don't think I can." She grimaced and grabbed her mother's hand as another pain began.

"Whatever you have to do, you can." The grandmother held her hand and leaned down close to the woman. "I give you my strength right here, right now."

"Your mother's right, Mrs. Wyatt. You're doing fine." Betty stepped up beside her too. "Think about your breathing to help the pain. You can do this. In and out." Betty glanced down at Fran. "Do we need to call in help to take her to the hospital?"

"I don't think we have time." Fran ducked under the sheet draped across Mrs. Wyatt's legs. Very gently she pushed on the woman's belly to see if she could move one baby back. The first baby's head was crowning already. At least it wasn't a breech birth.

Fran kept her eyes open as she silently prayed. *Lord, help my hands to safely guide this babe and the next one too through the rigors of birth, and give this mother strength and these babies love.*

Betty was still telling the mother to breathe and Fran realized she had been holding her breath along with the mother. She pulled in a deep breath and let it out. The first baby's head emerged along with a foot. Not his foot. Fran gently pushed it back and shifted the baby's shoulders a bit to let him slide on out. Not him at all.

"You have a sweet girl," Fran told Mrs. Wyatt as she wiped out the baby's mouth. The baby's first warbling cry was a joy to hear. She clipped the cord and handed the baby to Betty.

"Where's the other one?" the grandmother asked. "Or was you wrong about that?"

"Patience," Betty said. "Give her time."

"Patience. I'll call her that." The mother raised her head to look toward the baby girl.

"Don't be worryin' over names." The grandmother shook the mother's hand a little. "You got more birthing to do."

A few tense seconds went by. The mother was so exhausted that Fran wasn't sure she could push out the second baby, but she should have known better. Birthing takes over a woman's body and doesn't turn it loose until it's done.

A new contraction seized the mother and then she was pushing. Feet showed up first and then seemed to stall. Fran carefully slid her hand inside the birth canal to ease the baby's arms into a better birthing position. She guided the baby out as quickly as possible.

"A boy." Fran cleaned his mouth and patted his back. The first baby was still wailing, but this little fellow was silent with his skin looking blue. "Breathe, baby, breathe." Fran barely whispered the words as she massaged the baby's chest and then shifted him in her hands and thumped his back again with a bit more pressure. In desperation, she blew into the baby's face, as if she could give him her own breath.

Joy flooded through her as the baby's mouth opened and his chest moved. The newborn cry from his trembling lips was the sweetest sound. She closed her eyes for an instant as a thankful prayer rose up inside her.

"He's breathing." She wanted to laugh and dance around the room with the crying baby.

But instead she handed him off to Betty, who was smiling almost as much as Fran. The mother had fallen back against the pillow with a cry of relief, and the grandmother clapped her hands together, looked up at the ceiling, and praised the Lord.

Later after the mother was settled with the babies, the father fetched home the other children. The oldest stared at the two babies with wide eyes. Then she turned to her little brother. "See, this is why them nurses have saddlebags. To bring the babies."

On the way back to the center, Betty waited until they were able to ride side by side in one of the creeks before she said, "You handled that well, Fran. We could have lost that baby boy. Might not have been a big tragedy." Betty looked over at Fran. "Not that I wanted that to happen. I never want to lose a baby, but that poor woman has more than she can handle."

"Her mother will help her."

"And the older sister. They learn early to step up to chores here in the mountains, but even with these double babies, we'll be back up there with Mrs. Wyatt with more babies on the way before many months go by. These mountain people are fertile."

"You make them sound like a field." Fran frowned.

"Fertile simply means capable of producing a

fruitful crop, and Mrs. Wyatt is well on the way to that." Betty sounded matter-of-fact. "She has no issue with fecundity. That seems to be a mountain trait."

"Do they never think about limiting pregnancies? There are methods of birth control."

"That we are not allowed to offer to them. Mrs. B says how many children to have is not a decision we can make for them. If they ask about prevention, we can advise. Otherwise, we are simply there to help the mothers through the birthing experience and to make sure the baby gets the best start possible under the conditions."

"We didn't help her by missing that she was carrying twins."

"Unusual that we missed that, but it happens." Betty let Moses stop in the creek and take a long drink. Sarge sat down to wait.

When they started moving again, Betty gave a warning. "You won't be able to save them all, Fran. You have to accept that. Even with a million prayers, some babies don't take that first breath."

"I'm thankful this one did."

"As am I, but there will come a time when the outcome may be different. Keep that in mind."

32

October 24, 1945

Ben stepped up on the porch of the Beech Fork Center and knocked on the door. He should have sent Woody. Not come himself. He'd been staying away from Francine since Woody got shot. It was better that way. His mother had said it all. Francine wasn't mountain, and he was. Even if he left the mountains behind and lived in the biggest city in the country, he'd still be mountain. And no doubt, miserable.

Inside he heard Sarge bark, but just once. Then Fran called that she'd get the door. That was good. Better to not see Nurse Dawson's frown if she opened the door to see him standing there.

Nurse Dawson's voice came from farther back in the house. "Tell whoever it is we're closed."

Francine laughed. "But we're never closed."

That was true. The nurses were always ready to help. But he hadn't come for help. He wasn't sure why he'd come. Not really. He had a reason to tell her. He was going to offer to keep her dog. Becca told him Francine was going to the city.

That might be why he'd come. She was leaving the mountains. Supposedly only for a few days, but who knew if she'd come back? Mountain life was hard. And that was why he was standing there on her porch with his hands sweaty, waiting for her to open the door. He didn't like to think about her perhaps not coming back. Not that there was anything he could do about it. But he couldn't let her leave without seeing her one more time.

She was still smiling when she opened the door, but her smile faded. "Mr. Locke. Is something wrong with Woody or Becca? We were just up there."

"Nothing's wrong." He stepped back from the door. He twisted his hat in his hands and pushed a smile out on his face. Mr. Locke. Nurse Howard. Why couldn't they be Ben and Francine?

"That's good." Francine's smile came back when Sarge pushed past her to nuzzle Ben's hand. "Looks like Sarge remembers who rescued him, even if it's been a while since he's seen you." She gave him a questioning look.

Ben was grateful for the distraction of the dog. "I've been busy." He stroked the dog's head and down his back.

Sarge's tail thumped against Francine's legs. She stepped out on the porch. "It's a busy time of the year."

"Yes." Ben straightened up from rubbing the dog and looked directly at Francine. "If you aren't too busy right now, how about taking a walk down to the creek? There's still a little daylight before the edge of dark."

She hesitated and looked over her shoulder. He was ready to pull back the invitation when she grabbed her jacket from a hook inside the door and called back to Nurse Dawson. "I'll be back in a little bit. Go ahead and eat if you want. I have to see to the horses and chickens."

"You want to do that first?" Ben asked as she shut the door behind her.

"No. The horses would be surprised to see me until almost dark." She smiled up at him. "The edge of dark. I love the way you say things here."

"It's just talk to the folks up here."

"I suppose so, but to my ear it sounds poetic." She led the way down off the porch and across the yard to the path that led down the hill to Beech Fork.

He followed after her without saying anything. The air was cool as the sun dipped behind the hill and cast shadows across them. When the path broadened next to the creek, she paused to let him step up beside her.

"Are the winters here as bad as Nurse Dawson keeps warning me they are?" She started walking again.

"They can be, but I would take them anytime over the ones overseas. Leastways I knew what to expect from winters here. Over there it could be cold rain or snow. The rain was the worst.

Everything wet and no way to dry out for what seemed like weeks. The old-timers tell me we had it good compared to when they were in the trenches during the First World War."

"My father was in the First World War, but he never talked about it much."

"I guess that's the best way. Just leave it all behind." He couldn't believe he'd talked about the war with her. He hadn't talked to anybody about how it was over there. Then, here she asked a simple question about winter and he was dredging up memories she probably didn't even want to know.

"Could be. If you can." She glanced up at him and then away. She stopped and stared out at the water sliding past them. "I became a nurse with the intention of going overseas to serve, but after my father died, my mother couldn't bear the thought of being alone."

"But isn't your mother alone now? With you here?"

"Things changed. She remarried. I needed a new start."

He wanted to ask why she needed a new start, but he bit back the question. He didn't know her well enough to pry. "I guess this is pretty different from what you knew back in Ohio."

"Very different." She bent down and picked up a rock to throw in the stream. Sarge perked up his ears and she put her hand on his ruff to keep him from chasing after the rock. "I don't know that I've thanked you properly for Sarge. He is the best dog." She turned toward Ben.

"No thanks needed. As my sergeant used to say, I saw his potential and wanted him to have a chance to exercise it."

She was so close that he imagined he could feel her breath. He could put his hand on her shoulder and pull her an inch or two closer. Then he could tip up her chin and drop his lips down on hers. He could, but instead he turned away to look out at the creek. Maybe he should just wade out in it. The water would be cold and he definitely needed to cool down. Best to get to why he had come calling.

"Becca says you're going to the city."

"I am. I have to take an exam to be fully qualified in midwifery."

"You be gone long?"

"Until next Monday. I'm going to visit my mother, since it isn't that much farther to Cincinnati from Lexington by train."

"I reckon your mother is anxious to see you. You haven't been home in a while." He was sorry he said "home." He wanted her to be home here.

"Not since I came here in May. In some ways that doesn't seem long, but in other ways forever. So much has happened with all the people I've met and the babies I've helped deliver." She started walking again and he fell in beside her.

"Your mother must be proud of you."

Francine laughed. "Not really. She was totally against me coming to the mountains."

"Oh." He didn't know what to say to that.

She put her hand on his arm. "My mother is nothing like your mother. She wants people to take care of her instead of being the one to take care of others. But she is my mother and it will be good to see her."

"But you'll be back."

"God willing and the creek don't rise."

"The creeks always rise, but not too much in the fall of the year. Especially this year, since it's been dry. The tides come mostly in the spring or late winter."

"Tides? That's floods, isn't it?"

"I guess that does sound strange. Tides are in oceans. I've seen some of those now. Not much like flash floods."

She stopped and looked at the peaceful creek again. "Betty says this creek can turn into a torrent, but that Mrs. B made sure the center was on high enough ground that the waters don't reach it. She says sometimes you need a boat to get across. That's hard to imagine, since right now we could wade to the other side. Even Sarge wouldn't have to swim."

"When the rains come, you need to stay clear of rushing water. Folks can get swept away and drown."

"Does that happen often?"

"Not often, but sometimes folks are caught unaware."

"It can be a hard place here." Francine sighed a little. "Beautiful but hard."

She was what was beautiful, with nothing hard about her. Again, he reminded himself to stick to his excuse for being there as she turned back toward the center.

"Anyhow, when Becca said you were going, I thought maybe you needed me to take Sarge up to the house. I told you we could see to him if you needed us to."

"That's right. You did." She smiled at him. "But I think Sarge is winning Nurse Dawson over. And he has definitely already made Jeralene a lifelong friend. She's staying at the center to help out while I'm gone. She promises to watch out for Sarge."

"Then I guess you don't need us to take care of him." It was silly to feel rejected, but he did.

"Not this time, but I appreciate the offer." She laughed again. "Besides, I'm not sure Sarge would enjoy sharing space with Woody's Bruiser several days in a row. When we're up there, he growls whenever the pup gets close."

"Rufus has the same opinion. He hides out in the barn or under the porch most of the time these days. But Woody and Sadie love their pups."

"Sadie's been much better since you got back.

I'm so glad about that. And Woody is doing fine too. Nearly healed. That could have been so much worse."

"Yes." Ben didn't want to talk about Woody. He still hadn't come to terms with the sheriff's accidental shooting determination.

They were almost back to the center where Captain patiently waited in the shade of the tree out front. Ben hadn't seen the need in driving the truck.

She put her hand on his arm again to stop him. "What about you? Are you all right?"

His muscles tensed under her touch. "What do you mean? Why wouldn't I be all right?"

"I don't know." She didn't shrink from his angry tone. "No reason or maybe a dozen reasons. You seem a little on edge."

He narrowed his eyes on her. "You mean because somebody shot my little brother and nobody seems concerned about that. Not even my little brother. Or because my sister's husband left her at our mother's house and hasn't even bothered to write. And she doesn't seem bothered that he hasn't. Or because I sent in to go to school in January but can't see any way it can happen with two women, a boy, a girl, and a baby to get through the winter." He didn't add, *because I'm in love with a woman who would never consider loving me.* He'd already said too much. Again.

She didn't look away from him. "Some good reasons. I'm sorry."

"You don't have any call to be sorry. I'm the one sorry that I unloaded all that on you."

"No, no. I'm a nurse. People are supposed to tell me things."

"Not everything."

"Maybe not everything, but then I doubt you did tell me everything."

"So do you have a cure in your medicine bag?" Ben tried to lighten the moment.

"No. But I do have something my grandmother told me once. When things are the most confused in our lives, that's when the Lord can work best."

"I don't like confusion. I like things laid out in straight rows with everybody knowing which rows belong to them."

"But life is rarely that way. We make squiggles and turns and sometimes things work out and sometimes they don't. But either way the Lord has a plan and a purpose."

"If that's true, he hasn't let me in on what it is. That plan and purpose."

She smiled. "He will. When it's time. That's another thing she said. His time is not our time."

"You sound like a preacher."

"Oh heavens, I don't mean to. Mrs. B has rules against sounding like a preacher. No religion talk." She put her fingers over her lips.

"Don't worry. I won't tell on you."

"Or listen to me?" Her smile was back.

"To you? Or your grandmother?" He let his lips curl up to match hers. "She sounds like she might have been somebody worth listening to. Like my pa. He used to tell me to think about today and not to be reaching way ahead to borrow trouble. He claimed it had a way of coming soon enough. That's something you can count on."

"But good things happen too. Sometimes they go hand in hand."

"Trouble and joy." He stopped beside Captain and watched her walk on toward the center. He wasn't sure which she was. Trouble or joy. He just knew he didn't want her to disappear from his life until he found out. "Hope you do well on your exam."

She turned and waved. "Thank you."

Then she headed toward the barn. There was nothing for him to do but mount Captain and start for home. The same as her, he would have some nightly chores if his mother hadn't already done them.

33

October 28, 1945

Fran was glad to be done with the exam and also glad to have her visit to her mother almost over. She would catch the train to start the long journey back to the mountains early on Monday. Only Sunday to get through.

Nothing was the same. Her mother and her new husband had moved into a different house, and so the home Fran knew was gone. At this house, she slept in the spare bedroom that was all white and pink ruffles. A room for a little girl princess that she never was or wanted to be. Nothing from her old bedroom was there.

"Don't worry," her mother said when Fran asked about her clothes and books. "I packed up what was good and stored it in the attic. I wrote you we were moving. You should have come home and cleaned out your room yourself. I had no idea you had that many books."

"Are they in the attic too?"

"Oh no. We couldn't carry those up there. We gave them away."

"Even my copy of *Little Women* that Grandma Howard gave me?" Fran treasured that book. She and her grandmother had read it aloud to one another the summer she was twelve.

"Don't look at me like that. I didn't have time to look through all those dusty old books."

Fran pulled in a breath to calm herself, but the loss of that book was a stab to the heart. She had no reason to be surprised. Her mother had never paid much attention to what Fran liked. Her father might have known, but he was gone. His place was taken over by Harold Stephens, who was polite enough to Fran, but it was evident she had no permanent place at his house.

Early Sunday morning, Fran climbed into the attic to find a dress to wear to church. She dug through the clothes in the trunk. The red dress she had once worn to a dance with Seth was, of course, gone. Her mother would have never kept it. But there was a forest green dress with buttons down the front that would do. She gathered up stockings and underthings to take back to the mountains with her.

She sat back on her heels and closed her eyes. The stuffy attic disappeared and she could almost feel the mountain air against her face. She wished she could be getting ready to go to Wendover for chapel if no baby was ready to make an entrance. There they could show up in their nurse outfits. The service wasn't for wearing hats and gloves. It was for inspiring and empowering them to keep doing their best.

But it would be good to go to church here

too and see old friends. The one person she hadn't thought about seeing was Seth, but her mother obviously had other ideas.

When they started out for church and turned on a different street, not the one for the church they had always attended, Fran asked, "Aren't we going to Maple Avenue Church?"

"Not today, dear. I thought we'd go to the First Christian Church over on Midland today."

"Mother, what are you up to?"

"Why do you think I'm up to something? I'm just trying to make your visit home good. More of your friends from school go to church there."

Fran sank back in the seat. She knew which friend her mother wanted her to see, but it was useless to argue with her. Surely the Lord would forgive Fran's prayer that Seth would skip church today, but even if he didn't, she could smile and say hello. To him and his intended.

None of that mattered to her now. She had moved on. Tomorrow she would be on the way back to the mountains. There she was a different person, a nurse-midwife no longer consumed by the desire to marry and have a family. The Lord had given her a different purpose when he made a way for her to learn to catch babies. She smiled at that and remembered telling Ben Locke how much she liked mountain speak.

What was it she had told him her grandmother used to say? That when things got confused, that was when the Lord worked best. She'd depend on that to get her through the rest of this day. Her mother was obviously confused if she thought orchestrating a meeting between Seth and Fran would change anything. Especially since she didn't even have that red dress to wear any longer.

Fran smiled at the thought. She didn't need a red dress. She only needed her horse and dog and that important saddlebag. *A better sense of direction might be nice though, Lord,* she offered up silently. That could be her prayer today. That and somehow making it through the rest of the day without choking her mother.

The prayer that Seth might skip church wasn't answered. Her mother poked her and pointed when Seth's family came in. Thank goodness, none of them noticed, as Seth and his family continued on down the aisle toward the front of the church.

Seth looked different, but that was to be expected. Neither of them were schoolkids now. His hair was still short in a military style, and he moved with the easy confidence of a man, instead of the self-consciousness of a teen. The petite woman with him was as pretty as her picture. Her blonde hair curled around her face, and her bright red lipstick matched the red flower in her dress.

For just a moment, Fran thought how very

plain she must look in comparison, with her hair twisted in a tight roll on the back of her head and her dark green dress without the first adornment. But then she didn't care. She didn't want to compete with Cecelia. Fran might harbor some regret for their lost future, but Seth had made his choice. What Fran had hoped for them was lost months ago when Seth threw away her love. She had no intention of chasing after it.

Unfortunately, her mother wasn't ready to give up so easily. After the preacher said the final amen, Fran's mother delayed retrieving her purse. Then she dropped a glove in order to exit their pew directly behind Seth and his family. At least she had the good manners to wait until they were out of the church before she grabbed Fran's elbow and rushed after Seth.

"Seth," her mother called as they went down the steps. "Look who's home."

Fran wished for a way to escape what would surely be an awkward meeting. Not that Fran couldn't handle it. She had just ushered an unexpected twin into the world. She had stitched up a man's leg after his knife slipped while he was cleaning fish. She had wormed children and treated consumption. She had kept a boy from bleeding to death in the back of a truck. If she could do all that and more, she could look Seth Miller in the face without shrinking back.

"Hello, Seth. So good to see you home." She

had no trouble looking him in the eye and saying that. She was glad Seth had made it home from the war.

"Francine. I heard you were visiting your mother." Seth gave Fran the once-over. "It's been a while."

"Yes, it has." Fran shifted her eyes to the woman clinging to Seth's arm and held out a hand toward her. "And you must be Cecelia. Seth's sister showed me your picture before I went to the mountains, but it's good to meet you in person."

"Yes." The woman barely brushed her fingertips across Fran's hand. Perhaps English women thought it wasn't ladylike to shake hands. Perhaps it wasn't. She had a lovely English accent. "I've heard so much about you. Everyone considers you very brave to go off to become a frontier nurse."

"Not brave at all." Fran pulled her hand back. "Actually some of the nurse-midwives are from your home country. England."

"Oh really. How interesting." She didn't sound interested at all.

"Well, nice seeing you, Seth, and good to meet you, Cecelia." Her mother was still chatting with Seth's parents, but Fran eased past them with a wave to follow Harold, who had walked on toward the parking area. She didn't look back.

Then Seth was calling out for her to wait. When

she glanced around, he was pushing past the people on the walkway and hurrying after her. For what reason, she couldn't imagine. But she waited for him. Cecelia didn't come with him.

"Francine." He was panting a little when he caught up with her. "What's your rush? Can't you spare a few minutes for an old friend?"

"Of course." Francine kept a smile on her face. "So what are you doing since you got home from the service, old friend?" Those last two words had a bitter feel and she wished them back. But words said couldn't be retrieved.

Seth flinched. "I guess I deserved that."

Fran breathed out and let her smile slide off her face. "Look, Seth, we are old friends who have no reason to play games. You made your choice. And she's lovely. I wish you and Cecelia every happiness."

"You've changed." Seth moved closer to her. A little too close.

Fran stepped back. "It's been almost four years. We're not the kids fresh out of school that we were when you joined the army."

Funny how he wasn't as tall as she remembered. Maybe it was the shorter hair. But he had added muscle in his arms and shoulders. His light brown eyes were different too. More serious now than when he was a boy and always ready to pull a prank or tell a joke. Maybe that was all the talk of marriage had ever been to him.

A joke. If so, she had been too ready to fall for it.

"I appreciated all your letters," he said. "They kept me from being so homesick when I first went over."

"That's good." Fran cringed to think about some of the things she'd written in those letters about their plans when he got home. Her plans anyway. "My part of the war effort, I guess." She started walking toward her stepfather's car again. Seth fell in beside her.

"Yeah." He reached over and touched her hand. "Look, Francine, I don't blame you for thinking I'm a bum, but I really didn't mean to hurt you. It's just, I met Cecelia and, well, she was there and you were here and, well, you understand."

"Sure." Fran understood plenty, but sometimes it was best to take the high road. She let him off the hook. "My grandmother used to tell me things happen for a reason, and that's what the people at the Frontier Nursing Service say too. That nobody comes there by accident. So it all turned out for the best."

"Do you like it down there in the hills?" Seth frowned a little. "Your mother keeps talking about how awful it is. She says she expects to hear you've been shot or worse any day."

"Worse than shot?" Fran raised her eyebrows at him.

"Well, you know, with the sort of men in those

hills." He shrugged a little. "Moonshiners and all sorts of reprobates."

"There are some moonshiners for sure, but all the men, all the people treat us with the utmost respect."

"I guess your mother was relieved to hear that."

"She doesn't much like to hear anything about the mountains, but it's a beautiful place and the people are so true."

"True? What does that mean?" Seth gave her a puzzled look.

Fran thought a minute before she answered. "It's hard to explain to somebody who has never been there. But the way they live is tied somehow to the mountains. Growing their food or gleaning it off the land. They don't have much money, but they have things that matter more. Like family and roots. Some of their farms have been passed down for generations. They all work to survive, and each new baby is a gift, even if they already have a houseful of children."

"The mountain kids in the pictures in magazines look pretty ragged and dirty." Seth made a face.

"Baths aren't as easy to come by when you have to carry water from the creek or spring instead of turning a tap. And those photographers don't give the children time to run wash their faces or hands when they find them playing out in the dirt."

"You sound impassioned."

"I guess I do." Fran swept a stray strand of hair out of her face. "I'm sorry. I didn't mean to preach at you."

"No, no. Impassioned is a great look for you. Intense and beautiful."

Fran shot a quick look over at him to see if he was making fun of her, but he was studying her with serious eyes.

"There's a difference between pretty and beautiful. Did you know that?" he said.

"I've never really thought about it." At least she hadn't for a long time. She'd never felt she qualified for either description. But then Betty had talked about her being pretty. And just last week, Ben Locke had walked to the creek with her and let his gaze settle on her, as though she wasn't a bit hard on the eyes.

Now Seth was looking at her as though she were someone he'd never seen instead of the girl he'd dated all through high school. Fran wasn't sure she liked it. Not with his intended staring at them across the street. It was time to end this old friends' talk.

"I'm glad you're doing so well, Seth." Thank goodness, Harold's car was right in front of her and her mother was finally coming toward the parking lot. "I hope you and Cecelia will be very happy."

Then before her mother got close enough to stir up who knew what, Fran opened the car door and climbed into the back seat. She gave Seth a little wave before she closed the door and sat back with relief. A dozen memories poked her as she watched Seth turn away. School dances. Movies. Ball games. They had been so young and she'd had such dreams.

She gingerly peeked back at some of those dreams. She'd truly thought she would marry Seth and have his children.

"That your old boyfriend your mother keeps talking about?" Harold twisted around to look at Fran.

Fran was surprised. The man had rarely spoken to her since she'd been there. Perhaps that was because of her mother chattering nonstop. "Yes. We dated in high school."

"Your mother said you planned to get married."

"Sometimes plans go awry. I think most of the planning must have been my doing and not his. We were just kids."

"You're still a kid." Harold turned to peer out the window. "Where is that woman?"

"She's coming."

Her mother had stopped to talk to Seth, but now she was heading on toward the car. She didn't look happy.

Harold obviously thought the same. He ran his hands around the steering wheel. "Uh-oh. Get your ears ready. She looks like she has plenty to say."

Fran sighed. "Don't worry. I've heard it all before."

Harold chuckled. "Believe me. So have I. So have I. But she's generally satisfied if you just mumble something and nod now and again."

Fran laughed. "Thanks. Not sure that will work for me, but I might give it a try."

Harold got out and hurried around the car to open the door for Fran's mother. She'd barely settled in the seat before she twisted around to glare at Fran. "What in the world, Francine? The man trailed after you wanting to talk and you jump in the car and slam the door in his face. What is the matter with you?"

"We talked, Mother. And then I thought Harold was probably ready for lunch."

Harold clambered back in the car and shifted it into gear. "Lunch does sound good."

"Are you two teaming up against me?" Fran's mother shot a look toward Harold. "I wouldn't advise that."

"Not teaming up at all, Charlotte. Aren't you hungry? How about we take Francine out for lunch today?"

"That's fine. If you can find a decent restaurant open on Sunday." She seemed to have lost her irritation with Harold, but she wasn't so easily distracted from her upset at Fran. "Are you trying to throw away your chances with Seth?"

"Mother, Seth is engaged to Cecelia."

"I haven't seen a ring on her finger." Fran's mother raised her eyebrows. "I sense trouble in paradise there."

"If so, that trouble isn't coming from me. Nor should it come from you. Seth and I are old high school friends. Nothing more. His choice, but a choice I'm quite content with now." Fran kept her voice level and firm.

"Humph." Fran's mother turned around in her seat to stare forward. "You never have known what's best for you. I suppose you plan to head back to those hills where people don't even have running water."

"They have lots of running water. All in creeks and rivers." Fran should have kept quiet, but she was wishing she was in sight of some of those creeks and rivers now instead of facing a long afternoon listening to her mother.

"Don't be smart with me, Francine Elizabeth. You knew what I meant." She looked back at Fran again. "I can't believe you're that eager to go back there."

"I love what I do, Mother. Catching babies."

"What a peculiar way to talk about delivering babies." Fran's mother shook her head and sat back in her seat again. But she didn't quit talking. "Well, you'll never have any babies of your own for anybody else to catch. Not as long as you stay there. Because you surely have more sense than to fall for any of those hillbillies. You do, don't you?"

She didn't pause long enough for Fran to answer. That was just as well, since Ben Locke's image popped into Fran's head. Not that she had fallen for him. That surely wasn't true. But it had been good walking with him by the creek, and he had given her Sarge. A little smile lifted the corners of her lips. Thank goodness her mother didn't notice.

"I've seen plenty of pictures of those mountain people. Men with coal-dust skin and hungry eyes. And the women. Worn-out looking, with a dozen kids hanging on to them. None of them smiling. Ever. And I guess not. What would they have to smile about?"

Fran stayed silent as her mother chattered on. She didn't know about the mountains or the people. But Fran did know, and she wanted to know more. She shut her eyes and let her mother's words slide past her, mumbling an agreeable answer now and again. Harold was right. That was all she needed to do.

But come morning, Fran would be on the train and then the bus heading home. What was it people said? *Home is where the heart is*. Her eyes were anxious to see the mountains rising up in front of her again.

34

November 3, 1945

Ben kept from riding down the mountain all week. He knew Francine had returned to the center, and he told himself that was enough. She had given him no reason to think she wanted him showing up on her porch every other day. What he was hoping, as he worked to get ready for the cold weather slamming down on them soon, was that she would show up on his porch. After all, the nurses had been keeping a close eye on Becca.

Trouble was, Nurse Dawson was there on Monday to examine Becca and make sure Woody's wound continued to heal. She was capable, but looked like a smile might break her face. Not at all like Francine, with a smile that it up her eyes. But Nurse Dawson's visit meant the nurses wouldn't likely be back up the hill until another week went by.

Friday, the weather turned toward winter with a cold rain. Sadie woke up with a cough and Woody was sniffling. Ben had laid in enough wood for the weekend and carried water from the spring. He'd taken care of the animals and Captain. The roof wasn't leaking. There was absolutely nothing else for him to do, but he couldn't seem to sit down and relax. He paced back and forth as restless as a raccoon in a wire-cage trap.

His mother frowned at him from where she sat at the table, shelling popcorn to store in jars to keep the mice out of it. Woody had talked her into raising it. He'd been proud of figuring out when to plant the popcorn so it wouldn't be tasseled out with the bees pollinating it at the same time as the other corn. Woody said he had gathered plenty of gardening tips from wandering around the mountain. Besides seeing more than he needed to see and getting shot.

Maybe that was what Ben should do on this miserable weather day. Go confront Homer Caudill and get that squared away. Maybe he'd just take his gun and they could have a shoot-out. Ben looked at the gun on top of the cabinet. But that would do his family a lot of good. Getting killed. Or as the people here said, killed dead. He hadn't thought twice about how crazy that was to say somebody got killed when they were merely wounded until he went to the army. Wonder if Francine would think that mountain talk was poetic.

"For mercy's sake, Ben, settle somewhere. If you need something to do, sit down here and help us shell this corn." His mother nodded toward the basket full of popcorn ears beside her.

Woody and Sadie were already helping. To

avoid Woody's cold, Becca sat all the way across the room, hemming a baby blanket. Not that a body could avoid anything in this small house. Not even Sadie's pup that his mother let come inside. Woody's Bruiser didn't get the same treatment, so at least only one pup was underfoot. The pup went squeaking away when Ben almost stepped on it.

Sadie gave Ben an irritated look that so mirrored his mother's, Ben had to smile. He picked up a bowl and a couple of popcorn ears and sat down across from his mother. "Sorry," he said.

"No need," Ma said. "Your pa was the same way, except he could settle down and study the Bible. Maybe you should try that."

"Maybe so." Ben pushed some of the kernels off the cob to clink into his bowl.

Sadie coughed. Ma's brow furrowed at the hacking sound of the cough, but she kept shelling the corn.

"You think we should send for the nurse?" Ben looked at Sadie, then back at his mother.

"Not yet. Likely she just has a cold the same as Woody. The nurses can't cure a cold. I'll make up some ginger tea for her later. That always seems to help."

"Oh, Ma." Becca swished the baby blanket around in her lap and began stitching the hem on another side. "Ben's just wanting to get the nurses up here. One of them anyhows. That pretty Nurse Howard." Her voice went singsongy. "Froggie went a-courtin', he did ride, Uh-huh."

"Becca." Ma's voice was sharp. "Don't be botherin' your brother with that foolishness."

"Love ain't foolishness, but it can get you in some shapes." Becca stood up and stretched her back. "I don't see how you stood carrying five babies."

"You stand what you have to stand." Ma pitched a cob into a box to keep for fire starters. "Nary a one of you children would I give up, no matter how hard the task of bringing you into the world."

Becca cradled her abdomen with her hands. "I do know what you mean there. I already love this little feller."

"You're apt to have a girl," Ma warned her.

"I reckon you're right, but Carl was so set on a boy that I'm hopin' for him." She stepped closer to the fire.

"Have you heard from Carl?" Ben looked over at her.

"Not for a spell." Becca stared out the window almost as if she were watching for Carl to be stepping up on the porch. Then she sighed and shrugged. "Carl never was much for writing nothing. But he's a fine talker. He told me he'd be back to get me. And he will. Come the right time."

"When's the right time?" Woody asked.

"Some things you don't know till they happen." Becca settled back in the chair and picked up her needle and thread again. "Other things you can sort of guess when they might happen. Like a baby coming." She shot a look over at Ben. "Or when your brothers are going to get antsy over some girl."

"Well, if you're talking about me, don't be comparing me to that frog a-courting." Woody sneezed. "That frog and his mouse girlfriend came to some bad ends in that song."

Sadie giggled. "But it was fun when Nurse Howard sang it with us. I wish she was here to sing with us now. I like her."

"Me too," Woody said. "You like her too, don't you, Ben?"

"Nothing not to like." Ben pushed the last kernels off the ear of popcorn and pushed back from the table. "I got some things to do outside."

"But it's raining," Becca said. "You'll catch your death of cold."

"That's more likely to happen in here with everybody sneezing and coughing." Ben grabbed his jacket and hat.

When Becca opened her mouth to say more, Ma spoke up first. "Let him be, Becca. I don't expect he'll melt."

His mother's hands fell idle in her lap as she gave Ben a considering look. After a couple of seconds, she reached for another popcorn ear and began shelling again. Ben couldn't tell if she was worried or disgusted as she muttered, A man has to decide his own way."

The rain did have a bite to it as he stepped off the porch. No sleet. But the promise of it. Ben pulled his collar up and headed toward the barn. Bruiser followed him, but Rufus gave Ben the same kind of look as his mother and then dropped his head back down on his paws.

Ben looked back at the old dog. "You'd be warmer in the barn." The old dog didn't bother raising his head. He was where he wanted to be, satisfied with his lot in life. A front-porch dog guarding his people inside. Not that Rufus did more than stand up, bark once, and wag his tail when anybody rode up to the house. But that was enough.

Bruiser was another matter. He was a trial, the way he chased the hens and nipped at the cow's legs. He chewed on anything he could get his teeth around, even the porch posts. Rufus growled any time the pup got close, and Sadie's pup ran away with a whimper. Ben couldn't help but admire the pup's spirit as the rascal grabbed onto the bottom of Ben's jeans and tugged. He just never quit. He wanted attention and he found a way to get it. Not at all content to just lie down and hope somebody would notice him.

Ben leaned over and picked the pup up. It had grown a lot since he brought it home. "Why can't you be a good dog like Sarge?"

The pup climbed up Ben to lick his face while his tail beat against Ben's arm. He'd gotten what he wanted. Ben's attention.

Which dog was Ben like? The old dog on the porch, satisfied to hang around and get a pat on the head now and then, or the pup demanding to be noticed.

"Thinking about that nurse has made me addlebrained," he muttered as he put the pup down. Bruiser jumped back up on his legs. But when Ben pushed him off, he chased after a scent in the corner of the barn, digging down through a layer of old hay. Persistence in motion.

Nurse. It wasn't the nurse on his mind. It was Francine. Maybe he should chase after her. If she didn't favor that, she could tell him to get lost. At least then he'd know. She'd seemed friendly enough when they walked to the creek together.

Ben blew out a breath. No weather for creek walking this day. More the weather for hunting up Homer Caudill. A man couldn't completely ignore somebody shooting his little brother. He'd never read anything in the Bible about turning his brother's other cheek. Better to think about that than Francine.

The rain got colder and came down harder

as he started out on Captain. A few snowflakes mixed in with the rain. As best he remembered, the Caudill house was some distance high in the hills on the other side of Beech Fork up from Possum Bend. He passed up his truck. Who knew what kind of roads there were around Possum Bend? Best depend on Captain's sure steps on the muddy trail.

He turned a bend in the trail and up ahead was a nurse. Even swallowed up by a dark cloak, he knew it was Francine just by the way she sat the horse.

She was turning up a side trail and didn't know Ben was there. That was the trouble with wrapping up against the rain. The rain hitting the rain slickers covered up other noises a person might need to hear. But Sarge stopped in front of her horse and barked.

She reined in her horse and shifted in the saddle to look around. She waited until he rode closer before she said, "Mr. Locke."

"I'd count it a favor if you'd call me Ben." He locked his eyes on her face and finished. "Francine."

She blinked and looked down at her hands on the reins. Then a smile eased up the corners of her lips as she raised her eyes back to his. "All right. Ben."

An answering smile worked its way across Ben's face. He thought about reaching across to touch her hand, but maybe the names were enough for a start. They sat there on their horses without speaking anything more for a long moment until her horse grew restless.

"Were you looking for me?" she asked.

"Yes." He might as well be honest. He hadn't been going for her, but he was looking for her. All the time.

"Is something wrong at your house?" Her smile disappeared to be replaced by worry. Rain dripped down her cloak. "Nurse Dawson said I wouldn't need to visit Becca until next week. That she was doing fine."

"I shouldn't have said yes. I wasn't coming after you, even though Sadie does have a bad cough and Woody's catching cold. Ma says no need to trouble you about them yet."

"I can stop by after I call on Granny Em."

"Is that where you're headed on such a day?" A few more snowflakes mixed with the rain. "She send for you?"

"Granny Em would never send for one of us nurses." Francine stroked her horse's neck to steady her. "Jasmine doesn't like standing still." She took a firmer hold on the reins. "But I haven't seen Granny Em since I got back from the city. So I decided to ride up here. I thought I'd be more apt to find her at home on a day like this. Otherwise, she'd be who knows where on the mountain. I'm taking her something." She pointed to a gunnysack hanging down from her saddle horn. The sack moved.

"A dog?"

Francine laughed. A sound that felt like sunshine in the midst of the cold rain. She touched the sack. "No, a hen. The fox got her best hen."

"It might get this one too."

"True, but perhaps this one will be harder to catch. I best be on my way before we both get soaked." She turned her horse away.

"Have you ever been up to Granny Em's cabin?" Ben asked.

"Not yet. I generally see her at the center or at your house. Why?" She looked back at him.

"You're going the wrong way."

"Are you sure? I studied the map." She looked so crestfallen that Ben had to laugh.

"I'll ride up with you. Ma's been after me to go see if the old woman needs anything before winter sets in."

Ben led the way up the steep narrow trail to Granny Em's. In the years he'd been gone, the trees had almost taken over the small clearing around the old woman's cabin. The whole place was smaller than he remembered. A barn past repair tumbled down to the side of the house, with a corral fashioned out of poles around it.

"Are you sure she lives here?" Francine moved

her horse up beside his. "The chinking is gone between some of the logs."

"I'm sure. There's smoke coming out of her chimney."

"I suppose that means she's here." Francine slid off her horse and untied the gunnysack from her saddle horn. Then she grabbed her saddlebag.

Ben dismounted and took the gunnysack from her. The hen let out a muffled squawk. "Guess we better go see if she'll be glad to see us or chase us off. You never know with Granny Em."

35

Rocks made steps up to the small stoop in front of the door. Rain dripped through the sagging roof onto Fran as she knocked on the plank door. The cabin was so dilapidated that Fran didn't see how Granny Em or anybody could live there.

"Come on in if you're a mind to. Whoever you be." Granny Em's voice was low and hoarse. Her words were followed by a hacking cough.

Fran stepped into the dimly lit cabin. No light except the glow of a flickering fire in the fireplace. The windows were boarded over and yellowed newspapers covered the walls. Granny Em sat in a rocker pulled up close to the hearth with a ragged quilt draped around her shoulders. After she finally stopped coughing, she spit into a can.

"Granny Em, you're sick."

"Well, I'd a never believed it if'n I hadn't see'd it with my own eyes. You climbed all the way up here without going astray." The old woman peered over at Fran. "Or did you?"

"I would have gotten lost for sure, but I met Ben Locke on the hill and he led me up here." Fran pointed behind her toward Ben, coming through the door carrying the gunnysack.

When he set down the sack, Sarge sniffed it, then shook himself before he took up a guard post beside the hen. Fran peeled off her rain poncho and hung it on a hook next to the door. She was still wet and chilled. Ben had to be even wetter without any sort of rain gear.

"Appears chance meetings is a fine thing for the two of you. But kinda odd for you to be hanging out on the trail on a day sech as this." Granny Em stared at Ben.

"I was heading somewhere else when Nurse Howard came along." Ben took off his hat and ran his hand through his wet hair. "The other can wait."

"You ain't still thinking revenge, is you, Benjamin Locke?" Granny Em shook her finger at Ben.

"That's nothing for you to pay any mind to." Ben stepped over to poke the fire.

Fran looked at him, but he kept his face turned away from her. She couldn't worry about him now. Granny Em was the one who needed help. Fran pulled her stethoscope out of her saddlebag. "That sounds worse than a cold. You should have sent for me."

"Look around, girl." Granny choked out after she stopped coughing. "Ain't nobody here but me to send down the mountain." She eyed Fran as she moved toward her with the stethoscope.

"I just want to listen to your lungs."

"Ain't the first need in that. I can tell you I done got the lung suffering." She waved away Fran. "I get it from time to time, but ginger tea pulls me out of it."

"Do you have the tea now?" Fran looked around. She didn't see a stove, but a teapot sat on the fireplace hearth.

"I ain't felt like going to the spring, so's I've got a bucket out back to catch the runoff from the roof. Should be enough in it for the kettle now. Fire might not be hot enough to heat it up though." The old woman's voice sounded weak.

"Do you have more wood?" Ben asked.

"Not in here."

Ben picked up his hat and headed toward the door. "I'll get some water and hunt up something for the fire."

After he went out, Fran stepped nearer Granny Em and touched her forehead. "You're burning up."

"But feelin' cold."

"Will you let me listen to your breathing? You know there's a rhythm to that too. You remember telling me about the rhythm in most everything? I try to hear it now. Sometimes I do. Sometimes I don't. But I always hear that breathing rhythm."

"I reckon, 'cept when breathing stops." Granny Em coughed again. "But appears you ain't gonna let me be till you take a listen. So go ahead."

Her lungs sounded even more congested than Fran had feared. "You need to be in the hospital." She folded the stethoscope and put it back in her bag.

"You might as well hush about that. Ain't gonna go there. If'n it's my time, I'll meet my Maker on my own ground."

"You're too sick to stay here by yourself."

"And you're too young to tell me what to do." Another fit of coughing seized her. She had to wait awhile to get her breath after she finished coughing. "Some ginger tea and I'll be back up and going."

Fran put her hands on her hips and stared at Granny Em. The woman was right. She couldn't make her go to the hospital. "Tell you what. I'll make the tea for you if you tell me how, but you have to also take the medicine I give you."

"I can make my own tea."

"You can. But you can take the pills I give you too. You've got pneumonia. That's not something to mess around with."

"I told you before. When it's a body's time, it's their time. Naught you can do to change that."

"Except drink ginger tea and take these pills, because it just might not be your time right now."

"You're as worrisome as a pesky mosquito buzzing in a body's ear." She swiped at her ear as if hearing that mosquito.

"And I'm going to keep buzzing until you agree

to take these pills." Fran pulled out a packet of sulfapyridine pills from her saddlebag. If these didn't help Granny Em in a few days, she'd try to get her hands on that new drug, penicillin, she'd heard worked wonders. They probably had some at the hospital.

"All right. I'll wash down your pills with my ginger tea and won't neither of us know which thing to credit my healing to." A scrambling noise from the gunnysack caught her attention. "What's your dog got cornered over there in that sack? Have you brung me a snake?"

Fran shivered. "Never."

"Rattlers make right good eating. Better'n possum by a right smart sight."

"You'll have to catch your own rattlers for dinner." Fran went over and undid the top of the gunny sack and opened it wide to let the hen out. "I brought you a hen."

The brown hen flopped its wings at Sarge, who backed away. Then it cocked its head back and forth and stared at Granny Em. The old woman's laugh turned into a wheezing cough.

When she could talk again, she called, "Here, chickie, chickie." She pulled some crumbs out of a pocket somewhere under the quilt and held them out. The hen went straight over to eat out of her hand. Granny Em picked it up and stroked its feathers like it was a cat.

"I can't remember the last time anybody give

me a hen. Coulda been way back when I was still catching babies 'fore you nurses came around." She looked up at Fran. "You ain't got a baby you need catching, now does you?"

"Heavens no." Fran could feel her cheeks warming.

"Best not wait too many long years."

Ben came through the door with a bucket of water. "Too many long years for what?" he asked.

Fran busied herself fastening her saddlebag. No way could she answer Ben.

But Granny Em did. "For livin'. Ain't good to piddle around doing naught but countin' days. Ain't smart to wait too long on some things a feller wants."

At least the old woman didn't mention anything about babies. Fran straightened up and looked at the cabinet and table in the corner of the room that must pass as a kitchen. She opened the cabinet. A few dishes were on one shelf and some jars with various powders and herbs on another. The only food she saw was a few eggs in a bowl and a container of meal. She should have brought Granny Em some of those shucky beans. Fran hadn't really acquired a taste for them, but she couldn't deny they were filling.

"Where's the ginger for your tea?" she asked.

"That's just it." Granny Em put the hen down and pulled the quilt a little closer around her. "I run out of it last week. Ain't been up to going out to dig more roots." The hen scooted under her chair.

"I guess not." Fran dipped the glass into the bucket of water Ben set down on the table. She looked over at Ben. "You don't know where we could find ginger roots, do you?"

"Ginger roots?" Ben frowned at her.

"For Granny Em's tea. We made a deal. She'd take my pills if I made her tea." Fran took the water to Granny Em and shook a couple of pills out of the packet. "Here. You'll have to go ahead and take these. Then drink the tea later."

"I reckon I can do that." Granny Em reached a trembling hand out for the pills and put them in her mouth. She sipped at the water and made a terrible face. "I ain't never figured out why them town doctors think a body can swaller a horse pill." Granny Em handed the glass back to Fran.

"Drink a little more."

"I'll drink more when you make me that tea." Granny Em clamped her lips together.

Fran took the glass and turned back to Ben.

"We're not going out in this weather to hunt ginger roots." There was no give in his face.

"But I promised."

"Do you even know what ginger plants look like?" Ben said.

"No. Don't you?"

"I might find some in the spring, but not now." Granny Em shoved a corner of her quilt away.

"I'll jest have to go out and find them my own self."

Ben went over and put his hand on Granny Em's shoulder to keep her from getting up. "You aren't going root hunting. What you're going to do is come to my house. Nothing but windfall branches out there that won't do anything but sputter and put your fire out."

"You come home from the service awful bossy," Granny Em said.

"I did. But Ma would have my hide if I let you sit here and die in your stubborn spot."

Fran held her breath, expecting an explosion from Granny Em, but it didn't come. Instead the old woman's lips turned up a little.

"Ruthena is a fine woman. Generous to a fault." Granny Em had another coughing attack. When she was finished, she gave Fran a hard look. "Them pills ain't done a bit of good."

"You have to take them twice a day for ten days." Fran handed her the glass of water and got her to take another sip. "And drink lots of water. Or tea."

"And you could just let an old woman die in peace."

"You've never been the peaceful sort," Ben said.

"But I got this new chicken to keep away from the foxes and the cow to milk." Granny Em shook her head.

"I'll come back up here and see to your cow or Woody will. And we'll take that fetched hen with us, but Ma won't let it in the house. I can tell you that."

"Plenty of folks do." Granny Em peered up at him.

"Not Ma."

"She always was picky about her house." Granny Em let out a wheezy sigh. "But I reckon Silky can manage in your henhouse."

"Silky?" Fran said.

"Ain't you never stroked a chicken's feathers, girl? Got a sweet, silky feel to them." Granny Em looked at Fran and then back at Ben. "Tell you what. I'll head on down to your ma's soon as them pills the nurse girl give me make me feel up to it."

"That won't do," Ben said. "You're going now. Along with that hen."

"Should I find some clothes to take with you?" Fran looked around. A trunk sat at the end of the bed in the corner of the room.

"No need," Ben said. "Ma will find her something to wear."

"I reckon we better do what Mr. Bossy says, girl."

"I guess you're right." Fran reached under the chair and grabbed the hen. It squawked, but Fran stuck its head under its wing to stop its fight. "Back in the sack with you."

She wrapped her slicker around Granny Em while Ben scattered out the fire in the hearth. The flames sputtered out.

Granny Em watched him. "I ain't let that fire go dead out for more'n a year."

"I'll start it up for you again before you come back."

"If'n I ever come back." The old woman sounded sad. "It's a sorry time when a body can't be the one to decide where and when she's going."

"You'll be better soon. We'll figure out how to make that tea." Fran touched the old woman's shoulder.

"No problem about that." Ben stood up from the fireplace. "Ma was talking about making some up for Sadie before I came out today."

"The child got a cough?" Granny Em asked.

"She does," Ben said.

"Then the ginger tea is jest what she needs." Granny Em smiled. "Good your ma remembered that."

Fran helped Granny Em stand up, but when she swayed on her feet, Ben picked the old woman up like she was no heavier than Sadie. Outside the rain was turning to snow. Fran put her saddlebag on Jasmine and tied the gunnysack back to her saddle horn.

Ben let Granny Em stand down beside Fran while he climbed on his horse. Then he reached and gently pulled the old woman up to cradle her in front of him on Captain. He looked at Fran without her slicker now. "I'd give you my coat, but it's soaked through."

"I'll be fine." Fran fought against shivering.

"You can dry out at the house."

Granny Em started coughing again, and Ben tightened his arms around her, as though to help her get through the coughs. The very sight brought tears to Fran's eyes as she mounted Jasmine and followed Ben away from the cabin.

At Ben's house, the fire was warm and the air smelled deliciously of popped corn. Sadie and her pup ran to meet Fran, while Mrs. Locke fussed over Granny Em. Becca pulled Fran over to the fire. Sarge settled on a rug by the door to wait. When Sadie's pup crept over to him, Sarge gave him a friendly sniff and then licked the pup's face. Obviously he liked Buttons better than Bruiser.

In spite of being wet and cold from the ride down the hill, a warm feeling crept through Fran. This was family.

Ben hung his dripping coat on a chair by the fire. He smiled at Fran and then turned to his mother. "We need some ginger tea."

36

December 1945

The days slid by into winter. The weather bounced between nippy and bracing to brisk and cold. The houses, airy in the summer with open doors and windows, were now freezing even with the doors shut. The wintry winds sneaked in every crack between the logs and floorboards. Families gathered around their fireplaces or stoves to stay warm.

As she went about her rounds, Fran did her best to avoid getting wet crossing the creeks. But sometimes it rained. Whatever the weather, a nurse had to go when called out.

"Best get used to it," Betty warned Fran. "This is mild compared to what's coming. It might snow in December. Probably will, but January and February are the mean months. At times you have to shovel a path through the snow to the barn. Of course, the mountain men might show up to do that for you. They want you able to get to your horse if their wives are expecting."

After Betty left for New York, Jeralene came every day to help with the chores. Fran took care of the horses but gladly gave up milking Bella. Not only was Jeralene a happy face that made the days better, her being there was more than enough reason for Woody to show up, and rarely empty-handed. He might bring hickory nuts. Or fried apple pies or blackberry jam. And sometimes he brought his brother.

Ben always came with a purpose. Woody told him about the loose board on the shed or a window that needed new putty. Once, he appeared at her door to guide Fran up to a spot on the hill above the center where they watched the sun go down in flaming color. He claimed some things just needed sharing.

That evening as she stood shoulder to shoulder with Ben to soak in nature's beauty, she wanted to believe her heart was beating faster because of climbing the hill and that it had nothing to do with the man beside her. But she knew better.

On the way back down the trace of a path, she slipped and Ben reached out to steady her. His hand on her arm was strong yet gentle, and the picture came to mind of how he'd cradled Granny Em in front of him to take her to his house. She'd seen the same gentleness in him when he knelt to talk to Sadie or when he wouldn't let Woody carry water until his wound was completely healed.

Even as she kept her head turned away from Ben to hide her feelings, her mother's words echoed in her mind. *You surely have more sense than to fall for one of those hillbillies.*

Not only did her mother's disapproval poke her, but even though Betty was in New York, Fran had no trouble imagining her disapproving frown that spoke plain as words how nurses weren't there for romance.

Truly she had no reason to think romance. Ben never once reached for her hand or spoke a word out of line. And yet, she did sometimes catch him watching her with a look that took her breath.

Plus, there was the way Ben's mother settled her gaze on Fran now and again when she was at their house. A considering look that had a seed of sadness in it. Fran seemed to hear her thinking Fran didn't measure up. She might love the mountains, but she was city born.

The days slid one into another. Fran delivered Mrs. McReedy's baby. A nine-pound boy that had Mr. McReedy grinning all the way across his face, after three girls.

Whenever the call came, Fran threw on her coat, saddled Jasmine, and headed out to help, whatever the need. On clinic day, people lined up with various complaints. She managed to treat them all without Betty watching over her shoulder, and nobody died.

Not even Granny Em, who definitely flirted with death. But the pills Mrs. Locke made sure the old woman took, or perhaps the ginger tea, pulled her through. After a couple of weeks,

Granny Em climbed back up to her cabin that Ben and Woody had repaired to keep out the winter winds.

When Fran checked on her, a stack of wood was by the front door. Jars of food filled a shelf in her cabinet. Fresh lye soap was beside a new wash pan, and Silky had the run of the house.

"Don't look so rattled," Granny Em said when she saw Fran watching the hen. "I take her out to scratch around for bugs and sech."

"But has she laid any eggs?"

" 'Course she has. That's her reason for being." Granny Em looked at the hen. "Come spring, I'll carry her down to be with Ruthena's rooster so's she can hatch out some of them eggs. Just the way things is intended to be. A rooster. A hen. Chicks." The old woman fastened her eyes back on Fran. "Same as it is for folks."

"True. That way of things keeps me busy." Fran smiled.

"And now that my ginger tea done cured my breathin' trouble, I can be around to catch them babies of your'n when you decide on a rooster." Granny Em's lips curled up in a sly grin. "I've noted one that might be wantin' to do some crowing to get noticed."

"No time for a nurse-midwife to have a family." Fran busied herself packing up her instruments.

"Some folks can come up with a ready excuse

'bout near ev'rything. Come up with a few myself now and agin." Granny Em frowned. "Lived to regret some of 'em. But one thing I never did, and that was let somebody else tell me what I could or couldn't do."

Fran straightened up and looked directly at Granny Em. It almost sounded as if the old woman had read her mother's latest letters. Not that Fran planned to pack up and go back to Cincinnati the way her mother kept insisting, always ending with the news that Seth and Cecelia still weren't married. "I'm doing what I want."

"That's good to know." Granny Em rubbed her chin. "I was thinkin' maybe that Mary Breckinridge had done tol' you what you could and couldn't do when it come to certain parts of livin'. Like she tells you what you can talk about and what you can't. No religion, politics, or moonshine talk."

"She wants us to get along with the people here. That's all." Fran took up for Mrs. B.

"But maybe not get along too well?" Granny Em raised her eyebrows at Fran.

"I don't know what you mean." That wasn't entirely true, but it was better to skirt any talk about Ben. "Mrs. Breckinridge loves the people here and they love her."

"Uh-hum." Granny Em rocked back in her chair. "I reckon that's true enough and I ain't sayin' the woman ain't done some good for the folks hereabouts. Even me. Guess it's on account of her bringing in girls like you to pester me into getting that ginger tea that I'm still kicking."

"Ginger tea did help."

"After the snows melt, I'll show you how to find the roots. If'n you're still around."

"I expect to be. The Lord willing."

"Best be watching what you're saying. That verges on religious talk." The old woman shook a finger at Fran. "Reckon as how you better follow the rules."

"I try." Fran smiled and picked up her saddlebag. "You follow my rules and get better. I'll be back up to see you soon."

Granny Em's smile sank out of sight among her wrinkles as she grabbed Fran's arm. "Just one more thing, Nurse Girl. You keep in mind there's times to shrug off the rules and do what you know is true in your own insides."

"You mean follow my heart."

"Heart, gut, feet, whatever. Just don't let your oughta-dos mess up them long years ahead of you." She gave Fran's arm a shake. "Catching babies is a fine thing, but it ain't as fine as holding your own."

"Do you have children, Granny Em?"

Granny Em let go of Fran to stare down at her lap. Thinking maybe she had dozed off, Fran started to tiptoe out the door when the old woman spoke. "I caught one of mine. She was a pretty little thing. Not a thing like me or her pa. She come when the leaves were turning. The fevers took her and my man both before the trees put out new leaves."

"I'm sorry."

"No need. Weren't your doing. The Lord gives and the Lord takes away." She looked up with a sad smile. "Reckon I'm talkin' religion now. You watch out going down the hill. I look for the weather to turn bad. My old bones don't never lie bout that."

Granny Em's bones were right. By the time Fran got back to the center, a skiff of snow covered the ground. By the next morning, the snow measured four inches and was still falling.

Fran was pulling on her boots to go see to the animals when Jeralene came up on the porch.

"I wasn't sure you'd make it today," Fran said.

"I shoulda stayed over last night, but I thought the snow wasn't gonna amount to nothing. But then it set in." Jeralene stomped the snow off her feet before she stepped inside the door and stood on the little rug there. "If'n you'll hand me the bucket, I'll go on out and see to Bella. That way I won't be tracking all over the floor and have to mop it later."

Fran handed her the bucket and then shrugged on her own coat. "I'll see to the horses." Sarge bounced out the door, his ears up.

Jeralene laughed. "Looks like Sarge is a snow dog. I reckon that's good if he's gonna be following you all over the mountain. What with the way that wind's blowing today, you best hope nobody comes hollering for you. But Ma says babies are contrary little beings who have a way of picking the stormiest times to make an entrance into this old world."

"Babies come all times of the year and in all sorts of weather. Sunshine and moonshine."

Fran followed Jeralene off the porch. Only one mother was close to delivering. Becca. But she hadn't shown any signs of labor when she saw her yesterday. She complained with her back, but she'd been doing that for weeks. Her baby hadn't turned into the birth position. Fran was hoping something would shift before the next time she checked on Becca in a few days. If it didn't, she'd send Becca to the hospital to wait for the baby to come. A safer place for a breech birth.

"Even on Christmas Day," Jeralene said. "My little brother, Davey, was born on Christmas back when I was ten. It was like a special gift for us all. Such a sweet little thing. Then. Now he can be an ornery pest." She laughed as she held out a hand to catch a snowflake. "Christmas is next week."

"At home, we always wanted a white Christmas." Fran looked out over the yard and field toward the barn. Everything looked so pristine. "After we do the chores, I'll get some pine branches to bring inside to decorate and we can make cookies."

"Or candy. I saw some cocoa in the cabinet the other day." Jeralene turned back to Fran. "Who knows? We might have visitors. You know that Woody. A little snow won't stop him."

Fran followed her toward the barn. By the time she finished with the horses and went to the edge of the woods to break off a couple of pine branches, ice was mixing in the snow. Even Sarge started looking toward the house with longing. Snow was one thing. Ice another.

At least she had taken Jasmine and Moses to the blacksmith at Wendover to have special shoes with studs put on to be ready for winter weather.

By noon, the snow changed completely to ice and put a slippery skim on top of the snow. Then the wind started up, whistling down through the pines and rattling the windows. A good day to stay in and sample Jeralene's candy while she wrote her mother a Christmas letter.

When she thought about how her mother would be frantically decorating and planning for Christmas, Fran was glad to be in a cabin sitting by a warm fire with her dog at her feet. She had mailed her mother a pair of mittens Jeralene's mother knitted and sent Harold a jar of sorghum molasses. Christmas shopping done.

She might go to Wendover on Christmas Day if Becca wasn't having her baby. Or maybe she'd make cookies and stay right here at the center to hand out treats to anybody who came by. She could even wrap up some to take to Granny Em. That way she could stop in at the Locke house. Just thinking about that made her smile. She'd bought a little cloth sack of thumb-sized handkerchief dolls from one of the mountain women. Mrs. Jessup said they were church babies. Fran couldn't wait to give those to Sadie.

The snow and ice finally stopped late in the day. Jeralene had busied herself making soup, but Woody hadn't come down the mountain. Nor had his brother.

"Not a good day for traveling," Jeralene said. "Not less'n a body has to. I 'spect Woody will find his way here on the morrow before we eat all this candy."

Late that afternoon, Fran had just stepped out onto the porch, headed for the barn, when she heard that familiar call. "Hallooo."

At least she already had her coat and boots on.

37

December 19, 1945

Ben hated being stuck in the house. He'd already stacked more wood in the woodbox on the back porch and shoveled off the steps three times. He was restless. No doubt about it. Antsy. Even when the ice pellets started hitting the windowpanes, he still tried to think up a reason to head outside.

Not only outside. If he was honest with himself, it wasn't simply outside he wanted. He wanted to saddle up Captain and ride down the mountain. Shovel some paths for Francine. Maybe a path to her heart.

But he couldn't tell his mother that. She knew, but didn't either of them talk about it. Not anymore. She'd said her piece that night in the cornfield. She didn't approve. As far as that went, he didn't approve. He had better things to do than fall in love. Especially with a city girl who would never give him a second look.

That wasn't entirely true either. She did sometimes give him a second look. It might be easier to keep his wits about him if she didn't. But sometimes those soft eyes landed a look on him that made his stomach go all weak. It was a look he wanted to see again and again.

So any day he could come up with an excuse to ride down to the center, he did. Woody didn't need an excuse. He just went to see Jeralene. But Jeralene was one of them. If she and Woody ended up together, nobody would be the least bit bothered. Francine Howard and Ben Locke, that was a different matter.

He would have gone down the mountain today with or without an excuse, but first thing after breakfast, Ma said he needed to stay close at hand.

"I'm some worried it might be Becca's time." She kept her voice low so Becca couldn't hear.

"The nurse was just here yesterday. She said Becca was doing fine, didn't she?"

"Yesterday she was. Today things are looking different. I'm thinking it might be time, and I know those nurses have a heap of training, but I've had a heap of babies."

"You want me to go fetch the nurse?"

Ma frowned. "Not yet. But best stay close in case the need does arise. Being as how this is the first time for Becca, there'll be time and more to get the nurse when I'm sure it's the baby causing her to be punishing."

Across the room, Becca groaned as she shifted in her chair. "Ma, do you think a hot water bottle would help my back?"

Ben followed his mother into the kitchen where she picked up the teakettle to fill the hot water bottle. "Did you tell her about the letter you got from Ruthie?"

Ma shot a look into the next room at Becca. "Not yet. And don't you either. Let her get this baby here before she has to be worrying about where Carl has got off to."

Ben's sister had written that Carl had walked away from the factory job he'd found in Ohio and nobody had seen him since. Ruthie wrote that he should have a little money jingling in his pocket, but she wasn't sure if that was good or bad. The young man seemed unsettled in Ohio. Claimed being shut up in a factory was near as bad as being down in a mine. Ruthie hadn't been surprised when he went missing. She liked Carl, but some boys just didn't know how to start being men. She was fearful Carl was one of them.

So Ben had no choice except to hang around the house and wait out the day. Woody was reading an adventure book his schoolteacher had loaned him. Ma took the snowy day to work on the quilt she was making for Becca's baby. Sadie was learning stitches beside Ma. Becca lay down after the noon meal and went to sleep. That seemed to say the baby wasn't ready to come, but Ma said it didn't prove anything except Becca was worn out from carrying that baby load.

Ben tried to settle down. He leafed through his father's Bible, and his restlessness was somewhat eased by reading passages Pa had marked. Here and there he had made a notation about a sermon, and Ben wondered if it was one his father had heard or one he might have preached at a meeting when no preacher showed up. Then he was moved nearly to tears when he found a note stuck in the back of the Bible. A prayer list with the number of Ben's unit and the first names of some of the men Ben must have mentioned in letters home.

As he shifted in his chair, the envelope in his pocket crinkled. He'd been carrying around the letter from the college detailing the classes he'd signed up to take come January. The GI Bill seemed too good an opportunity to pass up. But now he didn't know how he could ride down off the mountain and over to Richmond every Monday morning and leave these here to shift for themselves all the week long. It was surely a crazy dream for him to think about studying long enough and hard enough to be a doctor.

He hadn't told anybody about considering medicine as his life's work. Best see if he could take the first step down the row, as his pa used to tell him, instead of wanting to skip to the end. If it was meant to happen, the Lord would open up a path. Another of his pa's sayings.

He supposed the same was true about Francine. If it was meant to happen, it would. At the same time, his pa did say a person had to do the stepping down the row toward whatever end he was searching out. But sometimes a path closed up.

That seemed to be what kept happening every time he thought about confronting Homer Caudill. He would set out to go have it out with the man, and something happened every time to change his direction. Maybe his mother was right and it was best to leave the thought of vengeance in the Lord's hands. He certainly had enough to keep a worry cloud over his head without stirring up trouble with the Caudills.

Still, a man shouldn't get away with sending his boy to shoot another boy without some justice being served. Even if the boy that got shot was ready to sweep it all under the rug. The thing was, Woody could have died. Some things shouldn't be forgiven without some kind of repentance. Ben didn't think Homer Caudill was sorrowful about anything he'd done.

He glanced down at the Bible, where it had fallen open to Colossians 3. His father had underlined verse 13. *Forbearing one another, and forgiving one another, if any man have a quarrel against any: even as Christ forgave you, so also do ye.*

Ben ran his finger over the verse. *It's not that easy, Pa.*

He could almost hear his father speaking inside his head. *Ain't nobody ever promised easy.*

Ben blew out a sigh. Pa was right. Ben had just been to war and lived to come home. No sense starting another war here on his home ground. The law would catch up with Homer Caudill.

Outside, Rufus barked and then Bruiser started in. That started up Sadie's pup inside.

Ma looked up from her stitching. "Somebody must be out there. Coming on a day like this. I hope it's not trouble."

Ben stood up. "I'll go see."

"Ma." Becca was up, leaning on the doorframe into the bedroom. "I'm having pains."

Ma shoved aside the quilt at the same time somebody banged on the door.

Ben pulled open the door to a man with a scarf wrapped around his head and snow on his hat. Before Ben could say anything, the man pulled his scarf down and stared across the room. "Becca."

"Carl, is that you?" Becca moved a couple of steps toward the door.

"I've come home to you."

Becca gasped, then grimaced and grabbed the back of a chair.

Ma was beside her at once with an arm around her. "Don't hold your breath, honey. The pain will pass in a minute."

410

Carl's eyes got wide, and Ben pulled the man inside before he could think about running back down the hill. "You're about to be a father. Get on in here and dry out so you can be some help."

Becca straightened up as the pain eased. A tear slid down her cheek as she looked at Carl. "I'm glad you're here. I wanted our son to have a daddy."

Carl shrugged off his wet coat and kicked off shoes that were soaked through. He squared his shoulders and headed across the room.

"I'm 'bout froze, Becca, but if'n you was to smile at me, I know my heart would warm right up." Carl reached out to brush the tear off Becca's cheek.

"Your hand's like ice." Becca grabbed Carl's hand and held it between both of hers.

"I ain't worried about that till I see you smile so's I know you ain't holdin' it agin me being gone so long."

"For a truth, I wasn't sure you'd ever come back."

Becca and Carl stood in the middle of the room paying no mind to Ben and the rest of the family watching them. Carl didn't even seem to notice Sadie's pup jerking on his pants leg. They were focused on one another as more tears flowed down Becca's cheeks.

"But I had to. My Becca is here. If'n only she'd

smile for me, I'd kiss away them tears right in front of her ma."

Becca laughed, but then she gasped as another pain grabbed her. Carl started to hold her, but Ma stepped between and pushed him back.

"No need getting her soaked. Woody, get Carl some dry clothes." Ma looked at Ben. "Best go for the nurse and don't be tarrying none."

"Right." Ben grabbed his coat.

"Take the horse. No sense getting stuck in that vehicle and having to walk."

"Yes'm."

The ice-encrusted snow crunched under Ben's feet as he made his way to the barn. His mother was probably right. The truck might slide off what passed for a road up the mountain. Captain was the better way.

Francine was on the porch of the center with Jeralene when he rode up. She rushed over to his horse before he could dismount.

"Becca?"

"Ma says it's time." He slid down off Captain to stand beside her.

She looked around at the snow-covered ground with a worried frown.

"The horses can make it," Ben said.

Her eyes came back to his face. "Yes. No need worrying about more until we have to." She turned away from him, but not before he noted her worried look hadn't eased. "I'll saddle up and be ready in a few minutes. At least the sleet has stopped, but it's still treacherous walking."

As if to prove her words, she slipped and nearly lost her footing. Ben stepped closer to take her arm. "Hold on to me."

Francine grabbed his arm as she slipped again. "I was ready for snow, but not this ice. And it's not even January when Betty says it'll be worse."

"Sometimes we have January weather in December." He hoped that if she noticed he sounded out of breath, she'd think it was due to how he was stomping through the snow and not the real reason. Her leaning so close against him. He wanted to put both arms around her and just hold her there in the middle of the snowy path. But he needed to think of Becca now.

With his help, Francine was riding out of the barn in minutes. The mare stepped gingerly into the snow at first, but then got more confident of her footing. After Francine got her saddlebag, Ben led the way on Captain. Sarge trailed behind Francine's mare.

The horses' hooves breaking through the ice crust made too much noise for them to talk. Better to concentrate on making it up the hill as fast as they could anyway, since they were at the edge of darkness. But the snow glistened in the fading light to keep night at bay.

When they passed the truck, snow was piled around the wheels and ice lay heavy on the windshield. As soon as the weather cleared, he needed to get that road cut through the trees to the house and build some kind of shed for the truck.

Maybe Carl could help with that. Carl being home might be a path opening up, the Lord making a way. Carl didn't like mining and factory work, but could be he would like keeping the farm going while Ben went off to school.

He glanced back at Francine as they rode into the yard. Maybe more paths would open up. Given more time.

38

Fran worried all the way up the hill, even though worry did no good at all. Better to think about what to do if the baby hadn't turned and was going to present a breech birth. She should have sent Becca on to the hospital yesterday. She wasn't due for a couple more weeks, but babies had a way of coming when they were ready. Now with the snowstorm, well, there was plenty to worry about.

The concern heightened when she saw Ben's truck snowed in. She couldn't see how anybody could make it down the hill in that without sliding where they didn't want to go. Thank goodness the horses were surefooted on the trail, but that might not help Becca.

If only Betty were still here riding beside her. She might have handled such situations in her years as nurse. But Betty was in New York. The lives of Becca and her baby were in Fran's hands.

Don't go borrowing trouble. Grandma Howard used to tell Fran that when she started worrying about something.

Prayers, that was what was needed. Every time she delivered a baby and especially this time.

At the house, Woody came out to take Jasmine

to the barn after Fran dismounted and pulled the saddlebag off.

Fran stopped Ben when he reached for the saddlebag to carry it inside for her. "You better dig out your truck. Becca may need to be in the hospital if the baby is still breech. That would be safer for both her and the baby."

Ben looked back at the trail they'd made through the snow to the house. He didn't say it wasn't possible to get to the hospital, even though she saw the uncertainty on his face. Instead he got back on his horse. "All right. Send Woody if you need me before I get back." Woody had already gone toward the barn with Jasmine.

"Do you think the truck can make it down the mountain?"

"It will if we need it to." The uncertainty was gone.

Fran didn't watch him ride back down the trail. Instead she hurried up the porch steps, where a man she didn't know opened the door.

"I'm Carl." He looked a little panicked. "You got to help Becca. She's punishing bad."

"So you're her husband?"

"That I am." The man glanced toward the bedroom at the sound of Becca crying out. He looked ready to cry himself. "I can't stand her hurting like that. You gotta help her."

Fran took off her coat and touched his arm.

"I'll do what I can. You best find a shovel and go help Ben dig out his truck. Just in case we need to take her to the hospital."

He looked relieved to have something to do as he grabbed a coat off a chair by the fire. Sadie was in the kitchen with a fresh towel for Fran to dry her hands after she scrubbed them with the lye soap.

Sadie stared up at Fran with wide eyes. "Is Becca going to die?"

"Having babies isn't easy, sweetheart. That's why they call these pains before birth 'laboring.' But with the Lord's help, Becca will have her baby soon."

"She says it's going to be a boy, but Ma says there's no way to know for sure till the baby comes." A guilty grin lifted the corners of Sadie's lips. "I hope Becca's wrong and it's a girl."

Fran hugged the girl. "Whichever it is, you'll be a fine help taking care of the baby. Now you have a job to do."

Her grin faded. "What's that?"

"You need to keep Buttons out of the bedroom and practice telling Priscilla the stories you'll be telling Becca's baby soon. Can you do that?"

Sadie's smile came back. "Yes'm. Ma told me to stay out here by the fire. I'll make Buttons sit with me. And Sarge too."

In the bedroom, Mrs. Locke held Becca's hands. "I think it's harder watching her than having my own." She pulled a hand free to stroke Becca's hair.

"I've heard other mothers say the same." Fran plastered a smile on her face as she leaned over Becca. "How do you feel, Becca?"

"He's wantin' out, Nurse Howard. Can't you do something to make him come faster? Get this punishing pain over and done." She stiffened as another pain seized her.

"Let me see what's happening and we'll do what we can."

The exam showed just what Fran feared. A breech presentation. A difficult birth, especially with a baby the size Becca was carrying.

She kept the worry out of her voice and off her face as she took Becca's hand. "You remember how I told you the baby needed to turn. Well, that didn't happen. You need to go to the hospital where a doctor will be at hand to help you."

"Can't we just send for the doctor to come here?" Becca said. "I don't see how I can go anywhere."

"That might take too long. Better to go in Ben's truck."

"You think that's what has to be done?" Mrs. Locke spoke up.

"It's best for Becca. And for the baby." Fran met Mrs. Locke's gaze straight on.

"It won't be no easy trip."

"No, ma'am. We'll need blankets to keep Becca

warm and some sort of pallet for her in the back of the truck."

Mrs. Locke stood up.

"Ma, you got to go with me." Becca reached for her mother's hand.

"Don't you worry, child. I'll be with you ev'ry step of the way." Mrs. Locke patted her hand. "Now rest best you can whilst I get things ready."

The Lord surely watched over them as they carried Becca on the pallet down the hill to the truck. Nobody slipped in the icy snow. Ben and Carl took the lead positions, with Woody and Mrs. Locke on the back. Fran hustled along beside Becca, who stoically bore up under the trip. The pains were closer together and Fran prayed they would have time to get to Hyden.

Woody headed back to the house to stay with Sadie and keep Sarge from following them. Carl got in the cab with Ben while Mrs. Locke and Fran climbed in the back to tuck quilts around Becca.

The sky had cleared and the moon on the snow made it nearly light as day. Fran kept her hand on Becca's abdomen to gauge her contractions as they slid down the hill.

Mrs. Locke held her daughter's hands and moved her lips in silent prayer. When she noticed Fran looking at her, she said, "I'm praying hard we make it down this mountain."

The truck fishtailed as she spoke and both Fran and Mrs. Locke held Becca to steady her. Ben got the truck back on what passed for a road. For a few minutes, Fran thought they might make it. But then Becca's pains were stronger as her body began to push out the baby.

"Tell Ben to stop." Fran looked at Mrs. Locke. "This baby isn't going to wait for the hospital."

After the truck stopped, Fran pulled a baby blanket out of her saddlebag and handed it to Mrs. Locke. "Put this up under your coat to get it as warm as possible." She turned to Ben and Carl, who climbed out of the truck to stare at her. "Make a tent with these quilts to keep Becca warm."

Fran warmed her hands under her armpits as she knelt beside Becca. "I'm going to help you, Becca, but you'll be doing the work. Work you can do." In her head, Fran added for herself, *You can do this.*

Moonlight filtered through the quilts as Fran positioned Becca and prayed the girl would be able to push the baby out quickly enough.

"Go ahead and scream if you need to," she told Becca. "That might help."

"Me a-screaming ain't gonna be the first thing this baby of mine hears," Becca gasped. "Ma, sing my baby here."

"Surely I can do that." Mrs. Locke leaned close to Becca under the quilts.

"Toora, loora, loora. Toora, loora, li.
Toora, loora, loora. Hush, now, don't you cry.
Ah, Toora, loora, loora. Toora, loora, li.
Toora, loora, loora. It's an Irish lullaby."

Mrs. Locke's clear, sure voice somehow calmed Fran as well as Becca. Grandma Howard used to sing that same lullaby. Then Ben's voice joined in with his mother's, and after another minute, Carl added his shaky voice. The sound of their voices sent a sweet shiver through Fran that had nothing to do with the cold as she guided Becca's baby into the world. As if they'd all been listening for it, they fell silent at the first thin wail from Becca's baby.

"It's a girl." Tears of relief rolled down Fran's cheeks. "A beautiful, healthy, strong girl."

Becca's mother pulled the blanket from under her coat to wrap around the baby. "Keep the baby warm, Mrs. Locke, while we finish what must be done here. Are you all right, Becca?"

Becca was crying too. "I knew she would be a girl. I knew it all along. I'm calling her Carlene Ruth."

"I've got a little girl." Carl jumped up and down and made the quilts flap. "I'm a daddy!"

"Stop that, Carl." Mrs. Locke's voice was sharp. The man stood still at once.

Becca shivered. She needed somewhere warm. A few minutes later, the afterbirth passed, Fran pulled the quilts down tight around Becca and looked at Ben. "How far to the hospital?"

"A good ways, but we're not far from the center." Ben pointed toward the creek glistening in the moonlight ahead of them.

"Go there then."

They slid the rest of the way down the hill and then spun back up the rise to the center. Ben and Carl carried Becca into the clinic area on the pallet. Mrs. Locke followed with the crying baby. A good sound since the cries were strong. But Becca was shaking with the cold, her lips trembling and pale.

Jeralene came from the extra bedroom with a lamp. Ben poked up the fire in the clinic's stove.

"Make some tea with extra sugar, Jeralene. And fix a hot water bottle."

Fran shrugged off her coat and let it land in the floor. Carl knelt by Becca.

"Rub her arms, Carl. We need to get her warm." Fran massaged Becca's legs and feet until her skin turned pink again and her teeth stopped chattering.

When Jeralene brought the tea, Fran raised Becca's head to let her have a sip.

Becca swallowed. "Moonshine might work better." The smile in her eyes was good to see.

"The tea will have to do."

Becca twisted to look for her baby. "Is she all right?"

Her mother spoke up. "She's a right pretty child. Takes after her mother." She peeled back the blanket from the baby and laid her beside Becca. Carl gently traced his new daughter's cheek with his fingertip.

When Fran looked up at Ben smiling down at Becca and her baby, her heart made a little sideways jump. She mentally shook herself and got back to business. "If you men will step into the other room, we'll make sure all is as it should be."

Later, after the baby was weighed and bathed and Becca was warm and comfortable on the clinic cot with Carl and her mother watching over her, Fran went out on the porch to clear her head. She stared up at the stars and thanked the Lord for the baby's safe delivery.

The door opened and Ben stepped out behind her. "My family has a new reason to be grateful to you."

"No, no." Fran glanced back at him, then turned her gaze back to the stars. "I should have had her go to the hospital yesterday. Things could have not turned out well."

He moved up beside her, his shoulder brushing hers at the porch railing. "But things did turn out well. The baby is fine. Becca is fine."

"But that could have happened at your house without that icy ride down the mountain."

"You did what you thought best. That's all anybody can do."

Fran looked over at him, but now he was staring up at the sky. "I guess you had plenty of times in the army where you could only do your best."

"I didn't save all of them. I wanted to, but I didn't."

"Not didn't. Couldn't." Fran put her hand on his arm.

He turned his eyes back to hers. Her breath caught in her throat as he stared down at her.

"Francine." He seemed ready to say more, but his mother called to him from inside. The moment was lost.

Fran shivered, more from being so near to him than the chill, but she didn't deny it when he said she must be cold. He slipped off his jacket and draped it around her shoulders. It carried his warmth.

For just an instant his hands rested on her shoulders, but then he pulled his hands away. "Ma's ready to go back up the hill. Carl's staying. I'll come down tomorrow to see if Becca can come to the house."

"All right."

A little frown creased Mrs. Locke's forehead when Ben followed Fran inside. The frown lines went a little deeper when Fran handed Ben his coat. She rubbed her hand across her forehead and replaced the frown with a smile. "We're beholding to you, Nurse Howard, for gettin' little Carlene here in trying circumstances."

"It could be we should have stayed at your house," Fran said. "Out of the cold."

"That could be, but some things is hard to see on down the road. It turned out right. That's what matters." She shifted her eyes to Ben. "Things turning out right."

"And they did." Ben met his mother's steady gaze.

After they left, Fran checked on Becca. She was dozing, her arm wrapped around the baby swaddled in a blanket with only her little round face showing. She too was sleeping peacefully. Carl sat on a pallet Jeralene must have fixed for him beside the bed, his gaze fastened on Becca.

"I love her, you know." He looked up at Fran. "That might not appear to be the truth of it, with me being gone so long, but I weren't never happy up there in Ohio without her. I don't intend to part from her again. I aim to be somebody she'll want to call her man."

"That's good to hear, Carl." She lightly touched Becca's forehead and observed her regular breathing and that of the baby. She peeked under the blanket. All was as it should be. "Call for me if Becca needs anything."

In her bedroom, she kicked off her boots and stripped off her soiled uniform. She put on a clean shirt and trousers to sleep in, since she'd be checking on the new mother and baby in a couple of hours. After she lay down, the silence of the house settled around her. Fran missed Sarge on the rug beside her bed. No sooner did she think that than she heard scratching on the front door.

She opened the door and Sarge slipped inside, as though he had just done his nightly turn around the yard instead of coming down the hill from the Lockes' house.

"Good dog." She dried off his paws with an old towel. "Did Ben let you out and tell you to come home?"

He gave her his doggie grin and danced his paws up and down, his toenails clicking on the wood floor.

Fran almost laughed. "You're too proud of yourself. Come on before you wake everybody up."

With Sarge on his rug as he should be, Fran lay back down, but she couldn't go to sleep. She kept seeing the look on Carl's face as he watched his wife and child. The same kind of look she'd seen on other men's faces after a baby was born. Would anyone ever look at her that way, or would she always be only an observer of that special kind of love?

She pushed away the thought and grabbed at sleep. She didn't have time for that kind of thinking. She was Nurse Howard.

39

December 20, 1945

Sun sneaking in through the window the next morning woke Fran. No more time for sleeping. Fran pulled the spread up over her bed. Outside, the eaves dripped as the snow melted. Weather could change quickly in Kentucky.

Becca was in the chair rocking her baby while Carl slept in the bed. "I told him he could, Nurse. He was plumb tuckered out from the walk home in that snowstorm yesterday." She smiled at the sleeping man. "Weren't it something him showin' up in time for the baby to come?" Becca shook her head a little. "Ma says that's how things work sometimes. God's doing. Fixing it so's folks show up when you 'specially need 'em to."

"He loves you." Fran looked over at Carl. "He told me so last night while you were sleeping."

"I ain't never doubted that for a minute." Becca's smile slipped away. "What I been ponderin' is whether he can be a passable husband and a daddy. Do for us, you know. A girl can jump off in love without a second thought, but a mother has to consider other things."

Fran had no answer for that. "I'll bring you

breakfast after I take care of the horses. Well, horse, since Jasmine is still up in your barn."

"Ben will see to her. He's a man who does what needs doing." Becca looked up at Fran. "You like him, don't you?"

"I like all of you." Fran sidestepped her question. "You've been so good to me."

"There's all kinds of ways of liking." Becca smiled down at her baby. "And loving. I'm finding out one of them ways right now with baby Carlene."

You like him, don't you? Becca's question followed Fran around all morning, but she kept avoiding an answer, even in her own thoughts.

Instead she busied herself checking on Becca, peeling potatoes for soup, and writing up notes for her records. Outside the snow melted almost as fast as it had fallen the day before.

Jeralene stared out the window and warned the creeks would be rising. "Tides don't generally happen this time of the year, but then it don't generally snow a foot in December. Getting anywheres is apt to be hard for a spell." Jeralene looked around at Fran. "You got any new babies near to coming?"

"Not for a while, but something's always happening."

"Ain't that the truth."

As if to prove their point, Sarge stood up and barked as somebody knocked. Fran rushed to open the door, expecting to see Ben coming for Becca. But it wasn't Ben.

"Seth." Fran blinked. Her eyes had to be playing tricks on her. "What in the world are you doing here?"

"I've come to take you home."

"What?" Fran was too surprised to see him standing there to make sense of his words.

"It's almost Christmas. You need to come home."

"Is something wrong with Mother?" An uneasy worry awakened inside her. What else could bring Seth all the way to the mountains?

"No, no. She's fine." Seth laid her worries to rest. "Other than missing her only daughter." He shivered a little. "I'm about froze. Are you going to let me come inside?"

He did look cold in spite of his heavy coat, but he didn't have a hat or boots. His shoes were soaked.

"Of course. I'm sorry. It's just that I can hardly believe you're actually here." When she pulled the door open wider, Sarge barked again. Fran touched the dog's head. "He's all right, Sarge."

"Sarge?" Seth frowned at the dog. "Odd name for a dog."

"He likes it." Fran kept her hand on Sarge. "Come over to the fire and take those wet shoes off." She scooted a chair closer to the fireplace in the front room. He had to have a reason to come all this way, but she couldn't imagine what it could be. Maybe something her mother cooked up to get Fran back to Cincinnati. Could her mother have paid him to come get her?

"I don't think I've ever been this cold. Not even in the army." He sat down without taking off his coat and leaned down to untie his shoes.

"Did you walk all the way here?"

"How else can you get to this godforsaken place?" Seth slipped off his shoe.

She wanted to tell him there was nothing godforsaken about it, but she bit back the words. He was obviously miserably cold. That could make a man cross. "So you came on the bus to Hyden?" She could still hardly believe he was sitting there in front of her eyes.

"No, I didn't come on the bus." He glared at her. "I came in my car. Got to what passes for a town in the middle of a snowstorm. Took my life in my hands driving that road up to the hospital and then you weren't there. Some short little nurse tells me you're out here in the hinterlands, a place I'd never be able to find in the dark. I'd end up killed or worse." Seth jerked off his wet sock. "Wasn't sure then what could be worse than killed, but that was before I spent the night shivering in my car."

Fran thought of her own night. Delivering a baby in the back of a truck. And of Becca having that baby. She caught the faint cry of the

430

newborn from the clinic and wanted to leave Seth by the fire to check on her. Instead, even though she wanted to tell him nobody had asked him to come, she summoned up a sympathetic look. "Sounds like you had a hard time."

"A hard time doesn't begin to describe it." He stared at his toes. "I think I have frostbite."

Fran doubted it, but if he did, he might need treatment. She leaned over to examine his foot. "No frostbite." She rubbed his toes to warm them.

He yanked off his other sock and poked that foot up toward her. "You better check this one too."

She didn't particularly like the way he grinned at her, as though she were touching his foot in a more personal way than simply as a nurse. This time she turned loose of his foot after examining it without trying to warm his toes.

"Nothing wrong that dry socks won't cure." She stepped back from him.

He kept his foot up in the air for a second. "You have good hands."

"A good thing for a nurse-midwife." She picked up his socks and spread them on the hearth near the fire. "Do you have other clothes with you?"

"Yeah, in my car maybe a mile from here. It's stuck in a ditch." His scowl was back. "There's probably not a wrecker to be found for miles."

"The men around here will help you."

"Are you sure they won't just shoot me and take my car? I hear they don't like outsiders."

"As long as they don't think you're a revenuer, you should be fine." Fran kept her face solemn.

"Should be?" Seth shook his head. "I don't like the sound of that."

Fran did smile then. "They'll help you if I tell them you're a friend."

"Are we friends, Fran?" His expression changed. "Like we used to be?"

Fran's smile disappeared. "What about Cecelia?"

"She's gone. Back to England. For good."

"I'm sorry," Fran said.

"Don't be. The parting was mutual. She wasn't the same Cecelia once she was here. Nothing like she was over in England. She didn't like my family. She didn't like Cincinnati. Wanted me to go to California." Seth frowned as he rubbed his toes. "What would I do in California?"

"I don't know. They say it's warm out there."

"That part would be good." He scooted nearer to the fire. "Can you put some more coal on the fire? Warm it up in here."

Fran dropped a chunk from the coal bucket beside the hearth onto the fire. The coal already glowing red in the fire broke apart and sent up sparks. She turned back to Seth. "Why are you here, Seth?"

"I told you. To take you home. Before

Christmas. Your mother says you won't pay any attention to her letters. That I needed to come get you." He stood up and stepped closer to her. "We, the two of us, can start over. See if we have as much fun together now as we used to before the war and everything." He reached and took her hand. "That's what you wanted, wasn't it? What you wrote about in all your letters to me."

It had been what she wanted. Or thought she did. She pulled her hand free and stepped back. "That was then. Things have changed."

"They don't have to be changed. We can make it work again." He followed her away from the fire. "All you have to do is come home with me."

"I can't do that. I have patients here who depend on me."

"They can put somebody else here. That nurse at the hospital said so. Said you could go home if you wanted to." When Fran didn't say anything, he went on. "Don't you want to have your own babies, our own babies, instead of merely helping others have babies?" He caught her hand again and raised it up to touch her fingers to his cheek.

He was right. She had been ready to marry him. Perhaps the feeling was still there inside her, but then why did she not like the way he kept grabbing her hand? She eased her hand free again. "I'm not going with you. At least not now."

A smile settled on his face. "But you will give it some consideration? I know I was a bum, but I've wanted to come after you ever since I saw you at church that day. Even before Cecelia left."

"I'll think about it."

A knock sounded on the door, but this time Sarge didn't bark. Instead he ran toward the door with his tail flapping happily. She knew before she opened the door that Ben would be standing there, and she wished Seth anywhere but beside her fire.

40

Ben pulled the truck as close to the center's door as he dared. He didn't want to get stuck. This driving in snow was tricky, but the way the temperature was rising, the snow wouldn't last long. In fact, the clouds gathering in the west looked more like rain than snow. Guess he'd find out then how his truck did in mud. Once he got Becca and her baby home, he'd just park the truck till time to go to Richmond to school. The chance of him actually getting to do that looked more promising with Carl back.

Until then, Ben wanted to see more of Francine. Lots more. Find out if there was any place for him in her heart. As much as he'd fought it, she'd already found a spot in his heart and mind.

When he noticed footprints through the snow to the porch, he hoped Francine hadn't been called out somewhere. With the way the creek was rising, he couldn't tarry here. He had to get his truck back across the water. He stared up at the clouds and hoped he was wrong about rain coming.

After he knocked on the door, he smiled at the sound of toenails on the floor. That meant Sarge found his way home. Even better, Sarge in the house meant Francine was surely there too.

Her smile was all wrong when she opened the door. "Mr. Locke. I guess you've come for Becca."

Ben's own smile faded. He started to say he thought they'd gotten past the Mr. Locke and Nurse Howard stage, but then he saw the man by her fire. Barefoot.

"If she's well enough for the ride, Nurse Howard." He followed her formal lead. "Ma's anxious to get hold of that baby again." He kept his eyes away from the man. "And the way the creek's rising, we might ought to go soon." With that man whoever he was there, he'd have no time for visiting Francine anyway. He wanted to think the man was a patient, but he looked like an outsider. Very much like one.

"Right." Francine stepped back from the door.

The man leaned forward to peer out the door. "Is that your truck?" When Ben nodded, the man said, "Then you could pull my car out of the ditch. It's down the road a little way."

"I don't think I know you." A man should wait until names were exchanged before he asked for favors.

"I'm Seth Miller. Francine and I are old friends. Practically engaged, weren't we, Frannie?" He grinned over at Francine.

"Before the war." Color spread across Francine's cheeks. "Seth, this is Ben Locke. He was in the service too."

"Good to meet you." The man stayed by the stove and didn't offer to shake Ben's hand. "So is that your baby I hear squalling back there?"

"My sister's." Ben turned to Francine. "Is the baby all right?"

"She's fine. A beautiful baby." Francine's voice softened and her smile came back. "I'll go help Becca get ready." She started toward the clinic.

"But what about my car?" The man pulled a couple of bills from his pocket to hold out toward Ben. "I'm willing to pay. I need my car to get back to civilization. Soon as I talk some sense into Francine, I'm ready to leave this place behind."

Francine turned back to Ben. "If you could help get Seth's car out of the ditch, I'd be grateful."

Ben hoped that meant so the man could be gone. He desperately also hoped she wasn't planning to pack up and go with him. He wanted to ask her that, but instead he spoke to the stranger. "You'll have to put on your boots and show me where it is."

"He just has shoes." She looked at the man. "Wait, I'll find you some socks."

Silence fell over the room after Francine left. Ben rubbed Sarge and ignored the man, but he knew the man was studying him.

After Francine came back and handed the socks to the man, she asked, "What about Jasmine? I might need her if somebody comes after me."

That sounded encouraging to Ben's ears. At least she wasn't ready to hop in this man's car and head back to Cincinnati today. She wanted her mare.

"Woody's bringing her down. He should be here anytime now if he doesn't dawdle."

"He won't dawdle. He'll want to see Jeralene."

"Jasmine? Jeralene?" the man asked. "How many people are in this place?"

Francine laughed. "Jasmine is my horse and Jeralene helps me with the cooking and chores. She's peeked out at you from the kitchen a few times already. Probably worried about whether the potato soup is going to be enough to go around."

"I don't like potato soup," the man said.

"Good. Then we'll have plenty. And you can find something better suited to your taste when you get back to civilization." Francine was smiling, but she didn't look particularly happy.

That had Ben feeling more like smiling as he looked directly at the man. "If you're anxious to get back to the city, you might want to get started as soon as you can. Those clouds out there look heavy with rain. The creeks get up, you might need a boat to get out of here unless you want to swim." Ben piled it on. The man didn't look like somebody who'd want to swim a creek and leave his car behind.

"Then maybe I'll just stick around here until

traveling is easier." The man smiled at Francine. "Give Fran and me time to hash over old times."

Francine looked uneasy again. "Of course, you can stay if you want to wait for better weather, Seth, but not here. I have to consider appearances and what Mrs. Breckinridge would think."

"Who is this Mrs. Breckinridge?" the man asked.

"My employer. She expects all her nurses to be above reproach."

"Above reproach, huh." The man gave Ben a sour look. "What about mountain men showing up at your door?"

"The people who live here are my patients. They have to come to my door." Francine kept her eyes on the man. "Mr. Locke and his family have been a great help to me here."

"I'll bet."

Ben balled his hands into fists and then stretched out his fingers. He wasn't going to punch the man. No matter what he said. Instead he would get his car out of the ditch. The sooner the better.

"So what am I supposed to do if I can't get out of here?" the man asked.

"I'll find a family willing to give you a bed for the night." Francine looked over at Ben. "Mr. Locke might know somebody who could take you in."

Before Ben could say anything, the man shook

his head. "I don't think so." He sat down and jerked on the socks Francine gave him and then shoved his feet into his shoes. "I want to see the sun rise in the morning."

"Seth, you don't even know these people."

The man did have enough grace about him to look a little shamefaced as he said, "I'm not meaning you, Locke. I'm sure you're a great fellow, but you hear about shootings and all happening down this way all the time. I managed to stay out of the way of bullets in the army. I aim to keep doing the same."

"Makes sense." Ben didn't care what the man thought of him. He just wanted to see his taillights going away from here. "We better get that car of yours out of the ditch before the rain comes."

As if to emphasize his words, a few drops plunked on the roof.

"I'll be out in a minute. Soon as I tell Francine goodbye." The man gave Ben a look, obviously wanting him to leave.

"Becca will be ready when you get back," Francine said.

Could be she wanted him to leave too.

"All right. I'll get Carl to come with us in case we need more help." Ben went back through the house to the clinic area. He told himself not to look back, but he did anyway.

The man had hold of Francine's hands. "You

will think about what I said. This is no place for you. We can start over. Me and you. Have that family you used to talk about."

He couldn't hear what Francine said, but it didn't look like no. Ben didn't slam the door when he went into the clinic, but he shut it firmly. Better he didn't hear whatever happened back in that other room.

Becca looked up from where she sat on the bed, her baby asleep beside her. "Uh-oh, looks like a storm's a-brewing."

"It does look like rain. We best get on home before the creeks tide."

"That's not the storm I meant." Becca stood up and glanced toward the closed door. "Who is that feller? Carl saw him come in a while ago."

"Where's Carl now?" Ben looked around.

"He went out to get some more coal for the fire. Got to keep babies warm. But you didn't answer me about that man."

"He's an old friend of Nurse Howard's."

"Come a-courtin'?"

"Appears that might be the way of it. Got his car in a ditch and wants me to pull him out. So it'll be a little while before we can head to the house. I came back here to get Carl to help us."

"And keep you from killing the guy?"

"Don't be silly. I'm not going to kill anybody."

"I know that," she said. "That don't mean you might not feel like you want to."

"Pa always told us the Bible said thinking it was as bad as doing it."

"Then I reckon you better be askin' forgiveness." Becca knew him too well. "And after that, could be you should consider doing some courtin' your own self."

"Could be you should mind your own business."

"Could be. But there are some things worth takin' a chance." She looked down at her baby with a tender smile. "Love is one of them."

"Ma advised against it."

Becca blew out a breath. "Ma wasn't happy when I run off and married Carl neither. Said I was too young and she was right about that. But things worked out. Leastways now that Carl has come home. Things might work out for you too, but not if you let that city man steal Nurse Howard right out from under your nose while you stand back with your hands in your pockets and your mouth clamped shut."

"I don't want to hear any more." Ben gave Becca a hard look. "You best be ready when I come back. If it rains much, the truck might not get across the creek and you'd have to stay here. You can't walk up the hill."

"Then don't take long getting that feller on the road again."

It didn't take long. They didn't even hook the truck up to it. With Carl and Woody helping, they just pushed it back up on the road. Woody reached for the money the man held out, but pulled his hand back when he saw Ben's frown. They got the man turned around and headed toward Hyden. Ben was glad when the car disappeared up the road. He was even gladder that Francine wasn't in the car with him. But would she be if the man came back another time?

She hadn't looked all that happy about the man being in her house, but then she had let him hold her hands. Both of them.

Could be Becca was right. He should just risk Francine's no and ask. But what was he going to say? *I think I'm in love with you. No, I am in love with you, but I don't have a house or a job. Would you be willing to put off getting married and having that family you want for a few years while I go to school?*

What kind of proposal was that? One no woman in her right mind would want to hear. But didn't they say love made a person crazy? Lose all good sense. If she loved him . . .

That was the big if, and not one he had time to figure out on this day. Not with the clouds building darker in the west. He had to get Becca and her baby to the house. Rain or shine, snow or sleet, he could come back down the hill tomorrow on Captain to see her. If he had the nerve. Another big if.

41

December 21, 1945

The rain was as unrelenting as the snow two days before. At the barn, Fran had to step with care to keep her boots from being sucked off in the mud.

Jeralene had gone home the day before and not shown up that morning. The creek was out of its banks and swallowing the paths the girl would have to walk to the center. So Fran milked Bella and hauled in coal for the fires.

She had people she needed to see. Becca and her baby were on the top of that list. And Granny Em. Then Jackson Perry might need a new round of pills if his pneumonia hadn't gotten better since she saw him last week. Fran walked down to the water's edge.

Sarge drooped along behind her, not nearly as excited by the rain as he'd been about the snow. Fran understood. Rain pounding down didn't have the same beauty. And now the creek, fed by that rain, was turning into a raging adversary.

There's beauty in everything if a person takes the time to look. Her grandmother's words. Fran couldn't remember what they'd been looking at then. Probably a garden spider and its web that Grandma Howard always admired and that gave Fran the shivers.

She did see beauty in the mad rush of the water chasing out to join up with the Middle Fork River. The river took longer to rise, so the Christmas celebrations at Wendover might still be happening. If so, they would happen without Fran. Better to stay put until the creeks stopped rising.

She looked across the rushing water up the hill toward Ben Locke's house. It wasn't just Becca and her baby girl she needed to see.

She blew out a long breath of air and turned back toward the center. Maybe she should just do as Seth said. Pack her bags and go home. She had loved Seth once. Had imagined having a family with him. Yesterday was not a good time to judge him. He was out of place here in the mountains.

The thing was, she wasn't. Out of place. She raised her head to look up at the mountains and then had to close her eyes to keep out the rain. But she didn't need to see. She knew what was there. Beauty. Raw, dangerous beauty. Rocks ready to slide down the hills. Snakes ready to slither out from under those rocks in the summertime. Snow and rain hiding the trails.

Still, she had told Seth she would think about his offer. He'd held her hands and looked sincere. But calling her Frannie? He hadn't done that since they were in elementary school.

So different from the way Ben Locke said Francine. And the way he let his eyes rest on her. But he never once tried to take her hands. He never once said anything about love. Never once. And even if he did, could she live in these mountains forever? Then again, could she ever leave them?

Sarge ran ahead of her up on the porch and shook the water off his fur. Fran climbed the porch steps behind him. "Don't act like you don't like the water. I've seen you in the creek."

The dog bared his teeth in his doggie grin. Wonder how Seth would like a house dog. But of course, if she went back to the city, the kindest thing would be to leave Sarge here for the next nurse. The very thought hurt Fran's heart, but a woman couldn't decide her future because of a dog. But then, perhaps when Ben Locke had brought her Sarge, that had set her feet on the path to her future.

Her mother's words echoed in her head. *Surely you have more sense than to fall for any of those hillbillies.* Yesterday with both Ben and Seth standing in her house, she knew which one her heart leaned toward. But was loving Ben the dangerous path while going back to the city and settling down with Seth the more sensible way? She'd always been sensible.

Fran shook her head. Ben had yet to ask her to step on that more dangerous path. She might be simply imagining his interest when it was nothing more than kindness.

She reached out and stroked Sarge. "Sensible or not, I'm not going anywhere right now. I'm here until May for sure."

That was in the agreement she had with the Frontier Nursing Service. She had to work that long in return for her training. That thought lifted her spirits, even with the rain still pounding down and the thought of January snows to come. She could handle it. In her sensible way.

Her hand was on the doorknob when she heard a faint voice over the sound of the rain.

"Hallooo."

"Oh well, Sarge, no drying off by the fire for us."

Fran turned to wait for whoever was hailing her. She couldn't think of anybody with an immediate need, but as she'd told Jeralene yesterday, something was always happening.

A boy on a mule came up from the creek. He wore a slouch hat and a plastic slicker. She thought she knew everybody in the Beech Fork area, but she didn't recognize the boy even after he got close enough for her to see his face. He was probably around Woody's age but bigger, and he looked in a panic.

"You got to come, Nurse. My pa's been killed."

"I'm sorry, but I can't do anything for him if he's dead." She tried to say the words as kindly as possible.

"I didn't say he'd been killed dead. He's still got breath in him."

"Right." Fran remembered the mountain way of saying somebody had been hurt. "What happened?"

"He got shot."

"Then it could be you should carry him to the hospital."

"Can't do that. He'd end up in the hoosegow for sure. You got to come and fix him up."

She didn't like to think about what the man might have done that would land him in jail, but that wasn't her business. Treating his wound was. "I can come, but I may still insist he go to the hospital." Fran made her voice firm.

"You can do your insistin', but Pa won't go."

No need arguing about it. "I'll get my saddle-bag and my horse."

The boy got down off his mule and handed her the reins. "Best take my mule. Safer across the tides. I'll bring your horse on behind you."

"I wouldn't know where to go." Fran gave the mule a sideways look. There wasn't even a saddle.

"The mule does. Jest give him his head. He'll take you straight to the house."

"What house? Who are you?"

"Coy Caudill. The one what everybody thought shot Woody Locke, but I wouldn't a never done that. Woody was always nice to me. Ma says he's probably gonna make a preacher like his pa sometimes was." The boy wiped the rain off his face. "We, me and Ma, was right glad Woody didn't die."

"Then who did shoot him if you didn't?"

The boy slid his eyes away from hers. "Can't say that I know. 'Tweren't Pa. I was with him. Coulda been Paps. He was a mean one. Put him in the ground last week so don't reckon we'll ever know." The boy looked back at her. "That keep you from coming to see about Pa?"

"No. I'll get my saddlebag, but I can't ride your mule without a saddle."

"Sure you can. Like sitting in a rockin' chair. Just grab hold of his neck when he's swimming the creek." The panicked look came on the boy's face again. "But you gotta hurry. Pa's killed bad."

She couldn't believe she was agreeing to the boy's plan, but she ran into the house to grab her saddlebag.

When Sarge followed her back out, Coy said, "Best leave your dog here. We've got some mean ones ready to fight most any other dog that comes around. Pa kin make 'em back off, but not me, and Pa ain't up to yellin' 'em down."

She took Sarge's collar and pulled him back in the house. He gave her a look as though she were betraying him before she shut the door. A niggling worry woke inside her of whether she'd ever see the dog or this place again. Going off on a mule to who knows where to treat a moonshiner.

Sarge barked and scratched the door, but Fran ignored him as she let the boy give her a leg up on the mule.

"You'll have to make him go into the creek, but once he gets out on the other side, he'll head straight for home."

The mule did balk at the creek, but she dug her toes into his side to make him step into the water. Once in, he swam across with stoic determination and only drifted a little way downstream. Fran was already soaked from the rain, so the creek soaking didn't make much difference. On the other side, the mule took off up the hillside in a trot just like the boy said he would.

Fran hung on and hoped the boy would catch up with her, because if he was wrong about the mule knowing its way, she'd be lost for sure.

She thought of the day Ben found her in a thunderstorm last summer and wished he was with her now. Then a new worry woke inside her. Had Ben taken justice into his own hands with the Caudills?

"You're a nurse. Not a lawman." She said the words out loud. She wasn't the one to dig into what happened. She just needed to treat the wound. But she did hope Ben Locke wasn't involved. Desperately.

She heard the dogs before she saw any sign of a house or barn. She had to be higher on the mountain than even Granny Em's place, and nothing looked familiar. She must have gone out of her territory into the Possum Bend district. Not that it mattered. The nurses went wherever they were called.

The cabin was perched on the hillside with pines thick around it. A person could ride past and never see it if the dogs didn't give it away. The mule went straight to the barn's breezeway. Fran slid off the animal, draped her saddlebag over her shoulder, and gave the dogs the eye as she headed for the cabin.

The dogs slinked along behind her, but none of them bit her. At the cabin, a woman with worried brown eyes surrounded by weather-hardened wrinkles opened the door.

Without waiting for Fran to speak, she pulled the door open wide and yelled over her shoulder. "The nurse is here, Homer. I told you she'd come." The woman turned back to Fran. "We done heard how you go all over the hills. Getting lost some too, but we knew old Pat would get you here. That ol' mule likes to be in his own barn lot more'n most."

"Don't talk her ear off, woman." The man's

451

voice sounded fairly strong, so maybe he wasn't hurt as badly as the boy had feared.

"I need to wash my hands and we might need some hot water."

"I ain't having a baby. I took a bullet." The man groaned.

Fran looked over at the man on a cot in front of the fireplace. "We need hot water for cleaning the wound, Mr. Caudill." She moved over to the wash pan the woman pointed out. The room was dark with the windows boarded over to keep out the cold. "Can you light a lamp?"

"Ain't got no lamps." The woman twisted her apron in a knot. "We go to bed come dark. I can hunt a candle, I reckon." She glanced around as though she didn't know where to look first.

"That's all right. I have a flashlight." Fran hoped the batteries hadn't gotten wet. She looked around as the woman handed her a towel. No children peeked out around the doors or from the loft.

"Is Coy your only child, Mrs. Caudill?" Fran hoped talking family might put the woman more at ease.

"Onliest one left to home. Others is some scattered."

"Ain't nothing to you where our boys is at," the man said. "Git on over here and see to my leg."

Fran approached the cot with some trepidation,

but Homer Caudill wasn't the first contrary patient she'd treated here in the hills. His pants leg was cut open at the seam and laid back. He held a blood-soaked towel down on the wound.

"What happened?"

"Don't see how that makes any matterance to you. Jest fix it. I'm bleeding like a stuck pig." His scowl grew fiercer. "The old woman said you kept that Locke boy from bleeding out after he was shot, so you could do the same for me."

"He went to the hospital, where the doctor treated his wound."

"I ain't goin' to no hospital." The man raised up off the pillow and glared at Fran a few seconds before he grimaced and fell back. "You're gonna fix me right here."

"I'll have to probe for the bullet. It will be painful."

"Jest get on with it. The boy kin hold my leg to keep it from jerking if'n that's what has you in a stir."

Right on cue, the door opened and the boy came in, bringing the damp smell of the rain with him. "Rain's lettin' up, but fog's a-rising."

Fran looked out before Coy shut the door. Outside the light was dim as though toward night. She squinted down at her watch. Barely past noon. Maybe the skies would clear a little

453

before she had to find her way back to the center. No time to worry about that now. She had a gunshot wound to treat. Whether or not she liked the patient had no bearing on the treatment.

Fran laid out the instruments she might need and, with a last glance at the man's stony face, began. He was as tough as he claimed, and though the boy did keep a firm grasp on his foot, it wouldn't have been necessary. The man flinched, but he didn't jerk away as she extracted the bullet and cleansed the wound.

"An unusual wound," she said as she stitched it up.

"That's 'cause he went and tripped on a root and shot hisself," Coy spoke up.

Relief rushed through Fran that Ben had nothing to do with the man getting shot.

"You talk too much, boy." The man's voice was weaker now. "It ain't like I done it a purpose. Leastways it wasn't a gut shot. If'n it had been, you might be putting me in the ground beside Pap."

"You're right. That would have been much worse." Fran packed up her saddlebag. "Leave the bandage on and keep it dry. I'll come check on it in a couple of days."

"Best you not come around agin." The man fixed his stare on her. "I knows where you're at if'n it don't heal up."

She hoped that wasn't a threat. "Then you need to watch it for signs of infections. Red streaks out from the wound or pus. Plus you'll need the stitches out in a few weeks."

"I got a knife."

Fran didn't argue. She was just glad to walk out of the house into the foggy afternoon.

Coy followed her to get her horse out of the barn. He had brought Moses and not Jasmine. He pointed down the hill. "Head toward the holler. The fog might not be so thick lower down."

Fran looked around. She should wait until the fog lifted, but she couldn't bear the thought of going back in the cabin with Homer Caudill. Coy was right. If she headed down and found a creek, she could follow it and get somewhere she knew.

"I'd guide you off the hill, but I got to stay here to tend to Pa. He's mean as a half-starved wildcat, but he's still my pa."

"I understand." Fran put her hand on his arm. "You're a good boy. You don't have to end up like him."

"Ma tells me the same. On the sly. Says the Feds are bound to get Pa sooner or later, and she don't want me to land in jail with him. I'd head off to the mines, but I don't want to leave Ma up here by her lonesome if'n Pa did come to bad. He don't let me help him at the still.

Him and Pap used to do it all so's I could stay out of trouble. He ain't all bad."

"That's good to know." Fran positioned her saddlebag on Moses and then mounted up. She looked down at Coy. "Is Granny Em's place near here?"

"Not so far. West a couple of miles as the crow flies, but that would be rough goin'. Ain't sure how far if'n you stick to trails. A good piece. In this soupy air, you'd be better served headin' down the hill. I hear tell you ain't good with directions, but up and down is easy enough."

"You're right. Down."

She started Moses down the trail. When she looked back, Coy was gone. Swallowed up by the fog. Ahead, she could make out a faint path. Nothing for it but to keep going and hope the fog lifted.

She was going to get so lost. She was already lost. If only Sarge were with her.

42

Ben didn't start down the hill to see Francine until noon. That morning he had to find the old cradle in the barn loft and work on it. Becca should have had him searching that out weeks ago. It wasn't like baby Carlene was a surprise. He told his mother as much.

"That's my fault," Ma said. "Feels like bad luck bringing the cradle in before the baby. Better to be sure all is well first."

Ben frowned. "You made a baby quilt and clothes."

"That's different."

"How so?" They were out on the back porch scrubbing the cradle while spatters of cold rain blew in on them.

His mother stopped working and stared out at the rain. "I ain't never told you young'uns this, but when I was expectin' my first, I wanted ev'rything to be perfect. Your pa made this cradle his own self." She stroked the side of the cradle. "I sat it in the middle of the house months before my laying-in time, and then the baby come too early. Tiny little thing never took a breath. Instead of laying him in this cradle, I had to put him in a box and bury him in the ground." Ben touched his mother's arm. "I'm sorry."

Ma tightened her lips and blinked a few times. "Anyhow, after that, your pa put the cradle out of sight in the barn. The next time I was carrying, I told him to leave it there until I had the babe safe in my arms, breathing and crying."

She looked over at Ben a little shamefaced. "I reckon it was silly me carrying over my superstitious fears to Becca, but I couldn't help myself. I kept telling Becca I'd get around to dragging the cradle out soon. Then when Nurse Howard had to deliver that baby in the truck, I feared the Lord might be punishing me for my faithless superstitions."

"Everything turned out all right. Carlene is doing fine." Ben could hear the baby crying inside the house.

"It was good the nurse was here." His mother started scrubbing on the cradle again. "She's a heap stronger than she looks. Strong in her spirit."

"She's a good nurse." Ben kept his eyes on the cradle.

"And pretty." When Ben stayed silent, she went on. "Becca tells me she had a feller from the city come see her. That she overheard they once considered marrying before the war."

"That's what the man said." Ben kept his voice level and kept washing the rockers of the cradle.

After they worked in silence a few minutes, Ma said, "Could be you should go put in your own bid 'fore the man comes down this way again."

Ben sat back on his heels and looked directly at his mother, who met his eyes without smiling. After a moment, he said, "Could be."

"Good." The corners of her lips turned up a bit as she bent back to the task of cleaning the cradle. "If'n I was you, I wouldn't wait overlong."

Ben rinsed out his rag in the bucket of soapy water. "She might chase me back up the hill."

"Could happen." Ma didn't look up, but her smile got a little wider. "But I'm thinkin' not. She's a sensible girl."

"That's just it. Sensible would go back to the city where life is easier."

"But without the mountains. I'm thinkin' Nurse Howard has done let her feet grow roots down in these mountains." Ma looked up at him. "One thing sure. You won't know if you don't ask."

She shook out her rag and stood up. She put her hands on her hips and stared down at the cradle. "I think we've got it in fine shape for my grandbaby. Carry it on in and then you can be on about whatever needs doing."

She held the door while he carried the cradle inside. Behind him, she started humming. It took him a minute to recognize the tune. Froggie went a-courting.

The tune circled around in his head all the way down the hill. It was beyond him why his mother would hum that and send him off courting. No happy endings there. The mouse the frog went courting got eaten by a black snake and a duck ate the frog.

The rain slacked off into a drizzle, with fog settling down on the mountains by the time he got to the creek. The water was still crashing along, but Captain was a strong swimmer and didn't have any problem getting across. On the other side of the creek, the horse headed straight for the center.

Ben heard Sarge barking before he got to the yard. Not his usual bark. Ben kicked Captain to a faster trot. Only a wisp of smoke rose up from one of the chimneys. None from the other. That didn't look right.

When barks were the only answer to his knock on the door, Ben pushed it open. Sarge tried to shove past him, but Ben held him back while he closed the door. The dog sat down and whined, his ears drooped down.

"Hold on, Sarge." Ben made a quick round of the center. Nobody there. The fire was nearly out in the fireplace and the cookstove was cold. Somebody must have come after her, but Sarge always went with her. Always.

The dog ran back to the door, whining. Sarge wanted to go after her. And why not? Ben could just build up the fire and wait. He could, but what if she was lost in that fog up on the mountain? That girl could get lost in the sunshine.

She could be in trouble. After all, big black snakes were out there. Maybe not the slithery kind here in late December, but plenty of other dangers. Especially in weather like this, with tides crashing down the mountain.

Plus, if he sat down and started thinking of all the reasons Francine should choose that city fellow over him, Ben might lose his courage and ride on back up the hill. Tell his mother Francine wasn't home. That she was probably never going to be home for him.

You won't know if you don't ask. His mother's words echoed in his head. She was right. He did need to ask Francine if she could ever look on him with favor. Better to know a yes or no so a man could face facts and move on. But first he had to find her.

As if reading his thoughts, Sarge started scratching on the door.

"All right, Sarge, let's go find her."

The dog sniffed around the yard and then took off for the creek. Without hesitation, he jumped in to swim for the other side. Ben followed on Captain. The current swept both the dog and the horse down creek. But once on the other side, Sarge put his nose to the ground and after a few minutes headed up the hill.

"Hope you know a horse can't always go where a dog can," Ben muttered as he followed. But then Francine would have been on a horse too. He should have checked her barn. What if both horses were there and she was lying hurt somewhere in the barn? But Sarge wouldn't be chasing up the hill if that was true. At least, Ben hoped it was.

At first the dog seemed to be heading toward his house. Francine could have gone to Granny Em's while he was helping his mother with the cradle. But then the dog took a turn to the east past a few houses without slowing down, even when a dog barked and rushed toward him.

On past the houses the trail got steeper and rougher. As far as Ben knew, only one family lived up this way. The Caudills. He'd started up this hill a half-dozen times, but something always stopped him. Providence, his mother would say. No need starting a feud when Woody could have been hit by a stray shot the way the sheriff decided. That could have been.

One of the Caudills might have come for Francine. Homer Caudill's wife appeared to be beyond childbearing age, but somebody said Homer's father was poorly. Maybe it was something moonshine couldn't cure.

The fog socked down on him like a curtain falling. One minute he could see the dog in front of him on the trail and the next he was swallowed up by gray. Ben slid off Captain and called Sarge. The dog came to him, his tail dragging.

He kept the dog next to him while he considered what to do. In fog like this, a man could step right over a cliff edge. Even a dog might take a wrong way, although animals generally had a better sense of the terrain than people.

Ben pulled a rope out of his saddlebag and attached it to Sarge's collar. "Just while we consider the best thing to do," he said.

Surely if Francine had gone to the Caudills' cabin she would stay there and wait out the fog. But then she might not know how fog could go from bad to impossible here in the mountains in a blink of the eye. Maybe he should go on to the Caudills' to see if Francine was there, but he wasn't all that certain he could find the cabin in this gray world.

Sarge whined and perked up his ears. Then he was back on his feet pulling at the rope. Ben listened but didn't hear anything except water dripping off the trees. But he turned toward where the dog's nose was pointing and shouted, "Halloooo!"

No sound came back to him, but the dog jerked against the rope. Ben took a better hold on it and followed Sarge across the hillside, leading Captain behind him. He held Sarge back and moved slowly to give Captain a chance to find his footing on the narrow path. Sarge dug at the ground to go faster, but Ben held on.

Then a rock turned under his boot and he slid down the hill. Nothing for it but to turn loose of the rope and the reins to keep the animals from going with him. He grabbed a tree to stop his slide. He scrambled back up the wet hillside to what passed for a path. Captain was there waiting, but Sarge was gone.

Ben whistled, but the dog didn't come back. Ben picked up Captain's reins and headed on along the path. But truth was, he was every bit as lost in this fog as Francine might be if she was here on this hill.

"What in the world am I going to do now?" he whispered.

All at once, his father's words were in his head, clear as the day he'd said them to Ben the week before he left for the army. *There's times in life when no way looks clear. You're bound to face some of them over there, but when you do, just put your trust in the Lord. He'll show you a way.*

Ben wasn't over there now, but the Lord was on this side of the ocean too. He was on this mountain. A prayer rose up inside him that the Lord would point the way.

43

Fran kept going for a while in the fog, but then Moses, always the steadier of the horses, tossed his head and stopped. Fran got off and gingerly stepped in front of the horse. The trail disappeared. They appeared to be on some kind of ledge.

She eased the horse back until she could turn him around. They backtracked to a couple of huge boulders. As good a place to wait out the fog as any. She backed up against one of the rocks and slipped off her slicker to drape between the boulders to make a little shelter over her head. Then she pulled Moses closer to lend her a little of his warmth. She rubbed her hands up and down her arms and stomped her feet.

"I'm sorry, boy," she told the horse. "We should have stayed in the Caudills' barn. But now we'll just have to wait it out."

A house could be just over the ridge and she wouldn't know it. Maybe even Granny Em's house. She had the feeling she was going in her direction.

The thought almost made her laugh. She couldn't keep her directions straight in the daylight. No way could she know where she was in this fog. What would Granny Em tell her? To listen for the rhythm of the mountain. She held her breath, but she didn't hear anything except water dripping off the trees. While that might make a rhythm, it wasn't going to help her find her way home.

But singing might make her feel better. The song that popped into her head was the one she'd sung with Sadie and Becca. Froggie went a-courting. What a silly song, but at least thinking about it made her smile.

Her smile faded as she thought about Seth coming courting. She still hadn't quite wrapped her mind around Seth wanting her to step back to the way they were before the war. Before Cecelia. Before Fran became a frontier nurse-midwife.

The gray fog pushed in on her. That was how she'd felt when Seth showed up at the center. That he was pushing in on her, not giving her the chance to think about what she wanted to do. Not caring what she wanted to do.

What did she want to do? With the rock cold and hard against her back, she had the feeling she was leaning against the mountain. That thought made her smile, even with the fog so thick around her that she felt a captive of it.

She blew out a breath and shut her eyes. If she could be anywhere in the world right at that moment, where would it be? She and Grandma

Howard used to play that game. Fran would dream of being in France or on the moon or wherever, but Grandma Howard always wanted to be right where she was on the farm. Now Fran knew how she felt. She wanted to be right here in the mountains, taking care of her people. By a fire might be nice though.

Not just any fire, but the Lockes' fire. She kept her eyes closed, letting her imagination go wild. By the fire, her hand in Ben Locke's with Sarge at her feet.

She shook her head a little and opened her eyes. That was dreaming. She couldn't let herself go to sleep and really dream. Hypothermia could sneak up on a person. She stomped her feet again and then rubbed her hands down the horse's back and up under the edge of the saddle.

Moses shifted his feet and nickered. He perked up his ears, and then Fran heard it too. Something coming. A bobcat maybe. She could be blocking its den here among the boulders. Or maybe a bear. Her heart pounded up in her ears.

She had her foot in the stirrup to at least be off the ground and have a chance of escaping whatever was coming when she heard a bark. A dog. She peered toward the sound and saw a flash of yellow fur through the fog.

"Sarge," she shouted.

She stepped back down to the ground as the dog exploded out of the fog. "I can't believe

467

you found me." He jumped up on her, his tail wag-ging almost off, and licked her face. "Did Jeralene let you out? Well, then I guess I'm glad to be lost here in the fog instead of at the Caudills' where their dogs might have hurt you."

See, good can come from everything. Her grandmother was always saying that, and maybe she was right, if being totally lost in the fog and about to freeze could have something good about it. She rubbed Sarge's head and spotted the rope dragging under him.

That changed things. Jeralene wouldn't have put a rope on Sarge. Maybe somebody had tried to come with Sarge. Maybe Woody. Maybe Ben. She looked out at the fog and thought she might see a bit farther than she could minutes ago.

She cupped her hands around her mouth and hollered the way the mountain men always did when they came after her. "Hallooo!"

She listened, but no sound came back to her. But then Sarge whipped around and barked. Maybe somebody was there. Somebody who would know how to get down the mountain. She remembered Ben finding her back in the summer, and even not knowing whether Ben might be out there in the fog looking for her or not, her heart started pounding harder again.

Ben went slow, practically feeling his way through the thick blanket of fog. He looked at his watch. Only half past three. With the rain over, the sun might break through the clouds and burn away the worst of the fog. He got back on Captain and gave him his head to pick the easiest path through the woods.

He yelled once, but the fog swallowed up the sound. What he needed was a foghorn. Or a conch shell like men used to call in their hounds after a hunt. Instead he put his fingers in his mouth and gave a sharp whistle.

He stopped Captain and listened. A dog's barks threaded through the damp air back to him. Maybe Sarge. He whistled again, and then he heard a voice. Francine's voice.

Captain made his way between boulders big as cars. Ben knew this place. Francine stepped into view on the other side of one of the boulders. He jumped off Captain and ran toward her, but stopped short of grabbing her in his arms the way he wanted to.

"Are you all right?"

She smiled a little. "Lost. And cold. But all right. What about you?"

He smiled back at her. "Lost. Cold. But all right."

"We're going to have to quit meeting like this." She laughed. "On the side of a mountain."

He started to say something, but she jumped in front of his words. "Wait. What did you say? You can't be lost too. I'm the one who gets lost."

"Anybody can get lost in the fog. Except Sarge there. He's quite a tracker."

"One of a kind." She reached down and rubbed Sarge's head.

Ben tried not to be jealous. "But actually I do know where I am now that I see these boulders."

"Then can you get us down off this hill back to civilization?" She looked up at him.

Her words made him remember the man who had come to convince her to go with him. Back to civilization. "Is that where you want to go? Back to the city?"

She frowned a little. "You mean Hyden?"

"Don't know that anybody would call that a city. No, Cincinnati."

"I'm soaked and about to freeze, Ben. Why are you talking about Cincinnati?"

Her lips were trembling and she was shivering. He unbuttoned his coat. It was wet on the outside, but the wool lining was still dry. He put his hands on her shoulders and gently pulled her toward him. "Come here and warm up."

She hesitated.

"Two bodies are warmer than one. In the army on cold nights we'd always buddy up with somebody to keep from freezing." He kept his arms open to her, but let her make the decision about stepping into his embrace.

"Sensible." She moved into his embrace and added in a whisper he barely heard. "Or not."

470

He wrapped the sides of his coat around her and held her close. After a minute, her shivers slowed. He rested his cheek on her head. Nothing sensible about that, but it felt good. "I don't want you to go back to Cincinnati."

"What do you want, Ben Locke?" She looked up at him. Her face was damp from the fog.

"I want you, Francine Howard. Only you."

When she looked at him without saying anything, he rushed on. "I know I don't have much to offer you. No reason to not go back to Cincinnati with that other fellow. No house of my own. No job. Planning to head off to school. And you hardly know me."

She slid her hand up out of his jacket and put her fingers over his lips. "Shh. Don't talk about the reasons I shouldn't stay. Tell me why I should."

"I love you." Three words he'd never said to any woman other than his ma when he was a little boy. But they were easy to say to Francine.

A smile lit up her eyes. "Then why don't you kiss me?" She slipped her hand away from his mouth and around behind his neck.

Her lips were cool at first but warmed under his. When at last he lifted his lips away from hers, he kissed her eyebrows and then the hair that peeked out from under her wool hat.

At first Fran wasn't sure if the sparkle of sunlight was really there or she was simply

471

imagining it because of the kiss. But no, the sun was pushing a sliver of light through the fog to hit on the boulder beside them. But she didn't move away from Ben. It felt too good to be in his arms.

She wasn't being sensible at all. Ben was right. She barely knew him, but she knew how he made her feel. And there would be time, plenty of time to get to know him better. More words between them. More kisses. She completely forgot about being so chilled. Here in Ben's arms, she felt warm and safe.

"You're still shivering." Ben rubbed his hands up and down her back. "We need to get you in front of a fire to warm up."

He was right. Warm and safe in her heart wasn't drying out her wet clothes and boots. Time to be sensible before her toes turned blue.

"Are we close to any houses?" she asked. "Coy told me Granny Em's house wasn't too far from theirs as the crow flies."

"So you were at the Caudills'." Ben's face turned hard.

"Mr. Caudill tripped on a root and shot himself in the leg."

"The old man?"

"No, Coy said they buried him last week." Fran studied Ben. "Coy said he didn't shoot Woody and that his father didn't either. He thinks his grandfather might have, but that we can never know now that he's dead."

"You believed him?"

"I did."

"And you patched up Homer Caudill?"

"I'm not a sheriff or a judge. I'm a nurse. Patching up people is what I do." She touched his cheek. "Does that bother you? That I treated him?"

Ben blew out a breath and took her hand in his. "I guess you can't turn away anybody needing help. Even somebody like Homer Caudill."

"I was glad you didn't shoot him."

"Did you think I might?" He answered his own question before she could say anything. "I guess that's a fair thought for you to have. I did consider confronting the man more than once, but something—Ma would say the good Lord's providence—kept turning me away from that path."

"And now we're on another path." Fran wanted to stop talking about Homer Caudill. "And I'm completely lost, as usual."

He laughed then, the uneasiness in his face disappearing the way the fog did in the sunshine. "I told you I know where we are. Now that the fog is lifting, we can head over that way and be at Granny Em's in half an hour. Or on down to our house in a little longer."

"Granny Em first. Then your house to see about Becca and little Carlene."

473

"Just a nurse on her rounds." He was still smiling. "Maybe I should always ride with you to keep you from getting lost."

"I wouldn't mind." She tiptoed up and brushed her lips across his cheek. "Thank you for finding me."

"I didn't. Sarge did."

"But you gave me Sarge." Sarge pushed his nose against her leg and wagged his tail at the sound of his name.

"So I did."

More sparkles of sunrays were pushing through the fog, bringing back the daylight. They mounted their horses and Fran followed after Ben. The horses' hooves plopped along the path. Water still showered down on them whenever they brushed against a branch. A squirrel chattered at them and a bird started singing. The rhythm of the mountains. It was part of her, and now she had a new song in her heart. A song of love.

She started singing.

"Froggie went a-courting,
He did ride, uh-huh, uh-huh."

Ben looked back over his shoulder at her and laughed. And then he started singing with her. They were going to make good music together.

FRONTIER NURSING
SERVICE READERS' NOTE

Born into an influential Kentucky family, Mary Breckinridge had a privileged childhood, but after the deaths of her two young children, she devoted her life to improving the health of women and children. A registered nurse, she went to France during World War I, where she met British nurse-midwives and decided a nurse-midwifery program would be the best way to bring better healthcare to rural areas. Perhaps due to having family roots in Kentucky, Breckinridge looked to the eastern Kentucky Appalachian area to start her nurse-midwife program. She went on horseback through the mountains, seeking out every "granny midwife" and talking with the people to understand their needs. In 1925, she established the Frontier Nursing Service in Leslie County, Kentucky.

She recruited the first midwives from England, where she received her own midwifery training. Since American physicians discouraged the use of midwives during that time period, there were few formally trained American midwives. When England became embroiled in World War II in 1939, several of those British midwives felt compelled to go home and use their nursing skills serving their country. The resulting shortage of midwives in the Frontier Nursing Service led Breckinridge to establish a midwifery school in 1939 at the small Hyden Hospital she'd helped the community build in 1928.

Mary Breckinridge traveled all over the country speaking about the frontier nurses, procuring millions of dollars in donations and recruiting nurses and volunteers called couriers. These couriers, mostly young women from socially prominent families, took care of the horses, ran errands, and assisted the nurse-midwives. The nurses traveled by horseback or on foot to provide in-home prenatal and childbirth care, functioning as both midwives and familynurses. The service's low fees could be paid in money or goods and no one was turned away. Maternal and infant mortality rates decreased dramatically in the area.

Breckinridge ran the Frontier Nursing Service until her death in 1965, but the FNS she established still serves southeastern Kentucky and the FNS School of Midwifery and Family Nursing continues to train nurse-midwives. Wendover, the headquarters and home of Mary Breckinridge, was selected as a National Historic Landmark in 1991. For more information, you can read Mary Breckinridge's own story, *Wide Neighborhoods: A Story of the Frontier Nursing Service.*

ACKNOWLEDGMENTS

The Frontier Nursing Service has a saying that nobody comes to the Service by accident. I think that might be true with writers too. We don't come to stories by accident. A writer is pulled to a story by some spark of an idea. For me that spark was learning about the nurse-midwives in the Frontier Nursing Service. Reading their first-person accounts allowed me to vicariously experience their adventures of riding Appalachian Mountain trails, fording rivers, and delivering babies in log cabins, and then let my characters have some of those same adventures.

I'm thankful for the opportunity to write this story. I appreciate my agent, Wendy Lawton, who was excited when I proposed the idea of writing about a midwife in the Appalachian Mountains of Kentucky. Her enthusiasm for the story helped me keep pushing through when the writing got hard.

I'm so blessed to work with a wonderful editor, Lonnie Hull DuPont, who is always ready with encouraging words and ways to improve my stories. Barb Barnes has made me a better writer with her careful editing. I appreciate the ready help available from Michele Misiak and Karen Steele with publicity, reviews, and more. Cheryl

Van Andel and her team never fail to design eye-catching covers for every story. The whole Revell team works to make my books be the best they can be and then find their way out to you, the readers.

I especially thank you, the readers, for picking up my books and letting my stories come to life in your imagination. Thank you for reading and for your friendship and prayers. I'm blessed beyond measure by you and by my loving family. Most of all, I thank the Lord for opening the door to let me write stories of faith, love, and life.

About the Author

Ann H. Gabhart is the bestselling author of many novels, including *Angel Sister*, *Small Town Girl*, and *Love Comes Home*, several Shaker novels such as *The Outsider*, *The Believer*, and *The Innocent*, and THE HEART OF HOLLYHILL series. As A. H. Gabhart, she is the author of THE HIDDEN SPRINGS MYSTERIES series. Ann's country roots go deep, and she and her husband still live on a Kentucky farm just over the hill from where she was born in a farmhouse built around a log cabin. Learn more at www.annhgabhart.com.

| Books are produced in the United States using U.S.-based materials | Books are printed using a revolutionary new process called THINKtech™ that lowers energy usage by 70% and increases overall quality | Books are durable and flexible because of smythe-sewing | Paper is sourced using environmentally responsible foresting methods and the paper is acid-free |

Center Point Large Print
600 Brooks Road / PO Box 1
Thorndike, ME 04986-0001 USA

(207) 568-3717

US & Canada:
1 800 929-9108
www.centerpointlargeprint.com